INNER
HARBOR

DEAR READER,

Home means different things to different people. Making a home can be both a challenge and a joy. Those of us who are lucky have fond memories of the place where we grew up, of the traditions set there. *Inner Harbor* deals with finding that home, making it, preserving it.

Ray and Stella Quinn had given Phillip a second chance at life. He'd never forgotten what they'd done for him. With his brothers, Cameron, Ethan, and now Seth, Phillip worked to maintain their home and keep a promise to a man he loved. Maybe he preferred his life in Annapolis, the museums, the restaurants, the crowds, but he'd keep his promise even if it meant splitting his time on the Shore, laboring over hulls and homework.

Home was what Ray had wanted for his sons, all of his sons. To keep his promise, and his home, Phillip must accept the boy Ray brought into their lives, and deal with a beautiful woman who has secrets that will affect all of them—a woman who needs both his trust and his heart.

To clear their father's name and keep a sacred vow, the Quinns will band together. A family formed by fate and the generous hearts of a special couple.

Nora Roberts

INNER
HARBOR

NORA ROBERTS

JOVE BOOKS, NEW YORK

INNER HARBOR

ISBN: 0-7394-0135-1

A JOVE BOOK®
Jove Books are published by The Berkley Publishing Group,
a member of Penguin Putnam Inc.,
375 Hudson Street, New York, New York 10014.
JOVE and the "J" design are trademarks belonging to
Jove Publications, Inc.

PRINTED IN THE UNITED STATES OF AMERICA

For Elaine and Beth, such devoted sisters—
even if they won't wear blue organdy and sing

PROLOGUE

PHILLIP QUINN DIED AT THE AGE
of thirteen. Since the overworked and underpaid staff at the Baltimore City Hospital emergency room zapped him back in less than
ninety seconds, he wasn't dead very long.

As far as he was concerned, it was plenty long enough.

What had killed him, briefly, were two .25-caliber bullets pumped
out of a Saturday night special shoved through the open window of a
stolen Toyota Celica. The finger on the trigger had belonged to a close
personal friend—or as near to a close personal friend as a thirteen-
year-old thief could claim on Baltimore's bad streets.

The bullets missed his heart. Not by much, but in later years Phillip
considered it just far enough.

That heart, young and strong, though sadly jaded, continued to beat
as he lay there, pouring blood over the used condoms and crack vials
in the stinking gutter on the corner of Fayette and Paca.

The pain was obscene, like sharp, burning icicles stabbing into his
chest. But that grinning pain refused to take him under, into the release of unconsciousness. He lay awake and aware, hearing the
screams of other victims or bystanders, the squeal of brakes, the rev-
ving of engines, and his own ragged and rapid breaths.

He'd just fenced a small haul of electronics that he'd stolen from a
third-story walk-up less than four blocks away. He had two hundred
fifty dollars in his pocket and had swaggered down to score a dime bag
to help him get through the night. Since he'd just been sprung from
ninety days in juvie for another B and E that hadn't gone quite so
smoothly, he'd been out of the loop. And out of cash.

Now it appeared he was out of luck.

Later, he would remember thinking, Shit, oh, shit, this *hurts*! But he couldn't seem to wrap his mind around another thought. He'd gotten in the way. He knew that. The bullets hadn't been meant for him in particular. He'd caught a glimpse of the gang colors in that frozen three seconds before the gun had fired. His own colors, when he bothered to associate himself with one of the gangs that roamed the streets and alleys of the city.

If he hadn't just popped out of the system, he wouldn't have been on that corner at that moment. He would have been told to stay clear, and he wouldn't now be sprawled out, pumping blood and staring into the dirty mouth of the gutter.

Lights flashed—blue, red, white. The scream of sirens pierced through human screams. Cops. Even through the slick haze of pain his instinct was to run. In his mind he sprang up, young, agile, street-smart, and melted into the shadows. But even the effort of the thought had cold sweat sliding down his face.

He felt a hand on his shoulder, and fingers probed until they reached the thready pulse in his throat.

This one's breathing. Get the paramedics over here.

Someone turned him over. The pain was unspeakable, but he couldn't release the scream that ripped through his head. He saw faces swimming over him, the hard eyes of a cop, the grim ones of the medical technician. Red, blue, and white lights burned his eyes. Someone wept in high, keening sobs.

Hang in there, kid.

Why? He wanted to ask why. It hurt to be there. He was never going to escape as he'd once promised himself he would. What was left of his life was running red into the gutter. What had come before was only ugliness. What was now was only pain.

What was the damn point?

HE WENT AWAY FOR A WHILE, sinking down below the pain, where the world was a dark and dingy red. From somewhere outside his world came the shriek of the sirens, the pressure on his chest, the speeding motion of the ambulance.

Then lights again, bright white to sear his closed lids. And he was flying while voices shouted on all sides of him.

Bullet wounds, chest. BP's eighty over fifty and falling, pulse thready and rapid. In and out. Pupils are good.

Type and cross-match. We need pictures. On three. One, two, three.

His body seemed to jerk, up then down. He no longer cared. Even the dingy red was going gray. A tube was pushing its way down his throat and he didn't bother to try to cough it out. He barely felt it. Barely felt anything and thanked God for it.

BP's dropping. We're losing him.

I've been lost a long time, he thought.

With vague interest he watched them, half a dozen green-suited people in a small room where a tall blond boy lay on a table. Blood was everywhere. His blood, he realized. He was on that table with his chest torn open. He looked down at himself with detached sympathy. No more pain now, and the quiet sense of relief nearly made him smile.

He floated higher, until the scene below took on a pearly sheen and the sounds were nothing but echoes.

Then the pain tore through him, an abrupt shock that made the body on the table jerk, that sucked him back. His struggle to pull away was brief and fruitless. He was inside again, feeling again, lost again.

The next thing he knew, he was riding in a drug-hazed blur. Someone was snoring. The room was dark and the bed narrow and hard. A backwash of light filtered through a pane of glass that was spotted with fingerprints. Machines beeped and sucked monotonously. Wanting only to escape the sounds, he rolled back under.

He was in and out for two days. He was very lucky. That's what they told him. There was a pretty nurse with tired eyes and a doctor with graying hair and thin lips. He wasn't ready to believe them, not when he was too weak to lift his head, not when the hideous pain swarmed back into him every two hours like clockwork.

When the two cops came in he was awake, and the pain was smothered under a few layers of morphine. He made them out to be cops at a glance. His instincts weren't so dulled that he didn't recognize the walk, the shoes, the eyes. He didn't need the identification they flashed at him.

"Gotta smoke?" Phillip asked it of everyone who passed through. He had a low-grade desperation for nicotine even though he doubted he could manage to suck on a cigarette.

"You're too young to smoke." The first cop pasted on an avuncular smile and stationed himself on one side of the bed. The Good Cop, Phillip thought wearily.

"I'm getting older every minute."

"You're lucky to be alive." The second cop kept his face hard as he pulled out a notebook.

And the Bad Cop, Phillip decided. He was nearly amused.

"That's what they keep telling me. So, what the hell happened?"

"You tell us." Bad Cop poised his pencil over a page of his book.

"I got the shit shot out of me."

"What were you doing on the street?"

"I think I was going home." He'd already decided how to play it, and he let his eyes close. "I can't remember exactly. I'd been . . . at the movies?" He made it a question, opening his eyes. He could see Bad Cop wasn't going to buy it, but what could they do?

"What movie did you see? Who were you with?"

"Look, I don't know. It's all messed up. One minute I was walking, the next I was lying facedown."

"Just tell us what you remember." Good Cop laid a hand on Phillip's shoulder. "Take your time."

"It happened fast. I heard shots—it must have been shots. Somebody was screaming, and it was like something exploded in my chest." That much was pretty close to the truth.

"Did you see a car? Did you see the shooter?"

Both were etched like acid on steel in his brain. "I think I saw a car—dark color. A flash."

"You belong to the Flames."

Phillip shifted his gaze to Bad Cop. "I hang with them sometimes."

"Three of the bodies we scraped off the street were members of the Tribe. They weren't as lucky as you. The Flames and the Tribe have a lot of bad blood between them."

"So I've heard."

"You took two bullets, Phil." Good Cop settled his face into concerned lines. "Another inch either way, you'd have been dead before you hit the pavement. You look like a smart kid. A smart kid doesn't fool himself into believing he needs to be loyal to assholes."

"I didn't see anything." It wasn't loyalty. It was survival. If he rolled over, he was dead.

"You had over two hundred in your wallet."

Phillip shrugged, regretting it as the movement stirred up the ghosts of pain. "Yeah? Well, maybe I can pay my bill here at the Hilton."

"Don't smart-mouth me, you little punk." Bad Cop leaned over the bed. "I see your kind every fucking day. You're not out of the system twenty hours before you end up bleeding into the gutter."

Phillip didn't flinch. "Is getting shot a violation of my parole?"

"Where'd you get the money?"

"I don't remember."

"You were down in Drug City to score."

"Did you find any drugs on me?"

"Maybe we did. You wouldn't remember, would you?"

Good one, Phillip mused. "I could sure as hell use some now."

"Ease off a little." Good Cop shifted his feet. "Look, son, you cooperate and we'll play square with you. You've been in and out of the system enough to know how it works."

"If the system worked I wouldn't be here, would I? You can't do anything to me that hasn't been done. For Christ's sake, if I'd known something was going down I wouldn't have been there."

The sudden disturbance out in the hall took the cops' attention away. Phillip merely closed his eyes. He recognized the voice raised in bitter fury.

Stoned, was his first and last thought. And when she stumbled into the room, he opened his eyes and saw that he'd been right on target.

She'd dressed up for the visit, he noted. Her yellow hair was teased and sprayed into submission, and she'd put on full makeup. Under it, she might have been a pretty woman, but the mask was hard and tough. Her body was good, it was what kept her in business. Strippers who moonlight as hookers need a good package. She'd peeled on a halter and jeans, and she clicked her way over to the bed on three-inch heels.

"Who the hell do you think's gonna pay for this? You're nothing but trouble."

"Hi, Ma, nice to see you, too."

"Don't you sass me. I got cops coming to the door 'cause of you. I'm sick of it." She flashed a look at the men on either side of the bed. Like her son, she recognized cops. "He's almost fourteen years old. I'm done with him. He ain't coming back on me this time. I ain't having cops and social workers breathing down my neck anymore."

She shrugged off the nurse who hustled in to grab her arm, then leaned over the bed. "Why the hell didn't you just die?"

"I don't know," Phillip said calmly. "I tried."

"You've never been any good." She hissed at Good Cop when he pulled her back. "Never been any damn good. Don't you come around looking for a place to stay when you get out of here," she shouted as she was dragged out of the room. "I'm done with you."

Phillip waited, listening to her swearing, shouting, demanding papers to sign to get him out of her life. Then he looked up at Bad Cop. "You think you can scare me? I live with that. Nothing's worse than living with that."

Two days later, strangers came into the room. The man was huge, with blue eyes bright in a wide face. The woman had wild red hair escaping from a messy knot at the nape of her neck and a face full of freckles. The woman took his chart from the foot of the bed, scanned it, then tapped it against her palm.

"Hello, Phillip. I'm Dr. Stella Quinn. This is my husband, Ray."

"Yeah, so?"

Ray pulled a chair up to the side of the bed and sat down with a sigh of pleasure. He angled his head, studied Phillip briefly. "You've got yourself into a hell of a mess here, haven't you? Want to get out of it?"

ONE

P HILLIP LOOSENED THE WIND-
sor knot in his Fendi tie. It was a long commute from Baltimore to
Maryland's Eastern Shore, and he'd programmed his CD player with
that in mind. He started out mellow with a little Tom Petty and the
Heartbreakers.

Thursday-evening traffic was as bad as predicted, made worse by
the sluggish rain and the rubberneckers who couldn't resist a long,
fascinated goggle at the three-car accident on the Baltimore Beltway.

By the time he was heading south on Route 50, even the hot licks of
vintage Stones couldn't completely lift his mood.

He'd brought work with him and somehow had to eke out time for
the Myerstone Tire account over the weekend. They wanted a whole
new look for this advertising campaign. Happy tires make happy driv-
ers, Phillip thought, drumming his fingers on the wheel to the rhythm
of Keith Richards's outlaw guitar.

Which was a crock, he decided. Nobody was happy driving in rainy
rush-hour traffic, no matter what rubber covered their wheels.

But he'd come up with something that would make the consumers
think that riding on Myerstones would make them happy, safe, and
sexy. It was his job, and he was good at it.

Good enough to juggle four major accounts, supervise the status of
six lesser ones, and never appear to break a sweat within the slick
corridors of Innovations, the well-heeled advertising firm where he
worked. The firm that demanded style, exuberance, and creativity
from its executives.

They didn't pay to see him sweat.

Alone, however, was a different matter.

He knew he'd been burning not a candle but a torch at both ends for months. With one hard slap of fate he'd gone from living for Phillip Quinn to wondering what had happened to his cheerfully upwardly mobile urban lifestyle.

His father's death six months before had turned his life upside down. The life that Ray and Stella Quinn had righted seventeen years ago. They'd walked into that dreary hospital room and offered him a chance and a choice. He'd taken the chance because he'd been smart enough to understand that he had no choice.

Going back on the streets wasn't as appealing as it had been before his chest had been ripped open by bullets. Living with his mother was no longer an option, not even if she changed her mind and let him buy his way back into the cramped apartment on Baltimore's Block. Social Services was taking a hard look at the situation, and he knew he'd be dumped into the system the minute he was back on his feet.

He had no intention of going back into the system, or back with his mother, or back to the gutter, for that matter. He'd already decided that. He felt that all he needed was a little time to work out a plan.

At the moment that time was buffered by some very fine drugs that he hadn't had to buy or steal. But he didn't figure that little benefit was going to last forever.

With the Demerol sliding through his system, he gave the Quinns a canny once-over and dismissed them as a couple of weirdo do-gooders. That was fine with him. They wanted to be Samaritans, give him a place to hang out until he was back to a hundred percent, good for them. Good for him.

They told him they had a house on the Eastern Shore, which for an inner-city kid was the other end of the world. But he figured a change of scene couldn't hurt. They had two sons about his age. Phillip decided he wouldn't have to worry about a couple of wimps that the do-gooders had raised.

They told him they had rules, and education was a priority. School didn't bother him any. He breezed his way through when he decided to go.

No drugs. Stella said that in a cool voice that made Phillip reevaluate her as he put on his most angelic expression and said a polite *No, ma'am.* He had no doubt that when he wanted a hit, he'd be able to find a source, even in some bumfuck town on the Bay.

Then Stella leaned over the bed, her eyes shrewd, her mouth smiling thinly.

You have a face that belongs on a Renaissance painting. But that doesn't make you less of a thief, a hoodlum, and a liar. We'll help you if you want to be helped. But don't treat us like imbeciles.

And Ray laughed his big, booming laugh. He squeezed Stella's shoulder and Phillip's at the same time. It would be, Phillip remembered he'd said, a rare treat to watch the two of them butt heads for the next little while.

They came back several times over the next two weeks. Phillip talked with them and with the social worker, who'd been much easier to con than the Quinns.

In the end they took him home from the hospital, to the pretty white house by the water. He met their sons, assessed the situation. When he learned that the other boys, Cameron and Ethan, had been taken in much as he had been, he was certain they were all lunatics.

He figured on biding his time. For a doctor and a college professor they hadn't collected an abundance of easily stolen or fenced valuables. But he scoped out what there was.

Instead of stealing from them, he fell in love with them. He took their name and spent the next ten years in the house by the water.

Then Stella had died, and part of his world dropped away. She had become the mother he'd never believed existed. Steady, strong, loving, and shrewd. He grieved for her, that first true loss of his life. He buried part of that grief in work, pushing his way through college, toward a goal of success and a sheen of sophistication—and an entry-level position at Innovations.

He didn't intend to remain on the bottom rung for long.

Taking the position at Innovations in Baltimore was a small personal triumph. He was going back to the city of his misery, but he was going back as a man of taste. No one seeing the man in the tailored suit would suspect that he'd once been a petty thief, a sometime drug dealer, and an occasional prostitute.

Everything he'd gained over the last seventeen years could be traced back to that moment when Ray and Stella Quinn had walked into his hospital room.

Then Ray had died suddenly, leaving shadows that had yet to be washed with the light. The man Phillip had loved as completely as a son could love a father had lost his life on a quiet stretch of road in the middle of the day when his car had met a telephone pole at high speed.

There was another hospital room. This time it was the Mighty Quinn lying broken in the bed with machines gasping. Phillip, along with his brothers, had made a promise to watch out for and to keep the last of Ray Quinn's strays, another lost boy.

But this boy had secrets, and he looked at you with Ray's eyes.

The talk around the waterfront and the neighborhoods of the little town of St. Christopher's on Maryland's Eastern Shore hinted of adultery, of suicide, of scandal. In the six months since the whispers had started, Phillip felt that he and his brothers had gotten no closer to finding the truth. Who was Seth DeLauter and what had he been to Raymond Quinn?

Another stray? Another half-grown boy drowning in a vicious sea of neglect and violence who so desperately needed a lifeline? Or was he more? A Quinn by blood as well as by circumstance?

All Phillip could be sure of was that ten-year-old Seth was his brother as much as Cam and Ethan were his brothers. Each of them had been snatched out of a nightmare and given a chance to change their lives.

With Seth, Ray and Stella weren't there to keep that choice open.

There was a part of Phillip, a part that had lived inside a young, careless thief, that resented even the possibility that Seth could be Ray's son by blood, a son conceived in adultery and abandoned in shame. It would be a betrayal of everything the Quinns had taught him, everything they had shown him by living their lives as they had.

He detested himself for considering it, for knowing that now and then he studied Seth with cool, appraising eyes and wondered if the boy's existence was the reason Ray Quinn was dead.

Whenever that nasty thought crept into his mind, Phillip shifted his concentration to Gloria DeLauter. Seth's mother was the woman who had accused Professor Raymond Quinn of sexual harassment. She claimed it had happened years before, while she was a student at the university. But there was no record of her ever attending classes there.

The same woman had sold her ten-year-old son to Ray as if he'd been a package of meat. The same woman, Phillip was certain, that Ray had been to Baltimore to see before he had driven home—and driven himself to his death.

She'd taken off. Women like Gloria were skilled in skipping out of harm's way. Weeks ago, she'd sent the Quinns a not-so-subtle blackmail letter: If you want to keep the kid, I need more. Phillip's jaw clenched when he remembered the naked fear on Seth's face when he'd learned of it.

She wasn't going to get her hands on the boy, he told himself. She was going to discover that the Quinn brothers were a tougher mark than one softhearted old man.

Not just the Quinn brothers now, either, he thought as he turned off onto the rural county road that would lead him home. He thought of family as he drove fast down a road flanked by fields of soybeans, of peas, of corn grown taller than a man. Now that Cam and Ethan were married, Seth had two determined women to stand with him as well.

Married. Phillip shook his head in amused wonder. Who would have thought it? Cam had hitched himself to the sexy social worker, and Ethan was married to sweet-eyed Grace. And had become an instant father, Phillip mused, to angel-faced Aubrey.

Well, good for them. In fact, he had to admit that Anna Spinelli and Grace Monroe were tailor-made for his brothers. It would only add to their strength as a family when it came time for the hearing on permanent guardianship of Seth. And marriage certainly appeared to suit them. Even if the word itself gave him the willies.

For himself, Phillip much preferred the single life and all its benefits. Not that he'd had much time to avail himself of all those benefits in the past few months. Weekends in St. Chris, supervising homework assignments, pounding a hull together for the fledgling Boats by Quinn, dealing with the books for the new business, hauling groceries—all of which had somehow become his domain—cramped a man's style.

He'd promised his father on his deathbed that he would take care of Seth. With his brothers he'd made a pact to move back to the Shore, to share the guardianship and the responsibilities. For Phillip that pact meant splitting his time between Baltimore and St. Chris, and his energies between maintaining his career—and his income—and tending to a new and often problematic brother and a new business.

It was all a risk. Raising a ten-year-old wasn't without headaches and fumbling mistakes under the best of circumstances, he imagined. Seth DeLauter, raised by a part-time hooker, full-time junkie, and amateur extortionist, had hardly come through the best of circumstances.

Getting a boatbuilding enterprise off the ground was a series of irksome details and backbreaking labor. Yet somehow it was working, and if he discounted the ridiculous demands on his time and energy, it was working fairly well.

Not so long ago his weekends had been spent in the company of any number of attractive, interesting women, having dinner at some new hot spot, an evening at the theater or a concert, and if the chemistry was right, a quiet Sunday brunch in bed.

He'd get back to that, Phillip promised himself. Once all the details were in place, he would have his life back again. But, as his father would have said, for the next little while . . .

He turned into the drive. The rain had stopped, leaving a light sheen of wet on the leaves and grass. Twilight was creeping in. He could see the light in the living room window glowing in a soft and steady welcome. Some of the summer flowers that Anna had babied along were hanging on, and early fall blooms shimmered in the shadows. He could hear the puppy barking, though at nine months Foolish had grown too big and sleek to be considered a puppy anymore.

It was Anna's night to cook, he remembered. Thank God. It meant a real meal would be served at the Quinns'. He rolled his shoulders, thought about pouring himself a glass of wine, then watched Foolish dash around the side of the house in pursuit of a mangy yellow tennis ball.

The sight of Phillip getting out of his car obviously distracted the dog from the game. He skidded to a halt and set up a din of wild, terrified barking.

"Idiot." But he grinned as he pulled his briefcase out of the Jeep.

At the familiar voice, the barking turned into mad joy. Foolish bounded up with a delighted look in his eyes and wet, muddy paws. "No jumping!" Phillip yelled, using his briefcase like a shield. "I mean it. Sit!"

Foolish quivered, but dropped his rump on the ground and lifted a paw. His tongue lolled, his eyes gleamed. "That's a good dog." Gingerly Phillip shook the filthy paw and scratched the dog's silky ears.

"Hey." Seth wandered into the front yard. His jeans were grubby from wrestling with the dog, his baseball cap was askew so that straw-straight blond hair spiked out of it. The smile, Phillip noted, came much more quickly and easily than it had a few months before. But there was a gap in it.

"Hey." Phillip butted a finger on the bill of the cap. "Lose something?"

"Huh?"

Phillip tapped a finger against his own straight, white teeth.

"Oh, yeah." With a typical Quinn shrug, Seth grinned, pushing his tongue into the gap. His face was fuller than it had been six months before, and his eyes less wary. "It was loose. Had to give it a yank a couple of days ago. Bled like a son of a bitch."

Phillip didn't bother to sigh over Seth's language. Some things, he determined, weren't going to be his problem. "So, did the Tooth Fairy bring you anything?"

"Get real."

"Hey, if you didn't squeeze a buck out of Cam, you're no brother of mine."

"I got two bucks out of it. One from Cam and one from Ethan."

Laughing, Phillip swung an arm over Seth's shoulders and headed toward the house. "Well, you're not getting one out of me, pal. I'm on to you. How was the first full week of school?"

"Boring." Though it hadn't been, Seth admitted silently. It had been exciting. All the new junk Anna had taken him shopping for. Sharp pencils, blank notebooks, pens full of ink. He'd refused the *X-Files* lunch box she'd wanted to get him. Only a dork carried a lunch box in middle school. But it had been really cool and tough to sneer at.

He had cool clothes and bitching sneakers. And best of all, for the first time in his life, he was in the same place, the same school, with the same people he'd left behind in June.

"Homework?" Phillip asked, raising his eyebrows as he opened the front door.

Seth rolled his eyes. "Man, don't you ever think about anything else?"

"Kid, I live for homework. Especially when it's yours." Foolish burst through the door ahead of Phillip, nearly knocking him down with enthusiasm. "You've still got some work to do on that dog." But the mild annoyance faded instantly. He could smell Anna's red sauce simmering, like ambrosia on the air. "God bless us, every one," he murmured.

"Manicotti," Seth informed him.

"Yeah? I've got a Chianti I've been saving just for this moment." He tossed his briefcase aside. "We'll hit the books after dinner."

He found his sister-in-law in the kitchen, filling pasta tubes with cheese. The sleeves of the crisp white shirt she'd worn to the office were rolled up, and a white butcher's apron covered her navy skirt. She'd taken off her heels and tapped a bare foot to the beat of the aria she was humming. *Carmen*, Phillip recognized. Her wonderful mass of curling black hair was still pinned up.

With a wink at Seth, Phillip came up behind her, caught her around the waist, and pressed a noisy kiss onto the top of her head. "Run away with me. We'll change our names. You can be Sophia and I'll be

Carlo. Let me take you to paradise where you can cook for me and me alone. None of these peasants appreciate you like I do."

"Let me just finish this tube, Carlo, and I'll go pack." She turned her head, her dark Italian eyes laughing. "Dinner in thirty minutes."

"I'll open the wine."

"Don't we have anything to eat now?" Seth wanted to know.

"There's antipasto in the fridge," she told him. "Go ahead and get it out."

"It's just vegetables and junk," Seth complained when he pulled out the platter.

"Yep."

"Jeez."

"Wash the dog off your hands before you start on that."

"Dog spit's cleaner than people spit," Seth informed her. "I read how if you get bit by another guy it's worse than getting bit by a dog."

"I'm thrilled to have that fascinating tidbit of information. Wash the dog spit off your hands anyway."

"Man." Disgusted, Seth clomped out, with Foolish slinking after him.

Phillip chose the wine from the small supply he kept in the pantry. Fine wines were one of his passions, and his palate was extremely discriminating. His apartment in Baltimore boasted an extensive and carefully chosen selection, which he kept in a closet he'd remodeled specifically for that purpose.

At the Shore, his beloved bottles of Bordeaux and Burgundy kept company with Rice Krispies and boxes of Jell-O Instant Pudding.

He'd learned to live with it.

"So how was your week?" he asked Anna.

"Busy. Whoever said women can have everything should be shot. Handling a career and a family is grueling." Then she looked up with a brilliant smile. "I'm loving it."

"It shows." He drew the cork expertly, sniffed it and approved, then set the bottle on the counter to breathe. "Where's Cam?"

"Should be on his way home from the boatyard. He and Ethan wanted to put in an extra hour. The first Boat by Quinn is finished. The owner's coming in tomorrow. It's finished, Phillip." Her smile flashed, brilliant and glowing with pride. "At dock, seaworthy and just gorgeous."

He felt a little tug of disappointment that he hadn't been in on the last day. "We should be having champagne."

Anna lifted a brow as she studied the label on the wine. "A bottle of Folonari, Ruffino?"

He considered one of Anna's finest traits to be her appreciation for good wine. "Seventy-five," he said with a broad grin.

"You won't hear any complaints from me. Congratulations, Mr. Quinn, on your first boat."

"It's not my deal. I just handle the details and pass for slave labor."

"Of course it's your deal. Details are necessary, and neither Cam nor Ethan could handle them with the finesse you do."

"I think the word they use, is 'nagging.' "

"They need to be nagged. You should be proud of what the three of you have accomplished in the last few months. Not just the new business, but the family. Each one of you has given up something that's important to you for Seth. And each one of you has gotten something important back."

"I never expected the kid to matter so much." While Anna smothered the filled tubes with sauce, Phillip opened a cupboard for wine-glasses. "I still have moments when the whole thing pisses me off."

"That's only natural, Phillip."

"Doesn't make me feel any better about it." He shrugged his shoulders in dismissal, then poured two glasses. "But most of the time, I look at him and think he's a pretty good deal for a kid brother."

Anna grated cheese over the casserole. Out of the corner of her eye she watched Phillip lift his glass, appreciate the bouquet. He was beautiful to look at, she mused. Physically, he was as close to male perfection as she could imagine. Bronze hair, thick and full, eyes more gold than brown. His face was long, narrow, thoughtful. Both sensual and angelic. His tall, trim build seemed to have been fashioned for Italian suits. But since she'd seen him stripped to the waist in faded Levi's she knew there was nothing soft about him.

Sophisticated, tough, erudite, shrewd. An interesting man, she mused.

She slipped the casserole into the oven, then turned to pick up her wine. Smiling at him, she tapped her glass on his. "You're a pretty good deal too, Phillip, for a big brother."

She leaned in to kiss him lightly as Cam walked in.

"Get your mouth off my wife."

Phillip merely smiled and slid an arm around Anna's waist. "She put hers on me. She likes me."

"She likes me better." To prove it, Cam hooked a hand in the tie of Anna's apron, spun her around, and pulled her into his arms to kiss her brainless. He grinned, nipped her bottom lip and patted her butt companionably. "Don'cha, sugar?"

Her head was still spinning. "Probably." She blew out a breath. "All things considered." But she wiggled free. "You're filthy."

"Just came in to grab a beer to take into the shower." Long and lean, dark and dangerous, he prowled over to the fridge. "And kiss my wife," he added with a smug look at Phillip. "Go get your own woman."

"Who has time?" Phillip said mournfully.

AFTER DINNER, AND AN HOUR spent slaving over long division, battles of the Revolutionary War, and sixth-grade vocabulary, Phillip settled down in his room with his laptop and his files.

It was the same room he'd been given when Ray and Stella Quinn had brought him home. The walls had been a pale green then. Sometime during his sixteenth year he'd gotten a wild hair and painted them magenta. God knew why. He remembered that his mother—for Stella had become his mother by then—had taken one look and warned him he'd have terminal indigestion.

He thought it was sexy. For about three months. Then he'd gone with a stark white for a while, accented with moody black-framed, black-and-white photographs.

Always looking for ambience, Phillip thought now, amused at himself. He'd circled back to that soft green right before he moved to Baltimore.

They'd been right all along, he supposed. His parents had usually been right.

They'd given him this room, in this house, in this place. He hadn't made it easy for them. The first three months were a battle of wills. He smuggled in drugs, picked fights, stole liquor, and stumbled in drunk at dawn.

It was clear to him now that he'd been testing them, daring them to kick him out. Toss him back. Go ahead, he'd thought. You can't handle me.

But they did. They had not only handled him, they had made him.

I wonder, Phillip, his father had said, *why you want to waste a good mind and a good body. Why you want to let the bastards win.*

Phillip, who was suffering from the raw gut and bursting head of a drug and alcohol hangover, didn't give a good damn.

Ray took him out on the boat, telling him that a good sail would clear his head. Sick as a dog, Phillip leaned over the rail, throwing up the remnants of the poisons he'd pumped into his system the night before.

He'd just turned fourteen.

Ray anchored the boat in a narrow gut. He held Phillip's head, wiped his face, then offered him a cold can of ginger ale.

"Sit down."

He didn't so much sit as collapse. His hands shook, his stomach shuddered at the first sip from the can. Ray sat across from him, his big hands on his knees, his silvering hair flowing in the light breeze. And those eyes, those brilliant blue eyes, level and considering.

"You've had a couple of months now to get your bearings around here. Stella says you've come around physically. You're strong, and healthy enough—though you aren't going to stay that way if you keep this up."

He pursed his lips, said nothing for a long moment. There was a heron in the tall grass, still as a painting. The air was bright and chill with late fall, the trees bare of leaves so that the hard blue sky spread overhead. Wind ruffled the grass and skimmed fingers over the water.

The man sat, apparently content with the silence and the scene. The boy slouched, pale of face and hard of eye.

"We can play this a lot of ways, Phil," Ray said at length. "We can be hard-asses. We can put you on a short leash, watch you every minute and bust your balls every time you screw up. Which is most of the time."

Considering, Ray picked up a fishing rod, absently baited it with a marshmallow. "Or we could all just say that this little experiment's a bust and you can go back into the system."

Phillip's stomach churned, making him swallow to hold down what he didn't quite recognize as fear. "I don't need you. I don't need anybody."

"Yeah, you do." Ray said it mildly as he dropped the line into the water. Ripples spread, endlessly. "You go back into the system, you'll stay there. Couple of years down the road, it won't be juvie anymore. You'll end up in a cell with the bad guys, the kind of guys who are going to take a real liking to that pretty face of yours. Some seven-foot con with hands like smoked hams is going to grab you in the showers one fine day and make you his bride."

Phillip yearned desperately for a cigarette. The image conjured by Ray's word made fresh sweat pop out on his forehead. "I can take care of myself."

"Son, they'll pass you around like canapés, and you know it. You talk a good game and you fight a good fight, but some things are inevitable. Up to this point your life has pretty much sucked. You're not responsible for that. But you are responsible for what happens from here on."

He fell into silence again, clamping the pole between his knees before reaching for a cold can of Pepsi. Taking his time, Ray popped the top, tipped the can back, and guzzled.

"Stella and I thought we saw something in you," he continued. "We still do," he added, looking at Phillip again. "But until you do, we're not going to get anywhere."

"What do you care?" Phillip tossed back miserably.

"Hard to say at the moment. Maybe you're not worth it. Maybe you'll just end up back on the streets hustling marks and turning tricks anyway."

For three months he'd had a decent bed, regular meals, and all the books he could read—one of his secret loves—at his disposal. At the thought of losing it his throat filled again, but he only shrugged. "I'll get by."

"If all you want to do is get by, that's your choice. Here you can have a home, a family. You can have a life and make something out of it. Or you can go on the way you are."

Ray reached over to Phillip quickly, and the boy braced himself for the blow, clenched his fists to return it. But Ray only pulled Phillip's shirt up to expose the livid scars on his chest. "You can go back to that," he said quietly.

Phillip looked into Ray's eyes. He saw compassion and hope. And he saw himself mirrored back, bleeding in a dirty gutter on a street where life was worth less than a dime bag.

Sick, tired, terrified, Phillip dropped his head into his hands. "What's the point?"

"You're the point, son." Ray ran his hand over Phillip's hair. "You're the point."

Things hadn't changed overnight, Phillip thought now. But they had begun to change. His parents had made him believe in himself, despite himself. It had become a point of pride for him to do well in school, to learn, to remake himself into Phillip Quinn.

He figured he'd done a good job of it. He'd coated that street kid with a sheen of class. He had a slick career, a well-appointed condo with a killer view of the Inner Harbor, and a wardrobe that suited both.

It seemed that he'd come full circle, spending his weekends back in this room with its green walls and sturdy furniture, with its windows that overlooked the trees and the marsh.

But this time, Seth was the point.

TWO

PHILLIP STOOD ON THE FORE-
deck of the yet-to-be-christened *Neptune's Lady*. He'd personally
sweated out nearly two thousand man-hours to take her from design
to finished sloop. Her decks were gleaming teak, her bright work
glinted in the yellow September sun.

Belowdecks her cabin was a woodworker's pride, Cam's for the
most part, Phillip mused. Glossy cabinets were fashioned of natural
wood, hand-fitted and custom-designed with sleeping room for four
close friends.

She was sound, he thought, and she was beautiful. Aesthetically
charming, with her fluid hull, glossy decks, and long waterline. Ethan's
early decision to use the smooth-lap method of planking had added
hours to the labor but had produced a gem.

The podiatrist from D.C. was going to pay handsomely for every
inch of her.

"Well . . . ?" Ethan, hands in the pockets of his faded jeans, eyes
squinting comfortably against the sun, left it an open-ended question.

Phillip ran a hand over the satin finish of the gunwale, an area he'd
spent many sweaty hours sanding and finishing. "She deserves a less
clichéd name."

"The owner's got more money than imagination. She takes the
wind." Ethan's lips curved into one of his slow, serious smiles. "Good
Christ, she goes, Phil. When Cam and I tested her out, I wasn't sure
he was going to bring her back in. Wasn't sure I wanted him to."

Phillip rubbed a thumb over his chin. "I've got a friend in Baltimore
who paints. Most of the stuff he does is strictly commercial, for hotels

and restaurants. But he does terrific stuff on the side. Every time he sells one, he bitches about it. Hates to let a canvas go. I didn't really understand how he felt until now."

"And she's our first."

"But not our last." Phillip hadn't expected to feel so attached. The boatbuilding business hadn't been his idea, or his choice. He liked to think his brothers had dragged him into it. He'd told them it was insane, ridiculous, doomed to fail.

Then, of course, he'd jumped in and negotiated for the rental of the building, applied for licenses, ordered the necessary utilities. During the construction of what was about to become *Neptune's Lady,* he'd dug splinters out of his fingers, nursed burns from hot creosote, soaked muscles that wept after hours of lifting planks. And had not suffered in silence.

But with this tangible result of long months of labor swaying gracefully under his feet, he had to admit it was all worth it.

Now they were about to start all over again.

"You and Cam made some headway this week on the next project."

"We want to have the hull ready to turn the end of October." Ethan took out a bandanna and methodically polished Phillip's fingerprints off the gunwale. "If we're going to keep to that killer schedule you worked up. Got a little bit more to do on this one, though."

"This one?" Eyes narrowed, Phillip tipped down his Wayfarers. "Damn it, Ethan, you said she was ready to go. The owner's coming in to take her. I was about to go in and work up the last of the papers on her."

"Just one little detail. Have to wait for Cam."

"What little detail?" Impatient, Phillip checked his watch. "The client's due here any minute."

"Won't take long." Ethan nodded toward the cargo doors of the building. "Here's Cam now."

"She's too good for this yahoo," Cam called out as he came down the narrow dock with a battery-operated drill. "I'm telling you we should get the wives and kids and sail her off to Bimini ourselves."

"She's good enough for the final draw he's going to give us today. Once he gives me that certified check, he's the captain." Phillip waited until Cam stepped nimbly aboard. "When I get to Bimini I don't want to see either of you."

"He's just jealous because we've got women," Cam told Ethan. "Here." He shoved the drill into Phillip's hand.

"What the hell am I supposed to do with this?"

"Finish her." Grinning, Cam pulled a brass cleat out of his back pocket. "We saved the last piece for you."

"Yeah?" Absurdly touched, Phillip took the cleat, watched it wink in the sun.

"We started her together," Ethan pointed out. "Seemed only right. It goes on the starboard."

Phillip took the screws Cam handed him and bent over the markings on the rail. "I figured we should celebrate after." The drill whirled in his hands. "I thought about a bottle of Dom," he said, raising his voice over the noise, "but figured it'd be wasted on the two of you. So I've got three Harps chilling down in the cooler."

They would go well, he thought, with the little surprise he was having delivered later that afternoon.

It WAS NEARLY NOON BEFORE the client had finished fussing over every inch of his new boat. Ethan had been elected to take the man out for a shakedown sail before they loaded the sloop onto its new trailer. From the dock, Phillip watched the butter-yellow sails—the client's choice—fill with the wind.

Ethan was right, he thought. She moved.

The sloop skimmed toward the waterfront, heeled in like a dream. He imagined the late-summer tourists would stop to watch, point out the pretty boat to each other. There was, he thought, no better advertising than a quality product.

"He'll run her aground the first time he sails her on his own," Cam said from behind him.

"Sure. But he'll have fun." He gave Cam a slap on the shoulder. "I'll just go write up that bill of sale."

The old brick building they rented and had modified for the boatyard didn't boast many amenities. The lion's share was a vast open space with fluorescent lights hanging from the rafters. The windows were small and always seemed to be coated with dust.

Power tools, lumber, equipment, gallons of epoxy and varnish and bottom paint were set up where they could be easily reached. The lofting platform was currently occupied by the bare skeleton of the hull for the custom-designed sport's fisher that was their second job.

The walls were pitted brick and unfinished Sheetrock. Up a steep flight of iron stairs was a cramped, windowless room that served as the office.

Despite its size and location, Phillip had it meticulously organized. The metal desk might have been a flea market special, but it was scrubbed clean. On its surface was a Month-at-a-Glance calendar, his old laptop computer, a wire in/out box, a two-line phone/answering machine and a Lucite holder for pens and pencils.

Crowded in with the desk were two file cabinets, a personal copier, and a plain-paper fax.

He settled in his chair and booted up the computer. The blinking light on the phone caught his eye. When he punched it for messages, he found two hang-ups and dismissed them.

Within moments, he'd brought up the program he'd customized for the business, and found himself grinning at the logo for Boats by Quinn.

They might be flying by the seat of their pants, he mused as he plugged in the data for the sale, but it didn't have to look that way. He'd justified the high-grade paper as an advertising expense. Desktop publishing was second nature to him. Creating stationery, receipts, bills was simple enough—he simply insisted that they have class.

He shot the job to the printer just as the phone rang.

"Boats by Quinn."

There was a hesitation, then the sound of throat clearing. "Sorry, wrong number." The voice was muffled and female and quickly gone.

"No problem, sweetheart," Phillip said to the dial tone as he plucked the printed bill of sale from the machine.

"THERE GOES A HAPPY MAN," Cam commented an hour later when the three of them watched their client drive off with the trailered sloop.

"We're happier." Phillip took the check out of his pocket and held it out. "Factoring in equipment, labor, overhead, supplies . . ." He folded the check in half again. "Well, we cleared enough to get by."

"Try to control your enthusiasm," Cam muttered. "You got a check for five figures in your hot little hand. Let's crack open those beers."

"The bulk of the profits have to go right back into the business," Phillip warned as they started inside. "Once the cold weather hits, our utility bill's going to go through the roof." He glanced up at the soaring ceiling. "Literally. And we've got quarterly taxes due next week."

Cam twisted the top off a bottle and pushed it at his brother. "Shut up, Phil."

"However," Phillip continued, ignoring him, "this is a fine moment in Quinn history." He lifted his beer, tapped the bottle to both Cam's and Ethan's. "To our foot doctor, the first of many happy clients. May he sail clean and heal many bunions."

"May he tell all his friends to call Boats by Quinn," Cam added.

"May he sail in Annapolis and keep out of my part of the Bay," Ethan finished with a shake of his head.

"Who's springing for lunch?" Cam wanted to know. "I'm starving."

"Grace made sandwiches," Ethan told him. "They're out in my cooler."

"God bless her."

"Might want to put off lunch just a bit." Phillip heard the sound of tires on gravel. "I think what I've been waiting for just got here." He strolled out, pleased to see the delivery truck.

The driver leaned out the window, worked a wad of gum into his cheek. "Quinn?"

"That's right."

"What'd you buy now?" Cam frowned at the truck, wondering how much of that brand-new check was flying away.

"Something we need. He's going to need a hand with it."

"You got that right." The driver huffed as he climbed out of the cab. "Took three of us to load her up. Son of a bitch weighs two hundred pounds if it weighs an ounce."

He hauled open the back doors. It lay on the bed on top of a padded cloth. It was easily ten feet long, six high, and three inches thick. Carved in simple block letters into treated oak were the words BOATS BY QUINN. A detailed image of a wooden skiff in full sail rode the top corner.

Lining the bottom corner were the names Cameron, Ethan, Phillip, and Seth Quinn.

"That's a damn fine sign," Ethan managed when he could find the words.

"I took one of Seth's sketches for the skiff. The same one we use for the logo on the letterhead. Put the design together on the computer at work." Phillip reached in to run a thumb along the side of the oak. "The sign company did a pretty good job of reproducing it."

"It's great." Cam rested his hand on Phillip's shoulder. "One of the details we've been missing. Christ, the kid's going to flip when he sees it."

"I put us down the way we came along. Works out alphabetical and chronological. I wanted to keep it clean and simple." He stepped back, his hands sliding into his pockets in an unconscious mirroring of his brothers' stances. "I thought this fit the building and what we're doing in it."

"It's good." Ethan nodded. "It's right."

The driver shoved at his gum again. "Well, you guys gonna admire it all day, or you want to get this heavy bastard out of the truck?"

THEY MADE A PICTURE, SHE thought. Three exceptional specimens of the male species engaged in manual labor on a warm afternoon in early September. The building certainly suited them. It was rough, the old brick faded and pitted, the grounds around it scrabbly—more weeds than grass.

Three different looks as well. One of the men was dark, with his hair long enough to pull back in a short ponytail. His jeans were black, fading to gray. There was something vaguely European about his style. She decided he would be Cameron Quinn, the one who'd made a name for himself on the racing circuit.

The second wore scuffed work boots that looked ancient. His sun-streaked hair tumbled out of a blue-billed ball cap. He moved fluidly and lifted his end of the sign with no visible effort. He would be Ethan Quinn, the waterman.

Which meant the third man was Phillip Quinn, the advertising executive, who worked at the top firm in Baltimore. He looked gilded, she thought. Wayfarers and Levi's, she mused. Bronzed hair that must be a joy to his stylist. A long, trim body that must see regular workouts at the health club.

Interesting. Physically they bore no resemblance to each other and through her research she knew they shared a name but not blood. Yet there was something in the body language, in the way they moved as a team, that indicated they were brothers.

She intended simply to pass by, to give the building where they based their business a quick look and evaluation. Though she'd known that at least one of them would be there, since he'd answered the phone, she hadn't expected to see them outside, as a group, to have this opportunity to study them.

She was a woman who appreciated the unexpected.

Nerves shimmered in her stomach. Out of habit, she took three slow breaths and rolled her shoulders to relax them. Casual, she reminded herself. There was nothing to be uneasy about. After all, she had the advantage here. She knew them, and they didn't know her.

It was typical behavior, she decided as she crossed the street. A person strolling along and seeing three men working to hang an impressive new sign would display curiosity and interest. Particularly a small-town tourist, which was, for this purpose, what she was. She was also a single female, and they were three very attractive men. A mild flirtation would be typical as well.

Still, when she reached the front of the building, she stood back. It seemed to be difficult and precarious work. The sign was bolted to thick black chains and wrapped in rope. They'd worked out a pulley system, with the ad exec on the roof guiding and his brothers on the ground hauling. Encouragement, curses, and directions were issued with equal enthusiasm.

There were certainly a lot of muscles rippling, she observed with a lift of her brow.

"Your end, Cam. Give me another inch. Goddamn." Grunting, Phillip dropped onto his belly and squirmed out far enough that she held her breath and waited for gravity to do its work.

But he managed to balance himself and snag the chain. She could see his mouth working as he fought to loop the heavy link around a thick hook, but she couldn't hear what he was saying. She thought that might be for the best.

"Got it. Hold it steady," he ordered, rising to tightwalk his way across the eaves to the other end. The sun struck his hair, gleamed over his skin. She caught herself goggling. This, she thought, was a prime example of sheer male beauty.

Then he was bellying over the edge again, grabbing for the chain, hauling it into place. And swearing ripely. When he rose, he scowled at the long tear down the front of his shirt where she supposed it had caught on something on the roof.

"I just bought this sucker."

"It was real pretty, too," Cam called up.

"Kiss my ass," Phillip suggested and tugged the shirt off to use it to mop sweat off his face.

Oh, well, now, she thought, appreciating the view on a purely personal level. The young American god, she decided. Designed to make females drool.

He hooked the ruined shirt in his back pocket, started for the ladder. And that's when he spotted her. She couldn't see his eyes, but she could tell by the momentary pause, the angle of the head, that he was looking at her. The evaluation would be instinctive, she knew. Male sees female, studies, considers, decides.

He'd seen her all right and, as he started down the ladder, was already considering. And hoping for a closer look. "We've got company," Phillip murmured, and Cam glanced over his shoulder.

"Hmmm. Very nice."

"Been there ten minutes." Ethan dusted his hands on his hips. "Watching the show."

Phillip stepped off the ladder, turned and smiled. "So," he called out to her, "how's it look?"

Curtain up, she thought and started forward. "Very impressive. I hope you don't mind the audience. I couldn't resist."

"Not at all. It's a big day for the Quinns." He held out a hand. "I'm Phillip."

"I'm Sybill. And you build boats."

"That's what the sign says."

"Fascinating. I'm spending some time in the area. I hadn't expected to stumble across boatbuilders. What sort of boats do you build?"

"Wooden sailing vessels."

"Really?" She turned her easy smile toward his brothers. "And you're partners?"

"Cam." He returned the smile, jerked a thumb. "My brother Ethan."

"Nice to meet you, Cameron," she began, shifting her gaze to read from the sign. "Ethan, Phillip." Her heartbeat accelerated, but she kept the polite smile in place. "Where's Seth?"

"In school," Phillip told her.

"Oh, college?"

"Middle. He's ten."

"I see." There were scars on his chest, she saw now. Old and shiny and riding dangerously close to his heart. "You have a very impressive sign, Boats by Quinn. I'd love to drop by sometime and see you and your brothers at work."

"Anytime. How long are you staying in St. Chris?"

"Depends. It was nice to meet you all." Time to retreat, she decided. Her throat was dry, her pulse unsteady. "Good luck with your boats."

"Drop by tomorrow," Phillip suggested as she walked away. "Catch all four Quinns at work."

She shot a look over her shoulder that she hoped revealed nothing more than amused interest. "I might just do that."

Seth, she thought, careful now to keep her eyes straight ahead. He'd just given her the open door to see Seth the following day.

Cam gave a quiet and male hum. "I gotta say, there's a woman who knows how to walk."

"Yes, indeed." Phillip hooked his hands in his pockets and enjoyed the view. Slim hips and slender legs in breezy maize-colored slacks, a snug little shirt the color of limes tucked into a narrow waist. A sleek and swinging fall of mink-colored hair just skimming strong shoulders.

And the face had been just as attractive. A classic oval with peaches-and-cream skin, a mobile and shapely mouth tinted with a soft, soft pink. Sexy eyebrows, he mused, dark and well arched. He hadn't been able to see the eyes under them, not through the trendy wire-framed sunglasses. They might be dark to match the hair, or light for contrast.

And that smooth contralto voice had set the whole package off nicely.

"You guys going to stand there watching that woman's butt all day?" Ethan wanted to know.

"Yeah, like you didn't notice it." Cam snorted.

"I noticed. I'm just not making a career out of it. Aren't we going to get anything done around here?"

"In a minute," Phillip murmured, smiling to himself when she turned the corner and disappeared. "Sybill. I sure hope you hang around St. Chris for a while."

SHE DIDN'T KNOW HOW LONG she would stay. Her time was her own. She could work where she chose, and for now she'd chosen this little water town on Maryland's southern Eastern Shore. Nearly all of her life had been spent in cities, initially because her parents had preferred them and then because she had.

New York, Boston, Chicago, Paris, London, Milan. She understood the urban landscape and its inhabitants. The fact was, Dr. Sybill Griffin had made a career out of the study of urban life. She'd gathered degrees in anthropology, sociology, and psychology along the way. Four years at Harvard, post-graduate work at Oxford, a doctorate from Columbia.

She'd thrived in academia, and now, six months before her thirtieth birthday, she could write her own ticket. Which was precisely what she'd chosen to do for a living. Write.

Her first book, *Urban Landscape*, had been well received, earned her critical acclaim and a modest income. But her second, *Familiar Strangers*, had rocketed onto the national lists, had taken her into the whirlwind of book tours, lectures, talk shows. Now that PBS was producing a documentary series based on her observations and theories of city life and customs, she was much more than financially secure. She was independent.

Her publisher had been open to her idea of a book on the dynamics and traditions of small towns. Initially, she'd considered it merely a cover, an excuse to travel to St. Christopher's, to spend time there on personal business.

But then she'd begun to think it through. It would make an interesting study. After all, she was a trained observer and skilled at documenting those observations.

Work might save her nerves in any case, she considered, pacing her pretty little hotel suite. Certainly it would be easier and more productive to approach this entire trip as a kind of project. She needed time, objectivity, and access to the subjects involved.

Thanks to convenient circumstance, it appeared she had all three now.

She stepped out onto the two-foot slab that the hotel loftily called a terrace. It offered a stunning view of the Chesapeake Bay and intriguing glimpses of life on the waterfront. Already she'd watched workboats chug into dock and unload tanks of the blue crabs the area was famous for. She'd watched the crab pickers at work, the sweep of gulls, the flight of egrets, but she had yet to wander into any of the little shops.

She wasn't in St. Chris for souvenirs.

Perhaps she would drag a table near the window and work with that view. When the breeze was right she could catch snippets of voices, a slower, more fluid dialect than she heard on the streets of New York, where she'd based herself for the last few years.

Not quite Southern, she thought, such as you would hear in Atlanta or Mobile or Charleston, but a long way from the clipped tones and hard consonants of the North.

On some sunny afternoons she could sit on one of the little iron benches that dotted the waterfront and watch the little world that had formed here out of water and fish and human sweat.

She would see how a small community of people like this, based on the Bay and tourists, interacted. What traditions, what habits, what clichés ran through them. Styles, she mused, of dress, of movements, of speech. Inhabitants so rarely realized how they conformed to unspoken rules of behavior dictated by place.

Rules, rules, rules. They existed everywhere. Sybill believed in them absolutely.

What rules did the Quinns live by? she wondered. What type of glue had fashioned them into a family? They would, of course, have their own codes, their own short-speak, with a pecking order and a reward and discipline standard.

Where and how would Seth fit into it?

Finding out, discreetly, was a priority.

There was no reason for the Quinns to know who she was, to suspect her connection. It would be better for all parties if no one knew. Otherwise, they could very well attempt, and possibly succeed in blocking her from Seth altogether. He'd been with them for months now. She couldn't be sure what he'd been told, what spin they might have put on the circumstances.

She needed to observe, to study, to consider, and to judge. Then she would act. She would not be pressured, she ordered herself. She would not be made to feel guilty or responsible. She would take her time.

After their meeting that afternoon, she thought it would be ridiculously simple to get to know the Quinns. All she had to do was wander into that big brick building and show an interest in the process of creating a wooden sailboat.

Phillip Quinn would be her entrée. He'd displayed all the typical behavioral patterns of early-stage attraction. It wouldn't be a hardship to take advantage of that. Since he only spent a few days a week in St. Chris, there was little danger of taking a casual flirtation into serious territory.

Wrangling an invitation to his home here wouldn't present a problem. She needed to see where and how Seth was living, who was in charge of his welfare.

Was he happy?

Gloria had said they'd stolen her son. That they'd used their influence and their money to snatch him away.

But Gloria was a liar. Sybill squeezed her eyes shut, struggling to be calm, to be objective, not to be hurt. Yes, Gloria was a liar, she thought again. A user. But she was also Seth's mother.

Going to the desk, Sybill opened her Filofax and slid the photograph out. A little boy with straw-colored hair and bright blue eyes smiled out at her. She'd taken the picture herself, the first and only time she'd seen Seth.

He must have been four, she thought now. Phillip had said he was ten now, and Sybill remembered it had been six years since Gloria showed up on her doorstep in New York with her son in tow.

She'd been desperate, of course. Broke, furious, weepy, begging. There'd been no choice but to take her in, not with the child staring up with those huge, haunted eyes. Sybill hadn't known anything about children. She'd never been around them. Perhaps that was why she'd fallen for Seth so quickly and so hard.

And when she'd come home three weeks later and found them gone, along with all the cash in the house, her jewelry, and her prized collection of Daum china, she'd been devastated.

She should have expected it, she told herself now. It had been classic Gloria behavior. But she'd believed, had needed to believe, that they could finally connect. That the child would make a difference. That she could help.

Well, this time, she thought as she tucked the photo away again, she would be more careful, less emotional. She knew that Gloria was telling at least part of the truth this time. Whatever she did from this point on would depend on her own judgment.

She would begin to judge when she saw her nephew again.

Sitting, she turned on her laptop and began to write her initial notes.

The Quinn brothers appear to have an easy, male-pattern relationship. From my single observation I would suspect they work together well. It will take additional study to determine what function each provides in this business partnership, and in their familial relations.

Both Cameron and Ethan Quinn are newly married. It will be necessary to meet their wives to understand the dynamics of this family. Logically one of them will represent the mother figure. Since Cameron's wife, Anna Spinelli Quinn, has a full-time career, one would suspect that Grace Monroe Quinn fulfills this function. However, it's a mistake to generalize such matters and this will require personal observations.

I found it telling that the business sign the Quinns hung this afternoon contained Seth's name, but as a Quinn. I can't say if this disposal of his legal name is for their benefit or his.

The boy must certainly be aware that the Quinns are filing for custody. I can't say as yet whether he has received any of the letters Gloria has written him. Perhaps the Quinns have disposed of them. Though I sympathize with her plight and her desperation to get her child back, it's best that she remain unaware that I've come here. Once I've documented my findings, I'll contact her. If there is a legal battle in the future, it's best to approach the matter with facts rather than raw emotion.

Hopefully the lawyer Gloria has engaged will contact the Quinns through the proper legal channels shortly.

For myself, I hope to see Seth tomorrow and gain some insight into the situation. It would be helpful to determine how much he knows about his parentage. As I have only recently become fully informed, I've not yet completely assimilated all the facts and their repercussions.

We will soon see if small towns are indeed a hotbed of information on their inhabitants. I intend to learn all I can learn about Professor Raymond Quinn before I'm done.

THREE

THE TYPICAL VENUE FOR SO-
cializing, information gathering, and mating rituals, small town or big
city, Sybill observed, was the local bar.

Whether it was decorated with brass and ferns or peanut shells and
tin ashtrays, whether the music was whiny country or heart-reeling
rock, it was the traditional spot for gathering and exchanging information.

Shiney's Pub in St. Christopher's certainly fit the bill. The decor
here was dark wood, cheap chrome, and faded posters of boats. The
music was loud, she decided, unable to fully identify the style booming
out of the towering amps flanking the small stage where four young
men pounded away at guitars and drums with more enthusiasm than
talent.

A trio of men at the bar kept their eyes glued to the baseball game
on the small-screen TV bracketed to the wall behind the bar. They
seemed content to watch the silent ballet of pitcher and batter while
they nursed brown bottles of beer and ate fistfuls of pretzels.

The dance floor was jammed. There were only four couples, but the
limited space caused several incidents of elbow rapping and hip bumping. No one seemed to mind.

The waitresses were decked out in foolish male-fantasy outfits—
short black skirts, tiny, tight V-neck blouses, fishnet stockings, and
stiletto heels.

Sybill felt instant sympathy.

She tucked herself into a wobbly table as far away from the amps as
humanly possible. The smoke and noise didn't bother her, nor did the

sticky floor or the jittery table. Her choice of seating afforded her the clearest view of the occupants.

She'd been desperate to escape her hotel room for a couple of hours. Now she was set to sit back, enjoy a glass of wine, and observe the natives.

The waitress who approached was a petite brunette with an enviable bustline and a cheery smile. "Hi. What can I get you?"

"A glass of Chardonnay and a side of ice."

"Coming right up." She set a black plastic bowl filled with pretzels on the table and picked her way back to the bar, taking orders as she went.

Sybill wondered if she'd just had her first encounter with Ethan's wife. Her information was that Grace Quinn worked at this bar. But there had been no wedding ring on the little brunette's finger, and Sybill assumed that a new bride would certainly wear one.

The other waitress? That one looked dangerous, she decided. Blond, built, and brooding. She was certainly attractive, in an obvious way. Still, nothing about her shouted newlywed either, particularly the way she leaned over an appreciative customer's table to give him the full benefit of her cleavage.

Sybill frowned and nibbled on a pretzel. If that was Grace Quinn, she would definitely be scratched from mother-figure status.

Something happened in the ball game, Sybill assumed, as the three men began to shout, cheering on someone named Eddie.

Out of habit she took out her notebook and began to record observations. The backslapping and arm punching of male companions. The body language of the females, leaning in for intimacy. The hair flipping, the eye shifting, hand gesturing. And of course, the mating ritual of the contemporary couple through the dance.

That was how Phillip saw her when he came in. She was smiling to herself, her gaze roaming, her hand scribbling. She looked, he thought, very cool, very remote. She might have been behind a thin sheet of one-way glass.

She'd pulled her hair back so that it lay in a sleek tail on her neck and left her face unframed. Gold drops studded with single colored stones swung at her ears. He watched her put her pen down to shrug out of a suede jacket of pale yellow.

He had driven in on impulse, giving in to restlessness. Now he blessed that vaguely dissatisfied mood that had dogged him all evening. She was, he decided, exactly what he'd been looking for.

"Sybill, right?" He saw the quick surprise flicker in her eyes when she glanced up. And he saw that those eyes were as clear and pure as lake water.

"That's right." Recovering, she closed her notebook and smiled. "Phillip, of Boats by Quinn."

"You here alone?"

"Yes . . . unless you'd like to sit down and have a drink."

"I'd love to." He pulled out a chair, nodding toward her notebook. "Did I interrupt you?"

"Not really." She shifted her smile to the waitress when her wine was served.

"Hey, Phil, want a draft?"

"Marsha, you read my mind."

Marsha, Sybill thought. That eliminated the perky brunette. "It's unusual music."

"The music here consistently sucks." He flashed a smile, quick, charming, and amused. "It's a tradition."

"Here's to tradition, then." She lifted her glass, sipped, then with a little hmmm began transferring ice into the wine.

"How would you rate the wine?"

"Well, it's basic, elemental, primitive." She sipped again, smiled winningly. "It sucks."

"That's also a proud Shiney's tradition. He's got Sam Adams on draft. It's a better bet."

"I'll remember that." Lips curved, she tilted her head. "Since you know the local traditions, I take it you've lived here for some time."

"Yeah." His eyes narrowed as he studied her, as something pushed at the edges of his memory. "I know you."

Her heart bounded hard into her throat. Taking her time, she picked up her glass again. Her hand remained steady, her voice even and easy. "I don't think so."

"No, I do. I know that face. It didn't click before, when you were wearing sunglasses. Something about . . ." He reached out, put a hand under her chin and angled her head again. "That look right there."

His fingertips were just a bit rough, his touch very confident and firm. The gesture itself warned her that this was a man used to touching women. And she was a woman unused to being touched.

In defense, Sybill arched an eyebrow. "A woman with a cynical bent would suspect that's a line, and not a very original one."

"I don't use lines," he murmured, concentrating on her face. "Except originals. I'm good with images, and I've seen that one. Clear, intelligent eyes, slightly amused smile. Sybill . . ." His gaze skimmed over her face, then his lips curved slowly. "Griffin. *Doctor* Sybill Griffin. *Familiar Strangers.*"

She let out the breath that had clogged in her lungs. Her success was still very new, and having her face recognized continued to surprise her. And, in this case, relieve her. There was no connection between Dr. Griffin and Seth DeLauter.

"You are good," she said lightly. "So, did you read the book or just look at my picture on the dust jacket?"

"I read it. Fascinating stuff. In fact, I liked it enough to go out and buy your first one. Haven't read it yet though."

"I'm flattered."

"You're good. Thanks, Marsha," he added when she set his beer in front of him.

"Y'all just holler if you need anything." Marsha winked. "Holler loud. This band's breaking sound records tonight."

Which gave him an excuse to edge his chair closer and lean in. Her scent was subtle, he noted. A man had to get very close to catch its message. "Tell me, Dr. Griffin, what's a renowned urbanite doing in an unapologetically rural water town like St. Chris?"

"Research. Behavioral patterns and traditions," she said, lifting her glass in a half toast. "Of small towns and rural communities."

"Quite a change of pace for you."

"Sociology and cultural interest aren't, and shouldn't be, limited to cities."

"Taking notes?"

"A few. The local tavern," she began, more comfortable now. "The regulars. The trio at the bar, obsessed with the ritual of male-dominated sports to the exclusion of the noise and activities around them. They could be home, kicked back in their Barcaloungers, but they prefer the bonding experience of passive participation in the event. In this way they have companionship, partners with whom to share the interest, who will either argue or agree. It doesn't matter which. It's the pattern that matters."

He found he enjoyed the way her voice took on a lecturing tone that brought out brisk Yankee. "The O's are in a hot pennant race, and you're deep in Orioles' territory. Maybe it's the game."

"The game is the vehicle. The pattern would remain fairly constant whether the vehicle was football or basketball." She shrugged. "The typical male gains more enjoyment from sports if he has at least one like-minded male companion with him. You have only to observe com-

mercials aimed primarily at the male consumer. Beer, for instance,"
she said, tapping a finger on his glass. "It's quite often sold by show-
casing a group of attractive men sharing some common experience. A
man then buys that brand of beer because he's been programmed to
believe that it will enhance his standing with his peer group."

Because he was grinning, she lifted her eyebrows. "You disagree?"

"Not at all. I'm in advertising, and that pretty much hit the nail."

"Advertising?" She ignored the little tug of guilt at the pretense. "I
wouldn't think there would be much call for that here."

"I work in Baltimore. I'm back here on weekends for a while. A
family thing. Long story."

"I'd like to hear it."

"Later." There was something, he thought, about those nearly
translucent blue eyes framed by long, inky lashes that made it nearly
impossible to look anywhere else. "Tell me what else you see."

"Well . . ." It was a fine skill, she decided. A masterwork. The way
he could look at a woman as if she were the most vital thing in the
world at that one moment. It made her heart bump pleasantly. "You
see the other waitress?"

Phillip glanced over, watched the frivolous bow on the back of the
woman's skirt swivel as she walked to the bar. "Hard to miss her."

"Yes. She fulfills certain primitive and typical male-fantasy require-
ments. But I'm referring to personality, not physicality."

"Okay." Phillip ran his tongue around his teeth. "What do you
see?"

"She's efficient, but she's already calculating the time until closing.
She knows how to size up the better tippers and play to them. She all
but ignores the table of college students there. They won't add much
to her bill. You'd see the same survival techniques from an experienced and cynical waitress in a New York bar."

"Linda Brewster," Phillip supplied. "Recently divorced, on the
prowl for a new, improved husband. Her family owns the pizza place,
so she's been waitressing off and on for years. Doesn't care for it. Do
you want to dance?"

"What?" Then that's not Grace either, she thought and struggled to
tune back in. "I'm sorry?"

"The band's slowed it down if they haven't turned it down. Would
you like to dance?"

"All right." She let him take her hand to lead her through the tables
to the dance floor, where they shoehorned themselves into the crowd.

"I think this is supposed to be a version of 'Angie,'" Phillip murmured.

"If Mick and the boys heard what they're doing to it, they'd shoot the entire band on sight."

"You like the Stones?"

"What's not to like?" Since they could do no more than sway, she tilted her head back to look at him. It wasn't a hardship to find his face so close to hers, or to be forced to press her body firmly to his. "Down-and-dirty rock and roll, no frills, no fuss. All sex."

"You like sex?"

She had to laugh. "What's not to like? And though I appreciate the thought, I don't intend to have any tonight."

"There's always tomorrow."

"There certainly is." She considered kissing him, letting him kiss her. As an experiment that would certainly include an aspect of enjoyment. Instead, she turned her head so cheeks brushed. He was entirely too attractive for an impulsive and uncalculated risk.

Better safe, she reminded herself, than stupid.

"Why don't I take you to dinner tomorrow?" Skillfully, he slid a hand up her spine, back down to her waist. "There's a nice place right in town. Terrific view of the Bay, best seafood on the Shore. We can have a conversation in normal tones, and you can tell me the story of your life."

His lips had brushed her ear, sending a shocking ripple of reaction down to her toes. She should have known, she thought, that anyone who looked like he did would be damn good at sexual maneuvers.

"I'll think about it," she murmured and, deciding to give as good as she got, skimmed her fingertips over the back of his neck. "And let you know."

When the song ended, and the next picked up on a blast of sound and speed, she eased away. "I have to go."

"What?" He leaned down so she could shout in his ear.

"I have to go. Thanks for the dance."

"I'll walk you out."

Back at the table, he pulled out some bills while she gathered her things. The first step outside into the cool and quiet air made her laugh. "Well, that was an experience. Thank you for adding to it."

"I wouldn't have missed it. It's not very late," he added, taking her hand.

"Late enough." She pulled out the keys to her car.

"Come by the boatyard tomorrow. I'll show you around."

"I might just do that. Good night, Phillip."

"Sybill." He didn't bother to resist, simply brought her hand to his lips. Over their joined fingers, his eyes locked with hers. "I'm glad you picked St. Chris."

"So am I."

She slipped into her car, relieved that she had to concentrate on the task of switching on the lights, releasing the brake, starting the engine. Driving wasn't second nature to a woman who had depended on public transportation or private car services most of her life.

She focused on reversing, on putting the car in drive to make the turn onto the road. And she firmly ignored the faint echo of pressure on her knuckles where his lips had touched.

But she didn't quite resist glancing in the rearview mirror and taking one last look at him before she drove away.

Phillip decided that going back into Shiney's would be absurdly anticlimactic. He thought about her as he drove home, the way her eyebrows arched when she made a point or enjoyed a comment. That subtle and intimate scent she wore that told a man that if he'd gotten close enough to catch a whiff, maybe, just maybe, he'd have a chance to get closer.

He told himself she was the perfect woman for him to invest some time in getting closer to. She was beautiful; she was smart; she was cultured and sophisticated.

And just sexy enough to make his hormones stand at attention.

He liked women, and missed having time for conversations with them. Not that he didn't enjoy talking with Anna and Grace. But let's face it, it wasn't quite the same as talking with a woman when you could also fantasize about taking her to bed.

And he'd been missing that particular area of male-female relationships just lately. He rarely had time to do more than stumble into his apartment after a ten- or twelve-hour workday. His once interesting and varied social calendar had taken some large hits since Seth had come to the family.

The week was dedicated to his accounts and consultations with the lawyer. The fight with the insurance company on payment of his father's death benefits was coming to a head. The resolution of permanent guardianship of Seth would be decided within ninety days. The responsibility of dealing with the mountain of paperwork and phone calls that sprang from those actions was his. Details were his strong point.

Weekends were consumed by household duties, the business, and whatever had slipped through the cracks during the week.

When you added it all up, he mused, it didn't leave much time for cozy dinners with attractive women, much less the ritual of slipping between the sheets with those women.

Which explained his recent restlessness and moodiness, he supposed. When a man's sex life virtually vanished, he was bound to get a little edgy.

The house was dark but for the single beam of the porch light when he pulled into the drive. Barely midnight on Friday night, he thought with a sigh. How the mighty have fallen. There would have been a time when he and his brothers would have been out cruising, looking for action. Well, he and Cam would have dragged Ethan along, but once they'd hounded him into it, Ethan would have held up his end.

The Quinn boys hadn't spent many Friday nights snoozing.

These days, he thought as he climbed out of the Jeep, Cam would be upstairs cozied up to his wife and Ethan would be tucked into Grace's little house. Undoubtedly they both had smiles on their faces.

Lucky bastards.

Knowing he wouldn't be able to sleep, he skirted the house and walked to where the edge of the trees met the edge of the water.

The moon was a fat ball riding the night sky. It shed its soft white light over the dark water, wet eelgrass, and thick leaves.

Cicadas were singing in their high, monotonous voices, and deep in those thick woods, an owl called out in tireless two-toned notes.

Perhaps he preferred the sounds of the city, voices and traffic muffled through glass. But he never failed to find this spot appealing. Though he missed the city's pace, the theater and museums, the eclectic mix of food and people, he could appreciate the peace and the stability found right here day after day. Year after year.

Without it, he had no doubt he would have found his way back to the gutter. And died there.

"You always wanted more for yourself than that."

The chill washed through him, from gut to fingertips. Where he had been standing, staring out at the moonlight showering through the trees, he was now staring at his father. The father he'd buried six months before.

"I only had one beer," he heard himself say.

"You're not drunk, son." Ray stepped forward so that the moonlight shimmered over his dramatic mane of silver hair and into the brilliant blue eyes that were bright with humor. "You're going to want to breathe now, before you pass out."

Phillip let out his breath in a *whoosh*, but his ears continued to ring. "I'm going to sit down now." He did, slowly, like a creaky old man, easing himself down onto the grass. "I don't believe in ghosts," he said to the water, "or reincarnation, the afterlife, visitations, or any form of psychic phenomenon."

"You always were the most pragmatic of the lot. Nothing was real unless you could see it, touch it, smell it."

Ray sat beside him with a contented sigh and stretched out long legs clad in frayed jeans. He crossed his ankles, and on his feet were the well-worn Dock-Sides that Phillip himself had packed into a box for the Salvation Army nearly six months before.

"Well," Ray said cheerfully, "you're seeing me, aren't you?"

"No. I'm having an episode most likely resulting from sexual deprivation and overwork."

"I won't argue with you. It's too pretty a night."

"I haven't reached closure yet," Phillip said to himself. "I'm still angry over the way he died, and why, and all the unanswered questions. So I'm projecting."

"I figured you'd be the toughest nut of the three. Always had an answer for everything. I know you've got questions, too. And I know you've got anger. You're entitled. You've had to change your life and take on responsibilities that shouldn't have been yours. But you did it, and I'm grateful."

"I don't have time for therapy right now. There's no place on the schedule to fit sessions in."

Ray let out a hoot of laughter. "Boy, you're not drunk, and you're not crazy either. You're just stubborn. Why don't you use that flexible mind of yours, Phillip, and consider a possibility?"

Bracing himself, Phillip turned his head. It was his father's face, wide and lined with life and filled with humor. Those bright-blue eyes were dancing, the silver hair ruffling in the night air. "This is an impossibility."

"Some people said when your mother and I took you and your brothers in, that it was an impossibility we'd make a family, make a difference. They were wrong. If we'd listened to them, if we'd gone by logic, none of you would have been ours. But fate doesn't give a horse's ass about logic. It just is. And you were meant to be ours."

"Okay." Phillip shot out a hand and jerked it back in shock. "How could I do that? How could I touch you if you're a ghost?"

"Because you need to." Casually, Ray gave Phillip's shoulder a quick pat. "I'm here, for the next little while."

Phillip's throat filled even as his stomach tightened into knots. "Why?"

"I didn't finish. I left it up to you and your brothers. I'm sorry for that, Phillip."

It wasn't happening, of course, Phillip told himself. He was probably in the first stages of a minor breakdown. He could feel the air against his face, warm and moist. The cicadas were still shrilling, the owl still hooting.

If he was having an episode, he thought again, it seemed only right to play it out. "They're trying to say it was suicide," he said slowly. "The insurance company's fighting the claim."

"I hope you know that's bullshit. I was careless, distracted. I had an accident." There was an edge to Ray's voice now, an impatience and annoyance that Phillip recognized. "I wouldn't have taken the easy way. And I had the boy to think about."

"Is Seth your son?"

"I can tell you that he belongs to me."

Both his head and his heart ached as he turned to stare out at the water again. "Mom was still alive when he was conceived."

"I know that. I was never unfaithful to your mother."

"Then how—"

"You need to accept him, for himself. I know you care for him. I know you're doing your best by him. You have that last step to take. Acceptance. He needs you, all of you."

"Nothing's going to happen to him," Phillip said grimly. "We'll see to that."

"He'll change your life, if you let him."

Phillip let out a short laugh. "Believe me, he already has."

"In a way that will make your life better. Don't close yourself off to those possibilities. And don't worry too much about this little visit." Ray patted him companionably on the knee. "Talk to your brothers."

"Yeah, like I'm going to tell them I sat outside in the middle of the night and talked to . . ." He looked over, saw nothing but the moonlight on the trees.

"Nobody," he finished and wearily laid down on the grass to stare up at the moon. "God, I need a vacation."

FOUR

It wouldn't do to appear too anxious, Sybill reminded herself. Or to get there too early. It had to be casual. She had to be relaxed.

She decided not to take her car. It would look more like a careless visit if she walked down from the waterfront. And if she included the visit to the boatyard in an afternoon of shopping and wandering, it would appear more impulsive than calculated.

To calm herself, she roamed the waterfront. A pretty Indian-summer Saturday morning drew tourists. They poked and strolled along as she did, dropping into the little shops, pausing to watch boats sail or motor on the Bay. No one seemed to be in a particular hurry or have a specific destination.

That in itself, she mused, made an interesting contrast to the usual urban Saturday when even the tourists seemed to be in a rush to get from one place to the next.

It would be something to consider and analyze and perhaps theorize over in her book. And because she *did* find it interesting, she slipped her mini recorder out of her bag and murmured a few verbal notes and observations.

"Families appear to be relaxed rather than harried or desperately seeking the entertainment they've traveled to find. The natives seem to be friendly and patient. Life is slow to reflect the pace set by the people who make their living here."

The little shops weren't doing what she'd term a bustling business, yet the merchants didn't have that anxious and sly-eyed look prevalent among the vendors where the crowds were thick and the wallets tightly guarded.

She bought a few postcards for friends and associates in New York, then, more out of habit than need, selected a book on the history of the area. It would help her in her research, she imagined. She lingered over a pewter fairy with a teardrop crystal hanging from her elegant fingers. But she resisted it, firmly reminding herself that she could purchase any sort of foolishness she wanted in New York.

Crawford's appeared to be a popular spot, so she strolled in and treated herself to an ice cream cone. It gave her something to do with her hands as she walked the few blocks to Boats by Quinn.

She appreciated the value of props. Everyone used them in the continuing play of living, she thought. A glass at a cocktail party, a paperback book on the subway. Jewelry, she realized when she caught herself twisting her necklace around her nervous fingers.

She dropped the chain, and concentrated on enjoying her scoop of raspberry sherbet.

It didn't take long to walk to the outskirts of town. She calculated that the waterfront area ran for barely a mile from end to end.

The neighborhoods ran west from the water. Narrow streets with tidy houses and tiny lawns. Low fences designed as much for backyard gossiping, she mused, as for boundary lines. Trees were large and leafy, still holding the deep, dark green of summer. It would be, she thought, an attractive sight when they turned with autumn.

Kids played in yards or rode bikes along the sloping sidewalks. She saw a teenage boy lovingly waxing an old Chevy compact, singing in a loud, just-out-of-tune voice to whatever played through his headphones.

A long-legged mutt with floppy ears rushed a fence as she passed, barking in deep, rusty clips. Her heart did a quick dance when he planted his huge paws on the top of the fence. And she kept walking.

She didn't know much about dogs.

She spotted Phillip's Jeep in the pothole-filled parking lot beside the boatyard. An aging pickup truck kept it company. The doors and several of the windows of the building were wide open. Through them came the buzz of saws and the Southern rock beat of John Fogerty.

Okay, Sybill, she thought and took a deep breath as she carefully swallowed the last of her cone. Now or never.

She stepped inside and found herself momentarily distracted by the look of the place. It was huge, and dusty and bright as a spotlighted stage. The Quinns were hard at work, with Ethan and Cam fitting a long, bent plank into place on what she assumed was a hull in progress. Phillip stood at a big, dangerous-looking power saw, running lumber through it.

She didn't see Seth.

For a moment she simply watched and wondered if she should slip back out again. If her nephew wasn't there, it would be more sensible to postpone the visit until she was sure he was.

He might be away for the day with friends. Did he have any friends? Or he could be home. Did he consider it his home?

Before she could decide, the saw switched off, leaving only John Fogerty crooning about a brown-eyed, handsome man. Phillip stepped back, pushed up his safety goggles, turned. And saw her.

His smile of welcome came so quickly, so sincerely, that she had to clamp down on a hard tug of guilt. "I'm interrupting." She raised her voice to compete with the music.

"Thank God." Dusting his hands on his jeans, Phillip started toward her. "I've been stuck with looking at these guys all day. You're a big improvement."

"I decided to play tourist." She jiggled the shopping bag she carried. "And I thought I'd take you up on the offer of a tour."

"I was hoping you would."

"So . . ." Deliberately, she shifted her gaze to the hull. It was safer, she decided, than looking into those tawny eyes for any length of time. "That's a boat?"

"It's a hull. Or will be." He took her hand, drew her forward. "It's going to be a sport's fisher."

"Which is?"

"One of those fancy boats men like to go out on to act manly, fish for marlin, and drink beer."

"Hey, Sybill." Cam shot her a grin. "Want a job?"

She looked at the tools, the sharp edges, the heavy lumber. "I don't think so." It was easy to smile back, to look over at Ethan. "It looks like the three of you know what you're doing."

"We know what we're doing." Cam wiggled his thumb between himself and Ethan. "We keep Phillip around for entertainment."

"I'm not appreciated around here."

She laughed and began to circle the hull. She could understand the basic shape but not the process. "I assume this is upside down."

"Good eye." Phillip only grinned when she cocked an eyebrow. "After she's planked, we'll turn her and start on the decking."

"Are your parents boatbuilders?"

"No, my mother was a doctor, my father a college professor. But we grew up around boats."

She heard it in his voice, the affection, the not-quite-settled grief. And hated herself. She'd intended to ask him more about his parents in some detail, but couldn't. "I've never been on a boat."

"Ever?"

"I imagine there are several million people in the world who haven't."

"Want to?"

"Maybe. I've enjoyed watching the boats from my hotel window." As she studied it, the hull became a puzzle she needed to solve. "How do you know where to begin to build this? I assume you work from a design, blueprints or schematics or whatever you call it."

"Ethan's been doing the bulk of the design work. Cam fiddles with it. Seth draws it up."

"Seth." Her fingers tightened on the strap of her purse. Props, she thought again. "Didn't you say he was in middle school?"

"That's right. The kid's got a real talent for drawing. Check these out."

Now she heard pride and it flustered her. Struggling for composure, she followed him to a far wall, where drawings of boats were roughly framed in raw wood. They were good—very, very good. Clever sketches done with pencil and care and talent.

"He . . . A young boy drew these?"

"Yes. Pretty great, huh? This is the one we just finished." He tapped a hand on the glass. "And this one's what we're working on now."

"He's very talented," she murmured around the lump in her throat. "He has excellent perspective."

"Do you draw?"

"A little, now and then. Just a hobby." She had to turn away to settle herself. "It relaxes me, and it helps in my work." Determined to smile again, she tossed her hair over her shoulder and aimed a bright, easy one at Phillip. "So, where's the artist today?"

"Oh, he's—"

He broke off as two dogs raced into the building. Sybill took an instinctive step back as the smaller of the two made a beeline in her direction. She made some strangled sound of distress just as Phillip jabbed out a finger and issued a sharp command.

"Hold it, you idiot. No jumping. No jumping," he repeated, but Foolish's forward motion proved too much for all of them. He was already up, already had his paws planted just under Sybill's breasts.

She staggered a bit, seeing only big, sharp teeth bared in what she took for fierceness rather than a sloppy doggie grin.

"Nice dog," she managed in a stutter. "Good dog."

"Stupid dog," Phillip corrected and hauled Foolish down by the collar. "No manners. Sit. Sorry," he said to Sybill when the dog obligingly plopped down and offered his paw. "He's Foolish."

"Well, he's enthusiastic."

"No, Foolish is his name—and his personality. He'll stay like that until you shake his paw."

"Oh. Hmm." Gingerly she took the paw with two fingers.

"He won't bite." Phillip angled his head, noting there was a good deal more distress than irritation in her eyes. "Sorry—are you afraid of dogs?"

"I . . . maybe a little—of large, strange dogs."

"He's strange, all right. The other one's Simon, and he's considerably more polite." Phillip scratched Simon's ears as the dog sat calmly studying Sybill. "He's Ethan's. The idiot belongs to Seth."

"I see." Seth had a dog, was all she could think as Foolish offered his paw yet again, eyeing her with what appeared abject adoration. "I don't know very much about dogs, I'm afraid."

"These are Chesapeake Bay retrievers—or Foolish mostly is. We're not sure what else he is. Seth, call off your dog before he slobbers all over the lady's shoes."

Sybill lifted her head quickly and saw the boy just inside the doorway. The sun was streaming at his back, and it cast his face into shadows. She saw only a tall, slightly built boy carrying a large brown bag and wearing a black-and-orange ball cap.

"He doesn't slobber much. Hey, Foolish!"

Instantly, both dogs scrambled to their feet and raced across the room. Seth waded through them, carrying the bag to a makeshift table fashioned from a sheet of plywood laid over two sawhorses.

"I don't know why I have to always go up for lunch and stuff," he complained.

"Because we're bigger than you," Cam told him and dived into the bag. "You get me the cold-cut sub loaded?"

"Yeah, yeah."

"Where's my change?"

Seth pulled a liter of Pepsi out of the bag, cracked the top and guzzled straight from the bottle. Then he grinned. "What change?"

"Look, you little thief, I've got at least two bucks coming back."

"Don't know what you're talking about. You must've forgotten to add on the carrying charges again."

Cam made a grab for him, and Seth danced agilely away, hooting with laughter.

"Brotherly love," Phillip said easily. "That's why I make sure I only give the kid the right change. You never see a nickel back otherwise. Want some lunch?"

"No, I . . . ." She couldn't take her eyes off Seth, knew she had to. He was talking with Ethan now, making wide, exaggerated gestures with his free hand while his dog took quick, playful leaps at his fingers. "I had something already. But you go ahead."

"A drink, then. Did you get my water, kid?"

"Yeah, fancy water. Waste of money. Man, Crawford's was packed."

Crawford's. With a sensation she couldn't quite define, Sybill realized they might have been in the store at the same time. Might have walked right by each other. She would have passed him on the street without a clue.

Seth glanced from Phillip to Sybill, studied her with mild interest. "You buying a boat?"

"No." He didn't recognize her, she thought. Of course he wouldn't. He'd been hardly more than a baby the only time they'd seen each other. There was no stunned familial awareness in his eyes, any more than there would have been in hers. But she knew. "I'm just looking around."

"That's cool." He went back to the bag and pulled out his own sandwich.

"Ah . . . ." Talk to him, she ordered herself. Say something. Anything. "Phillip was just showing me your drawings. They're wonderful."

"They're okay." He jerked a shoulder, but she thought she saw a faint flush of pleasure on his cheeks. "I could do better, but they're always rushing me."

Casually—she hoped it was casually—she crossed to him. She could see him clearly now. His eyes were blue, but a deeper, darker blue than hers or her sister's. His hair was a darker blond than the little boy's in the picture she carried. He'd been nearly a towhead at four, and now his hair was a richer blond and very straight.

The mouth, she thought. Wasn't there some resemblance around the mouth and chin?

"Is that what you want to be?" She needed to keep him talking. "An artist?"

"Maybe, but that's mostly for kicks." He took a huge bite of his sandwich, then talked through it. "We're boatbuilders."

His hands were far from clean, she noted, and his face wasn't much better. She imagined such niceties as washing up before meals went by the wayside in a household of males. "Maybe you'll go into design work."

"Seth, this is Dr. Sybill Griffin." Phillip offered Sybill a plastic cup of bubbling water over ice. "She writes books."

"Like stories?"

"Not exactly," she told him. "Like observations. Right now I'm spending some time in the area, observing."

He wiped his mouth with a swipe from the back of his hand. The hand Foolish had enthusiastically licked, before and after, Sybill noted with an inward wince.

"You going to do a book about boats?" he asked her.

"No, about people. People who live in small towns, and right now people who live in small towns by the water. How do you like it—living here, I mean?"

"I like it okay. Living in the city sucks." He picked up the soft drink bottle, glugged again. "People who live there are nuts." He grinned. "Like Phil."

"You're a peasant, Seth. I worry about you."

With a snort, Seth bit into his sandwich again. "I'm going out on the dock. We got some ducks hanging out."

He bounced out, dogs trailing behind him.

"Seth's got very definite opinions," Phillip said dryly. "I guess the world's pretty black and white when you're ten."

"He doesn't care for the urban experience." Nerves, she noted, had been drowned out by sheer curiosity. "Has he spent time with you in Baltimore?"

"No. He lived there for a while with his mother." His tone had darkened, making Sybill raise an eyebrow. "Part of that long story I mentioned."

"I believe I mentioned I'd enjoy hearing it."

"Then have dinner with me tonight, and we'll exchange those life stories."

She looked toward the cargo doors. Seth had gone out through them, very much at home. She needed to spend more time with him. Observing. And, she decided, she needed to hear what the Quinns had to say about the situation. Why not start with Phillip?

"All right. I'd like that."

"I'll pick you up at seven."

She shook her head. He seemed perfectly safe, perfectly fine, but she knew better than to take chances. "No, I'll meet you there. Where's the restaurant?"

"I'll write it down for you. We can start the tour in my office."

IT WAS EASY ENOUGH, AND SHE had to admit it was interesting. The tour itself didn't take long. Other than the huge work area, there was little to the boatyard—just Phillip's closet-size office, a small bathroom, and a dark, dingy storeroom.

It was obvious even to the untrained eye that the work center of the operation was its heart and soul.

It was Ethan who patiently instructed her on smooth-lap planking, about waterlines and bow shapes. She thought he would have made an excellent teacher, with his clear, simple phrasing and willingness to answer what must have been very basic questions.

She watched, genuinely fascinated, as the men held timber in a box and pumped out steam until the plank bowed into the shape they desired. Cam demonstrated how the ends were rabbeted together to form the smooth joints.

Watching Cam with Seth, she was forced to admit there was a definite bond between them. If she had come across them knowing nothing, she would have assumed they were brothers, or perhaps father and son. It was all in the attitude, she decided.

Then again, they had an audience, she mused, and were likely on their best behavior.

She would see how they acted once they became used to her.

CAM LET OUT A LONG, LOW whistle when Sybill left the building. He wiggled his eyebrows meaningfully at Phillip. "Very nice, bro. Very nice, indeed."

Phillip flashed a grin, then lifted his bottle of water to his lips. "Can't complain."

"She going to be around long enough to, ah . . ."

"If there's a God."

Seth laid a plank down by the saw, let out a huff. "Shit, you mean you're going to start poking at her? Is that all you guys think about?"

"Other than pounding on you?" Phillip whipped off Seth's hat and bopped the boy over the head with it. "Sure, what else?"

"You guys are always getting married," Seth said in disgust and tried to grab his hat.

"I don't want to marry her, I just want to have a nice, civilized dinner with her."

"Then bounce on her," Seth finished.

"Christ. He gets that from you," Phillip accused Cam.

"He came that way." Cam wrapped an arm around Seth's neck. "Didn't you, brat?"

The panic didn't come now, as it used to whenever Seth was touched or held. Instead he wriggled and grinned. "At least I think of something besides girls all the time. You guys are really lame."

"Lame?" Phillip put Seth's hat on his own head to free his hands, then rubbed them together. "Let's toss this runt fish off the dock."

"Can you do that later?" Ethan asked while Seth shouted in wild and delighted objection. "Or do I have to build this damn boat by myself?"

"Later, then." Phillip leaned down until he and Seth were nose to nose. "And you won't know when, you won't know where, you won't know why."

"Man, I'm shaking now."

I *SAW SETH TODAY.*

At her laptop, Sybill gnawed her bottom lip, then deleted the first sentence she'd typed.

I made contact with the subject this afternoon.

Better, she decided. More objective. To approach this situation properly, it would be best if she thought of Seth as the subject.

There was no recognition on either side. This is, of course, as expected. He appears to be healthy. He's attractive, slimly built yet sturdy. Gloria was always thin, so I suspect he's inherited her basic body type. He's blond, as she is—or was when I last saw her.

He seemed to be comfortable with me. I'm aware that some children are shy around strangers. That doesn't appear to be the case here.

Though he was not at the boatyard when I arrived, he came in shortly after. He'd been sent to the store for lunch. From the ensuing complaints and conversation, I can assume he is often expected to run errands. This could be construed two ways. One that the Quinns take advantage of having a young boy available and use him accordingly. Or two, that they are instilling a sense of responsibility.

The truth likely resides in the middle.

He has a dog. I believe this to be a usual, even traditional occurrence for a child living in suburban or rural areas.

He also has a talent for drawing. I was somewhat taken by surprise by this. I have some talent for it myself, as does my mother. Gloria, however, never showed any skill or interest in art. This shared interest may be a way to develop a rapport with the boy. It will be necessary to have some time alone with him to assist me in choosing the correct course to take.

The subject is, in my opinion, comfortable with the Quinns. He seems to be content and secure. There is, however, a certain roughness, a mild crudeness in him. Several times during the hour or so I spent with him, I heard him swear. Once or twice he was rather absently corrected, otherwise his language was ignored.

He was not required to wash his hands before eating, nor did any of the Quinns correct him for speaking with his mouth full or for feeding the dogs bits of his lunch. His manners are by no means appalling, but they are far from strictly polite.

He mentioned preferring living here to the city. In fact, he was most disdainful of urban life. I have agreed to have dinner with Phillip Quinn tonight and will urge him to tell me the facts of how Seth came to be with the Quinns.

How those facts agree with, and differ from, the facts I received from Gloria will help me assimilate the situation.

The next step will be to obtain an invitation to the Quinn house. I'm very interested to see where the boy is living, to see him and the Quinns on this stage. And to meet the women who are now a part of his foster family.

I hesitate to contact Social Services and identify myself until I have completed this personal study.

Sybill sat back, tapping her fingers on the desk as she skimmed over her notes. It was so little, really, she thought. And her own fault. She'd thought she was prepared for that first meeting, but she wasn't.

Seeing him had left her dry-mouthed and sad. The boy was her nephew, her family. Yet they were strangers. And wasn't that nearly as much her fault as it was Gloria's? Had she ever really tried to make a connection, to bring him into her life?

True, she had rarely known where he was, but had she ever gone out of her way to find him, or her sister?

The few times Gloria had contacted her over the years for money, always for money, she had asked about Seth. But hadn't she simply taken Gloria's word that the child was fine? Had she ever demanded to speak with him, to see him?

Hadn't it simply been easier for her to send money over the wire and forget about them again?

Easier, she admitted. Because the one time she had let him in, the one time she had let herself open her home and her heart, he'd been taken away. And she had suffered.

This time she would do something. She would do whatever was right, whatever was best. She wouldn't allow herself to become too emotionally involved, however. After all, he wasn't her child. If Gloria retained custody, he would still move out of her life again.

But she would make the effort, take the time, see that he was situated well. Then she would get on with her life and her work.

Satisfied, she saved the document and shifted to another to continue her notes for her book. Before she could begin, the phone on her desk rang.

"Yes. Dr. Griffin."

"Sybill. It took me a great deal of time and trouble to track you down."

"Mother." On a long sigh Sybill closed her eyes. "Hello."

"Would you mind telling me what you're doing?"

"Not at all. I'm researching a new book. How are you? How's Father?"

"Please, don't insult my intelligence. I thought we'd agreed you would stay out of this sordid little affair."

"No." As it always did when faced with a family confrontation, Sybill's stomach pitched. "We agreed that you would prefer I stay out of it. I decided I prefer not to. I've seen Seth."

"I'm not interested in Gloria, or her son."

"I am. I'm sorry that upsets you."

"Can you expect it to do otherwise? Your sister has chosen her own life and is no longer a part of mine. I will not be dragged into this."

"I have no intention of dragging you into this." Resigned, Sybill reached into her purse and found the small cloisonné box she used to store aspirin. "No one knows who I am. And even if I'm connected to

Dr. and Mrs. Walter Griffin, that hardly follows to Gloria and Seth
DeLauter."

"It can be followed, if anyone becomes interested enough to pursue
it. You can't accomplish anything by staying there and interfering in
this situation, Sybill. I want you to leave. Go back to New York, or
come here to Paris. Perhaps you'll listen to your father if not to me."

Sybill washed down the aspirin with water, then dug out antacids.
"I'm going to see this through. I'm sorry."

There was a long silence ripe with temper and frustration. Sybill
closed her eyes, left them closed, and waited.

"You were always a joy to me. I never expected this kind of betrayal.
I very much regret that I spoke with you about this matter. I wouldn't
have if I'd known you would react so outrageously."

"He's a ten-year-old boy, Mother. He's your grandson."

"He is nothing to me, or to you. If you continue this, Gloria will
make you pay for what you see as kindness."

"I can handle Gloria."

There was a laugh now, short and brittle as glass. "So you always
believed. And you were always wrong. Please don't contact me, or
your father, about any of this. I'll expect to hear from you when you've
come to your senses."

"Mother—" The dial tone made Sybill wince. Barbara Griffin was a
master at having the last word. Very carefully, Sybill set the receiver
on the hook. Very deliberately, she swallowed the antacid.

Then, very defiantly, she turned back to her screen and buried herself in work.

FIVE

SINCE SYBILL WAS ALWAYS ON time and nearly everyone else in the world, as far as she was concerned, never was, she was surprised to find Phillip already sitting at the table he'd reserved for dinner.

He rose, offered her a killer smile and a single yellow rose. Both charmed her and made her suspicious.

"Thank you."

"My pleasure. Sincerely. You look wonderful."

She'd gone to some trouble in that area, but more for herself than for him. The call from her mother had left her miserably depressed and guilty. She'd tried to fight off both emotions by taking a great deal of time and putting a great deal of effort into her appearance.

The simple black dress with its square neck and long, snug sleeves was one of her favorites. The single strand of pearls was a legacy from her paternal grandmother and much loved. She'd swept her hair up in a smooth twist and added sapphire cabochon earrings that she'd bought in London years before.

She knew it was the sort of feminine armor that women slipped into for confidence and power. She'd wanted both. "Thank you again." She slid into the booth across from him and sniffed the rose. "And so do you."

"I know the wine list here," he told her. "Trust me?"

"On wine? Why not?"

"Good." He glanced toward the server. "We'll have a bottle of the number 103."

She laid the rose beside the leather-bound menu. "Which is?"

"A very nice Pouilly Fuisse. I remember from Shiney's that you like white. I think you'll find this a few very important steps up from what you had there."

"Almost anything would be."

He cocked his head, took her hand. "Something's wrong."

"No." Deliberately she curved her lips. "What could be wrong? It's just as advertised." She turned her head to look out the window beside her, where the Bay stretched, dark blue and excitingly choppy under a sky going rosy with sunset. "A lovely view, a pretty spot." She turned back. "An interesting companion for the evening."

No, he thought, watching her eyes. Something was just a little off. On impulse he slid over, cupped her chin in his hand, and laid his lips lightly on hers.

She didn't draw away, but allowed herself to experience. The kiss was easy, smooth, skilled. And very soothing. When he drew back, she raised an eyebrow. "And that was because?"

"You looked like you needed it."

She didn't sigh, but she wanted to. Instead, she put her hands in her lap. "Thank you once again."

"Any time. In fact . . ." His fingers tightened just a little on her face, and this time the kiss moved a bit deeper, lasted a bit longer.

Her lips parted under his before she realized that she'd meant it to happen. Her breath caught, released, and her pulse shivered as his teeth scraped lightly, as his tongue teased hers into a slow, seductive dance.

Her fingers were linked and gripped tight, her mind just beginning to blur when he eased away.

"And that was because?" she managed.

"I guess I needed it."

His lips brushed over hers once, then again, before she found the presence of mind to lay a hand on his chest. A hand, she realized, that wanted to ball into a fist on that soft shirt and hold him in place rather than nudge him away.

But she nudged him away. It was simply a matter of handling him, she reminded herself. Of staying in control.

"I think as appetizers go, that was very appealing. But we should order."

"Tell me what's wrong." He wanted to know, he realized. Wanted to help, wanted to smooth those shadows out of her incredibly clear eyes and make them smile.

He hadn't expected to develop a taste for her so quickly.

"It's nothing."

"Of course it is. And there can't be anything much more therapeutic than dumping on a relative stranger."

"You're right." She opened her menu. "But most relative strangers aren't particularly interested in someone else's minor problems."

"I'm interested in you."

She smiled as she shifted her gaze from the entrées to his face. "You're attracted to me. That's not always the same thing."

"I think I'm both."

He took her hand, held it as the wine was brought to the table, as the label was turned for his approval. He waited while a sample was poured into his glass, watching her in that steady, all-else-aside way she'd discovered he had. He lifted it, sipped, still looking at her.

"It's perfect. You'll like it," he murmured to her while their glasses were being filled.

"You're right," she told him after she sipped. "I like it very much."

"Shall I tell you tonight's specials," their waiter began in a cheerful voice. While he recited, they sat, hands linked, eyes locked.

Sybill decided she heard about every third word and didn't really give a damn. He had the most incredible eyes. Like old gold, like something she'd seen in a painting in Rome. "I'll have the mixed salad, with the vinaigrette, and the fish of the day, grilled."

He kept watching her, his lips curving slowly as he drew her hand across the table to kiss her palm. "The same. And take your time. I'm very attracted," he said to Sybill as the waiter rolled his eyes and walked away. "And I'm very interested. Talk to me."

"All right." What harm could it do? she decided. Since, sooner or later, they would have to deal with each other on a different sort of level, it might be helpful if they understood one another now. "I'm the good daughter." Amused at herself, she smiled a little. "Obedient, respectful, polite, academically skilled, professionally successful."

"It's a burden."

"Yes, it can be. Of course, I know better, intellectually, than to allow myself to be ruled by parental expectations at this stage of my life."

"But," Phillip said, giving her fingers a squeeze, "you are. We all are."

"Are you?"

He thought of sitting by the water in the moonlight and having a conversation with his dead father. "More than I might have believed. In my case, my parents didn't give me life. They gave me *the* life. This life. In yours," he considered, "since you're the good daughter, is there a bad daughter?"

"My sister has always been difficult. Certainly she's been a disappointment to my parents. And the more disappointed they've become in her, the more they expect from me."

"You're supposed to be perfect."

"Exactly, and I can't be." Wanted to be, tried to be, couldn't be. Which, of course, equaled failure. How could it be otherwise? she mused.

"Perfect is boring," Phillip commented. "And intimidating. Why try to be either? So what happened?" he asked when she only frowned.

"It's nothing, really. My mother is angry with me just now. If I give in and do what she wants . . . well, I can't. I just can't."

"So you feel guilty and sad and sorry."

"And afraid that nothing will ever be the same between us again."

"As bad as that?"

"It could be," Sybill murmured. "I'm grateful for all the opportunities they gave me, the structure, the education. We traveled quite a bit, so I saw a great deal of the world, of different cultures, while I was still a child. It's been invaluable in my work."

Opportunities, Phillip thought. Structure, education, and travel. Nowhere had she listed love, affection, fun. He wondered if she realized she'd described a school more than a family. "Where did you grow up?"

"Um. Here and there. New York, Boston, Chicago, Paris, Milan, London. My father lectured and held consultations. He's a psychiatrist. They live in Paris now. It was always my mother's favorite city."

"Long-distance guilt."

It made her laugh. "Yes." She sat back as their salads were served. Oddly enough, she did feel a little better. It seemed slightly less deceptive to have told him something about herself. "And you grew up here."

"I came here when I was thirteen, when the Quinns became my parents."

"Became?"

"It's part of that long story." He lifted his wineglass, studying her over its rim. Normally if he brought up that period of his life with a woman, what he told was a carefully edited version. Not a lie, but a less-than-detailed account of his life before the Quinns.

Oddly enough, he was tempted to tell Sybill the whole, the ugly and unvarnished truth. He hesitated, then settled on something between the two.

"I grew up in Baltimore, on the rough side. I got into trouble, pretty serious trouble. By the time I was thirteen, I was headed for worse. The Quinns gave me a chance to change that. They took me in, brought me to St. Chris. Became my family."

"They adopted you." She'd had that much information, from researching everything she could find on Raymond Quinn. But it didn't give her the why.

"Yeah. They already had Cam and Ethan, and they made room for one more. I didn't make it easy for them initially, but they stuck with me. I never knew either of them to back off from a problem."

He thought of his father, broken and dying in a hospital bed. Even then Ray's concerns had been for his sons, for Seth. For family.

"When I first saw you," Sybill began, "the three of you, I knew you were brothers. No real physical resemblance, but something less tangible. I'd say you're an example of how environment can offset heredity."

"More an example of what two generous and determined people can do for three lost boys."

She sipped her wine to soothe her throat before she spoke. "And Seth."

"Lost boy number four. We're trying to do for him what my parents would have done, what our father asked us to do. My mother died several years ago. It left the four of us floundering some. She was an incredible woman. We couldn't have appreciated her enough when we had her."

"I think you did." And moved by the sound of his voice, she smiled at him. "I'm sure she felt very loved."

"I hope so. After we lost her, Cam took off for Europe. Racing—boats, cars, whatever. He did pretty well at it. Ethan stayed. Bought his own house, but he's locked into the Bay. I moved back to Baltimore. Once an urbanite," he added with a quick smile.

"The Inner Harbor, Camden Yards."

"Exactly. I came down here off and on. Holidays, the occasional weekend. But it's not the same."

Curious, she tilted her head. "Would you want it to be?" She remembered her secret thrill when she'd gone off to college. To be on her own, not to have every movement and word weighed and judged. Freedom.

"No, but there were times, are times, I miss the way it was. Don't you ever think back to some perfect summer? You're sixteen, your driver's license is shiny and new in your wallet, and the world is all yours."

She laughed, but shook her head. She hadn't had a driver's license at sixteen. They'd been living in London that year, as she recalled. There had been a uniformed driver to take her where she'd been allowed to go, unless she managed to slip out and ride the Tube. That had been her small rebellion.

"Sixteen-year-old boys," she said, while their salad plates were removed, their entrées served, "are more emotionally attached to their cars than sixteen-year-old girls are."

"It's easier for that boy to get himself a girl if he has wheels."

"I doubt you had any trouble in that area, with or without a car."

"It's tough to neck in the backseat until you've got one."

"True enough. And now you're back here, and so are your brothers."

"Yeah. My father had Seth through complicated and not entirely clear circumstances. Seth's mother . . . well, you'll hear talk if you stay in the area for any length of time."

"Oh?" Sybill cut into her fish, hoping that she could swallow it.

"My father taught English lit at the university, the Eastern Shore campus of Maryland. A little less than a year ago a woman came to see him. It was a private meeting, so we don't have the details, but from all accounts it wasn't pleasant. She went to the dean and accused my father of sexual harassment."

Sybill's fork clattered onto her plate. As casually as she could, she lifted it again. "That must have been very difficult for him, for all of you."

"Difficult isn't quite the word for it. She claimed to have been a student here years back and said that at that time he had demanded sex for grades, intimidated her, had an affair with her."

No, she couldn't swallow, Sybill realized, gripping her fork until her fingers ached. "She had an affair with your father?"

"No, she said she did. My mother would still have been alive," he said half to himself. "In any case, there was no record of her ever attending the university. My father taught on that campus for more than twenty-five years, without a whisper of improper behavior. She took a shot at destroying his reputation. And it left a smear."

Of course there'd be no truth to it, Sybill thought wearily. It was Gloria's usual pattern. Accuse, damage, run. But she herself still had a part to play. "Why? Why would she do that?"

"Money."

"I don't understand."

"My father gave her money, a great deal of it. For Seth. She's Seth's mother."

"You're saying that she . . . she traded her son for money?" Not even Gloria could do something so appalling, she told herself. Surely, not even Gloria. "That's difficult to believe."

"Not all mothers are maternal." He jerked a shoulder. "He had a check for several thousand made out to Gloria DeLauter—that's her name—and he went away for a few days, then came back with Seth."

Saying nothing, she picked up her water glass, cooled her throat. *He came and got Seth,* Gloria had sobbed to her. *They've got Seth. You have to help me.*

"A few months later," Phillip continued, "he drew almost all his savings out into a cashier's check. He was on his way back from Baltimore when he had an accident. He didn't make it."

"I'm so sorry." She murmured the words, recognizing their inadequacy.

"He hung on until Cam got in from Europe. He asked the three of us to keep Seth, to look out for him. We're doing everything we can to keep that promise. I can't say it wasn't rough for a while," he added, smiling a little now. "But it's never been dull. Moving back here, starting the boat business, not such a bad deal. Cam got a wife out of it," he added with a grin. "Anna is Seth's caseworker."

"Really? They couldn't have known each other very long."

"I guess when it hits, it hits. Time doesn't factor in."

She'd always believed it did, vitally. To be successful, marriage took planning and dedication and a strong, solid knowledge of one's partner, an assurance of compatibility, an assessment of personal goals.

Then again, that portion of the Quinn dynamics wasn't her concern.

"That's quite a story." How much was true? she wondered, sick at heart. How much was slanted? Was she supposed to believe that her sister had sold her own son?

Somewhere in the middle, she decided. The real truth could generally be found somewhere between two opposing stories.

Phillip didn't know, she was sure of that now. He had no clue what Gloria had been to Raymond Quinn. When that single fact was added to the mix, how did it change everything else?

"At this point it's working out. The kid's happy. Another couple of months and the permanent guardianship should be wrapped. And this big brother stuff has its advantages. Gives me somebody to boss around."

She needed to think. She had to put emotion aside and think. But she had to get through the evening first. "How does he feel about that?"

"It's a perfect setup. He can bitch to Cam or Ethan about me, to me about Cam or Ethan. He knows how to play it. Seth's incredibly smart. They did placement tests when my father enrolled him in school here. He's practically off the charts. His final report card for last year? Straight A's."

"Really?" She found herself smiling. "You're proud of him."

"Sure. And me. I'm the one who got roped into being homework monitor. Until recently I'd forgotten how much I hate fractions. Now that I've told you my long story, why don't you tell me what you think of St. Chris?"

"I'm just getting my bearings."

"Does that mean you'll be staying a while yet?"

"Yes. A while."

"You can't really judge a water town unless you spend some time on the water. Why don't you go sailing with me tomorrow?"

"Don't you have to get back to Baltimore?"

"Monday."

She hesitated, then reminded herself that this was exactly why she was here. If she was to find that real truth, she couldn't back away now. "I'd like that. I can't guarantee what kind of sailor I'll be."

"We'll find out. I'll pick you up. Ten, ten-thirty?"

"That'll be fine. All of you sail, I imagine."

"Right down to the dogs." He laughed at the expression on her face. "We won't bring them along."

"I'm not afraid of them. I'm just not used to them."

"You never had a puppy."

"No."

"Cat?"

"No."

"Goldfish?"

She laughed, shook her head. "No. We moved around quite a bit. Once I had a schoolmate in Boston whose dog had puppies. They were darling." Odd, she thought, to have remembered that now. She'd wanted one of those pups desperately.

It had been impossible, of course. Antique furniture, important guests, social obligations. Out of the question, her mother had said. And that had been the end of it.

"Now I move around quite a bit. It's not practical."

"Where do you like best?" he asked her.

"I'm flexible. Wherever I end up tends to suit me, until I'm somewhere else."

"So right now it's St. Chris."

"Apparently. It's interesting." She gazed out the window, where the rising moon glittered light onto the water. "The pace is slow, but it's not stagnant. The mood varies, as the weather varies. After only a few days, I'm able to separate the natives from the tourists. And the watermen from everyone else."

"How?"

"How?" Distracted, she looked back at him.

"How can you tell one from the other?"

"Just basic observation. I can look out of my window onto the waterfront. The tourists are couples, more likely families, occasionally a single. They stroll, or they shop. They rent a boat. They interact with each other, the ones in their group. They're out of their milieu. Most will have camera, map, maybe binoculars. Most of the natives have a purpose for being there. A job, an errand. They might stop and say hello to a neighbor. You can see them easing back on their way as they end the conversation."

"Why are you watching from the window?"

"I don't understand the question."

"Why aren't you down on the waterfront?"

"I have been. But you usually get a purer study when you, the observer, aren't part of the scene."

"I'd think you'd get more varied and more personal input if you were." He glanced up as the waiter arrived to top off their wine and offer them dessert.

"Just coffee," Sybill decided. "Decaf."

"The same." Phillip leaned forward. "In your book, the section on isolation as a survival technique, the example you used of having someone lying on the sidewalk. How people would look away, walk around. Some might hesitate before hurrying past."

"Noninvolvement. Disassociation."

"Exactly. But one person would eventually stop, try to help. Once one person broke the isolation, others would begin to stop, too."

"Once the isolation is breached, it becomes easier, even necessary for others to join. It's the first step that's the most difficult. I conducted that study in New York and London and Budapest, all with similar results. It follows the urban survival technique of avoiding eye contact on the street, of blocking the homeless out of our line of sight."

"What makes that first person who stops to help different from everyone else?"

"Their survival instincts aren't as well honed as their compassion. Or their impulse button is more easily pushed."

"Yeah, that. And they're involved. They're not just walking through, not just there. They're involved."

"And you think that because I observe, I'm not."

"I don't know. But I think that observing from a distance isn't nearly as rewarding as experiencing up close."

"Observing's what I do, and I find it rewarding."

He slid closer and kept his eyes on hers, ignoring the waiter who tidily served their coffee. "But you're a scientist. You experiment. Why don't you give experiencing a try? With me."

She looked down, watched his fingertip toy with hers. And felt the slow heat of response creep into her blood. "That's a very novel, if roundabout, way of suggesting that I sleep with you."

"Actually, that wasn't what I meant—though if the answer's yes, I'm all for it." He flashed her a grin as she shifted her gaze warily to his. "I was going to suggest that we take a walk on the waterfront when we've finished our coffee. But if you'd rather sleep with me, we can be in your hotel room in, oh, five minutes flat."

She didn't evade when his head lowered to hers, when his lips slid lazily into a lovely fit over hers. The taste of him was cool, with an underlying promise of heat. If she wanted it. And she did. It surprised her how much, just at that one moment, she wanted the flash and burn—the demand that would override the tension inside her, the worry, the doubts.

But she'd had a lifetime of training against self-indulgence, and now she laid a hand lightly on his chest to end the kiss, and the temptation.

"I think a walk would be pleasant."

"Then we'll walk."

H E WANTED MORE PHILLIP TOLD himself he should have known that a few tastes of her would stir up the need. But he hadn't expected that need to be quite so sharp, quite so edgy. Maybe part of it was sheer ego, he mused as he took her hand to walk with her along the quiet waterfront. Her response had been so cool and controlled. It made him wonder what it would be like to peel that intellect away, layer by layer, and find the woman beneath. To work his way down to pure emotion and instinct.

He nearly laughed at himself. Ego, indeed. For all he knew, that formal, slightly distant response was precisely all that Dr. Sybill Griffin intended to give him.

If so, that made her a challenge he was going to have a very difficult time resisting.

"I see why Shiney's is a popular spot." She slanted him a smiling look. "It's barely nine-thirty and the shops are closed, the boats are moored. A few people strolling along, but for the most part everything here is tucked in for the night."

"It's a little livelier during the summer. Not much, but a little. It's cooling off. Are you warm enough?"

"Mmm. Plenty. It's a lovely breeze." She stopped to look out at the swaying masts of boats. "Do you keep your boat here?"

"No, we have a dock at home. That's Ethan's skipjack."

"Where?"

"It's the only skipjack in St. Chris. There are only a couple of dozen left on the Bay. There." He gestured. "The single mast."

To her untrained eye, one sailboat looked very much the same as the next. Size varied, of course, and gloss, but essentially they were all boats. "What's a skipjack?"

"It evolved from the flat-bottomed bay-crabbing skiffs." He drew her closer as he spoke. "They were enlarged, designed with a V-shaped hull. Had to be easily and inexpensively built."

"So they go out crabbing in them."

"No, mostly the watermen use motor-powered workboats for crabbing. The skipjack is for oysters. Back in the early 1800s they passed a law in Maryland that allowed only sail-powered vessels to dredge for oysters."

"Conservation?"

"Exactly. The skipjack came out of that, and it still survives. But there aren't many of them. There aren't many oysters either."

"Does your brother still use it?"

"Yeah. It's miserable, cold, hard, frustrating work."

"You sound like the voice of experience."

"I've put in some time on her." He stopped near the bow and slipped an arm around Sybill's waist. "Sailing out in February, with that wind cutting through you, bouncing on the high chop of a winter storm . . . all in all, I'd rather be in Baltimore."

She chuckled, studying the boat. It looked ancient and rough, like something out of an earlier time. "Without having set foot on it, I'm going to agree with you. So why were you bouncing on the high chop of a winter storm instead of in Baltimore?"

"Beats the hell out of me."

"I take it this isn't the boat you invited me out on tomorrow."

"No. That one's a tidy little pleasure sloop. Do you swim?"

She arched an eyebrow. "Is that a statement on your sailing abilities?"

"No, it's a suggestion. The water's cool, but not so cold you couldn't take a dip if you like."

"I didn't bring a bathing suit with me."

"And your point is?"

She laughed and started walking again. "I think a sail's enough for one day. I've got some work I want to finish up tonight. I enjoyed dinner."

"So did I. I'll walk you to your hotel."

"There's no need. It's just around the corner."

"Nonetheless."

She didn't argue. She had no intention of allowing him to walk her to her door, or to talk his way into her suite. All in all, she felt she was handling him, and a difficult, confusing situation, very well. An early night, she mused, would give her time to sort out her thoughts and feelings before she saw him again the next day.

And since the boat was docked at his home, the odds were good that she would see Seth again, too.

"I'll come down in the morning," she began as she stopped a few feet from the lobby entrance. "Ten or so?"

"Fine."

"Is there anything I should bring? Besides Dramamine?"

He shot her a grin. "I'll take care of it. Sleep well."

"You, too."

She prepared herself for the easy and expected good-night kiss. His lips were soft, undemanding. Pleased with both of them, she relaxed, started to back away.

Then his hand cupped the back of her neck firmly, his head changed angles, and for one staggering moment, the kiss went hot and wild and threatening. The hand she'd laid on his shoulder curled into a fist, gripping his jacket, hanging on for balance as her feet all but swept out from under her. Her mind went blank as her pulse leapt to roar in her spinning head.

Someone moaned, low and deep and long.

It lasted only seconds, but it was as shocking and burning as a brand. He saw the stunned arousal in her eyes when they opened and stared into his. And he felt that basic need claw to a new level inside him.

Not a cool, controlled, and distant response this time, he decided. One layer down, he mused, and skimmed his thumb along her jawline.

"I'll see you in the morning."

"Yes—good night." She recovered quickly and sent him a smile before turning. But she pressed an unsteady hand to her jittery stomach as she slipped into the lobby.

She'd miscalculated that one, she admitted, fighting to take slow, even breaths as she walked to the elevator. He wasn't as smooth, polished, and harmless as he appeared on the surface.

There was something much more primitive and much more dangerous inside that attractive package than she'd realized.

And whatever it was, she found it entirely too compelling for her own good.

Six

It was like riding a bike. Or sex, Phillip mused as he tacked, threading through the light traffic on the Bay toward an available slip on the waterfront. It had been a while since he'd done any solo sailing, but he hadn't forgotten how. If anything, he'd forgotten how much he enjoyed being out on the water on a breezy Sunday morning, with the sun warm and the water blue and the wicked screams of gulls echoing on the air.

He was going to have to start finding time for simple pleasures again. Since this was the first full day he'd taken off in more than two months, he intended to make the most of it.

He certainly intended to make the most of a few golden hours on the Bay with the intriguing Dr. Griffin.

He looked over at the hotel, idly trying to calculate which window might be hers. From what she'd told him, he knew it faced the water, giving her a view of the life that pulsed there and enough distance for her research.

Then he saw her, standing on a tiny balcony, her glossy, mink-colored hair sleeked back and haloed in the sunlight, her face aloof and unreadable from so far away.

Not so aloof close up, he thought, replaying their last sizzle of a kiss in his mind. No, there'd been nothing aloof in that long, throaty moan, nothing distant in that quick, hard tremble her body had made against his. That instinctive, involuntary signal of blood calling to blood.

Her eyes, that water-clear blue, hadn't been cool; nor had they been intriguingly remote when he'd lifted his mouth from hers and looked into them. Instead, they'd been just a little clouded, just a little confused. And all the more intriguing.

He hadn't quite been able to get her taste out of his system, not on the drive home, not through the night, not now, seeing her again. And knowing she stood and watched him.

What, he wondered, do you observe, Dr. Griffin? And what do you intend to do about it?

Phillip flashed her a quick smile, snapped her a salute to let her know he'd seen her. Then he shifted his attention away from her and maneuvered into dock.

His brows lifted in surprise as he saw Seth standing on dock waiting to secure the lines. "What're you doing here?"

Expertly, Seth looped the bow line over the post. "Playing errand boy again." There was a hint of disgust in the tone, but Seth had to work to put it there. "They sent me down from the boatyard. Donuts."

"Yeah?" Phillip stepped nimbly onto the dock. "Artery cloggers."

"Real people don't eat tree bark for breakfast," Seth sneered. "Just you."

"And I'll still be strong and good-looking when you're a wheezing old man."

"Maybe, but I'll have more fun."

Phillip tugged Seth's ball cap off, batted him lightly with it. "Depends, pal, on your definition of fun."

"I guess yours is poking at city girls."

"That's one of them. Another is hounding you over your homework. You finish *Johnny Tremaine* for your book report?"

"Yeah, yeah, yeah." Seth rolled his eyes. "Man, don't you ever take a day off?"

"What, when my life is devoted to you?" He grinned at Seth's snort. "So, what'd you think of it?"

"It was okay." Then he jerked a shoulder, a purely Quinn movement. "It was pretty good."

"We'll put together some notes for your oral report later tonight."

"Sunday night's my favorite night of the week," Seth said. "It means you'll be gone for four days."

"Come on, you know you miss me."

"Shit."

"You count the hours until I come home."

Seth barely suppressed a giggle. "Like hell." Then he did giggle as Phillip snagged him around the waist for a tussle.

Sybill heard the bright, happy sound as she walked toward them.

She saw the wide grin on Seth's face. Her heart did a long, slow roll in her chest. What was she doing here? she asked herself. What did she hope to accomplish?

And how could she walk away until she found out?

"Good morning."

Distracted by her voice, Phillip glanced over, dropping his guard just long enough for Seth's elbow to slip through and into his gut. He grunted, wrapped an arm around Seth's neck, and leaned down. "I'll have to beat you up later," he said in a stage whisper. "When there aren't any witnesses."

"You wish." Flushed with pleasure, Seth settled his cap securely on his head and feigned disinterest. "Some of us gotta work today."

"And some of us don't."

"I thought you were going with us," Sybill said to Seth. "Would you like to?"

"I'm just a slave around here." Seth looked longingly at the boat, then shrugged. "We got a hull to build. Besides, Pretty Boy here will probably capsize her."

"Smart-ass." Phillip made a grab, but Seth danced laughingly out of reach.

"Hope she can swim!" he called out, then raced away.

When Phillip looked back at Sybill, she was gnawing her bottom lip. "I'm not going to capsize her."

"Well . . ." Sybill glanced toward the boat. It seemed awfully small and fragile. "I can swim, so I suppose it's all right."

"Christ, kid comes along and completely smears my rep. I've been sailing longer than the brat's been alive."

"Don't be angry with him."

"Huh?"

"Please, don't be angry with him. I'm sure he was just joking with you. He didn't mean to be disrespectful."

Phillip just stared at her. She'd actually gone pale, and her hand was nervously twisting the thin gold chain she wore around her neck. There was active and acute distress in her voice. "Sybill, I'm not mad at him. We were just fooling around. Relax." Baffled, he rubbed his knuckles lightly over her jaw. "Razzing each other is just our clever male way of showing affection."

"Oh." She wasn't certain whether to be embarrassed or relieved. "I guess that shows I didn't have any brothers."

"It would have been their job to make your life a living hell." He leaned down, touched her lips lightly with his. "It's traditional."

He stepped onto the boat, held out a hand. After the briefest of hesitations, she let him take hers.

"Welcome aboard."

The deck rocked under her feet. She did her best to ignore it. "Thank you. Do I have an assignment?"

"For now, sit, relax, and enjoy."

"I should be able to manage that."

At least she hoped so. She sat on one of the padded benches, gripping it tightly as he stepped out again to release the lines. It would be fine, she assured herself. It would be fun.

Hadn't she watched him sail into port, or dock, or whatever you would call it? He'd seemed very competent. Even a bit cocky, she decided, the way he'd scanned the hotel until he saw her standing out on her balcony.

There had been something foolishly romantic about that, she thought now. The way he had sailed across the sun-splashed water, searching for her, finding her. Then the quick smile and wave. If her pulse had bumped a little, it was an understandable and human response.

He made such a picture, after all. The faded jeans, the crisp T-shirt tucked into them as blindingly white as the sails, that gilded hair, and the warmly tanned, sleekly muscled arms. What woman wouldn't feel a bump at the prospect of spending a few hours alone with a man who looked like Phillip Quinn?

And kissed like Phillip Quinn.

Though she had promised herself she wouldn't dwell on that particular talent of his. He'd shown her just a little too much of that skill the night before.

Now with the sails lowered, he motored gently away from the dock. She found some security in the low rumble of the engine. Not that different from a car, really, she supposed. This vehicle just happened to drive over water.

Nor were they really alone. Her hands relaxed their death grip on the bench as she watched other boats skim and glide. She saw a boy who was surely no older than Seth, tucked into a tiny boat with a triangular red sail. If it was an activity considered safe for children, surely she could handle it.

"Hoisting sails."

She turned her head, smiled absently at Phillip. "What did you say?"

"Watch."

He moved gracefully over the deck, working the lines. Then suddenly the sails rose, snapped in the wind, filled with it. Her heartbeat skipped and scrambled, and her fingers tightened once more on the bench.

No, she'd been wrong, she saw that now. This was nothing at all like a car. It was primitive and beautiful and thrilling. The boat no longer seemed small, or fragile, but powerful, just a little dangerous. And breathtaking.

Very much like the man who captained her.

"It's lovely from down here." Though she kept her hands firmly locked on the bench, she smiled over at Phillip. "They always look pretty when I watch from the window. But it's lovely to see the sails from below."

"You're sitting," Phillip commented as he took the wheel. "And you're enjoying, but I don't think you're relaxing."

"Not yet. I might get there." She turned her face to the wind. It tugged and teased at her hair, trying to free it from the band. "Where are we going?"

"Nowhere in particular."

Her smile warmed and widened. "I rarely have a chance to go there."

She hadn't smiled at him just that way before, Phillip thought. Without thinking, without weighing. He doubted she realized how that easy smile transformed her coolly beautiful face into something softer, more approachable. Wanting to touch her, he held out a hand.

"Come on up here, check out the view."

Her smile faded. "Stand up?"

"Yeah. There's no chop today. It's a smooth ride."

"Stand up," she repeated, giving each word separate weight. "And walk over there. On the boat."

"Two steps." He couldn't stop the grin. "You don't want to just be a bystander, do you?"

"Actually, yes." Her eyes widened when he stepped away from the wheel. "No, don't." She stifled a scream when he laughed and snagged her hand. Before she could dig in, he'd pulled her to her feet. Off balance, she fell against him and held on in terror and defense.

"Couldn't have planned that one better," he murmured and holding her, stepped back to the wheel. "I like getting close enough to smell you. A man has to get almost right here . . ." He turned his head, nuzzled his lips on her throat.

"Stop." Thrills and fears raced through her. "Pay attention."

"Oh, believe me"—his teeth caught and nipped her earlobe—"I am."

"To the boat. Pay attention to the boat."

"Oh, yeah." But he kept one arm snug around her waist. "Look out over the bow, to port. The left," he explained. "That little swash there goes back into the marsh. You'll see herons and wild turkey."

"Where?"

"Sometimes you have to go in to find them. But you can catch sight of them now and then, the herons standing like a sculpture in the high grass or rising up from it, the turkeys bobbling their way out of the trees."

She wanted to see, she discovered. She hoped she would see.

"In another month, we'll have geese flying over. From their view this area wouldn't look much different from the Everglades."

Her heart was still jumping, but she inhaled slowly, exhaled deliberately. "Why?"

"The marshland. It's too far from the beaches for the developers to be very interested. It's largely undisturbed. Just one of the Bay's assets, one of the factors that makes it an estuary. A finer one for watermen than the fjords of Norway."

She inhaled again, exhaled. "Why?"

"The shallows, for one thing. A good estuary needs shallows so the sun can nourish aquatic plants, plankton. And the marshlands, for another. They add the tidal creeks, the coves. There." He brushed a kiss over the crown on her head. "Now you're relaxing."

With some surprise, she realized she wasn't simply relaxing. She'd already gotten there. "So, you were appealing to the scientist."

"Took your mind off your nerves."

"Yes, it did." Odd, she thought, that he would know so quickly which switch to throw. "I don't think I have my sea legs yet, but it is a pretty view. Still so green." She watched the passing of big, leafy trees, the deep pockets of shadows in the marsh. They sailed by markers topped with huge, scruffy nests. "What birds build those?"

"Osprey. Now they're experts at those disassociation techniques. You can sail right by one when it's sitting on its nest, and it'll look right through you."

"Survival instinct," she murmured. She'd like to see that, too. An osprey roosting on that rough circular nest, ignoring the humans.

"See those orange buoys? Crab pots. The workboat putting down that gut? He's going to check his pots, rebait. Over there, to starboard." He nudged her head to the right. "The little outboard. Looks to me like they're hoping to catch some rockfish for Sunday dinner."

"It's a busy place," she commented. "I didn't realize there was so much going on."

"On and under the water."

He adjusted the sails and, heeling in, skimmed around a thick line of trees leaning out from shore. As they cleared the trees, a narrow dock came into view. Behind it was a sloping lawn, flower beds just starting to lose their summer brilliance. The house was simple, white with blue trim. A rocker sat on the wide covered porch, and bronze-toned mums speared out of an old crockery tub.

Sybill could hear the light, drifting notes of music floating through the open windows. Chopin, she realized after a moment.

"It's charming." She angled her head, shifting slightly to keep the house in view. "All it needs is a dog, a couple of kids tossing a ball, and a tire swing."

"We were too old for tire swings, but we always had the dog. That's our house," he told her, absently running his hand down her long, smooth ponytail.

"Yours?" She strained, wanting to see more. Where Seth lived, she thought, struck by dozens of conflicting emotions.

"We spent plenty of time tossing balls, or each other, in the back-yard. We'll come back later and you can meet the rest of the family."

She closed her eyes and squashed the guilt. "I'd like that."

H E   HAD   A   PLACE   IN   MIND. THE quiet cove with its lapping water and dappled shade was a perfect spot for a romantic picnic. He dropped anchor where the eelgrass gleamed wetly, and the sky canopied in unbroken autumnal blue overhead.

"Obviously my research on this area was lacking."

"Oh?" Phillip opened a large cooler and retrieved a bottle of wine. "It's full of surprises."

"Pleasant ones, I hope."

"Very pleasant ones." She smiled, raising a brow at the label on the wine he opened. "Very pleasant."

"You struck me as a woman who'd appreciate a fine dry Sancerre."

"You're very astute."

"Indeed I am." From a wicker hamper he took two wineglasses and poured. "To pleasant surprises," he said and tapped his glass to hers.

"Are there more?"

He took her hand, kissed her fingers. "We've barely started." Setting his glass aside, he unfolded a white cloth and spread it on the deck. "Your table's ready."

"Ah." Enjoying herself, she sat, shaded her eyes against the sun, and smiled up at him. "What's today's special?"

"Some rather nice paté to stir the appetite." To demonstrate, he opened a small container and a box of stoned wheat crackers. He spread one for her and held it to her lips.

"Mmm." She nodded after the first bite. "Very nice."

"To be followed by crab salad à la Quinn."

"Sounds intriguing. And did you make it with your own two hands?"

"I did." He grinned at her. "I'm a hell of a cook."

"The man cooks, has excellent taste in wine, appreciates ambience, and wears his Levi's very well." She bit into the paté again, relaxed now, the ground familiar and easily negotiated. "You appear to be quite a catch, Mr. Quinn."

"I am indeed, Dr. Griffin."

She laughed into her wine. "And how often have you brought some lucky woman to this spot for crab salad à la Quinn?"

"Actually, I haven't been here with a woman since the summer of my sophomore year in college. Then it was a fairly decent Chablis, chilled shrimp, and Marianne Teasdale."

"I suppose I should be flattered."

"I don't know. Marianne was pretty hot." He flashed that killer grin again. "But being callow and shortsighted, I threw her over for a pre-med student with a sexy lisp and big brown eyes."

"Lisps do weaken a man. Did Marianne recover?"

"Enough to marry a plumber from Princess Anne and bear him two children. But, of course, we know she secretly yearns for me."

Laughing, Sybill spread a cracker for him. "I like you."

"I like you, too." He caught her wrist, holding it as he nibbled at the cracker she held. "And you don't even lisp."

When his fingers continued to nibble, at the tips of her fingers now, it wasn't quite as easy to breathe. "You're very smooth," she murmured.

"You're very lovely."

"Thank you. What I should say," she continued, and eased her hand out of his, "is that while you're very smooth, and very attractive, and I'm enjoying spending time with you, I don't intend to be seduced."

"You know what they say about intentions."

"I tend to hold to mine. And while I do enjoy your company, I also recognize your type." She smiled again and gestured with her glass. "A hundred years ago, the word 'rogue' would have come to mind."

He considered a moment. "That didn't sound like an insult."

"It wasn't meant to be. Rogues are invariably charming and very rarely serious."

"I have to object there. There are some issues that I'm very serious about."

"Let's try this." She peeked in the cooler and took out another container. "Have you ever been married?"

"No."

"Engaged?" she asked as she opened the lid and discovered a beautifully prepared crab salad.

"No."

"Have you ever lived with a woman for a consecutive period of six months or more?"

With a shrug, he took plates out of the hamper, passed her a pale-blue linen napkin. "No."

"So, we can theorize that one of the issues about which you are not serious is relationships."

"Or we can theorize that I have yet to meet the woman I want a serious relationship with."

"We could. However . . ." She narrowed her eyes at his face as he scooped salad onto the plates. "You're what, thirty?"

"One." He added a thick slice of French bread to each plate.

"Thirty-one. Typically, by the age of thirty a man in this culture would have experienced at least one serious, long-term, monogamous relationship."

"I wouldn't care to be typical. Olives?"

"Yes, thanks. Typical is not necessarily an unattractive trait. Nor is conformity. Everyone conforms. Even those who consider themselves the rebels of society conform to certain codes and standards."

Enjoying her, he tilted his head. "Is that so, Dr. Griffin?"

"Quite so. Gang members in the inner city have internal rules, codes, standards. Colors," she added, selecting an olive from her plate. "In that way they don't differ much from members of the city council."

"You had to be there," Phillip mumbled.

"Excuse me?"

"Nothing. What about serial killers?"

"They follow patterns." Enjoying herself, she tore a chunk off her slice of bread. "The FBI studies them, catalogs them, profiles them. Society wouldn't term them standards certainly, but in the strictest sense of the word, that's precisely what they are."

Damned if she didn't have a point, he decided. And found himself only more fascinated. "So you, the observer, size people up by noting what rules, codes, patterns they follow."

"More or less. People aren't so very difficult to understand, if you pay attention."

"What about those surprises?"

She smiled, appreciating the question as much as she appreciated that he would think to ask it. Most laymen she'd socialized with weren't really interested in her work. "They're factored in. There's always margin for error, and for adjustments. This is wonderful salad." She sampled another bite. "And the surprise, a pleasant one, is that you would have gone to the trouble to prepare it."

"Don't you find that people are usually willing to go to some trouble for someone they care for?" When she only blinked at him, he tilted his head. "Well, well, that threw you off."

"You barely know me." She picked up her wine, a purely defensive gesture. "There's a difference between being attracted to and caring for. The latter takes more time."

"Some of us move fast." He enjoyed seeing her flustered. It would be, he decided, a rare event. Taking advantage of it, he slid closer. "I do."

"So I've already observed. However—"

"However. I like hearing you laugh. I like feeling you tremble just slightly when I kiss you. I like hearing your voice slide into that didactic tone when you expand on a theory."

At the last comment she frowned. "I'm not didactic."

"Charmingly," he murmured, skimming his lips over her temple. "And I like seeing your eyes in that moment when I start to confuse you. Therefore, I believe I've crossed over into the care-for stage. So let's try your earlier hypothesis out on you and see where that leaves us. Have you ever been married?"

His mouth was cruising just under her ear, making it very difficult to think clearly. "No. Well, not really."

He paused, leaned back, narrowed his eyes. "No or not really?"

"It was an impulse, an error in judgment. It was less than six months. It didn't count." Her brain was fogged, she decided, trying to inch away for some breathing room. He only scooted her back.

"You were married?"

"Only technically. It didn't . . ." She turned her head to make her point, and his mouth was there. Right there to meet hers, to urge her lips to part and warm and soften.

It was like sliding under a slow-moving wave, being taken down into silky, shimmering water. Everything inside her went fluid. A surprise, she would realize later, that she'd neglected to factor into this particular pattern.

"It didn't count," she managed as her head fell back, as his lips trailed smoothly down her throat.

"Okay."

If he'd taken her by surprise, she'd done exactly the same to him. At her sudden and utter surrender to the moment, his need churned to the surface, thrashing there. He had to touch her, to fill his hands with her, to mold those pretty curves through the thin, crisp cotton of her blouse.

He had to taste her, deeper now, while those little hums of shock and pleasure sounded in her throat. As he did, as he touched and as he tasted, her arms came around him, her hands sliding into his hair, her body turning to fit itself against him.

He felt her heart thud in time with his own.

Panic punched through pleasure when she felt him tug at the buttons of her blouse. "No." Her own fingers shook as she covered his. "It's too fast." She squeezed her eyes shut, struggling to find her control, her sense, her purpose. "I'm sorry. I don't go this fast. I can't."

It wasn't easy to check the urge to ignore the rules, to simply press her under him on the deck until she was pliant and willing again. He put his tense fingers under her chin and lifted her face to his. No, it wasn't easy, he thought again as he saw both desire and denial in her eyes. But it was necessary.

"Okay. No rush." He rubbed his thumb over her bottom lip. "Tell me about the one that didn't count."

Her thoughts had scattered to the edges of her mind. She couldn't begin to draw them together while he was looking at her with those tawny eyes. "What?"

"The husband."

"Oh." She looked away, concentrated on her breathing.

"What are you doing?"

"Relaxation technique."

Humor danced back and made him grin at her. "Does it work?"

"Eventually."

"Cool." He shifted until they were hip to hip and timed his breathing to hers. "So this guy you were technically married to . . ."

"It was in college, at Harvard. He was a chemistry major." Eyes shut, she ordered her toes to relax, then her arches, her ankles. "We were barely twenty and just lost our heads for a short time."

"Eloped."

"Yes. We didn't even live together, because we were in different dorms. So it wasn't really a marriage. It was weeks before we told our families, and then, naturally, there were several difficult scenes."

"Why?"

"Because . . ." She blinked her eyes open, found the sun dazzling. Something plopped in the water behind her, then there was only the lap of it, kissing the hull. "We weren't suited, we had no feasible plans. We were too young. The divorce was very quiet and quick and civilized."

"Did you love him?"

"I was twenty." Her relaxation level was reaching her shoulders. "Of course I thought I did. Love has little complexity at that age."

"So spoken from the advanced age of what twenty-seven, twenty-eight?"

"Twenty-nine and counting." She let out a last long breath. Satisfied and steady, she turned to look at him again. "I haven't thought of Rob in years. He was a very nice boy. I hope he's happy."

"And that's it for you?"

"It has to be."

He nodded, but found her story strangely sad. "Then I have to say, Dr. Griffin, that using your own scale, you don't take relationships seriously."

She opened her mouth to protest, then wisely, shut it again. Casually, she picked up the wine bottle and topped off both glasses. "You may be right. I'll have to give that some thought."

SEVEN

SETH DIDN'T MIND RUNNING
herd on Aubrey. She was kind of his niece now that Ethan and Grace
were married. Being an uncle made him feel adult and responsible.
Besides, all she really wanted to do was race around the yard. Every
time he threw a ball or a stick for one of the dogs, she went into gales
of laughter. A guy couldn't help but get a kick out of it.

She was pretty cute, too, with her curly gold hair and her big green
eyes that looked amazed at everything he did. Spending an hour or
two on a Sunday entertaining her wasn't a bad deal.

He hadn't forgotten where he had been a year ago. There'd been no
big backyard that fell off into the water, no woods to explore, no dogs
to wrestle with, no little girl who looked at him like he was Fox Mul-
der, all the Power Rangers and Superman rolled into one.

Instead, there'd been grungy rooms three flights up from the street.
And those streets had been a dark carnival at night, a place where
everything had its price. Sex, drugs, weapons, misery.

He'd learned that no matter what went on in those grungy rooms,
he shouldn't go out after dark.

There'd been no one to care if he was clean or fed, if he was sick or
scared. He'd never felt like a hero there, or even very much like a kid.
He'd felt like a thing, and he'd learned quickly that things are often
hunted.

Gloria had ridden all the rides in that carnival, again and again.
She'd brought the freaks and the hustlers into those rooms, selling
herself to whoever would pay the price of her next spin.

A year ago Seth hadn't believed his life would ever be any different.

Then Ray came and took him to the house by the water. Ray showed him a different world and promised he would never have to go back to the old one.

Ray had died, but he had kept his promise all the same. Now Seth could stand in the big backyard with water lapping at its edges and throw balls and sticks for the dogs to chase while an angel-faced toddler laughed.

"Seth, let me! Let me!" Aubrey danced on her sturdy little legs, holding up both hands for the mangled ball.

"Okay, you throw it."

He grinned while she screwed up her face with concentration and effort. The ball bounced inches away from the toes of her bright-red sneakers. Simon snapped it up, making her squeal with delight, then politely offered it back.

"Oooh, good doggie." Aubrey batted the patient Simon on either side of his jaw. Angling for attention, Foolish nudged his way in, shoved her down on her butt. She rewarded him with a fierce hug. "Now you," she ordered Seth. "You do it."

Obliging her, Seth winged the ball. He laughed as the dogs raced after it, bumping their bodies like two football players rushing downfield. They crashed into the woods, sending a pair of birds squawking skyward.

At that moment, with Aubrey bouncing with giggles, the dogs barking, the fresh September air on his cheeks, Seth was completely happy. A part of his mind focused on it, snatched at it to keep. The angle of the sun, the brilliance of light on the water, the creamy sound of Otis Redding drifting through the kitchen window, the bitchy complaints of the birds, and the rich salty scent of the bay.

He was home.

Then the putt of a motor caught his attention. When he turned he saw the family sloop angling in toward the dock. At the wheel, Phillip raised a hand in greeting. Even as Seth returned the wave, his gaze shifted to the woman standing beside Phillip. It felt as if something brushed over the nape of his neck, light and cagey as the legs of a spider. Absently he rubbed at it, shrugged his shoulders, then took Aubrey firmly by the hand.

"Remember, you have to stay in the middle of the dock."

She gazed up at him adoringly. "Okay. I will. Mama says never, never go by the water by myself."

"That's right." He stepped onto the dock with her and waited for Phillip to come alongside. It was the woman who, awkwardly, tossed him the bow line. Sybill something, he thought. For a moment, as she balanced herself, as their eyes met, he felt that sly tickle on the nape of his neck again.

Then the dogs were bounding onto the dock and Aubrey was laughing again.

"Hey, Angel Baby." Phillip helped Sybill step onto the dock, then winked down at Aubrey.

"Up," she demanded.

"You bet." He swung her onto his hip and planted a smacking kiss on her cheek. "When are you going to grow up and marry me?"

"Tomorrow!"

"That's what you always say. This is Sybill. Sybill, meet Aubrey, my best girl."

"She's pretty," Aubrey stated and flashed her dimples.

"Thank you. So are you." As the dogs bumped her legs, Sybill jolted and took a step back. Phillip shot out a hand to grab her arm before she backed her way off the dock and into the water.

"Steady there. Seth, call off the dogs. Sybill's a little uneasy around them."

"They won't hurt you," Seth said with a shake of his head that warned Sybill she'd just dropped several notches in his estimation. But he snagged both dogs by the collar, holding them back until she could ease by.

"Everybody inside?" Phillip asked Seth.

"Yeah, just hanging until dinner. Grace brought over a monster chocolate cake. Cam sweet-talked Anna into making lasagna."

"God bless him. My sister-in-law's lasagna is a work of art," he told Sybill.

"Speaking of art, I wanted to tell you again, Seth, how much I liked the sketches you've done for the boatyard. They're very good."

He shrugged his shoulders, then bent down to scoop up two sticks to toss and distract the dogs. "I just draw sometimes."

"Me, too." She knew it was foolish, but Sybill felt her cheeks go warm at the way Seth studied her, measured and judged. "It's something I like to do in my spare time," she went on. "I find it relaxing and satisfying."

"Yeah, I guess."

"Maybe you'll show me more of your work sometime."

"If you want." He pushed open the door to the kitchen and headed straight to the refrigerator. A telling sign, Sybill mused. He was at home here.

She took a quick scan of the room, filing impressions. There was a pot simmering on what seemed to be an ancient stove. The scent was impossibly aromatic. Several small clay pots lined the windowsill over the sink. Fresh herbs thrived in them.

The counters were clean, if a bit worn. A pile of papers was stacked on the end beneath a wall phone and anchored with a set of keys. A shallow bowl was centered on the table and filled with glossy red and green apples. A mug of coffee, half full, stood in front of a chair under which someone had kicked off shoes.

"Goddamn it! That ump ought to be shot in the head. That pitch was a mile high."

Sybill arched an eyebrow at the furious male voice from the next room. Phillip merely smiled and jiggled Aubrey on his hip. "Ball game. Cam's taking this year's pennant race personally."

"The game! I forgot." Seth slammed the refrigerator door and raced out of the kitchen. "What's the score, what inning is it, who's up?"

"Three to two, A's, bottom of the sixth, two outs, a man on second. Now sit down and shut up."

"Very personally," Phillip added, then set Aubrey down when she wiggled.

"Baseball often becomes a personal challenge between the audience and the opposing team. Especially," Sybill added with a sober nod, "during the September pennant race."

"You like baseball?"

"What's not to like?" she said and laughed. "It's a fascinating study of men, of teamwork, of battle. Speed, cunning, finesse, and always pitcher against batter. In the end it all comes down to style, endurance. And math."

"We're going to have to take in a game at Camden Yards," he decided. "I'd just love to hear your play-by-play technique. Can I get you anything?"

"No, I'm fine." More shouts, more cursing burst out of the living room. "But I think it might be dangerous to leave this room as long as your brother's team is down a run."

"You're perceptive." Phillip reached out to curve his hand over her cheek. "So, why don't we stay right here and—"

"Way to go, Cal!" Cam shouted from the living room. "That son of a bitch is amazing."

"Shit." Seth's voice was cocky and smug. "No stinking California outfielder's going to blow one by Ripken."

Phillip let out a sigh. "Or maybe we should head out back and take a walk for a few innings."

"Seth, I believe we've discussed acceptable word usage in this house."

"Anna," Phillip murmured. "Coming downstairs to lay down the law."

"Cameron, you're supposed to be an adult."

"It's baseball, sugar."

"If the pair of you don't watch your language, the TV goes off."

"She's very strict," Phillip informed Sybill. "We're all terrified of her."

"Really?" Sybill considered as she glanced toward the living room. She heard another voice, lower, softer, then Aubrey's firm response. "No, Mama, please. I want Seth."

"She's okay, Grace. She can stay with me."

The easy, absent tone of Seth's voice had Sybill considering. "It's unusual, I'd think, for a boy Seth's age to be so patient with a toddler."

Phillip shrugged his shoulders and walked to the stove to start a pot of fresh coffee. "They hit it off right away. Aubrey adores him. That has to boost the kid's ego, and he's really good with her."

He turned, smiling as two women walked into the room. "Ah, the ones who got away. Sybill, these are the women my brothers stole from me. Anna, Grace, Dr. Sybill Griffin."

"He only wanted us to cook for him," Anna said with a laugh and held out a hand. "It's nice to meet you. I've read your books. I think they're brilliant."

Taken by surprise, both by the statement and the lush and outrageous beauty of Anna Spinelli Quinn, Sybill nearly fumbled. "Thank you. I appreciate you tolerating a Sunday-evening intrusion."

"It's no intrusion. We're delighted."

And, Anna thought, incredibly curious. In the seven months she'd known Phillip, this was the first woman he'd brought home to Sunday dinner.

"Phillip, go watch baseball." She waved him toward the doorway with the back of her hand. "Grace and Sybill and I can get acquainted."

"She's bossy, too," Phillip warned Sybill. "Just yell if you need help, and I'll come rescue you." He gave her a hard, firm kiss on the mouth before she could think to evade it, then deserted her.

Anna gave a long, interested hum, then smiled brightly. "Let's have some wine."

Grace pulled out a chair. "Phillip said you were going to stay in St. Chris a while and write a book about it."

"Something like that." Sybill took a deep breath. They were just women, after all. A stunning dark-eyed brunette and a cool lovely blonde. There was no need to be nervous. "Actually, I plan to write about the culture and traditions and social landscapes of small towns and rural communities."

"We have both on the Shore."

"So I see. You and Ethan are recently married."

Grace's smile warmed, and her gaze shifted to the gold band on her finger. "Just last month."

"And you grew up here, together."

"I was born here. Ethan moved here when he was about twelve."

"Are you from the area, too?" she asked Anna, more comfortable in the role of interviewer.

"No, I'm from Pittsburgh. I moved to D.C., wandered down to Princess Anne. I work for Social Services, as a caseworker. That's one of the reasons I was so interested in your books." She set a glass of deep-red wine in front of Sybill.

"Oh, yes, you're Seth's caseworker. Phillip told me a little about the situation."

"Mmm," was Anna's only comment as she turned to take a bib apron from a hook. "Did you enjoy your sail?"

So, Sybill realized, discussing Seth with outsiders was off-limits. She ordered herself to accept that, for now. "Yes, very much. More than I'd expected to. I can't believe I've gone so long without trying it."

"I had my first sail a few months ago." Anna set a huge pot of water on the stove to boil. "Grace has been sailing all her life."

"Do you work here, in St. Christopher's?"

"Yes, I clean houses."

"Including this one, thank the Lord," Anna put in. "I was telling Grace she ought to start a company. Maids Are Us or something." When Grace laughed, Anna shook her head. "I'm serious. It would be a terrific service, to the working woman in particular. You could even do commercial buildings. If you trained two or three people, word of mouth alone would get it going."

"You think bigger than I do. I don't know how to run a business."

"I bet you do. Your family's been running the crab house for generations."

"Crab house?" Sybill interrupted.

"Picking, packing, shipping." Grace lifted a hand. "Odds are, if you've had crab while you've been here, it came to you via my father's company. But I've never been involved in the business end."

"That doesn't mean you couldn't handle your own business." Anna took a chunk of mozzarella out of the refrigerator and began to grate it. "A lot of people out there are more than willing to pay for good, reliable, and trustworthy domestic services. They don't want to spend what little free time they might have cleaning the house, cooking meals, separating laundry. Traditional roles are shifting—don't you agree, Sybill? Women can't spend every spare second of their time in the kitchen."

"Well, I would agree, but . . . well, here you are."

Anna stopped, blinked, then threw back her head and laughed. She looked, Sybill thought, like a woman who should be dancing around a campfire to the sound of violins rather than cozily grating cheese in a fragrant kitchen.

"You're right, absolutely." Still chuckling, Anna shook her head. "Here I am, while my man lounges in front of the TV, deaf and blind to anything but the game. And this is often the scene on Sundays around here. I don't mind. I love to cook."

"Really?"

Hearing the suspicion in Sybill's voice, Anna laughed again. "Really. I find it satisfying, but not when I have to rush in from work and toss something together. That's why we take turns around here. Mondays are leftovers from whatever I've cooked Sunday. Tuesdays we all suffer through whatever Cam cooks, because he's simply dreadful in the kitchen. Wednesdays we do takeout, Thursdays I cook, Fridays Phillip cooks, and Saturdays are up for grabs. It's a very workable system when it works."

"Anna's planning on having Seth take over as chef on Wednesdays within the year."

"At his age?"

Anna shook back her hair. "He'll be eleven in a couple of weeks. By the time I was his age, I could make a killer red sauce. The time and effort it takes to teach him and to convince him he's still a male if he knows how to make a meal will be worth it in the end. And," she added, sliding wide, flat noodles into the boiling water, "if I use the fact that he can outdo Cam in any area, he'll be an A student."

"They don't get along."

"They're wonderful together." Anna tilted her head as the living room exploded with shouts, cheers, stomping. "And Seth likes nothing more than to impress his big brother. Which means, of course, they argue and prod each other constantly." She smiled again. "I take it you don't have any brothers."

"No. No, I don't."

"Sisters?" Grace asked and wondered why Sybill's eyes went so cool.

"One."

"I always wanted a sister." Grace smiled over at Anna. "Now I've got one."

"Grace and I were both only children." Anna squeezed Grace's shoulder as she walked by to mix her cheeses. Something in that easy, intimate gesture stirred a tug of envy inside Sybill. "Since we fell in with the Quinns, we've been making up rapidly for coming from small families. Does your sister live in New York?"

"No." Sybill's stomach clenched reflexively. "We're not terribly close. Excuse me." She pushed away from the table. "Can I use the bathroom?"

"Sure. Down the hall, first door on the left." Anna waited until Sybill walked out, then pursed her lips at Grace. "I can't decide what I think about her."

"She seems a little uncomfortable."

Anna shrugged her shoulders. "Well, I guess we'll have to wait and see, won't we?"

In the little powder room off the hall, Sybill splashed water on her face. She was hot, nervous, and vaguely sick to her stomach. She didn't understand this family, she thought. They were loud, occasionally crude, pieced together from different origins. Yet they seemed happy, at ease with each other, and very affectionate.

As she patted her face dry, she met her own eyes in the mirror. Her family had never been loud or crude. Except for those ugly moments when Gloria had pushed the limits. Just now she couldn't honestly say for certain if they had ever been happy, ever been at ease with each other. And affection had never been a priority or something that was expressed in an overt manner.

It was simply that none of them were very emotional people, she told herself. She had always been more cerebral, out of inclination, she decided, and in defense against Gloria's baffling volatility. Life was calmer if one depended on the intellect. She knew that. Believed that absolutely.

But it was her emotions that were churning now. She felt like a liar, a spy, a sneak. Reminding herself that she was doing what she was doing for the welfare of a child helped. Telling herself that the child was her own nephew and she had every right to be there, to form opinions, soothed.

Objectivity, she told herself, pressing her fingertips against her temples to smother the nagging ache. That's what would get her through until she'd gathered all the facts, all the data, and formed her opinion.

She stepped out quietly and took the few steps down the hall toward the blaring noise of the ball game. She saw Seth sprawled on the floor at Cam's feet and shouting abuse at the set across the room. Cam was gesturing with his beer and arguing the last call with Phillip. Ethan simply watched the game, with Aubrey curled in his lap, dozing despite the noise.

The room itself was homey, slightly shabby, and appeared comfortable. A piano was angled out from the corner. A vase of zinnias and dozens of small-framed snapshots crowded its polished surface. A half empty bowl of potato chips sat at Seth's elbow. The rug was littered with crumbs, shoes, the Sunday paper, and a grubby, well-gnawed hunk of rope.

The light had faded, but no one had bothered to switch on a lamp.

She started to step back, but Phillip glanced over. Smiled. Held out a hand. She walked to him, let him draw her down to the arm of his chair. "Bottom of the ninth," he murmured. "We're up by one."

"Watch this reliever kick this guy's sorry ass." Seth kept his voice down, but it rang with glee. He didn't even flinch when Cam slapped him on the head with his own ball cap. "Oh, yeah! Struck him *out!*" He leaped up, did a victory boogie. "We are number one. Man, I'm starving." He raced off to the kitchen and soon could be heard begging for food.

"Winning ball games works up an appetite," Phillip decided, absently kissing Sybill's hand. "How's she doing in there?"

"She appeared to be on top of things."

"Let's go see if she made antipasto."

He pulled her into the kitchen, and within moments it was crowded with people. Aubrey rested her head on Ethan's shoulder and blinked like an owl. Seth stuffed his mouth with tidbits from an elaborate tray and did a play-by-play of the game.

Everyone seemed to be moving, talking, eating at the same time, Sybill thought. Phillip put another glass of wine in her hand before he was drafted to deal with the bread. Because she felt slightly less confused by him than by the others, Sybill stuck to his side as chaos reigned.

He cut thick slices of Italian bread, then doctored them with butter and garlic.

"Is it always like this?" she murmured to him.

"No." He picked up his own glass of wine, touched it lightly to hers. "Sometimes it's really loud and disorganized."

By THE TIME HE DROVE HER BACK to her hotel, Sybill's head was ringing. There was so much to process. Sights, sounds, personalities, impressions. She had survived complex state dinners with less confusion than a Sunday dinner with the Quinns.

She needed time, she decided, to analyze. Once she was able to write down her thoughts, her observations, she would align them, dissect them, and begin to draw her initial conclusions.

"Tired?"

She sighed once. "A little. It was quite a day. A fascinating one." Blew out a breath. "And a fattening one. I'm definitely going to make use of the hotel's health club in the morning. I enjoyed myself," she added as he parked near the lobby entrance. "Very much."

"Good. Then you'll be willing to do it again." He climbed out, skirted the hood, then took her hand as she stepped onto the curb.

"There's no need for you to take me up. I know the way."

"I'll take you up anyway."

"I'm not going to ask you to come in."

"I'm still going to walk you to your door, Sybill."

She let it go, crossing with him to the elevators, stepping inside with him when the doors opened. "So, you'll drive to Baltimore in the morning?" She pushed the button for her floor.

"Tonight. When things are fairly settled here, I drive back Sunday nights. There's rarely any traffic, and I can get an earlier start on Mondays."

"It can't be easy for you, the commute, the demands on your time, and the tug-of-war of responsibilities."

"A lot of things aren't easy. But they're worth working for." He caressed her hair. "I don't mind putting time and effort into something I enjoy."

"Well . . ." She cleared her throat and walked out of the elevator the minute the doors opened. "I appreciate the time and effort you put into today."

"I'll be back Thursday night. I want to see you."

She slipped her key card out of her purse. "I can't be sure right now what I'll be doing at the end of the week."

He simply framed her face with his hands, moved in and covered her mouth with his. The taste of her, he thought. He couldn't seem to get enough of the taste of her. "I want to see you," he murmured against her lips.

She'd always been so good at staying in control, at distancing herself from attempts at seduction, from resisting the persuasions of physical attractions. But with him, each time she could feel herself slipping a little farther, a little deeper.

"I'm not ready for this," she heard herself say.

"Neither am I." Still, he drew her closer, held her tighter and took the kiss toward desperation. "I want you. Maybe it's a good thing we both have a few days to think about what happens next."

She looked up at him, shaken, yearning, and just a little frightened of what was happening inside her. "Yes, I think it's a very good thing." She turned, had to use both hands to shove the key card into its slot. "Drive carefully." She stepped inside, closed the door quickly, then leaned back against it until she was certain her heart wasn't going to pump its way out of her chest.

It was insane, she thought, absolutely insane to get this involved this quickly. She was honest enough with herself, scientist enough not to skew the results with incorrect data, to admit that what was happening to her where Phillip Quinn was concerned had nothing whatsoever to do with Seth.

It should be stopped. She closed her eyes and felt the pressure of his mouth still vibrating on her lips. And she was afraid it couldn't be stopped.

EIGHT

It was probably a chancy step to take. Sybill wondered if it could possibly be illegal. Loitering near St. Christopher's Middle School certainly made her feel like some sort of criminal, no matter how firmly she told herself she was doing nothing wrong.

She was simply walking on a public street in the middle of the afternoon. It wasn't as though she was stalking Seth, or planning to abduct him. She only wanted to talk to him, to see him alone for a little while.

She'd waited until the middle of the week, watching from a careful distance on Monday and Tuesday to gauge his routine, and the timing. Habitually, she now knew, the buses lumbered up to school several minutes before the doors opened and children began pouring out.

Elementary first, then middle, then the high school students.

That alone was a lesson in the process of childhood, she mused. The compact little bodies and fresh round faces of the elementary children, then the more gangling, somewhat awkward forms of those who hovered around puberty. And last, the astonishingly adult and more individual young people who strolled out of the high school.

It was a study in itself, she decided. From dangling shoelaces and gap-toothed smiles to cowlicks and ball jackets to baggy jeans and shining falls of hair.

Children had never been a part of her life, or her interests. She'd grown up in a world of adults and had been expected to acclimate, to conform. There had been no big yellow school buses, no wild rebel yells when bursting out of the school doors into freedom, no lingering in the parking lot with some leather-jacketed bad boy.

So she observed all those things here like an audience at a play and found the mix of drama and comedy both amusing and informative.

When Seth hurried out, bumping bodies with the dark-haired boy she'd decided was his most usual companion, her pulse quickened. He whipped his ball cap out of his pocket and put it on his head the moment he was through the doors. A ritual, she thought, symbolizing the change of rules. The other boy fished in his pocket and pulled out a fistful of bubblegum. In seconds it was wadded into his mouth.

The noise level rose, making it impossible for her to hear their conversation, but it appeared to be animated and included a great deal of elbow jabbing and shoulder punching.

Typical male affection pattern, she concluded.

They turned their backs on the buses and began to walk down the sidewalk. Moments later, a smaller boy raced up to them. He bounced, Sybill noted, and seemed to have a great deal to say for himself.

She waited a moment longer, then casually took a path that would intersect with theirs.

"Shit, man, that geography test was nothing. A bozo could've aced it." Seth shrugged to distribute the weight of his backpack.

The other boy blew an impressive candy-pink bubble, popped it, then sucked it in. "I don't know what's the big damn deal about knowing all the states and capitals. It's not like I'm going to live in North Dakota."

"Seth, hello."

Sybill watched him stop, adjust his train of thought, and focus on her. "Oh, yeah, hi."

"I guess school's done for the day. You heading home?"

"The boatyard." There was that little dance on the nape of his neck again. It irritated him. "We got work."

"I'm going that way myself." She tried a smile on the other boys. "Hi, I'm Sybill."

"I'm Danny," the other boy told her. "That's Will."

"Nice to meet you."

"We had vegetable soup for lunch," Will informed everyone grandly. "And Lisa Harbough threw up *all over*. And Mr. Jim had to clean it up, and her mom came to get her, and we couldn't write our vocabulary words." He danced around Sybill as he relayed the information, then shot her an amazingly innocent, wonderfully bright smile that she was helpless to resist.

"I hope Lisa's feeling better soon."

"Once when I threw up I got to stay home and watch TV all day. Me and Danny live over there on Heron Lane. Where do you live?"

"I'm just visiting."

"My Uncle John and Aunt Margie moved to South Carolina and we got to visit them. They have two dogs and a baby named Mike. Do you have dogs and babies?"

"No . . . no, I don't."

"You can get them," he told her. "You can go right to the animal shelter and get a dog—that's what we did. And you can get married and make a baby so it lives in your stomach. There's nothing to it."

"Jeez, Will." Seth rolled his eyes, while Sybill only managed to blink.

"Well, I'm going to have dogs and babies when I grow up. As many as I want." He flashed that hundred-watt smile again, then raced away. " 'Bye."

"He's such a geek," Danny said with the shuddering disdain of older brother for younger. "See you, Seth." He bounded after Will, turned briefly to run backward and flipped a wave toward Sybill. " 'Bye."

"Will's not really a geek," Seth told Sybill. "He's just a kid, and he's got diarrhea of the mouth, but he's pretty cool."

"He's certainly friendly." She shifted her shoulder bag, smiled down at him. "Do you mind if I walk the rest of the way with you?"

"It's okay."

"I thought I heard you say something about a geography test."

"Yeah, we took one today. It was nothing."

"You like school?"

"It's there." He jerked his shoulder. "You gotta go."

"I always enjoyed it. Learning new things." She laughed lightly. "I suppose I was a geek."

Seth angled his head, narrowing his eyes as he studied her face. A looker, Phillip had called her, he remembered. He guessed she was. She had nice eyes, the light color a sharp contrast to the dark lashes. Her hair wasn't as dark as Anna's, nor light like Grace's. It was really shiny, he noted, and the way she pulled it back all smooth and stuff left her face right out there.

She might be cool to draw sometime.

"You don't look like a geek," Seth announced just as Sybill felt heat begin to rise into her cheeks under his long, intense study. "Anyway, that would be a nerd."

"Oh." She wasn't sure if she'd just qualified for nerd status and decided not to ask. "What do you like studying best?"

"I don't know. Mostly it's just a bunch of—stuff," he decided, quickly censoring his opinion. "I guess I like it better when we get to read about people instead of things."

"I've always liked to study people." She stopped and gestured toward a small two-story gray house with a trim front yard. "My theory would be that a young family lives there. Both husband and wife work outside the home and they have a preschooler, most likely a boy. Odds are that they've known each other a number of years and have been married less than seven."

"How come?"

"Well, it's the middle of the day and no one's home. No cars in the drive, and the house looks empty. But there's a tricycle there and several large toy trucks. The house isn't new, but it's well kept. Most young couples both work today in order to buy a home, have a family. They live in a small community. Younger people rarely settle in small towns unless one or both of them grew up there. So I'd theorize that this couple lived here, knew each other, eventually married. It's likely they had their first child within the first three years of marriage and the toys indicate he's three to five."

"That's pretty cool," Seth decided after a moment.

However foolish it was, she felt a surge of pride that she might have avoided nerddom after all. "But I'd want to know more, wouldn't you?"

She'd caught his interest. "Like what?"

"Why did they choose this particular house. What are their goals? What is the status of their relationship? Who handles the money, which indicates the disposition of power, and why? If you study people, you see the patterns."

"How come it matters?"

"I don't understand."

"Who cares?"

She considered. "Well, if you understand the patterns, the social picture on a large scale, you learn why people behave in certain manners."

"What if they don't fit?"

Bright boy, she thought on another, deeper wave of pride. "Everyone fits some pattern. You factor in background, genetics, education, social strata, religious and cultural roots."

"You get paid for that?"

"Yes, I suppose I do."

"Weird."

Now, she concluded, she had definitely been relegated to nerd status. "It can be interesting." She racked her brain to come up with an example that would salvage his opinion of her. "I did this experiment once in several cities. I arranged for a man to stand on the street and stare up at a building."

"Just stare at it?"

"That's right. He stood there and stared up, shading his eyes from the sun when he had to. Before long someone stopped beside him and stared up at the same building. Then another and another, until there was a crowd of people, all looking up at that building. It took much longer for anyone to actually ask what was going on, what were they looking at. No one really wanted to be the first to ask because that was an admission that you didn't see what you assumed everyone else was seeing. We want to conform, we want to fit in, we want to know and see and understand what the person beside us knows and sees and understands."

"I bet some of them thought someone was going to jump out of a window."

"Very likely. The average time an individual stood, looking, interrupting their schedule, was two minutes." She believed she'd caught his imagination again, and so she hurried on. "That's actually quite a long time to stare at a perfectly ordinary building."

"That's pretty cool. But it's still weird."

They were coming to the point where he would have to veer off to go to the boatyard. She thought quickly and in a rare move went with impulse. "What do you think would happen if you conducted the same experiment in St. Christopher's?"

"I don't know. The same thing?"

"I doubt it." She sent him a conspirator's smile. "Want to try it?"

"Maybe."

"We can head over to the waterfront now. Will your brother worry if you're a few minutes late? Should you go tell him you're with me?"

"Nah. Cam doesn't keep me on a leash. He cuts me some slack time."

She wasn't sure how she felt about the loose discipline in that area, but at the moment she was happy to take advantage of it. "Let's try it, then. I'll pay you in ice cream."

"You got a deal."

They turned away from the boatyard. "You can pick a spot," she began. "It's necessary to stand. People don't generally pay attention to someone who's sitting and looking. They often assume the person is simply daydreaming or resting."

"I get it."

"It's more effective if you look up at something. Is it okay if I videotape?"

He raised his eyebrows as she took a neat compact video recorder out of her bag. "Yeah, I guess. You carry that around all the time?"

"When I'm working, I do. And a notebook, and a micro audio tape recorder, backup batteries and tapes, extra pencils. My cell phone." She laughed at herself. "I like being prepared. And the day they make a computer small enough to fit in a purse, I'm going to be the first in line."

"Phil likes all that electronic stuff, too."

"The baggage of the urbanite. We're desperate not to waste a minute. Then, of course, we can't get away from anything because we're plugged in every second of the day."

"You could just turn everything off."

"Yes." Oddly she found the simplicity of his statement profound. "I suppose I could."

Pedestrian traffic was light on the waterfront. She saw a workboat unloading the day's catch and a family taking advantage of the balmy afternoon by splurging on ice cream sundaes at one of the little outdoor tables. Two old men, their faces nut brown and deeply seamed, sat on an iron bench with a checkerboard between them. Neither seemed inclined to make a move. A trio of women chatted in the doorway of one of the shops, but only one of them carried a bag.

"I'm going to stand over there." Seth pointed to his spot. "And look up at the hotel."

"Good choice." Sybill stayed where she was as he strolled off. Distance was necessary to keep the experiment pure. She lifted the camera, zoomed in as Seth moved away. He turned once, shot her a quick, cocky smile.

And when his face filled her view screen, emotions she hadn't been prepared for flooded her. He was so handsome, so bright. So happy. She struggled to pull herself back from a dangerous edge that she was afraid was despair.

She could walk away, she thought, pack up and leave, never see him again. He would never know who she was or what they were to each other. He would never miss whatever she could bring into his life. She was nothing to him.

She'd never really tried to be.

It was different now, she reminded herself. She was making it different now. Deliberately she ordered her fingers to relax, her neck, her arms. She was causing no harm by getting to know him, spending some time studying his situation.

She taped him as he settled on his spot, lifted his face. His profile was finer, more angled than Gloria's, Sybill decided. Perhaps his bone structure had come from his father.

His build wasn't Gloria's either, as she'd first assumed, but more like her own, and her mother's. He would be tall when he finished growing, mostly leg, and on the slim side.

His body language, she saw with a slight jolt, was typical Quinn. Already, he'd taken on some of the traits of his foster family. That hip-shot stance, hands tucked into pockets, head angled.

She fought back an annoying spurt of resentment and ordered herself to focus on the experiment.

It took just over a minute for the first person to stop beside Seth. She recognized the big woman with the gray-streaked hair who manned the counter at Crawford's. Everyone called her Mother. As expected, the woman shifted her gaze, tilted her face up to follow Seth's line of sight. But after a quick scan, she patted Seth on the shoulder.

"What're you looking at, boy?"

"Nothing."

He muttered it so that Sybill edged closer to try to pick up his voice on the tape.

"Well, hell, you stand there for long looking at nothing, people're going to think you're pixilated. Why aren't you down to the boat-yard?"

"I'm going in a minute."

"Hey, Mother. Hi, Seth." A pretty young woman with dark hair stepped into the frame, glanced up at the hotel. "Something going on up there? I don't see anything."

"Nothing to see," Mother informed her. "Boy's just standing looking at nothing. How's your mama, Julie?"

"Oh, she's a little under the weather. She's got a sore throat and a little cough."

"Chicken soup, hot tea and honey."

"Grace brought some soup over this morning."

"You see she eats it. Hey, there, Jim."

"Afternoon." A short, stocky man in white rubber boots clumped over, gave Seth a friendly swat on the head. "What you staring at up there, boy?"

"Jeez, can't a guy just stand around?" Seth turned his face to the camera, rolled his eyes for Sybill and made her chuckle.

"Stand here long, gulls'll light on you." Jim winked at him. "Cap'n's in for the day," he added, referring to Ethan. "He gets to the boatyard before you, he's gonna want to know why."

"I'm going, I'm going. Man." Shoulders rounded, head down, Seth stalked back to Sybill. "Nobody's falling for it."

"Because everyone knows you." She switched off the camera, lowered it. "It changes the pattern."

"You figured that would happen?"

"I theorized," she corrected, "that in a closely knit area where the subject was known, the pattern would be that an individual would stop. They would probably look first, then question. There's no risk, no loss of ego when questioning a familiar person, and a young one at that."

He frowned over toward where the trio continued to chat. "So, I still get paid."

"Absolutely, and you'll likely rate a section in my book."

"Cool. I'll take a cookie dough cone. I've got to get to the boatyard before Cam and Ethan hassle me."

"If they're going to be angry with you, I'll explain. It's my fault you're late."

"They won't be pissed or anything. Beside, I'll tell them it was, like, for science, right?" When he flashed that grin she had to resist an unexpected urge to hug him.

"That's exactly right." She risked laying a hand on his shoulder as they started toward Crawford's. She thought she felt him stiffen and casually let her hand drop away. "And we can always call them on my cell phone."

"Yeah? Way cool. Can I do it?"

"Sure, why not?"

•   •   •

TWENTY MINUTES LATER SYBILL
was at her desk, fingers racing over her keyboard.

*Though I spent less than an hour with him, I would conclude that
the subject is extremely bright. Phillip informed me that he achieves
high grades academically, which is admirable. It was satisfying to
discover that he has a questioning mind. His manners are perhaps a
bit rough, but not unpleasant. He appears to be considerably more
outgoing socially than his mother or I were at his age. In that, I
mean he seems quite natural with relative strangers without the
polite formality that was stressed in my own upbringing. Part of this
may be due to the influence of the Quinns. They are, as I have
noted previously, informal, casual people.*

*I would also conclude from watching both the children and the
adults with whom he interacted today, that he is generally well liked
in this community and accepted as part of it. Naturally I cannot, at
this early stage, conclude whether or not his best interest would be
served by remaining here.*

*It's simply not possible to ignore Gloria's rights, nor have I at-
tempted, as yet, to discover the boy's wishes as concern his mother.*

*I would prefer that he grow accustomed to me, feel comfortable
around me, before he learns of our family connection.*

I need more time to . . .

She broke off as the phone rang and, scanning her hastily typed
notes, picked up the receiver.

"Dr. Griffin."

"Hello, Dr. Griffin. Why do I suspect I've interrupted your work?"

She recognized Phillip's voice, the amusement in it, and with a flare
of guilt lowered the top of her computer. "Because you're a perceptive man. But I can spare a few minutes. How are things in Baltimore?"

"Busy. How's this? The visual is a handsome young couple, beaming
smiles as they carry their laughing toddler to a mid-size sedan. Cap-
tion: 'Myerstone Tires. Your family matters to us.' "

"Manipulative. The consumer is led to believe that if he or she buys
another brand, the family doesn't matter to that other company."

"Yeah. It works. Of course, we're hitting the car mags with a different image. Screaming convertible in kick-ass red, long, winding road,
sexy blonde at the wheel. 'Myerstone Tires. You can drive there, or
you can BE there.' "

"Clever."

"The client likes it, and that takes a load off. How's life in St. Chris?"

"Quiet." She bit her lip. "I ran into Seth a bit ago. Actually, I drafted him to help me with an experiment. It went well."

"Oh, yeah? How much did you have to pay him?"

"An ice cream cone, double scoop."

"You got off cheap. The kid's an operator. How about dinner tomorrow night, a bottle of champagne to celebrate our mutual successes?"

"Speaking of operators."

"I've been thinking about you all week."

"Three days," she corrected and, picking up a pencil, began to doodle on her pad.

"And nights. With this account settled, I can get out a little earlier tomorrow. Why don't I pick you up at seven?"

"I'm not sure where we're going, Phillip."

"Neither am I. Do you need to be?"

She understood that neither of them was speaking of restaurants. "It's less confusing that way."

"Then we'll talk about it, and maybe we'll get past the confusion. Seven o'clock."

She glanced down, noticed that she'd unconsciously sketched his face on her notepad. A bad sign, she thought. A very dangerous sign. "All right." It was best to face complications head-on. "I'll see you tomorrow."

"Do me a favor?"

"If I can."

"Think of me tonight."

She doubted she had any choice in the matter. " 'Bye."

IN HIS OFFICE FOURTEEN STO-ries above the streets of Baltimore, Phillip pushed back from his slick black desk, ignored the beep on his computer that signaled an interoffice e-mail and turned toward his wide window.

He loved his view of the city, the renovated buildings, the glimpses of the harbor, the hustle of cars and people below. But just now he didn't see any of it.

He literally couldn't get Sybill out of his mind. It was a new experience for him, this continual tug on his thoughts and concentration. It wasn't as if she was interfering with his routine, he reflected. He could work, eat, brainstorm, do his presentations as skillfully as he had before he'd met her.

But she was simply there, he decided. A tickle at the back of his mind through the day, that inched forward to the front when his energies weren't otherwise occupied.

He wasn't quite sure if he enjoyed having a woman demand so much of his attention, particularly a woman who was doing very little to encourage him.

Maybe he considered that light sheen of formality, that cautious distance she tried to maintain, a challenge. He thought he could live with that. It was just another of the entertaining and varied games men and women played.

But he worried that something was happening on a level he'd never explored. And if he was any judge, she was just as unsettled by it as he.

"It's just like you," Ray said from behind him.

"Oh, Jesus." Phillip didn't spin around, didn't goggle. He simply shut his eyes.

"Pretty fancy office you got here. Been a while since I got in." Ray prowled the room casually, pursing his lips at a black-framed canvas splashed with reds and blues. "Not bad," he decided. "Brain stimulator. I'd guess that's why you put it in your office, get the juices going."

"I refuse to believe that my dead father is standing in my office critiquing art."

"Well, that wasn't what I wanted to talk about anyway." But he paused by a metal sculpture in the corner. "But I like this piece, too. You always had high-class taste. Art, food, women." He grinned cheerfully as Phillip turned. "The woman you've got on your mind now, for instance. Very high-class."

"I need to take some time off."

"I'd agree with you there. You've been up to and over your head for months. She's an interesting woman, Phillip. There's more to her than you see, or than she knows. I hope when the time comes you'll listen to her, really listen to her."

"What are you talking about?" He held up a hand, palm out. "Why am I asking you what you're talking about when you're not here?"

"I'm hoping that the pair of you will stop analyzing the steps and stages and accept what is." Ray shrugged, slipped his hands into the pockets of his Orioles fielder's jacket. "But you have to go your own way. It's going to be hard. There's not much time left before it gets a lot harder. You'll stand between Seth and what hurts him. I know that. I want to tell you that you can trust her. When it's down to the sticking point, Phillip, you trust yourself, and you trust her."

A new chill skidded down his spine. "What does Sybill have to do with Seth?"

"It's not for me to tell you that." He smiled again, but his eyes didn't match the curve of his lips. "You haven't talked to your brothers about me. You need to. You need to stop feeling you have to control all the buttons. You're good at it, God knows, but give a little."

He drew in a deep breath, turned a slow circle. "Christ, your mother would've gotten a kick out of this place. You've done a hell of a job with your life so far." Now his eyes smiled. "I'm proud of you. I know you'll handle what comes next."

"You did a hell of a job with my life," Phillip murmured. "You and Mom."

"Damn right we did." Ray winked. "Keep it up." When the phone rang, Ray sighed. "Everything that happens needs to happen. It's what you do about it that makes the difference. Answer the phone, Phillip, and remember Seth needs you."

Then there was nothing but the ringing of the phone and an empty office. With his gaze locked on where his father had been, Phillip reached for the phone.

"Phillip Quinn."

As he listened, his eyes hardened. He grabbed a pen, and began to take notes on the detective's report on the most recent movements of Gloria DeLauter.

NINE

"SHE'S IN HAMPTON." PHILLIP kept his eyes on Seth as he relayed the information. He watched Cam lay a hand on the boy's rigid shoulder, an unspoken sign of protection. "She was picked up by the police—drunk and disorderly, possession."

"She's in jail." Seth's face was white as bone. "They can keep her in jail."

"She's there now." How long she would stay there, Phillip thought, was another matter. "She probably has enough money to post bond."

"You mean she can pay them money and they'll let her go?" Beneath Cam's hand, Seth began to tremble. "No matter what?"

"I don't know. But for now we know exactly where she is. I'm going down to talk to her."

"Don't! Don't go there."

"Seth, we've talked about this." Cam massaged the shaking shoulder as he turned Seth to face him. "The only way we're going to fix this for good is to deal with her."

"I won't go back." It was said in a whisper, but a furious one. "I'll never go back."

"You won't go back." Ethan unhitched his tool belt, laid it on the workbench. "You can stay with Grace until Anna gets home." He looked at Phillip and Cam. "We'll go to Hampton."

"What if the cops say I have to? What if they come while you're gone and—"

"Seth." Phillip interrupted the rising desperation. He crouched, took Seth's arms firmly. "You have to trust us."

Seth stared back at him with Ray Quinn's eyes, and those eyes were glazed with tears and terror. For the first time, Phillip looked into them and felt no shadowy resentment, no doubts.

"You belong with us," he said quietly. "Nothing's going to change that."

On a long, shuddering breath Seth nodded. He had no choice, could do nothing but hope. And fear.

"We'll take my car," Phillip stated.

"GRACE AND ANNA WILL CALM him down." Cam shifted restlessly in the passenger seat of Phillip's Jeep.

"It's hell being that scared." From the backseat, Ethan glanced at the speedometer and noted that Phillip was pushing eighty. "Not being able to do anything but wait and see."

"She's fucked herself," Phillip said flatly. "Getting arrested isn't going to help her custody case, if she tries to make one."

"She doesn't want the kid."

Phillip spared a brief glance at Cam. "No, she wants money. She isn't going to bleed any out of us. But we're going to get some answers. We're going to end it."

She'd lie, Phillip thought. He had no doubt that she would lie and wheedle and maneuver. But she was wrong, dead wrong, if she thought she could get past the three of them to Seth.

You'll handle what comes next, Ray had said.

Phillip's hands tightened on the wheel. He kept his eyes on the road. He'd handle it, all right. One way or the other.

WITH HER HEAD THROBBING, her stomach rolling, Sybill walked into the small county police station. Gloria had called her, weeping and desperate, begging her to send money for bail.

For bail, Sybill thought now, fighting off a shudder.

Gloria said it was a mistake, she reminded herself, a terrible misunderstanding. Of course, what else could it have been? She'd nearly wired the money. She still wasn't sure what had stopped her, what had pushed her to get into her car and drive.

To help, of course, she told herself. She only wanted to help.

"I'm here for Gloria DeLauter," she told the uniformed officer who sat behind a narrow, cluttered counter. "I'd like to see her, if possible."

"Your name?"

"Griffin. Dr. Sybill Griffin. I'm her sister. I'll post her bond, but I'd . . . I'd like to see her."

"Can I see some ID?"

"Oh, yes." She fumbled in her purse for her wallet. Her hands were damp and shaky, but the cop simply watched her with cool eyes until she offered identification.

"Why don't you have a seat?" he suggested, then scraped back his own chair and slipped into an adjoining room.

Her throat was dry and desperate for water. She wandered the small waiting area with its grouping of hard plastic chairs in industrial beige until she found a water fountain. But the water hit her tortured stomach like frigid balls of lead.

Had they put her in a cell? Oh, God, had they actually put her sister in a cell? Is that where she would have to see Gloria?

But under the sorrow, her mind was working coolly, pragmatically. How had Gloria known where to reach her? What was she doing so close to St. Christopher's? Why was she accused of having drugs?

That was why she hadn't wired the money, she admitted now. She wanted the answers first.

"Dr. Griffin."

She jolted, turned to the officer with her eyes wide as a doe's caught in headlights. "Yes. Can I see her now?"

"I'll need to take your purse. I'll give you a receipt."

"All right."

She handed it over to him, signed the log where he indicated, accepted the receipt for her belongings.

"This way."

He gestured toward a side door, then opened it into a narrow corridor. On the left was a small room furnished only with a single table and a few chairs. Gloria sat at one, her right wrist cuffed to a bolt.

Sybill's first thought was that they'd made a mistake. This wasn't her sister. They'd brought the wrong woman into the room. This one looked far too old, far too hard, with her bony body, the shoulders like points of wings, the contrast of breasts pressing against a tiny, snug sweater so hard that the nipples stood out in arrogant relief.

Her frizzed mass of straw-colored hair had a dark streak shooting up the center, deep lines dug in around her mouth, and the calculation in her eyes was as sharp as those shoulders.

Then those eyes filled, that mouth trembled.

"Syb." Her voice cracked as she held out an imploring hand. "Thank God you've come."

"Gloria." She stepped forward quickly, took that shaking hand in her own. "What happened?"

"I don't know. I don't understand any of it. I'm so scared." She laid her head on the table and began to weep in loud, racking sobs.

"Please." Instinctively Sybill sat and draped her arm around her sister as she looked over at the cop. "Can we be alone?"

"I'll be right outside." He looked back at Gloria. If he thought what a change this was from the screaming, cursing woman who'd been pulled in a few hours ago, his face revealed nothing.

He stepped out, shut the door, and left them alone.

"Let me get you some water."

Sybill rose, hurried over to the water jug in the corner, and filled a thin triangle of paper. She cupped her hands around her sister's, holding it steady.

"Did you pay the bail? Why can't we just go? I don't want to stay here."

"I'll take care of it. Tell me what happened."

"I said I don't know. I was with this guy. I was lonely." She sniffed, accepting the tissue that Sybill passed her. "We were just talking for a while. We were going to go out to lunch, then the cops came up. He ran away and they grabbed me. It all happened so fast."

She buried her face in her hands. "They found drugs in my purse. He must have put them there. I just wanted someone to talk to."

"All right. I'm sure we'll straighten it all out." Sybill wanted to believe, to accept, and she hated herself because she couldn't. Not quite. "What was his name?"

"John. John Barlow. He seemed so sweet, Sybill. So understanding. I was feeling really low. Because of Seth." She lowered her hands and her eyes were tragic. "I miss my little boy so much."

"Were you coming to St. Christopher's?"

Gloria lowered her gaze. "I thought, if I just had a chance to see him."

"Is that what the lawyer suggested?"

"The—oh . . ." The hesitation was brief, but it set off warning bells in Sybill's head. "No, but lawyers don't understand. They just keep asking for money."

"What's your lawyer's name? I'll call him. He may be able to help straighten this out."

"He's not from around here. Look, Sybill, I just want to get out of here. You can't believe how horrible it is. That cop out there?" She nodded toward the door. "He put his hands on me."

Sybill's stomach began to pitch again. "What do you mean?"

"You know what I mean." The first hint of annoyance sliced through. "He felt me up, and he said he'd be back later for more. He's going to rape me."

Sybill shut her eyes, pressed her fingers to them. When they were teenagers, Gloria had accused more than a dozen boys and men of molesting her, including her high school counselor and principal. Even their own father.

"Gloria, don't do this. I said I would help you."

"I'm telling you that bastard put his hands all over me. As soon as I'm out of here, I'm filing charges." She crumpled the paper cup, heaved it. "I don't give a damn if you believe me or not. I know what happened."

"All right, but let's deal with now. How did you know where to find me?"

"What?" A dark rage had been sliding over her brain, and she had to struggle to remember her role. "What do you mean?"

"I didn't tell you where I was going, where I would be. I said I would contact you. How did you know to call me at the hotel in St. Christopher's?"

It had been a mistake, which Gloria had realized shortly after making the call. But she'd been drunk and furious. And damn it, she didn't have the cash on her to make bail. What she had left was safely tucked away. Until the Quinns added to it.

She wasn't thinking when she called Sybill, but she'd had time to think since. The way to play sister Sybill, she knew, was to tug on the guilt and responsibility strings.

"I know you." She offered a watery smile. "I knew that when I told you what happened with Seth, you'd help. I tried your apartment in New York." Which she had, more than a week ago. "And when your answering service said you were out of town, I explained how I was your sister and there was an emergency. They gave me the number of the hotel."

"I see." It was plausible, Sybill decided, even logical. "I'll take care of the bail, Gloria, but there are conditions."

"Yeah." She gave a short laugh. "That sounds familiar."

"I need the name of your lawyer so I can contact him. I want to be brought up to date on the status of this situation with Seth. I want you to talk to me. We'll have dinner and you can explain to me about the Quinns. You can explain to me why they claim Ray Quinn gave you money for Seth."

"The bastards are liars."

"I've met them," she said calmly. "And their wives. I've seen Seth. It's very difficult for me to equate what you told me with what I've seen."

"You can't put everything all neat and tidy into reports. Christ, you're just like the old man." She started to get up, snarled at the jerk of the cuff on her wrist. "The two eminent Dr. Griffins."

"This has nothing to do with my father," Sybill said quietly. "And everything, I suspect, to do with yours."

"Fuck this." Gloria twisted her lips into a vicious smile. "And fuck you. The perfect daughter, the perfect student, the perfect goddamn robot. Just pay the fucking bail. I got money put by. You'll get it back. I'll get my kid back without your help, sister dear. My kid. You want to take the word of a bunch of strangers over your own flesh and blood, you go right ahead. You always hated me anyway."

"I don't hate you, Gloria. I never have." But she could, she realized, as the ache began in her head and heart. She was afraid she very easily could. "And I'm not taking anyone's word over yours. I'm just trying to understand."

Deliberately Gloria turned her face away so Sybill wouldn't see her smile of satisfaction. She'd found the right button to push after all, she decided. "I need to get out of here. I need to get cleaned up." She made certain her voice broke. "I can't talk about this anymore. I'm so tired."

"I'll go deal with the paperwork. I'm sure it won't take long."

As she rose, Gloria grabbed her hand again, pressed it to her cheek. "I'm sorry. I'm so sorry I said those things to you. I didn't mean them. I'm just upset and confused. I feel so alone."

"It's all right." Sybill pulled her hand free and walked to the door on legs that felt as brittle as glass.

Outside, she downed two aspirin and chased them with antacids as she waited for the bail to be processed. Physically, she thought, Gloria had changed. The once astonishingly pretty girl had hardened, toughened like dried leather. But emotionally, Sybill feared, she was exactly the same unhappy, manipulative, and disturbed child that had taken dark joy in disrupting their home.

She would insist that Gloria agree to therapy, she decided. And if drug abuse was part of the problem, she would see to it that Gloria went into rehab. Certainly the woman she'd just spoken with wasn't capable of taking custody of a young boy. She would explore the possibilities of what was best for him until Gloria was back on track.

She would need to see a lawyer, of course. First thing in the morning she would find a lawyer and discuss Gloria's rights and Seth's welfare.

She would have to face the Quinns.

The thought of that had her stomach clutching again. A confrontation was inevitable, unavoidable. Nothing left her feeling more miserable and vulnerable than angry words and hateful emotions.

But she would be prepared. She would take the time to think through what had to be said, anticipate their questions and demands so she would have the proper responses. She would, above all, remain calm and objective.

When she saw Phillip walk into the building, her mind went blank. Every ounce of color drained out of her face. She stood frozen when his gaze whipped to hers, when it narrowed and hardened.

"What are you doing here, Sybill?"

"I . . ." It wasn't panic that spurted through her but embarrassment. Shame. "I had business."

"Really?" He stepped closer, while his brothers stood back in speculative silence. He saw it in her face—guilt and more than a little fear. "What kind of business would that be?" When she didn't answer, he angled his head. "What's Gloria DeLauter to you, Dr. Griffin?"

She ordered herself to keep her gaze steady, her voice even. "She's my sister."

His fury was ice cold and deadly. He balled his hands into his pockets to keep from using them in a way that was unforgivable. "That's cozy, isn't it? You bitch," he said softly, but she flinched as if he had struck her. "You used me to get to Seth."

She shook her head, but she couldn't voice the denial. It was true, wasn't it? She had used him, had used all of them. "I only wanted to see him. He's my sister's son. I had to know he was being cared for."

"Then where the hell have you been for the last ten years?"

She opened her mouth, but swallowed the excuses and explanations as Gloria was led out.

"Let's get the hell out of here. You buy me a drink, Syb." Gloria hitched a cherry-red shoulder bag over her arm, aimed an invitational smile at Phillip. "We'll talk all you want. Hi, there, handsome." She shifted her weight, put a fist on her hip, and let the smile spread to the other men. "How's it going?"

Under other circumstances the contrasts between the women might have been laughable. Sybill stood pale and quiet, her glossy brown hair brushed smoothly back, her mouth unpainted, her eyes shadowed. She exuded simple elegance in a tailored gray blazer and slacks and a white silk blouse, while Gloria offered sharp bones and overblown curves poured into black jeans and a snug T-shirt that plunged between her breasts.

She'd taken the time to repair her makeup, and her lips were as slickly red as her handbag, her eyes darkly lined. She looked, Phillip decided, like precisely what she was: an aging whore looking for an angle.

She fished a cigarette out of a crumpled pack in her bag, then wiggled it between her fingers. "Got a light, big guy?"

"Gloria, this is Phillip Quinn." The formal introduction echoed hollowly in her ears. "His brothers, Cameron and Ethan."

"Well, well, well." Gloria's smile went sharp and ugly. "Ray Quinn's wicked trio. What the hell do you want?"

"Answers," Phillip said shortly. "Let's take this outside."

"I got nothing to say to you. You make one move I don't like, I'll start screaming." She jabbed with the unlit cigarette. "There's a houseful of cops in here. We'll see how you like spending some time in a cage."

"Gloria." Sybill put a restraining hand on her arm. "The only way to straighten this out is to discuss it rationally."

"They don't look like they want a rational discussion to me. They want to hurt me." She shifted tacks skillfully, throwing her arms around Sybill, clinging to her. "I'm afraid of them. Sybill, please help me."

"I'm trying to. Gloria, no one's going to hurt you. We'll find a place where we can all sit down and talk this through. I'll be right there with you."

"I'm going to be sick." She yanked back, wrapped her arms around her stomach, and dashed into the bathroom.

"Quite a performance," Phillip decided.

"She's upset." Sybill linked her hands together, twisted her fingers. "She's not in any shape to deal with this tonight."

He shifted his gaze back to Sybill's, and it was ripe with derision. "Do you want me to believe you bought that? Either you're incredibly gullible, or you think I am."

"She spent most of the afternoon in jail," Sybill snapped back. "Anyone would be upset. Can't we discuss all of this tomorrow? It's waited this long, surely it can wait one more day."

"We're here now," Cam put in. "We'll deal with it now. Are you going to go in there and bring her out, or am I?"

"Is that how you plan to resolve this? By bullying her. And me?"

"You don't want to get me started on how I plan to resolve this," Cam began, and shrugged off Ethan's calming hand. "After what she put Seth through, there's nothing we can do to her that she hasn't earned."

Sybill glanced uncomfortably behind her at the uniformed officer manning the desk. "I don't think any of us want to cause a scene in a police station."

"Fine." Phillip took her arm. "Let's just step outside and cause one."

She held her ground, partly out of fear, partly common sense. "We'll meet tomorrow, at whatever time is convenient for you. I'll bring her to my hotel."

"You keep her out of St. Chris."

Sybill winced when Phillip's fingers tightened on her arm. "All right. Where do you suggest?"

"I'll tell you what I suggest," Cam began, but Phillip held up a hand.

"Princess Anne. You bring her into Anna's office at Social Services. Nine o'clock. That keeps everything official, doesn't it? Everything aboveboard."

"Yes." Relief trickled through her. "I can agree to that. I'll bring her. You have my word."

"I wouldn't give you two cents for your word, Sybill." Phillip leaned in slightly. "But if you don't bring her, we'll find her. Meanwhile, if either of you tries to get within a mile of Seth, you'll both be spending time in a cell." He dropped her arm and stepped back.

"We'll be there at nine," she said, resisting the urge to rub her aching arm. Then she turned and went into the bathroom to get her sister.

"Why the hell did you agree to that?" Cam demanded as he stalked outside behind Phillip. "We've got her, here and now."

"We'll get more out of her tomorrow."

"Bullshit."

"Phillip's right." As much as he detested it, Ethan accepted the change of plans. "We keep it in official surroundings. We keep our heads. It's better for Seth."

"Why? So his bitch of a mother and his lying auntie have more time to put their heads together? Christ, when I think Sybill was alone with Seth for a good hour today, I want to—"

"It's done," Phillip snapped. "He's fine. We're fine." With fury bubbling through his blood, he slammed into the Jeep. "And there are five of us. They won't get their hands on Seth."

"He didn't recognize her," Ethan pointed out. "That's funny, isn't it? He didn't know who Sybill was."

"Neither did I," Phillip murmured and shoved the Jeep into gear. "But I do now."

SYBILL'S PRIORITY WAS TO GET Gloria a hot meal, keep her calm, and question her carefully. The little Italian restaurant was only a few blocks from the police station, and after a hurried glance, Sybill decided it would fill the bill.

"My nerves are shot to hell." Gloria puffed greedily on a cigarette while Sybill maneuvered into a parking spot. "The nerve of those bastards, coming after me like that. You know what they'd have done if I'd been alone, don't you?"

Sybill only sighed and stepped out of the car. "You need to eat."

"Yeah, sure." Gloria sniffed at the decor the minute they stepped inside. It was bright and cheerful, with colorful Italian pottery, thick candles, striped tablecloths, and decorative bottles of herbed vinegars. "I'd rather have a steak than Wop food."

"Please." Forcing back irritation, she took Gloria's arm and requested a table for two.

"Smoking section," Gloria added, already pulling out another cigarette as they were led to the noisier bar area. "Gin and tonic, a double."

Sybill rubbed her temples. "Just mineral water. Thank you."

"Loosen up," Gloria suggested when the hostess left them alone. "You look like you could use a drink."

"I'm driving. I don't want one anyway." She shifted away from the smoke Gloria blew toward her face. "We have to talk, seriously."

"Let me get some lubrication, will you?" Gloria smoked and

scanned the men at the bar, toying with which one she'd pick up if she didn't have her deadly dull sister along.

Christ, Sybill was a bore. Always had been, she mused, drumming her fingers on the table and wanting her goddamn drink. But she was useful, and always had been. If you played her right, laid on plenty of tears, she came through.

She needed a hammer with the Quinns, and Sybill was the perfect choice. Upstanding, fucking respectable Dr. Griffin. "Gloria, you haven't even asked about Seth?"

"What about him?"

"I've seen him several times, spoken with him. I've seen where he's living, where he goes to school. I met some of his friends."

Gloria clicked into the tone of her sister's voice, adjusted her attitude. "How is he?" She worked up a shaky smile. "Did he ask about me?"

"He's fine. Really wonderful, actually. He's grown so much since I saw him."

Ate like a horse, Gloria remembered, and was always growing out of his clothes and shoes. Like she was made of fucking money or something.

"He didn't know who I was."

"What do you mean?" Gloria snatched up her drink the minute it was set on the table. "You didn't tell him?"

"No, I didn't." Sybill glanced up at the waitress. "We need a few more minutes before ordering."

"So you were poking around incognito." Gloria let out a long, hoarse laugh. "You surprise me, Syb."

"I thought it best that I observe the situation before changing the dynamics."

Gloria snorted. "Now that sounds just like you. Man, you don't change. 'Observe the situation before changing the dynamics,'" she repeated in her imitation of a snooty voice. "Christ. The situation is those sons of bitches have my kid. They threatened me, and God knows what they're doing to him. I want some dough to work on getting him back."

"I sent you money for the lawyer," Sybill reminded her.

Gloria clinked ice against her teeth as she drank. And the five thousand had come in handy, she thought now. How the hell could she have known how fast the money she'd bled out of Ray would slip away? She had expenses, didn't she? She'd wanted to have some fun for a change. Should have demanded twice as much from him, she decided.

Well, she'd get it out of those bastards he'd raised.

"You got the money I wired for your lawyer, didn't you, Gloria?"

Gloria took another deep drink. "Yeah, well, lawyers suck you dry, don't they? Hey!" She called out, signaling to the waitress and pointing at her empty glass. "Hit me again, will you?"

"If you drink like that and you don't eat, you're going to be sick again."

Like hell, Gloria sneered as she snatched up her menu. She didn't intend to stick her finger down her throat again. Once was more than enough. "Hey, they got steak Florentine. I can handle that. Remember when the old man took us off to Italy that summer? All those hot-looking dudes on motorbikes. Holy God, I had a hell of a time with that guy, what was his name. Carlo or Leo or whatever. I snuck him into the bedroom. You were too shy to stay and watch, so you slept in the parlor while we did the deed half the night."

She snatched up her fresh glass, lifted it in toast. "God bless the Italians."

"I'll have the linguini with pesto and the insalada mista."

"Give me the steak, bloody." Gloria held out the menu without looking at the waitress. "Skip the rabbit food. Been a while, hasn't it, Syb? What, four, five years?"

"Six," Sybill corrected. "It's been just over six since I came home to find you and Seth gone, along with a number of my personal possessions."

"Yeah, sorry about that. I was messed up. It's tough raising a kid on your own. Money's always tight."

"You never told me very much about his father."

"What's to tell? Old news." She shrugged it off and rattled the ice in her glass.

"All right, then, let's deal with current events. I need to know everything that happened. I need to understand it in order to help you and to know how to handle our meeting with the Quinns tomorrow."

The gin and tonic thudded onto the table. "What meeting?"

"We're going in to Social Services tomorrow morning to air out the problems, discuss the situation, and try to reach a solution."

"The hell I am. The only thing they want is to fuck me over."

"Keep your voice down," Sybill ordered sharply. "And listen to me. If you want to straighten yourself out, if you want your son back, this has to be done calmly and legally. Gloria, you need help, and I'm willing to help you. From what I can see, you're not in any shape to take Seth back right now."

"Whose side are you on?"

"His." It came out of her mouth before she realized that it was the absolute truth. "I'm on his side, and I hope that puts me on yours. We need to resolve what happened today."

"I told you I was set up."

"Fine. It still needs to be resolved. The courts aren't going to be very sympathetic to a woman who's facing charges of possession."

"Great, why don't you get on the witness stand and tell them how worthless I am? That's what you think anyway. That's what all of you always thought."

"Please, stop it." Lowering her voice to a murmur, Sybill leaned over the table. "I'm doing everything I know how to do. If you want to prove to me you want to make this work, you have to cooperate. You have to give something back, Gloria."

"Nothing's ever been free with you."

"We're not talking about me. I'll pay your legal fees, I'll talk to Social Services, I'll work to make the Quinns understand your needs and your rights. I want you to agree to rehab."

"For what?"

"You drink too much."

She sneered, deliberately gulping down more gin. "I've had a rough day."

"You had drugs in your possession."

"I said they weren't fucking mine."

"You've said that before," Sybill said, coolly now. "You get counseling, you get therapy, you get rehab. I'll arrange it, I'll foot the bill. I'll help you find a job, a place to stay."

"As long as it's your way." Gloria tossed back the rest of her drink. "Therapy. You and the old man used that to solve everything."

"Those are the conditions."

"So you're running the show. Jesus, order me another drink. I've gotta piss." She swung her purse over her shoulder and strode past the bar.

Sybill sat back and closed her eyes. She wasn't going to order Gloria another drink, not when her sister's words were already beginning to slur. That would be another bitter little battle, she imagined.

The aspirin she'd taken had failed miserably. Pain was drumming at both temples in a sick and consistent rhythm. Across her forehead was a squeezing band of iron. She wanted nothing quite so much as to stretch out on a soft bed in a dark room and sink into oblivion.

He despised her now. It made her ache with regret and shame to remember the contempt she'd seen in Phillip's eyes. Maybe she deserved it. At that moment she simply couldn't think clearly enough to be sure. But she was sorry for it.

More than that, she was furious with herself for letting him and his opinion of her come to matter so much in such a short time. She'd known him for only a matter of days and had never, never intended to allow his emotions or hers to become entangled.

A casual physical attraction, a few mutually enjoyable hours in each other's company. That was all it was supposed to be. How had it become more?

But she knew when he'd held her, when he'd sent her blood swimming with those long, intimate kisses, she'd wanted more. Now she, who had never considered herself particularly sexy or overly emotional, was a frustrated, pitiful wreck because one man had jiggled a lock he was no longer interested in opening.

There was nothing to be done about it, she reminded herself. Certainly, considering the circumstances, she and Phillip Quinn had never been meant to develop a personal relationship of any kind. If they managed to have one now, it would be because of the child. They would both be adult, coldly polite, and—in the end, she hoped—reasonable.

For Seth's sake.

She opened her eyes as the waitress served her salad and hated the pity she saw on a stranger's face.

"Can I get you anything else? More water?"

"No. I'm fine, thank you. You could take that," she added, indicating Gloria's empty glass.

Her stomach rebelled at the thought of food, but she ordered herself to pick up her fork. For five minutes she toyed with the salad, poking at it while her gaze drifted regularly toward the rear of the restaurant.

She must be ill again, Sybill thought wearily. Now she would have to go back, hold Gloria's head, listen to her whining, and mop up the mess. One more pattern.

Battling both resentment and the shame that trickled from it, she rose and walked back to the ladies' room.

"Gloria, are you all right?" There was no one at the sinks and no answer from any of the stalls. Resigned, Sybill began to nudge doors open. "Gloria?"

In the last stall she saw her own wallet lying open on the closed lid of the toilet. Stunned, she snatched it up, flipped through it. Her various identifications were there, and her credit cards.

But all her cash was gone, along with her sister.

TEN

With her mind jumbled with pain, her hands unsteady, and her system begging to shut down for the night, Sybill keyed open her hotel door. If she could just get to her migraine medication, to a dark room, to oblivion, she would find a way to deal with tomorrow.

She would find a way to face the Quinns, alone, with the shameful sting of failure.

They would believe she'd helped Gloria run away. How could she blame them? She was already a liar and a sneak in their eyes. In Seth's.

And, she admitted, in her own.

With slow deliberation, she turned the bolt, fixed the safety lock, then leaned back against the door until she could will her legs to move again.

When the light switched on, she stifled a yelp and covered her eyes in defense.

"You're right about the view," Phillip said from her terrace doors. "It's spectacular."

She lowered her hand, forced her mind to engage. He'd removed his jacket and tie, she noted, but otherwise he looked just as he had when he'd confronted her at the police station. Polished, urbane, and bitterly angry.

"How did you get in?"

His smile was cold, turning his eyes a hard, chilly gold. The color of an icy winter sun. "You disappoint me, Sybill. I'd have thought your research on your subject would have included the fact that one of my formative skills was breaking and entering."

She stayed where she was, supported by the door. "You were a thief?"

"Among other things. But enough about me." He stepped forward to settle on the arm of the sofa, like a casual friend making himself comfortable for a chatty visit. "You fascinate me. Your notes are incredibly revealing, even to a layman."

"You read my notes?" Her gaze swung toward the desk and her laptop. She couldn't quite find outrage through the prickly blanket of pain enveloping her head, but she knew it must be there. "You had no right to come in here, uninvited. To break into my computer and read my work."

So calm, Phillip thought, and rose to help himself to a beer from her mini bar. What kind of woman was she? "As far as I'm concerned, Sybill, all bets are off. You lied to me, you used me. You had it all worked out, didn't you? When you waltzed into the boatyard last week, your agenda was set."

He couldn't stay calm. The longer she stood, staring at him with no expression on her face, the higher his temper spiked. "Infiltrate the enemy camp." He slammed the beer onto the table. The crack of glass on wood split through her head like an axe. "Observe and report, pass information to your sister. And if being with me helped you slide more smoothly behind the lines, you were willing to make the sacrifice. Would you have slept with me?"

"No." She pressed a hand to her head and nearly gave in to the need to slip to the floor and curl into a ball. "I never meant for things . . ."

"I think you're lying." He crossed to her, taking her arms and drawing her up to her toes. "I think you'd have done anything. Just one more object lesson, right? And with the added benefit of helping your bitch of a sister bleed us for more money. Seth doesn't mean any more to you than he does to her. Just a means to an end for both of you."

"No, that's not—I can't think." The pain was excruciating. If he hadn't been holding her up, she would have gone to her knees and begged. "I—we'll discuss it tomorrow. I'm not well."

"You and Gloria have that in common too. I'm not falling for it, Sybill."

Her breath began to hitch, her vision to blur. "I'm sorry. I can't stand it. I have to sit down. Please, I have to sit down."

He focused in, past his fury. Her cheeks were dead pale, her eyes glassy, her breath coming fast and uneven. If she was faking illness, he decided, Hollywood had missed a major star.

Muttering an oath, he pulled her to the sofa. She all but melted onto the cushions.

Too ill to be embarrassed, she closed her eyes. "My briefcase. My pills are in my briefcase."

He picked up the soft black leather case beside the desk, riffled through it and found the prescription bottle. "Imitrex?" He looked over at her. She had her head back, her eyes closed, and her hands fisted in her lap as if she could center the pain there and squeeze it to death. "Major migraine drugs."

"Yes. I get them now and again." She had to focus, she ordered herself, had to relax. But nothing she did eased her past the vicious pain. "I should have had them with me. If I'd had them with me it wouldn't have gone this far."

"Here." He handed her a pill and water he'd taken from the mini bar.

"Thank you." She nearly bobbled the water in her rush. "It takes a while, but it's better than the injection." She closed her eyes again and prayed he would just leave her alone.

"Have you eaten?"

"What? No. I'll be all right."

She looked fragile, terrifyingly so. Part of him thought she deserved to hurt, was tempted to leave her with her misery. But he picked up the phone and asked for room service.

"I don't want anything."

"Just be quiet." He ordered up soup and tea, then began to prowl the room.

How could he have misjudged her so completely? Pegging people quickly and accurately was one of his most finely honed skills. He'd seen an intelligent, interesting woman. A classy one, with humor and taste. But beneath the glossy surface, she was a liar, a cheat, and an opportunist.

He nearly laughed. He'd just described the boy he'd worked half his life to bury.

"In your notes you say you haven't seen Seth since he was about four. Why did you come here now?"

"I thought I could help."

"Who?"

The hope that the pain would begin to recede gave her the strength to open her eyes. "I don't know. I thought I could help him, and Gloria."

"You help one, you hurt the other. I read your notes, Sybill. Are you going to try to tell me you care about him? 'The subject appears healthy.' He's not a fucking subject, he's a child."

"It's necessary to be objective."

"It's necessary to be human."

It was a dart, sharp enough to strike her heart and make it ache as well. "I'm not very good with emotions. Reactions and behavioral patterns are more my forte than feelings. I'd hoped to be able to keep a certain distance from the situation, to analyze it, to determine what was best for all involved. I haven't been doing a good job of it."

"Why didn't you do anything before?" he demanded. "Why didn't you do anything to analyze the situation when Seth was with your sister?"

"I didn't know where they were." Then she let out a breath and shook her head. It was no time for excuses, and the man staring at her with those cold eyes wouldn't accept them in any case. "I never seriously tried to find out. I sent her money now and again if she contacted me and asked for it. My connection with Gloria was usually unproductive and unpleasant."

"For Christ's sake, Sybill, we're talking about a little boy here, not your views on sibling rivalry."

"I was afraid to get attached," she snapped out. "The one time I did, she took him away. He was her child, not mine. There was nothing I could do about it. I asked her to let me help, but she wouldn't. She's been raising him all alone. My parents have disinherited her. My mother won't even acknowledge that she has a grandson. I know Gloria has problems, but it can't be easy for her."

He simply stared at her. "Are you serious?"

"She's had no one to depend on," Sybill began, then closed her eyes again as a knock sounded on the door. "I'm sorry, but I don't think I can eat."

"Yes, you can."

Phillip opened the door for the room service waiter, directed him to set the tray on the table in front of the sofa. He dispatched him quickly, with cash and a generous tip.

"Try the soup," he ordered. "You need something in your system or the medication's going to end up making you nauseous. My mother was a doctor, remember."

"All right." She spooned it up slowly, telling herself it was just more medicine. "Thank you. I'm sure you're not in the mood to be kind."

"It's harder for me to kick you when you're down. Eat up, Sybill, and we'll go a round or two."

She sighed. The leading edge of the headache was dulling. She could handle it now, she thought. And him as well. "I hope you'll at least attempt to understand my point of view on this. Gloria called me a few weeks ago. She was desperate, terrified. She told me she'd lost Seth."

"Lost him?" Phillip let out a short, sarcastic laugh. "Oh, that's rich."

"I thought abduction at first, but I was able to get some of the details out of her. She explained that your family had him, had taken him from her. She was almost hysterical, so afraid she'd never get him back. She didn't have the money to pay her lawyer. She was fighting an entire family, an entire system all alone. I wired her the money for the lawyer, and I told her I'd help. That she should wait until I contacted her."

As her system began to settle again, she reached for one of the rolls in the basket beside her bowl and broke it open. "I decided to come and see the situation for myself. I know Gloria doesn't always tell the entire truth, that she can slant things to suit her position. But the fact remains that your family had Seth and she didn't."

"Thank God for that."

She stared at the bread in her hand, wondered if she could manage to put it in her mouth and chew. "I know you're providing him with a good home, but she's his mother, Phillip. She has a right to keep her own son."

He watched her face carefully, measured the tone of her voice. He didn't know whether to be furious or baffled by both. "You actually believe that, don't you?"

Color was seeping back into her cheeks. Her eyes had cleared and now met his steadily. "What do you mean?"

"You believe that my family took Seth, that we took advantage of some poor single mother down on her luck and snatched the kid, that she wants him back. That she even has a lawyer working on custody."

"You do have him," Sybill pointed out.

"That's right. And he's exactly where he belongs and is going to stay. Let me give you some facts. She blackmailed my father, and she sold Seth to him."

"I know you believe that, but—"

"I said *facts*, Sybill. Less than a year ago, Seth was living in a set of filthy rooms on the Block in Baltimore, and your sister was on the stroll."

"On the stroll?"

"God, where do you come from? She was hooking. This isn't a whore with a heart of gold here, this isn't a desperate, down-on-her-luck unwed mother doing anything she has to to survive and keep her child fed. She was keeping her habit fed."

She only shook her head, slowly, side to side, even as part of her mind accepted everything he said. "You can't know all this."

"Yes, I can know it. Because I live with Seth. I've talked with him, I've listened to him."

Her hands went icy. She lifted the pot of tea to warm them, poured some slowly into a cup. "He's just a boy. He could have misunderstood."

"Sure. I bet that's it. He just misunderstood when she brought a john up to the place, when she got so stoned she sprawled on the floor and he wondered if she was dead. He just misunderstood when she beat the hell out of him when she was feeling testy."

"She hit him." The cup rattled into the saucer. "She hit him?"

"She beat him. No controversial yet civilized spanking, Dr. Griffin. Fists, belts, the back of the hand. Have you ever had a fist in the face?" He held his up to hers. "Figure it out. Proportionately, this would be about right, comparing a grown woman's fist to, say, a five-, six-year-old boy. Put liquor and drugs into that fist and it comes faster and harder. I've been there."

He angled his fist away, studied it. "My mother preferred smack—to the uninitiated that's heroin. If she missed her fix, you learned to stay far out of her way. I know just what it is to have a vicious, fucked-up female take her fists to me." His gaze whipped back to Sybill's. "Your sister won't ever have the chance to use them on Seth again."

"I—she needs to go into therapy. I never . . . He was fine when I saw him. If I'd known she was abusing him—"

"I haven't finished. He's a good-looking kid, isn't he? Some of Gloria's clients thought so."

The color that had come back to her cheeks fell away. "No." Shaking her head, she pushed away from him and staggered to her feet. "No, I don't believe that. That's hideous. That's impossible."

"She didn't do anything to stop it." He ignored the pale cheeks and fragility now and pushed. Hard. "She didn't do a goddamn thing to protect him. Seth was on his own there. He fought them off or hid.

Sooner or later, there would have been one he couldn't fight off or hide from."

"That's not possible. She couldn't."

"She could—especially if it earned her a few extra bucks. It took months with us before he could stand to be touched in even the most casual way. He has nightmares still. And if you say his mother's name, it makes you sick to see the fear that comes into his eyes. That's your situation, Dr. Griffin."

"God. How can you expect me to accept all that? To believe she's capable of that?" She pressed a hand to her heart. "I grew up with her. I've known you less than a week, and you expect me to accept this horror story, this vileness as fact?"

"I think you believe it," he said after a moment. "I think, under it all, you're smart enough, and let's say observant enough to know the truth."

She was terrified. "If it is the truth, why didn't the authorities do anything? Why wasn't he helped?"

"Sybill, have you lived on that smooth plateau so long that you really don't know what life's like on the street? How many Seths there are out there? The system works some of the time, for the few and the lucky. It didn't work for me. It didn't work for Seth. Ray and Stella Quinn worked for me. And just under a year ago, my father paid your sister the first installment on a ten-year-old boy. He brought Seth home, he gave him a life, a decent one."

"She said—she said he took Seth."

"Yeah, he took him. Ten thousand the first time, a couple of other payments of about the same. Then last March she wrote him a letter demanding a lump-sum payment. A hundred fifty thousand, cash, and she'd walk away."

"A hundred and—" Appalled, she broke off, struggled to concentrate on verifiable facts. "She wrote a letter?"

"I've read it. It was in the car with my father when he was killed. He was on his way back from Baltimore. He'd cleaned out most of his bank accounts. I'd have to guess she's gone through a big chunk of it by now. She wrote us, demanding more money, just a few months ago."

She turned away, walked quickly to the terrace doors, and flung them open. The need for air was urgent, and she gulped it in like water. "I'm supposed to accept that Gloria has done all of this, and her primary motive is money?"

"You sent her money for her lawyer. What's his name? Why hasn't our lawyer been contacted by him?"

She squeezed her eyes shut. It wouldn't help to feel betrayed, she reminded herself. "She evaded the question when I asked her. Obviously, she doesn't have a lawyer, and it's doubtful she ever intended to consult one."

"Well, you're slow"—the sarcasm rang clearly—"but you do catch on."

"I wanted to believe her. We were never close as children, and that has to be as much my fault as hers. I'd hoped I could help her, and Seth. I thought this was the way."

"So, she played you."

"I felt responsible. My mother is so unbending on this. She's angry that I came here. She has refused to acknowledge Gloria since she ran off at eighteen. Gloria claimed to have been molested by the counselor at our school. She was always claiming to have been molested. They had a terrible row, my mother and she, and Gloria was gone the next day. She'd taken some of my mother's jewelry, my father's coin collection, some cash. I didn't hear from her for nearly five years. Those five years were a relief."

"She hated me," Sybill said quietly and continued to stare out at the lights on the water. "Always, as long as I can remember. It didn't matter what I did, whether I fought with her or stepped back and let her have her way, she detested me. It was easier for me to keep my distance. I didn't hate her, I simply felt nothing. And when I brush everything else aside right now, it's exactly the same. I can't feel anything for her. It must be a flaw," she murmured. "Maybe it's genetic."

With a weak smile, she turned around again. "It might make an interesting study one day."

"You never had a clue, did you, of what she was doing?"

"No. So much for my renowned observational skills. I'm sorry, Phillip. I'm so terribly sorry for what I've done, and haven't done. I promise you I didn't come here to harm Seth. And I give you my word I'll do whatever I can to help. If I can go into Social Services in the morning, speak with Anna, your family. If you'll allow it, I'd like to see Seth, try to explain."

"We won't be taking him to Anna's office. We're not letting Gloria near him."

"She won't be there."

His eyes flickered. "I beg your pardon?"

"I don't know where she is." Defeated, she spread her hands. "I promised I'd bring her. I meant to."

"You just let her walk? Goddamn it."

"I didn't—not intentionally." She sank down onto the sofa again. "I took her to a restaurant. I wanted to get her a meal, talk to her. She was agitated and drinking too much. I was annoyed with her. I told her we were going to straighten everything out, that we were going to have a meeting in the morning. I made ultimatums. I should have known better. She didn't like it, but I didn't see what she could do about it."

"What sort of ultimatums?"

"That she would get counseling, go into rehab. That she would get help, get herself straightened out before she tried to gain custody of Seth. She went to the ladies' room, and when she didn't come back out, I went in looking for her."

She lifted her hands, let them fall uselessly. "I found my wallet. She must have taken it out of my purse. She left me my credit cards," she added with a wry smile. "She'd know I would cancel them straight off. She only took the cash. It's not the first time she's stolen from me, but it always surprises me." She sighed, shrugged it off. "I drove around for nearly two hours, hoping I'd find her. But I didn't, and I don't know where she is. I don't know what she intends to do."

"She messed you over pretty good, didn't she?"

"I'm an adult. I can take care of myself, and I'm responsible for myself. But Seth . . . if even a part of what you've told me is true . . . he'll hate me. I understand that and I'll have to accept it. I'd like the chance to talk to him."

"That'll be up to him."

"Fair enough. I need to see the files, the paperwork." She linked her fingers together. "I realize you can require me to get a court order, but I'd like to avoid that. I'd process this better if I had it all in black and white."

"It's not as simple as black and white when you're dealing with people's lives and feelings."

"Maybe not. But I need facts, documentation, reports. Once I have them, if I'm persuaded that Seth's best interest is to remain with your family, through legal guardianship or adoption, I'll do whatever I can to help that happen."

She had to push now, she told herself. She had to push to make him give her another chance. Just one more chance. "I'm a psychologist, and I'm the birth mother's sister. I'd think my opinion would bear weight in court."

He studied her objectively. Details, he thought. He was the man who handled the details, after all. Those she was adding would only help settle everything the way he wanted it settled. "I imagine it would, and I'll discuss it with my family. But I don't think you get it, Sybill. She isn't going to fight for Seth. She's never intended to fight for him. She's just trying to use him to get more money. She's not going to get that, either, not another dime."

"So I'm superfluous."

"Maybe. I haven't decided." He rose, jingling the change in his pockets as he paced. "How are you feeling?"

"Better. Fine. Thank you. I'm sorry to have fallen apart like that, but the migraine was a full-blown one."

"You get them often?"

"A few times a year. I'm usually able to get to the medication at onset, so they're not too bad. When I left this evening I was distracted."

"Yeah, bailing your sister out of jail would be a distraction." He glanced back at her with mild curiosity. "How much did it take to spring her?"

"Bail was set at five thousand."

"Well, I'd say you can kiss that good-bye."

"Most likely. The money isn't important."

"What is?" He stopped, turned toward her. She looked exhausted and disconcertingly fragile still. An unfair advantage was still an advantage, he decided, and pressed. "What is important to you, Sybill?"

"Finishing what I've started. You may not need my help, but I don't intend to walk away until I've done what I can."

"If Seth doesn't want to see you or speak to you, he won't. That's bottom line. He's had enough."

She straightened her shoulders before they could slump. "Regardless of whether he agrees to see or speak with me, I intend to stay until the legalities are settled. You can't force me to leave, Phillip. You can make it difficult for me, uncomfortable, but you can't make me leave until I'm satisfied."

"Yeah, I can make it difficult for you. I can make it damn near impossible for you. And I'm considering just that." He leaned over, ignoring her instinctive jerk, and caught her chin firmly in his hand. "Would you have slept with me?"

"Under the circumstances, I believe that's moot."

"Not to me it isn't. Answer the question."

She kept her eyes level with his. That was a matter of pride, though she felt she had little of that or her dignity left intact. "Yes." When his eyes flared, she jerked her chin away. "But not because of Seth or Gloria. I would have slept with you because I wanted you. Because I was attracted to you and when I was around you for any length of time my priorities became blurred."

"Your priorities became blurred." He rocked back on his heels, dipped his hands into his pockets. "Jesus, you're a case. Why do I find that snotty attitude intriguing?"

"I don't have a snotty attitude. You asked a question, I answered it honestly. And, you'll note, in the past tense."

"Now I've got something else to consider. If I want to change that to present tense. Don't say it's moot, Sybill," he warned when she opened her mouth. "I'm bound to take that as a dare. If we end up in bed tonight, neither one of us is going to like ourselves in the morning."

"I don't like you very much right now."

"We're on the same curve there, honey." He jingled his change again, then shrugged. "We'll keep the meeting at Anna's office in the morning. As far as I'm concerned, you can see all the paperwork, including your sister's blackmail letters. As far as Seth goes, I don't make any promises. If you try to go around me and my family to get to him, you'll regret it."

"Don't threaten me."

"I'm not. I'm giving you facts. It's your family who likes threats." His smile was sharp, dangerous, and without an ounce of humor. "The Quinns make promises, and they keep them."

"I'm not Gloria."

"No, but we still have to see just who you are. Nine o'clock," he added. "Oh, and Dr. Griffin, you may want to look over your own notes again. When you do it might be interesting, psychologically speaking, to ask yourself why you find it so much more rewarding to observe than to participate. Get some sleep," he suggested as he walked to the door. "You're going to want to be sharp tomorrow."

"Phillip." Going with the impulse of temper, she rose and waited for him to turn around, with the door open at his back. "Isn't it fortunate that circumstances changed before we made the mistake of sex?"

He angled his head, both impressed and amused that she'd dared such a dangerous parting shot. "Darling, I'm counting my blessings."

He closed the door with a quiet snap.

ELEVEN

SETH NEEDED TO BE TOLD. There was only one way to do it, and that was straight out, as a family. Ethan and Grace would bring him home as soon as Aubrey was settled with the baby-sitter.

"We shouldn't have let her out of our sight." Cam paced the kitchen, hands jammed in his pockets, gray eyes hard as flint. "God knows where she took off to, and instead of having answers, instead of straightening her ass out, we've got nothing."

"That's not entirely true." Anna brewed coffee. It wouldn't help to settle nerves, she thought, but everyone would want it. "I'll have a police report for the file. You couldn't very well drag her out of the station house, Cameron, and force her to talk to you."

"It would've been a hell of a lot more satisfying than watching her walk."

"Momentarily, perhaps. But it remains in Seth's best interest, and ours, to handle everything in an official, by-the-book manner."

"How do you think Seth's going to feel about that?" He whirled, and the leading edge of his temper whipped out at his wife and his brother. "Do you think he's going to feel it's in his best interest that we had Gloria and did nothing?"

"You did do something." Because she understood his frustration, Anna kept her voice calm. "You agreed to meet her in my office. If she doesn't keep the appointment, it's another strike against her."

"She won't be anywhere near Social Services tomorrow," Phillip began, "but Sybill will."

"And we're supposed to trust her?" Cam snapped out. "All she's done so far is lie."

"You didn't see her tonight," Phillip said evenly. "I did."

"Yeah, and we know what part of your anatomy you're looking with, bro."

"Stop it." Anna stepped quickly between them as two pairs of fists curled, two pairs of eyes flashed. "You're not going to beat each other brainless in this house." She slapped a hand on Cam's chest, then Phillip's, found them both immovable. "It's not going to help anyone if you rip pieces off each other. We need a united front. Seth needs it," she added, pushing harder when she heard the front door open. "Now, both of you sit down. Sit down!" She hissed it, the image of those ready fists swinging over her head, adding both urgency and authority to her voice.

With their gazes still heated and locked, both men dragged out chairs and sat. Anna had time for one relieved breath before Seth came in, trailed by two dogs with cheerfully swatting tails.

"Hey, what's up?" His cheerful grin vanished immediately. A lifetime of living with Gloria's wildly swinging moods had taught him to gauge atmosphere. The air in the kitchen was simmering with tension and temper.

He took a step back, then froze as Ethan came in behind him and laid a hand on his shoulder. "Coffee smells good," he said mildly, and the hand on Seth's shoulder remained, part restraint, part support.

"I'll get some cups." Grace hurried past them to the cupboard. She knew she'd be better off with her hands busy. "Seth, do you want a Coke?"

"What happened?" His lips felt stiff and his hands cold.

"It's going to take a little while to explain it all." Anna walked to him, put her hands on his cheeks. The first order of business, she determined, was to erase the fear that had come into his eyes. "But you don't have to worry."

"Did she ask for more money again? Is she coming here? Did they let her out of jail?"

"No. Come sit down. We'll explain everything." She shook her head at Cam before he could speak and locked her eyes with Phillip's as she guided Seth toward the table. He had more firsthand information, she decided. It was best that it come from him.

Where the hell was he supposed to start? Phillip dragged a hand through his hair. "Seth, do you know anything about your mother's family?"

"No. She used to tell me stuff. One day she'd say how her parents were rich, really rolling in it, but they died and some slick lawyer stole all the money. Another day she'd say how she was an orphan and she'd run away from this foster home because the father tried to rape her. Or how her mother was this movie star who gave her up for adoption so she wouldn't lose her career. She was always changing it."

His gaze shifted around the room as he spoke, trying to read faces. "Who cares?" he demanded, ignoring the soft drink Grace set in front of him. "Who the hell cares, anyway? There wasn't anybody or she'd've tapped them for money."

"There is somebody, and it seems she did tap them for money off and on." Phillip kept his voice quiet and calm, as a person would when soothing a frantic puppy. "We found out today that she has parents, and a sister."

"I don't have to go with them." Alarm rang in his head as he surged out of his chair. "I don't know them. I don't have to go with them."

"No, you don't." Phillip took Seth's arm. "But you need to know about them."

"I don't want to." His gaze flew to Cam's, pleaded. "I don't want to know. You said I could stay. You said nothing was going to change that."

It made Cam sick to see that desperation, but he pointed to the chair. "You are staying. Nothing is going to change that. Sit down. You never solve anything by running."

"Look around, Seth." Ethan's tone was soft, the voice of reason. "You've got five people here, standing with you."

He wanted to believe it. He didn't know how to explain that it was so much easier to believe in lies and threats than in promises. "What are they going to do? How did they find me?"

"Gloria called her sister a few weeks ago," Phillip began when Seth sat again. "You don't remember her sister?"

"I don't remember anybody," Seth muttered and hunched his shoulders.

"Well, it seems she spun a tale for the sister, told her that we'd stolen you from her."

"She's full of shit."

"Seth." Anna drilled him with a look that made him squirm.

"She conned the sister out of some money for a lawyer," Phillip continued. "Said she was broke and desperate, that we'd threatened her. She needed the money to get you back."

Seth wiped his mouth with the back of his hand. "She bought it? She must be an idiot."

"Maybe. Or maybe she's a soft touch. Either way, the sister didn't buy the whole package. She wanted to check things out for herself. So she came to St. Chris."

"She's here?" Seth's head whipped up. "I don't want to see her. I don't want to talk to her."

"You already have. Sybill is Gloria's sister."

Seth's dark-blue eyes widened, and the angry flush faded from his cheeks. "She can't be. She's a doctor. She writes books."

"Nonetheless, she is. When Cam and Ethan and I drove down to Hampton, we saw her."

"You saw her? You saw Gloria?"

"Yeah, we saw her. Hold on." Phillip laid a hand over Seth's rigid one. "Sybill was there, too. She was posting bail. So it all came out."

"She's a liar." Seth's voice began to hitch. "Just like Gloria. She's a damn liar."

"Let me finish. We agreed to meet them both in the morning, in Anna's office. We have to get the facts, Seth," he added when the boy snatched his hands free. "It's the only way we're going to fix this for good."

"I'm not going."

"You can decide that for yourself. We don't think Gloria's going to show. I saw Sybill just a little while ago. Gloria had given her the slip."

"She's gone." Relief and hope struggled to beat back fear. "She's gone again?"

"It looks that way. She took money out of Sybill's wallet and split." Phillip glanced over at Ethan, judged his brother's reaction to the news as angry resignation. "Sybill will be in Anna's office in the morning. I think it would be better if you went in with us, talked to her there."

"I don't have anything to say to her. I don't know her. I don't care about her. She should just go away and leave me alone."

"She can't hurt you, Seth."

"I hate her. She's probably just like Gloria, only she pretends to be different."

Phillip thought of the fatigue, the guilt, the misery he'd seen on Sybill's face. But he said, "That's for you to decide, too. But you need to see her and hear what she has to say to do that. She said she'd only seen you once. Gloria came to New York and you stayed at Sybill's place for a little while. You were about four."

"I don't remember." His face went stony with stubbornness. "We stayed in a lot of places."

"Seth, I know it doesn't seem fair." Grace reached over to give the hands he had balled into fists on the table a quick, reassuring squeeze. "But your aunt may be able to help. We'll all be there with you."

Cam saw the refusal in Seth's eyes and leaned forward. "Quinns don't walk away from a fight." He paused until Seth's gaze shifted to his. "Until they win it."

It was pride and the fear of not living up to the name they'd given him that stiffened his shoulders. "I'll go, but nothing she says is going to mean dick to me." With eyes hot and brooding, he turned to Phillip. "Did you have sex with her?"

"Seth!" Anna's voice was sharp as a slap, but Phillip only raised a hand.

Maybe his first instinct was to tell the boy it was none of his business, but he knew how to think past the quick retort and study the whole. "No, I didn't."

Seth gave a stiff shrug. "That's something, then."

"You come first." Phillip saw the surprise flicker in Seth's eyes at the statement. "I made a promise that you would, so you do. Nothing and no one changes that."

Beneath the warm thrill, Seth felt a greasy tug of shame. "Sorry," he mumbled it and stared down at his own hands.

"Fine." Phillip sipped at the coffee that had gone cold in his cup. "We'll hear what she has to say in the morning, then she'll hear what we have to say. What you have to say. We'll go from there."

SHE DIDN'T KNOW WHAT SHE WAS going to say. She felt sick inside. The dregs of a migraine hangover fuzzed her brain, and her nerves were stretched to the breaking point at the prospect of facing the Quinns. And Seth.

They had to hate her. She doubted very much they could feel more contempt for her than she felt for herself. If what Phillip had told her was true—the drugs, the beatings, the men—she had by the sin of omission left her own nephew in hell.

There was nothing they could say to her that was worse than what she had said to herself during the endless, sleepless night. But she was sick with anticipation of what was to come as she pulled into the small parking lot attached to Social Services.

It was bound to become ugly, she thought, as she tilted her rearview mirror and carefully applied lipstick. Hard words, cold looks—and she was so pitifully vulnerable to both.

She could stand against them, she told herself. She could maintain that outward calm no matter what was happening to her insides. She'd learned that defense over the years. Remain aloof and detached, and survive.

She would survive this. And if she could somehow ease Seth's mind, whatever wounds she suffered would be worth it.

She stepped out of the car, a cool and composed woman in an elegantly simple silk suit the color of mourning. Her hair was swept up in a sleek twist, her makeup was subtle and flawless.

Her stomach was raw and burning.

She stepped inside the lobby. Already the waiting area contained a scattering of people. An infant whimpered restlessly in the arms of a woman whose eyes were glazed with fatigue. A man in a flannel shirt and jeans sat with his face grim and his fisted hands dangling between his knees. Two other women sat in a corner. Mother and daughter, Sybill deduced. The younger woman had her head cradled on the other's shoulder and wept silently out of eyes blackened by fists.

Sybill turned away.

"Dr. Griffin," she told the receptionist. "I have an appointment with Anna Spinelli."

"Yes, she's expecting you. Down this hall, second door on your left."

"Thank you." Sybill closed her hand around the strap of her purse and walked briskly to Anna's office.

Her heart plummeted to her stomach when she reached the doorway. They were all there, waiting. Anna sat behind the desk, looking professional in a navy blazer, her hair pinned up. She was scanning an open file.

Grace sat with her hand swallowed by Ethan's. Cam stood at the narrow window, scowling, while Phillip sat, flipping through a magazine.

Seth sat between them, staring down at the floor, his eyes curtained by his lashes, his mouth set, his shoulders hunched.

She gathered her courage, started to speak. But Phillip's eyes flicked up and found hers. The one long look warned her he hadn't softened overnight. She ignored her trembling pulse and angled her head in acknowledgment.

"You're prompt, Dr. Griffin," he said, and instantly all eyes were on her.

She felt scalded and pinned all at once, but she took the last step over the threshold into what she fully understood was Quinn turf. "Thank you for seeing me."

"Oh, we're looking forward to it." Cam's voice was dangerously soft. His hand, Sybill noted, had gone to Seth's shoulder in a gesture that was both possessive and protective.

"Ethan, would you close the door?" Anna folded her hands on the open file. "Please sit down, Dr. Griffin."

It wouldn't be Sybill and Anna here. All the friendly female connection that came from cozy kitchens and simmering pots was gone.

Accepting that, Sybill took the vacant seat facing Anna's desk. She set her purse in her lap, clutched it with boneless fingers, and smoothly, casually, crossed her legs.

"Before we begin, I'd like to say something." She took a slow breath when Anna nodded in agreement. Sybill shifted and looked directly at Seth. He kept his eyes on the floor. "I didn't come here to hurt you, Seth, or to make you unhappy. I'm sorry that I seem to have done both. If living with the Quinns is what you want, what you need, then I want to help see that you stay with them."

Seth lifted his head now and stared at her with eyes that were stunningly adult and harsh. "I don't want your help."

"But you may need it," she murmured, then turned back to Anna. Sybill saw speculation there, and what she hoped was an open mind. "I don't know where Gloria is. I'm sorry. I gave my word I would bring her here this morning. It's been a very long time since I'd seen her, and I . . . I hadn't realized how much she'd . . . how unstable she is."

" 'Unstable.' " Cam snorted at the term. "That's a rich one."

"She contacted you," Anna began, shooting her husband one warning look.

"Yes, a few weeks ago. She was very upset, claimed that Seth had been stolen from her and that she needed money for her lawyer, who was going to fight a custody case. She was crying, nearly hysterical. She begged me to help her. I got as much information as I could. Who had Seth, and where he was living. I sent her five thousand dollars."

Sybill lifted her hands. "I realized yesterday when I spoke with her that there was no lawyer. Gloria has always been a clever actress. I'd forgotten that, or I chose to forget that."

"Were you aware that she had a drug problem?"

"No—again, not until yesterday. When I saw her, and spoke with her, it became clear that she's not capable at this time of handling the responsibility of a child."

"She doesn't want the responsibility of a child," Phillip commented.

"So you said," Sybill responded coolly. "You indicated that she wanted money. I'm aware that money is important to Gloria. I'm also aware that she's not stable. But it's difficult for me to believe, without proof, that she's done all that you claim."

"You want proof?" Cam stepped forward, fury all but visible in waves around him. "You got it, sugar. Show her the letters, Anna."

"Cam, sit down." Anna's order was firm before she turned back to Sybill. "Would you recognize your sister's handwriting?"

"I don't know. I suppose I might."

"I have a copy of the letter found in Raymond Quinn's car when he was killed, and one of the letters sent to us more recently."

She took them out of the file and passed them over the desk into Sybill's hands.

Words and phrases leaped out at her, burned into her mind.

Quinn, I'm tired of playing nickel and dime. You want the kid so bad, then it's time to pay for him. . . . A hundred and fifty grand's a pretty good bargain for a good-looking boy like Seth.

Oh, God, was all Sybill could think. Dear God.

The letter to the Quinns after Ray's death was no better.

Ray and me had an agreement.

If you're set on keeping him . . . I'm going to need some money . . .

Sybill willed her hands to remain steady.

"She took this money?"

"Professor Quinn drew out cashier's checks to Gloria DeLauter, twice for ten thousand dollars, once for five." Anna spoke clearly and without emotion. "He brought Seth DeLauter to St. Christopher's late last year. The letter you have is postmarked March tenth. The following day Professor Quinn arranged to cash out his bonds, some stock, and he drew large sums of cash out of his bank account. On March twelfth, he told Ethan he had business in Baltimore. On his return, he was killed in a single-car accident. There were just over forty dollars in his wallet. No other money was found."

"He promised I wouldn't have to go back," Seth said dully. "He was decent. He promised, and she knew he'd pay her."

"She asked for more. From you. From all of you."

"And miscalculated." Phillip leaned back, studying Sybill. Nothing showed, he noted, but her pallor. "She won't bleed us, Dr. Griffin. She can threaten all she wants, but she won't bleed us, and she won't get Seth."

"You also have a copy of the letter I wrote to Gloria DeLauter,"

Anna stated. "I informed her that Seth was under the protection of Social Services, that an investigation by this office was under way on charges of child abuse. If she comes into the county, she'll be served with a restraining order and a warrant."

"She was furious," Grace spoke up. "She called the house right after she got Anna's letter. She threatened and demanded. She said she wanted money or she'd take Seth. I told her she was wrong." Grace looked over, held Seth's gaze. "He's ours now."

She'd sold her son, was all Sybill could think. It was just as Phillip had said. All of it was just as he'd said. "You have temporary guardianship."

"It'll be permanent shortly," Phillip informed her. "We intend to see to that."

Sybill laid the papers back on Anna's desk. Inside she was cold, brutally cold, but she linked her fingers lightly on top of her purse and spoke evenly to Seth. "Did she hit you?"

"What the hell do you care?"

"Answer the question, Seth," Phillip ordered. "Tell your aunt what life was like with her sister."

"Okay, fine." He bit the words off, but his sneer was wobbly around the edges. "Sure, she knocked me around when she felt like it. If I was lucky, she was too drunk or stoned for it to hurt much. I could usually get away, anyhow." He shrugged as if it didn't matter in the least. "Sometimes she got me by surprise. Maybe she hadn't been able to turn enough tricks to score. So she'd wake me up and pound on me a while. Or she'd cry all over me."

She wanted to turn away from that image, as she'd turned away from the desperate strangers in the waiting area. Instead she kept her gaze steady on Seth's face. "Why didn't you tell anyone, find someone to help you?"

"Like who?" Was she stupid, Seth thought? "The cops? She told me what the cops would do. I'd end up in juvie and some guy would use me like some of her johns wanted to. They could do whatever they wanted once I was inside. As long as I was out, I could get away."

"She lied to you," Anna said softly while Sybill tried to find words, any words. "The police would have helped."

"She knew?" Sybill managed. "About the men who tried to . . . touch you?"

"Sure, she thought it was funny. Hell, when she's stoned, she thinks most everything is funny. It's when she's drunk that she gets mean."

Could this monster the boy spoke of so casually be her sister?

"How . . . Do you know why she decided to contact Professor Quinn?"

"No, I don't know anything about it. She got wired up one day, started talking about hitting a gold mine. She took off for a few days."

"She left you alone?" Why that should horrify her, after everything else she'd heard, Sybill couldn't say.

"Hey, I can take care of myself. When she came back, she was flying. Said I was finally going to be of some use. She had some money—real money, because she went out and scored a lot of dope without hooking. She stayed stoned and happy for days. Then Ray came. He said I could come with him. At first I thought he was like the guys she brought home. But he wasn't. I could tell. He looked sad and tired."

His voice had changed, she noted, softened. So, she thought, he grieves, too. Then she saw the ripe disgust come into his eyes.

"She came on to him," Seth said shortly, "and he got real upset. He didn't yell or anything, but he got real hard in the eyes. He made her leave. He had money with him, and he said if she wanted it, to leave. So she took it and went. He told me he had a house by the water, and a dog, and that I could live there if I wanted. And no one would mess with me."

"You went with him."

"He was old," Seth said with a shrug. "I figured I could get away from him if he tried anything. But you could trust Ray. He was decent. He said I'd never have to go back to the way things were. And I won't. No matter what, I won't go back. And I don't trust you." His eyes were adult again, his voice controlled and derisive. "Because you lied, you pretended to be decent. All you were doing was spying on us."

"You're right." She thought it the hardest thing she'd ever done, or would ever have to do, to meet those scornful eyes in a child's face and admit her own sins. "You have no reason to trust me. I didn't help you. I could have, all those years ago when she brought you to New York. I didn't want to see. It was easier not to. And when I came home one day and both of you were gone, I didn't do anything about that, either. I told myself it wasn't my concern, that you weren't my responsibility. That wasn't just wrong, it was cowardly."

He didn't want to believe her, didn't want to hear the regret and the apology in her voice. He balled his hands into fists on his knees. "It doesn't have anything to do with you now, either."

"She's my sister. I can't change that." Because it hurt to see the contempt in his eyes, she turned back to Anna. "What can I do to help? Can I make a statement to you? Talk to your lawyer? I'm a licensed psychologist, and Gloria's sister. I would assume that my opinion might carry some weight toward the guardianship."

"I'm sure it would," Anna murmured. "It won't be easy for you."

"I have no feelings for her. I'm not proud to say that, but it's the simple truth. I feel nothing toward her whatsoever, and the sense of responsibility I thought I should feel to her is over. As much as he may wish it otherwise, I'm Seth's aunt. I intend to help."

She rose and scanned the faces in the room while her stomach pitched and rolled. "I'm terribly sorry, for all of this. I realize an apology is useless. I have no excuse for what I did. Reasons, but no excuses. It's perfectly clear that Seth is where he belongs, where he's happy. If you'll give me a moment to gather my thoughts, I'll give you a statement."

She walked out, without hurry, and continued to the outside, where she could find air.

"Well, she went about it wrong, but she seems level right now." Cam got up, paced off some of his energy in the crowded office. "She sure doesn't shake easily."

"I wonder," Anna murmured. She, too, was a trained observer, and instinct told her there was a great deal more going on under that placid surface than any of them might guess. "Having her on our side will, without question, help. It might be best if you left the two of us alone so I can talk with her. Phillip, you'll want to call the lawyer, explain the situation, and see if he wants to depose her."

"Yeah, I'll take care of it." He frowned thoughtfully at the fingers drumming on his knee. "She had a picture of Seth in her Filofax."

"What?" Anna blinked at him.

"I went through her things before she got back to the hotel last night." He smiled a little, then shrugged as his sister-in-law closed her eyes. "Seemed like the thing to do at the time. She's got this snapshot of Seth when he was little, tucked in her Filofax."

"So what?" Seth demanded.

"So, it was the only picture I found anywhere. It's interesting." He lifted his hands, dropped them again. "On another path, it could be that Sybill knows something about Gloria's connection to Dad. Since we can't question Gloria, we ought to ask her."

"Seems to me," Ethan said slowly, "that whatever she knows would've come from Gloria. Be tough to believe it. I think she'd tell us what she knows," he continued, "but what she knows might not be fact."

"We don't know fact or fiction," Phillip pointed out, "until we ask her."

"Ask me what?" Steadier, determined now to finish it out, Sybill stepped back into the room and closed the door quietly at her back.

"The reason Gloria hit on our father." Phillip rose so their eyes were level. "The reason she knew he would pay to protect Seth."

"Seth said he was a decent man." Sybill's gaze roamed the faces of the men. "I think you're proof of that."

"Decent men don't have adulterous affairs with women half their age, then walk away from a child conceived from that affair." Bitterness coated Phillip's voice as he took another step toward Sybill. "And there's no way you're going to convince us that Ray slept with your sister behind our mother's back, then walked away from his son."

"What?" Without realizing it, Sybill shot a hand out to grip his arm, as much in shock as to keep her balance as she reeled from it. "Of course he didn't. You told me you didn't believe that Gloria and your father . . ."

"Others do."

"But that's—where did you get the idea that Seth was his son, his son by Gloria?"

"It's easy enough to hear it in town if you keep your ears open." Phillip narrowed his eyes at her face. "It's something your sister planted. She claimed he molested her, then she blackmails him, sells him her son." He looked back at Seth, into Ray Quinn's eyes. "I say it's a lie."

"Of course it's a lie. It's a horrible lie."

Desperate to do at least this one thing right and well, she went to Seth, crouched in front of him. She wanted badly to take his hand, but resisted her impulse when he leaned away from her.

"Ray Quinn wasn't your father, Seth. He was your grandfather. Gloria's his daughter."

His lips trembled, and those deep-blue eyes shimmered. "My grandfather?"

"Yes. I'm sorry she didn't tell you, so sorry you didn't know before he . . ." She shook her head, straightened. "I didn't realize there was confusion about this. I should have. I only learned about it myself a few weeks ago."

She took her seat again, prepared herself. "I'll tell you everything I know."

TWELVE

It was easier now, almost like a lecture. Sybill was used to giving lectures on social topics. All she had to do was divorce herself from the subject and relay information in a clear and cohesive manner.

"Professor Quinn had a relationship with Barbara Harrow," she began. She put her back to the window so that she could face all of them as she spoke. "They met at American University in Washington. I don't have a great many of the details, but what I do know indicates that he was teaching there and she was a graduate student. Barbara Harrow is my mother. Gloria's mother."

"My father," Phillip said. "Your mother."

"Yes. Nearly thirty-five years ago. I assume they were attracted to each other, physically at least. My mother . . ." She cleared her throat. "My mother indicated that she believed he had a great deal of potential, that he would rise up the ranks in academia quickly. Status is an essential requirement to my mother's contentment. However, she found herself disappointed in his . . . what she saw as his lack of ambition. He was content to teach. Apparently he wasn't particularly interested in the social obligations that are necessary for advancement. And his politics were too liberal for her tastes."

"She wanted a rich, important husband." Cueing in quickly, Phillip raised his eyebrows. "And she discovered he wasn't going to be it."

"That's essentially true," Sybill agreed in a cool, steady voice. "Thirty-five years ago, the country was experiencing unrest, its own internal war between youth and establishment. Colleges were teeming with minds that questioned not only an unpopular war, but the status quo. Professor Quinn, it would seem, had a lot of questions."

"He believed in using the brain," Cam muttered. "And in taking a stand."

"According to my mother, he took stands." Sybill managed a small smile. "Often unpopular with the administration of the university. He and my mother disagreed, strongly, on basic principles and beliefs. At the end of the term, she went home to Boston, disillusioned, angry, and, she was to discover, pregnant."

"Bullshit. Sorry," Cam said shortly when Anna hissed at him. "But it's bullshit. There's no way he would have ignored responsibility for a kid. No way in hell."

"She never told him." Sybill folded her hands as all eyes swung back to her. "She was furious. Perhaps she was frightened as well, but she was furious to find herself pregnant by a man she'd decided was unsuitable. She considered terminating the pregnancy. She'd met my father, and they had clicked."

"He was suitable," Cam concluded.

"I believe they suited each other." Her voice chilled. They were her parents, damn it. She had to be left with something. "My mother was in a difficult and frightening position. She wasn't a child. She was nearly twenty-five, but an unwanted and unplanned pregnancy is a wrenching episode for a woman of any age. In a moment of weakness, or despair, she confessed all of it to my father. And he offered her marriage. He loved her," Sybill said quietly. "He must have loved her very much. They were married quickly and quietly. She never went back to Washington. She never looked back."

"Dad never knew he had a daughter?" Ethan covered Grace's hand with his.

"No, he couldn't have. Gloria was three, nearly four when I was born. I can't say what the relationship between her and my parents was like in those early years. I know that later on, she felt excluded. She was difficult and temperamental, demanding. Certainly she was wild. Certain standards of behavior were expected, and she refused to meet them."

It sounded so cold, Sybill thought now. So unyielding. "In any case, she left home when she was still a teenager. Later, I discovered that both of my parents, and myself, sent her money, independently of each other. She would contact one of us and plead, demand, threaten, whichever worked. I wasn't aware of any of this until Gloria called me last month, about Seth."

Sybill paused a moment until she could compose her thoughts. "Before I came here, I flew to Paris to see my parents. I felt they needed to know. Seth was their grandchild, and as far as I knew, he'd been taken away from Gloria and was living with strangers. When I told my mother what had happened, and she refused to become involved, to offer any assistance, I was stunned and angry. We argued." Sybill let out a short laugh. "She was surprised enough by that, I think, to tell me what I've just told you."

"Gloria had to know," Phillip pointed out. "She had to know Ray Quinn was her father or she'd never have come here."

"Yes, she knew. A couple of years ago, she went to my mother when my parents were staying in D.C. for a few months. I can assume it was an ugly scene. From what my mother told me, Gloria demanded a large sum of money or she'd go to the press, to the police, to whoever would listen and accuse my father of sexual abuse, my mother of collusion in it. None of that is true," Sybill said wearily. "Gloria always equated sex with power, and acceptance. She routinely accused men, particularly men in positions of authority, of molesting her.

"In this instance, my mother gave her several thousand dollars and the story I've just told you. She promised Gloria that it was the last penny she would ever see from her, the last word she would ever speak to her. My mother rarely, very rarely, goes back on a promise of any kind. Gloria would have known that."

"So she hit on Ray Quinn instead," Phillip concluded.

"I don't know when she decided to find him. It may have stewed in her mind for a time. Now she would consider this the reason she was never loved, never wanted, never accepted as she felt she deserved to be. I imagine she blamed your father for that. Someone else is always to blame when Gloria has difficulties."

"So she found him." Phillip rose from his chair to pace. "And, true to form, demanded money, made accusations, threatened. Only this time she used her own son as the hammer."

"Apparently. I'm sorry. I should have realized you weren't aware of all the facts. I suppose I assumed your father had told you more of it."

"He didn't have time." Cam's voice was cold and bitter.

"He told me he was waiting for some information," Ethan remembered. "That he'd explain everything once he found out."

"He must have tried contacting your mother." Phillip pinned Sybill with a look. "He would have wanted to speak with her, to know."

"I can't tell you that. I simply don't know."

"I know," Phillip said shortly. "He would have done what he felt was right. For Seth first, because he's a child. But he would have wanted to help Gloria. To do that, he needed to talk to her mother, find out what had happened. It would have mattered to him."

"I can only tell you what I know or what's been told to me." Sybill lifted her hands, let them fall. "My family has behaved badly." It was weak, she knew. "All of us," she said to Seth. "I apologize for myself, and for them. I don't expect you to . . ." What? she wondered, and let it go. "I'll do anything I can to help."

"I want people to know." Seth's eyes swam when he lifted them to her face. "I want people to know he was my grandfather. They're saying things about him, and it's wrong. I want people to know I'm a Quinn."

Sybill could only nod. If this was all he asked of her, she would make certain she gave it. Drawing a breath, she looked at Anna. "What can I do?"

"You've made a good start already." Anna glanced at her watch. She had other cases and another appointment scheduled in ten minutes. "Are you willing to make the information you've given us official, and public?"

"Yes."

"I have an idea how to start that ball rolling."

The embarrassment factor couldn't be weighed, Sybill reminded herself. She could and would live with the whispers and the speculative looks that were bound to come her way once she followed through on Anna's suggestion.

SHE'D TYPED UP HER STATEMENT herself, spending two hours in her room choosing the right words and phrasing. The information had to be clear, the details of her mother's actions, of Gloria's, even her own.

When it was proofed and printed out, she didn't hesitate. She took the pages down to the front desk, and calmly requested that they be faxed to Anna's office.

"I'll need the originals back," she told the clerk. "And I expect a reply by return fax."

"I'll take care of this for you." The young, fresh-faced clerk smiled professionally before she slipped into the office behind the desk.

Sybill closed her eyes briefly. No turning back now, she reminded herself. She folded her hands, composed her features, and waited.

It didn't take long. And there was no mistaking from the wide eyes of the clerk that at least part of the transmission had been scanned. "Do you want to wait for the reply, Dr. Griffin?"

"Yes, thank you." Sybill held out a hand for the papers, nearly smiling as the clerk jolted, then quickly passed them across the desk.

"Are you, ah, enjoying your stay?"

Can't wait to pass on what you read, can you? Sybill thought. Typical, and totally expected human behavior. "It's been an interesting experience so far."

"Well, excuse me a moment." The clerk dashed into the back room again.

Sybill was just releasing a sigh when her shoulders tensed. She knew Phillip was behind her before she turned to face him. "I sent the fax to Anna," she said stiffly. "I'm waiting for her reply. If she finds it satisfactory, I'll have time to go to the bank before it closes and have the document notarized. I gave my word."

"I'm not here as a guard dog, Sybill. I thought you could use a little moral support."

She all but sniffed. "I'm perfectly fine."

"No, you're not." To prove it to both of them, he rested a hand on the rigid cords in her neck. "But you put on a hell of a show."

"I prefer to do this alone."

"Well, you can't always get what you want. As the song says." He glanced over with an easy smile, his hand still on Sybill's nape, as the clerk hurried out with an envelope. "Hi, there, Karen. How's it going?"

The clerk blushed clear to the hairline, her eyes darting from his face to Sybill's. "Fine. Um . . . here's your fax, Dr. Griffin."

"Thank you." Without flinching Sybill took the envelope and tucked it into her bag. "You'll bill my account for the service."

"Yes, of course."

"See you around, Karen." Smoothly, Phillip slid his hand from Sybill's neck to the small of her back to guide her across the lobby.

"She'll have told her six best friends by her next break," Sybill murmured.

"At the very least. The wonders of small towns. The Quinns will be the hot topic of discussion over a number of dinner tables tonight. By breakfast, the gossip mill will be in full swing."

"That amuses you," Sybill said tightly.

"It reassures me, Dr. Griffin. Traditions are meant to reassure. I spoke to our lawyer," he continued as they crossed the waterfront.

Gulls swooped, dogging a workboat on its way to dock. "The notarized statement will help, but he'd like to take your deposition, early next week if you can manage it."

"I'll make an appointment." In front of the bank she stopped and turned toward him. He'd changed into casual clothes, and the wind off the water ruffled his hair. His eyes were concealed behind shaded lenses, but she wasn't certain she cared to see the expression in them. "It might look less as if I'm under house arrest if I go in alone."

He merely lifted his hands, palms out, and stepped back. She was a tough nut, he decided when she strode into the bank. But he had a feeling that, once cracked, there was something soft, even delectable inside.

He was surprised that someone as intelligent, as highly trained in the human condition as she was couldn't see her own distress, couldn't or wouldn't admit that there had been something lacking in her own upbringing that forced her to build walls.

He'd nearly been fooled, he mused, into believing she was cold and distant and untouched by the messier emotions. He couldn't be sure what it was that insisted he believe differently. Maybe it was nothing more than wishful thinking, but he was determined to find out for himself. And soon.

He knew that making her family secrets accessible and so informally public would be humiliating for her, and perhaps painful. But she'd agreed without condition and was following through without hesitation.

Standards, he thought. Integrity. She had them. And he believed that she had heart as well.

Sybill offered a thin smile as she came back out. "Well, that's the first time I've seen a notary's eyes nearly pop out of her head. I think that should—"

The rest of her babbling statement was lost as his mouth rushed to cover hers. She lifted a hand to his shoulder, but her fingers only curled into the soft material of his sweater.

"You looked like you needed it," he murmured, and skimmed a hand over her cheek.

"Regardless—"

"Hell, Sybill, we've already got them talking. Why not add to the mystery?"

Her emotions were rocking, making it difficult for her to hold on to any threads of composure. "I've no intention of standing here making a spectacle of myself. So if you'll—"

"Fine. Let's go somewhere else. I've got the boat."

"The boat? I can't go out on the boat. I'm not dressed for it. I have work." I need to think, she told herself, but he was already pulling her to the dock.

"A sail will do you good. You're starting on another headache. The fresh air should help."

"I don't have a headache." Only the nasty, simmering threat of one. "And I don't want to—" She nearly yelped, so stunned was she when he simply plucked her off her feet and set her down on the deck.

"Consider yourself shanghaied, doc." Quickly, competently, he freed the lines and leaped aboard. "I have a feeling you haven't had nearly enough of that kind of treatment in your short, sheltered life."

"You don't know anything about my life, or what I've had. If you start that engine, I'm going to—" She broke off, grinding her teeth as the motor putted to life. "Phillip, I want to go back to my hotel. Now."

"Hardly anybody ever says no to you, do they?" He said it cheerfully as he gave her a firm nudge onto the port bench. "Just sit back and enjoy the ride."

Since she didn't intend to leap overboard and swim back to shore in a silk suit and Italian shoes, she folded her arms. It was his way of paying her back, she supposed, by taking away her freedom of choice, asserting his will and his physical dominance.

Typical.

She turned her head to stare out over the light chop. She wasn't afraid of him, not physically. He had a tougher side than she'd originally thought, but he wouldn't hurt her. And because he cared for Seth, deeply, she'd come to believe, he needed her cooperation.

She refused to be thrilled when he hoisted the sails. The sound of the canvas opening itself to the wind, the sight of the sun beating against the rippling white, the sudden and smooth angling of the boat, meant nothing to her, she insisted.

She would simply tolerate this little game of his, give him no reaction. Undoubtedly, he would grow weary of her silence and inattention and take her back.

"Here." He tossed something, making her jump. She looked down and saw the sunglasses that had landed neatly in her lap. "Sun's fierce today, even if the temperature's cooling. Indian summer's around the corner."

He smiled to himself when she said nothing, only slid the sunglasses primly on her nose and continued to stare in the opposite direction.

"We need a good hard frost first," he continued conversationally.

"When the leaves start to turn, the shoreline near the house is a picture. Golds and scarlets. You get that deep blue sky behind them, and the water mirror-bright, that spice of fall on the air, and you could start to believe there's no place else on the planet you'd ever want to be."

She kept her mouth firmly shut, tightened the fold of her arms across her breasts.

Phillip merely tucked his tongue in his cheek. "Even a couple of avowed urbanites like you and I can appreciate a fine fall day in the country. Seth's birthday's coming up."

Out of the corner of his eye he saw her head jerk around, her mouth tremble open. She shut it again, but this time when she turned away, her shoulders were hunched defensively.

Oh, she felt all right, Phillip mused. There were plenty of messy emotions stewing inside that cool package of hers.

"We thought we'd throw him a party, have some of his pals over to raise hell. You already know Grace bakes a hell of a chocolate cake. We've got his present taken care of. But just the other day I saw these art supplies in this shop in Baltimore. Not a kid's setup, a real one. Chalk, pencils, charcoal, brushes, watercolors, paper, palettes. It's a specialty shop a few blocks from my office. Somebody who knew something about art could breeze in there and pick out just the right things."

He'd intended to do so himself, but he saw now that his instincts to tell her about it had been true. She was facing him now, and though the sun flashed off her sunglasses, he could see from the angle of her head that he had her full attention.

"He wouldn't want anything from me."

"You're not giving him enough credit. Maybe you're not giving yourself enough either."

He trimmed the sails, caught the wind, and saw the instant she recognized the curve of trees along the shore. She got unsteadily to her feet. "Phillip, however you may feel about me right now, it can't help the situation for you to push me at Seth again so soon."

"I'm not taking you home." He scanned the yard as they passed. "Seth's at the boatyard with Cam and Ethan, in any case. You need a distraction, Sybill, not a confrontation. And for the record, I don't know how I feel about you at the moment."

"I've told you everything I know."

"Yeah, I think you've given me the facts. You haven't told me how you feel, how those facts affect you personally, emotionally."

"It isn't the issue."

"I'm making it an issue. We're tangled up here, Sybill, whether we like it or not. Seth's your nephew, and he's mine. My father and your mother had an affair. And we're about to."

"No," she said definitely, "we're not."

He turned his head long enough to shoot her a glittering look. "You know better than that. You're in my system, and I know when a woman's got me in hers."

"And we're both old enough to control our more basic urges."

He stared at her another moment, then laughed. "Hell we are. And it's not the sex that worries you. It's the intimacy."

He was hitting all the targets. It didn't anger her nearly as much as it frightened her. "You don't know me."

"I'm beginning to," he said quietly. "And I'm someone else who finishes what I start. I'm coming about." His voice was mild now. "Watch the boom."

She stepped out of the way, sat. She recognized the little cove where they had shared wine and paté. Only a week ago, she thought dully. Now so much had changed. Everything had changed.

She couldn't be here with him, couldn't risk it. The idea of handling him now was absurd. Still, she could do nothing but try.

Coolly, she eyed him. Casually, she smoothed her hand over the sophisticated twist the wind had disordered. Caustically, she smiled. "What, no wine this time? No music, no neat gourmet lunch?"

He dropped the sails, secured the boat. "You're scared."

"You're arrogant. And you don't worry me."

"Now you're lying." While the boat swayed gently underfoot, he stepped forward and took the sunglasses from her. "I worry you, quite a bit. You keep thinking you have me pegged, then I don't follow the script. I imagine most of the men you've let hover around your life have been fairly predictable. Easier for you."

"Is this your definition of a distraction?" she countered. "It fits my definition of a confrontation."

"You're right." He pulled his own sunglasses off, tossed them aside. "We'll analyze later."

He moved quickly. She knew he was capable of lightning motion but hadn't expected him to snap from cynic to lover in the blink of an eye. His mouth was hot, hungry, and hard on hers. His hands gripped her arms, pressing her against him so that as the heat and the need poured out, she couldn't tell if it came from him or from herself.

He'd spoken no less than the truth when he told her she was in his system. Whether she was poison or salvation didn't seem to matter. She was in there and he couldn't stop the flow.

He jerked her back so that their lips parted, but their faces remained close. His eyes were as gold and powerful as the flare of the sun. "You tell me you don't want me, you don't want this. Tell me and mean it, and it stops here."

"I—"

"No." Impatient, suffering, he shook her until her gaze lifted to his again. "No, you look at me and say it."

She'd already lied, and the lies weighed on her like lead. She couldn't bear another. "This will only complicate things, make them more difficult."

Unmistakable triumph flashed into those tawny eyes. "Damn right it will," he muttered. "Just now, I don't give a damn. Kiss me back," he demanded. "And mean it."

She couldn't stop herself. This kind of raw, wicked need was new to her, and left her defenseless. Her mouth met his, just as hungry now, just as desperate. And the low, primal moan that escaped was an echo to the beat of desire between her legs.

She stopped thinking. Found herself swamped and spinning with sensations, emotions, yearnings. The kiss roughened, teetered toward pain as his teeth scraped and nipped. She clutched at his hair, gasping for air, shaking with shock as that skillful mouth streaked down her throat and sent wild chills over her skin.

For the first time in her life, she surrendered utterly to the physical. And craved the taking.

He pulled at her jacket, tugging the soft silk off her shoulders and tossing it heedlessly aside. He wanted flesh, the feel of it under his hands, the taste of it in his mouth. He yanked the slim ivory shell over her head and filled his hands with her trembling lace-covered breasts.

Her skin was warmer than the silk, and somehow smoother. With one impatient flick he opened her bra, then dragged it aside. And satisfied his need to taste.

The sun blinded her. Even with her eyes tightly shut, the strength of it pounded on her lids. She couldn't see, only feel. That busy, almost brutal mouth devoured her, those rough and demanding hands doing as they pleased. The whimper in her throat was a scream in her head.

Now, now, now!

Fumbling, she dragged at his sweater, finding the muscle and scars and flesh beneath as he yanked her skirt down her hips. Her stockings ended with thin bands of stretchy lace high on her thighs. Another time he might have appreciated the mix of practicality and femininity. But now he was driven to possess, and he thrilled darkly at her stunned gasp when he ripped aside the thin triangle blocking him from her. Before she could draw the next breath, he plunged his fingers into her and shot her violently over the edge.

She cried out, shocked, staggered at that vicious slap of heat. It sliced through her without warning, sending her flying, flailing.

"Oh, God. Phillip." When her head dropped weakly on his shoulder, her body going from spring-taut to limp, he swept her off her feet and pressed her down on one of the narrow benches.

The blood was pounding in his head. His loins screamed for release. His heart hammered like a dull axe against his ribs.

His breath was ragged, his vision focused on her face like a laser as he freed himself. His fingers dug into her hips as he lifted and opened them. And he plunged. Hard and deep so that his long, long groan melted into hers.

She closed around him, a tight, hot glove. Moved under him, a trembling, eager woman. Breathed his name, a breathless, aching sigh.

He drove into her again, again, strong, steady strokes that she rose to meet. Her hair escaped its pins, flowed like rich mink. He buried his face in it, lost in her scent, in her heat, in the sheer, shimmering glory of a woman aroused beyond reason.

Her nails dug into his back, her cry muffled against his shoulder as she came. Her muscles clamped around him, owned him, destroyed him.

He was as limp as she, wrecked, struggling to fill his burning lungs with air. Beneath him, her body continued to quake, the aftershock of hard, satisfying sex.

When his vision cleared, he could see the three pieces of her pretty businesswoman's suit scattered along the deck. And one black high heel. It made him grin even as he shifted just enough to nip lightly at her shoulder.

"I usually try for more finesse," he said. Slyly, he skimmed a hand down to toy with the thin lace at the top of her stocking, experimenting with textures. "Oh, you're full of surprises, Dr. Griffin."

She was floating, somewhere just above reality. She couldn't seem to open her eyes, to move her hand. "What?"

At the dreamy, distant sound of her voice, he lifted his head to study her face. Her cheeks were flushed, her mouth swollen, her hair a tumbling mass. "As an objective observation, I have to conclude you've never been ravished before."

There was amusement in his tone, and just enough male arrogance to snap her back to earth. She opened her eyes now, and saw the sleepy smile of victory in his. "You're heavy," she said shortly.

"Okay." he shifted, sat up, but pulled her up and around until she straddled his lap. "You're still wearing your stockings, and one of your shoes." He grinned and began to knead the muscles of her tight little butt. "Christ, that's sexy."

"Stop it." The heat was pouring back, a combination of embarrassment and fresh desire. "Let me up."

"I haven't finished with you yet." He dipped his head, circled his tongue lazily around her nipple. "You're still soft and warm. Tasty," he added, flicking his tongue over her stiffened nipple, sucking lightly until her breathing thickened yet again. "I want more. So do you."

Her body arched back, beautifully fluid as he trailed his mouth up to the hammering pulse in her neck. Oh, yes, yes, she wanted more.

"But this time," he promised, "it'll take a little longer."

On a yielding moan, she lowered her mouth to his. "I guess there's time."

THE SUN WAS ANGLED LOW when he shifted her yet again. Her body felt golden and bruised, energized and exhausted. She'd had no idea she could claim such a sexual appetite, and now that she did, she hadn't a clue what she would do about it.

"We have to discuss . . ." She frowned at herself, draped an arm over her body. She was half naked and damp from him. And more confused than she'd ever been in her life. "We—this—can't continue."

"Not right this minute," he agreed. "Even I have my limitations."

"I didn't mean . . . This was just a diversion, as you said. Something we both apparently needed on a physical level. And now—"

"Shut up, Sybill." He said it mildly, but she caught the edge of annoyance. "It was a hell of a lot more than a diversion, and we'll discuss it to pieces later."

He scooped the hair out of his eyes, studied her. She was just beginning to feel awkward, he realized, uneasy with being naked, and with the situation. So he smiled. "Right now, we're a mess. So there's only one thing to do before we get dressed and head in."

"What?"

Still smiling, he pulled off her shoe, then scooped her up into his arms. "Just this," he said, and tossed her over the side.

She managed one scream before she hit. What surfaced was a furious woman with tangles of wet hair in her eyes. "You son of a bitch! You idiot!"

"I knew it." He stepped onto the gunwale and laughed like a loon. "I just knew you'd be gorgeous when you're angry."

He dived in to join her.

THIRTEEN

No one had ever treated her
the way Phillip Quinn had treated her. Sybill couldn't decide what she
thought of that, much less what to do about it.

He'd been rough, careless, demanding. He had, in his own words,
ravished her—and more than once. Though she couldn't claim to have
put up even what could remotely be termed a struggle, it had been a
long way from a civilized seduction.

Never in her life had she slept with a man she'd known for such a
short time. To do so was reckless, potentially dangerous, and certainly
irresponsible. Even factoring in the overwhelming and unprecedented
chemistry between them, it was foolish behavior.

Worse than foolish, she admitted, because she very much wanted to
be reckless, with him, again.

She would have to consider the matter carefully, as soon as she
could get her mind off her body and the incredible pleasure it had
experienced under those fast, take-charge hands.

Now he was sailing her back to the waterfront at St. Christopher's,
completely at ease with himself, and with her. She never would have
guessed he'd just spent more than an hour engaged in wild, frantic sex.

If she hadn't been a party to it.

There was no doubt in her mind that what they'd done would further complicate an already horribly complicated situation. Both of
them would have to be coldly sensible now, and carefully practical.
She did her best to tidy her damp, tangled hair as the wind whipped at
it.

Conversation, she decided, to bridge the gap between sex and sensibility.

"How did you get the scars?"

"Which ones?" He tossed the question over his shoulder, but he thought he knew. Most women wanted to know.

"On your chest. They look surgical."

"Mmm. Long story." This time he threw a smile back with the look. "I'll bore you with it tonight."

"Tonight?"

Oh, he just loved it when her brows buckled together, forming that little concentration line between them. "We have a date, remember?"

"But I . . . hmmm."

"I confuse the hell out of you, don't I?"

Annoyed, she slapped at the hair that insisted on blowing over her eyes. "And you enjoy that?"

"Darling, I can't begin to tell you how much. You keep trying to slip me into one of your slots, Sybill, and I'll keep sliding back out again. You figured on a fairly safe, one-dimensional urban professional who likes his wine aged and his women cultured. But that's only part of the picture."

As he entered the harbor, he dropped the sails, switched to motor. "First glance at you, I have to figure well-bred, well-educated, career-oriented city woman who likes her wine white and her men at a safe distance. But that's only part of the picture, too."

He cut the engine, let the boat bump gently at dock. Gave her hair a friendly tug before he climbed out to secure the lines. "I think we'll both be well entertained while we uncover the rest of the canvas."

"A continuation of a physical relationship is—"

"Inevitable," he finished, and offered her a hand. "Let's not waste time or energy pretending otherwise. We can call it basic chemistry for now." He tugged her to him the minute her feet hit the dock, and proved his point with one long, fiery kiss. "It works for me."

"Your family won't approve."

"Family approval's important to you."

"Of course."

"I don't discount it either. Normally, this wouldn't be any of their business. In this case, it is." It bothered him, more than a little. "But it's my family, and my concern, not yours."

"This may sound hypocritical at this point, but I don't want to do anything else that will hurt or disturb Seth."

"Neither do I. But I'm not going to let a ten-year-old take charge of my personal life. Relax, Sybill." He skimmed his fingers over her jaw. "This isn't the Montagues and the Capulets."

"I'm hardly thinking of you as Romeo," she said, so dryly that he laughed and kissed her again.

"You might, darling, if I put my mind to it. But for now, let's just be who we are. You're tired." He rubbed his thumb gently under her eye. "You've got thin skin, Sybill, the shadows show. Go take a nap. We can make do with room service later."

"With—"

"I'll bring the wine," he said cheerfully and leaped back into the boat. "I've got a bottle of Chateau Olivier I've been wanting to sample," he shouted over the motor. "No need to dress up," he added with a wicked grin as he maneuvered the boat away from the dock and out of earshot.

She wasn't sure what she would have shouted at him if she'd lost what was left of her control. Instead she stood on the dock in her wrinkled but elegant silk suit, her hair a damp mess and her dignity as shaky as her heart.

CAM RECOGNIZED THE SIGNS. A fast sail on a breezy afternoon might relax a man, loosen his muscles, clear his head. But he only knew one thing that put that lazy, satisfied gleam in a man's eyes.

He recognized that gleam in his brother's eyes when Phillip slid up to the dock to toss him the lines. You son of a bitch, was his first thought.

He caught the stern line, yanked it taut. "You son of a bitch."

Phillip only lifted his eyebrows. He'd been expecting that reaction, though not quite so quickly. He'd already ordered himself to hold on to his temper, to explain his position. "Always a friendly welcome at the Quinns'."

"I figured you were past the stage where you thought with your dick."

Not quite as calm as he'd planned to be, Phillip stepped off the boat and stood facing his brother. He recognized the signs, too. Cam was spoiling for a fight. "Actually, I tend to let my dick think for itself. Though we often agree."

"You're either crazy or stupid, or you just don't give a damn. A kid's life is in the balance here, his peace of mind, his trust."

"Nothing's going to happen to Seth. I'm doing everything I can to make sure of that."

"Oh, I get it. You fucked her for his sake."

Phillip's hands shot out, and before the bright fury fully registered he had them gripped on Cam's jacket. Now their faces were close, and both were warrior hard. "You were tearing up the sheets with Anna last spring. How much were you thinking about Seth when you had her under you?"

Cam's fist rammed up, under Phillip's guard. The blow rocked his head back but didn't loosen his hold. Instinct blanked out reason as he shoved Cam back and prepared to tear in.

He swore viciously when Ethan clamped an arm around his throat from behind.

"Cool off," Ethan ordered on more of a sigh than a snarl. "Both of you—or I'll toss you in until you do." He tightened his hold on Phillip's windpipe just enough to show he meant it and scowled at Cam. "Get ahold of yourself, damn it. Seth's had a rough day. You want to add to it?"

"No, I don't want to add to it," Cam said bitterly. "This one doesn't give a good damn, but I do."

"My relationship with Sybill and my concern for Seth are two separate matters."

"Like hell."

"Let go of me, Ethan." Because Phillip's tone was cool and deliberate, Ethan released him. "You know, Cam, I don't remember you being so interested in my sex life since we both had our sights set on Jenny Malone."

"We're not in high school anymore, pal."

"No, we're not. And you're not my keeper. Either of you," he added, shifting so that he could look at both of them. He would explain himself because it mattered. Because they mattered. "I've got feelings for her, and I'm going to take the time to figure out what they are. I've made a lot of changes in my life over the last few months, and I've gone along with what the two of you wanted. But goddamn it, I'm entitled to a personal life."

"I wouldn't argue with that, Phil." Ethan glanced toward the house, hoping Seth was busy with his homework or his drawings and not spying out the window. "I don't know how Seth's going to feel about this part of your personal life."

"There's something none of you are taking into consideration. Sybill is Seth's aunt."

"That's exactly what I am taking into consideration," Cam shot back. "She's Gloria's sister, and she came in here on a lie."

"She came in here believing a lie." It was an important distinction, Phillip thought. A vital distinction. "Did you read the statement she faxed to Anna?"

Cam hissed between his teeth, hooked his thumbs in his pockets. "Yeah, I saw it."

"What do you think it cost her to put that down in black and white, to know everybody in town would be talking about it, about her, within twenty-four hours?" Phillip waited a beat, noting that the muscle in Cam's jaw relaxed, fractionally. "How much more do you want her to pay?"

"I'm not thinking about her. I'm thinking about Seth."

"And she's the best defense we've got against Gloria DeLauter."

"You think she'll stand up to it?" Ethan wondered. "When push comes to shove?"

"Yeah, I do. He needs his family, all his family. That's what Dad would want. He told me . . ." Catching himself, Phillip frowned out over the dark water.

Cam pursed his lips, exchanged a look with Ethan, and nearly smiled. "Been feeling a little odd lately, Phillip?"

"I'm fine."

"Maybe you're stressed out some." Since he'd only gotten in one punch, Cam felt entitled to enjoy himself. "I thought I saw you talking to yourself a couple of times."

"I don't talk to myself."

"Maybe you think you're talking to somebody who isn't there." He did smile now, widely and wickedly. "Stress is a killer. Eats at the mind."

Ethan didn't quite swallow a chuckle, and Phillip glared at him. "You got something to say about the state of my mental health?"

"Well . . ." Ethan scratched at his chin, "you've been looking a little tense lately."

"For Christ's sake, I'm entitled to look a little tense." He threw out his arms as if to encompass the world that too often weighed on his shoulders. "I put in ten, twelve hours a day in Baltimore, then come down here and sweat like a goddamn galley slave in the boatyard. That's when I'm not frying my brains over the books and the bills or playing housewife at the grocery store or making sure Seth doesn't slide out of his homework."

"Always was bitchy," Cam mumbled.

"You want bitchy?" Phillip took one threatening step forward, but this time Cam grinned and spread his hands.

"Ethan'll just toss you off the dock. Me, I don't feel like a swim just now."

"First few times with me, I thought I was dreaming."

Confused, unsure if he wanted to punch Cam or just sit down for a while, Phillip looked back at Ethan. "What the hell are you talking about?"

"I thought we were discussing your mental health." Ethan's tone was mild, conversational now. "It was good to see him. Hard to know you'd have to let him go again, but it was worth it."

A chill danced up Phillip's spine, and he put his suddenly unsteady hands safely in his pockets. "Maybe we should be talking about your mental health."

"We figured when it was your turn, you'd head for the therapist's couch." Cam grinned again. "Or Aruba."

"I don't know what you're talking about."

"Yes, you do." Ethan spoke calmly, then settled down on the dock, legs dangling, to take out a cigar. "It's your turn. Looks like he took us in the same order he took us in."

"Symmetry," Cam decided, dropping down beside Ethan. "He'd have liked the symmetry of it. I talked to him the first time the day I met Anna." He thought back to it, the way he'd seen her cross the back lawn with that knockout face and that ugly suit. "I guess that's a kind of symmetry, too."

The chill was still dancing, tapping fast now, up and down Phillip's spine. "What do you mean, 'talked to him'?"

"Had a conversation." Cam plucked the cigar out of Ethan's mouth and helped himself to a puff. "Of course, I figured I'd cracked." He glanced up, smiled. "You figure you've cracked, Phil?"

"No. I've just been working too hard."

"Shit, drawing pictures, coming up with jingles. Big deal."

"Kiss ass." But with a sigh, he sat on the dock. "Are the two of you trying to tell me you've talked to Dad? The one who died in March? The one we buried a few miles from here?"

In an easy gesture Cam passed Phillip the cigar. "You trying to tell us you haven't?"

"I don't believe in that sort of thing."

"Doesn't much matter what you believe when it happens," Ethan pointed out and took back his cigar. "Last time I saw him was the night I asked Grace to marry me. He had a bag of peanuts."

"Christ Jesus," Phillip murmured.

"I could smell them, the same way I can smell this cigar smoke, the water, Cam's leather jacket."

"When people die, that's it. They don't come back." Phillip paused a moment, waiting until the cigar came back down the line to him. "Did you—touch him?"

Cam angled his head. "Did you?"

"He was solid. He couldn't be."

"It's either that," Ethan pointed out, "or we're all crazy."

"We barely had time to say good-bye, and no time to understand." Cam let out a breath. His grief had eased and softened. "He bought us each a little more time. That's what I think."

"He and Mom bought us all time when they made us Quinns." He couldn't think about it, Phillip decided. Not now, at any rate. "It must have ripped him when he found out he had a daughter he'd never known."

"He'd have wanted to help her, save her," Ethan murmured.

"He'd have seen it was too late for her. But not for Seth," Cam concluded. "So he'd have done whatever he could do to save Seth."

"His grandson." Phillip watched an egret soar, then slide silently into the dark. And he was no longer cold. "He'd have seen himself in the eyes, but he would've wanted answers. I've been thinking about that. The logical step would have been for him to try to locate Gloria's mother, have her confirm it."

"It would have taken time." Cam considered it. "She's married, she's living in Europe, and from what Sybill said, she wasn't interested in contacting him."

"And he ran out of time," Phillip concluded. "But now we know. And now, we make it stick."

S HE HADN'T MEANT TO SLEEP
Sybill indulged in a long, hot shower, then wrapped herself in a robe with the intention of adding to her notes. She ordered herself to drum up the courage to call her mother, to speak her mind and demand a written corroboration of her own notarized statement.

She did neither. Instead she fell face down on the bed, closed her eyes, and escaped.

The knocking at the door pulled her out of sleep into groggy. She stumbled out of bed, fumbled for the light switch. With her mind still fuzzy, she walked through the parlor and barely had the presence of mind to check the peephole.

She let out a self-directed annoyed sigh as she flipped off the locks.

Phillip took one look at her tousled hair, sleepy eyes, and practical navy terry robe, and smiled. "Well, I did tell you not to dress up."

"I'm sorry. I fell asleep." Distracted, she pushed at her hair. She hated being mussed, particularly when he looked so fresh and alert. And gorgeous.

"If you're tired, I'll take a rain check."

"No, I . . . if I sleep any more now I'll end up wide awake at three A.M. I hate hotel rooms at three A.M." She stepped back to let him in. "I'll just get dressed."

"Stay comfortable," he suggested, and used his free hand to cup the nape of her neck and bring her forward for a casual kiss. "I've already seen you naked. And a very appealing sight it was."

It appeared, she decided, that her dignity was still just out of reach. "I'm not going to claim that was a mistake."

"Good." He set the wine he carried on her coffee table.

"But," she said, with what she considered admirable patience, "neither was it wise. We're both sensible people."

"Speak for yourself, doc. I stop feeling sensible every time I get a whiff of you. What *is* that you wear?"

She leaned back when he leaned in to sniff at her. "Phillip."

"Sybill." And he laughed. "How about if I attempt to be civilized and not cart you off to bed until you're a little more awake?"

"I appreciate your restraint," she said tightly.

"And so you should. Hungry?"

"What is this almost pathological need of yours to feed me?"

"You're the analyst," he told her with a shrug. "I've got the wine. You got some glasses?"

She might have sighed, but it wouldn't have been constructive. She did want to talk to him, to put their relationship on an even footing again. To ask his advice. And, she hoped, to enlist his help in persuading Seth to accept her friendship.

She took the two short, thick glasses the hotel provided, lifting her eyebrow when Phillip sneered at them. He had a damn sexy sneer.

"They're an insult to this very delightful wine," he said, as he opened the bottle with the stainless-steel corkscrew he'd brought with him. "But if they're the best you can offer we'll just have to make do."

"I forgot to pack my Waterford."

"Next time." He poured the pretty straw-colored wine into the glasses, handed her one. "To beginnings, middles, and endings. We seem to be at all three."

"Which means?"

"The charade's ended, the teamwork is established, and we've just become lovers. I'm happy with all three aspects of our very interesting relationship."

"Teamwork?" She picked the aspect that didn't shame her or make her nervous.

"Seth's a Quinn. With your help we'll make that legal and permanent, and soon."

She stared down into her wine. "It's important to you that he have your name."

"His grandfather's name," Phillip corrected. "And it can't be nearly as important to me as it is to Seth."

"Yes, you're right. I saw his face when I told him. He looked almost awed. Professor Quinn must have been an extraordinary man."

"My parents were special. They had the kind of marriage you rarely see. A true partnership, based on trust, respect, love, passion. It hasn't been easy wondering if my father broke that trust."

"You were afraid that he had cheated on your mother with Gloria, fathered a child with her." Sybill sat down. "It was hideous of her to plant that seed."

"It was also hell living with the seeds in me that I couldn't quite stomp out. Resentment for Seth. Was he my father's son? His true son, while I was just one of the substitutes? I knew better," he added as he sat beside her. "In my heart. But it's one of those mind games that nag at you at three A.M."

If nothing else, she realized, she'd eased his mind on that one point. But it wasn't enough. "I'm going to ask my mother to corroborate my statement in writing. I don't know that she will. I doubt that she will," Sybill admitted. "But I'll ask, I'll try."

"Teamwork, see." He took her hand in his, nuzzling it, which had her turning her head to study him warily.

"Your jaw's bruised."

"Yeah." He grimaced, wiggled it. "Cam still has a damn sneaky left."

"He hit you?"

The absolute shock in her voice made him laugh. Obviously the good doctor didn't come from a world where fists flew. "I was going to hit him first, but he beat me to it. Which means I owe him one. I'd have paid him back then and there, but Ethan got me in a choke hold."

"Oh, God." Swamped with distress, she got to her feet. "This was about us. About what happened today on the boat. It should never have happened. I knew it would cause trouble between you and your family."

"Yes," he said evenly, "it was about us. And we worked it out. Sybill, my brothers and I have been pounding on each other as long as we've been brothers. It's a Quinn family tradition. Like my father's waffle recipe."

Distress continued to ripple through her. But confusion ran with it. Fists and waffles? she wondered, pulling a hand through her disordered hair. "You fight with them, physically?"

"Sure."

To try to compute it, she pressed her fingers to her temples. It didn't help a bit. "Why?"

He considered, smiled. "Because they're there?" he suggested.

"And your parents allowed this type of violent behavior."

"My mother was a pediatrician. She always stitched us up." He leaned forward to pour himself more wine. "I think I'd better explain the whole picture. You know that Cam, Ethan, and I are adopted."

"Yes. I did some research before I came . . ." She trailed off, glanced back at her laptop. "Well, you know that already."

"Yeah. And you know some of the facts, but not the meaning. You asked me about my scars. It doesn't start there," he mused. "Not really. Cam was the first. Ray caught him trying to steal my mother's car one morning."

"Her car? Steal her car?"

"Right out of the driveway. He was twelve. He'd run away from home and was planning on going to Mexico."

"At twelve he was stealing cars with plans to go to Mexico."

"That's right. The first of the Quinn bad boys." He lifted his glass to toast his absent sibling. "He'd been beaten, again, by his drunk father, and he'd figured it was time to run or die."

"Oh." She braced a hand on the arm of the sofa as she lowered herself again.

"He passed out, and my father carried him inside. My mother treated him."

"They didn't call the police?"

"No. Cam was terrified, and my mother recognized the signs of continual physical abuse. They made inquiries, arrangements, worked with the system and circumvented it. And they gave him a home."

"They just made him their son?"

"My mother said once that we were all hers already. We just hadn't found each other before. Then there was Ethan. His mother was a hooker in Baltimore, a junkie. She relieved boredom by knocking him around. And then she got the bright idea that she could supplement her income by selling her eight-year-old son to perverts."

Sybill clutched her glass in both hands and rocked. She said nothing, could say nothing.

"He had a few years of that. One night one of her customers finished with Ethan, and with her, and got violent. Since his target was her and not her kid, she objected. Stabbed him. She ran, and when the cops got there they took Ethan to the hospital. My mother was doing guest rounds."

"They took him, too," Sybill murmured.

"Yeah, that's the long and short of it."

She raised her glass, sipped slowly, watched him over the rim. She didn't know the world he was describing. Logically, she knew it existed, but it had never touched hers. Until now. "And you?"

"My mother worked the Block in Baltimore. Strip joints, turned tricks on the side. A little bait and switch now and then, some short cons." He shrugged. "My father was long gone. He did some time in Jessup for armed robbery, and when he got out he didn't look us up."

"Did she . . . did she beat you?"

"Now and then, until I got big enough, strong enough, that she worried I might hit back." His smile was thin and sharp. "She was right to worry. We didn't care for each other much. But if I wanted a roof over my head, and I did, I needed her, and I had to pull my weight. I picked pockets, lifted locks. I was pretty good at it. Hell," he said with a faint stir of pride, "I was damn good at it. Still, I stuck with small shit. The kind you turn into easy cash or drugs. If things were really tight, I sold myself."

He saw her eyes widen in shock, flick away from his.

"Survival's not always pretty," he said shortly. "Most of the time I had my freedom. I was tough, and I was mean, and I was smart. Maybe I got picked up once in a while and rattled through the system, but I always popped out again. Another few years of that life, and I'd have been in Jessup—or the morgue. Another few years of that life," he continued, watching her face, "and Seth would have gone the same way."

Struggling to absorb it, she stared into her wine. "You see your situations as similar, but—"

"I recognized Gloria yesterday," he interrupted. "A pretty woman gone brittle. Hard and sharp at the eyes, bitter at the mouth. She and my mother would have recognized each other, too."

What could she say, how could she argue when she'd seen the same thing, felt the same? "I didn't recognize her," she said quickly. "For a moment I thought there was a mistake."

"She recognized you. And she played the angles, pushed the buttons. She'd know how." He paused a moment. "She'd know exactly how. So do I."

She looked at him then, noted he was studying her coolly. "Is that what you're doing? Pushing buttons, playing angles?"

Maybe it was, he thought. They would both have to figure that out before much longer. "Right now I'm answering your question. Do you want the rest?"

"Yes." She didn't hesitate, for she'd discovered she very much wanted to hear it all.

"When I was thirteen, I thought I had it handled. I figured I was just fine. Until I found myself face down in the gutter, bleeding to death. Drive-by shooting. Wrong place, wrong time."

"Shot?" Her gaze whipped back to his. "You were shot."

"In the chest. Probably should have killed me. One of the doctors who made sure I didn't die knew Stella Quinn. She and Ray came to see me in the hospital. I figured them for weirdos, do-gooders, your basic assholes. But I played along with them. My mother was done with me, and I was going to end up solid in the system. I thought I'd use them until I was steady on my feet again. Then I'd take what I needed and cut out."

Who was this boy he described to her? And how was she to reconcile him with the man beside her? "You were going to rob them?"

"It's what I did. What I was. But they . . ." How to explain it? he wondered. The miracle of them. "They just wore that away. Until I fell in love with them. Until I'd have done anything, been anything, to make them proud of me. It wasn't the paramedics or the surgical team that saved my life. It was Ray and Stella Quinn."

"How old were you when they took you in?"

"Thirteen. But I wasn't a kid like Seth. I wasn't a victim like Cam and Ethan. I made my choices."

"You're wrong." For the first time, she reached out and, taking his face in her hands, she kissed him gently.

He lifted his hands to her wrists, had to concentrate on not squeezing her skin the way that soft kiss had squeezed his heart. "That's not the reaction I expected."

It wasn't the one she'd expected to have. But she found herself feeling pity for the boy he described to her and admiration for the man he'd made himself into. "What reaction do you usually get?"

"I've never told anyone outside the family." He managed a smile. "Bad for the image."

Touched, she rested her forehead against his. "You're right. It could have been Seth," she murmured. "What happened to you, it could have been Seth. Your father saved him from that. You and your family saved him, while mine's done nothing. And worse than nothing."

"You're doing something."

"I hope it's enough." When his mouth came to hers, she let herself slide into comfort.

FOURTEEN

PHILLIP UNLOCKED THE BOAT-
yard at seven A.M. The very fact that his brothers hadn't given him
grief about not working the day before, or about taking a full Sunday
off the previous week, had his guilt quota at peak.

He expected he had a good hour, maybe a little more before Cam
showed up to continue work on the hull of the sport's fisher. Ethan
would put in a morning of crabbing, taking advantage of the fall sea-
son, before heading in to work that afternoon.

So he would have the place to himself, and the quiet and solitude to
deal with the paperwork he'd neglected the week before.

Quiet didn't mean silence. His first act when entering his cramped
office was to hit the lights. The next was to switch on the radio. Ten
minutes later, he was nose-deep in accounts and very much at home.

Well, they owed just about everybody, he concluded. Rent, utilities,
insurance premiums, the lumberyard, and the ever popular Master-
Card.

The government had demanded its share in the middle of September, and the bite had been just a little nasty. The next tax nibble wasn't
far enough away to let him relax.

He juggled figures, toyed with them, stroked them, and decided red
wasn't such a bad color. They'd made a tidy profit on their first job,
the bulk of which had been poured back into the business. Once they
turned the hull, they would get another draw from their current client.
That would keep their heads above water.

But they weren't going to see a lot of the color black for a time yet.
Dutifully, he cut checks, updated the spreadsheet, reconciled fig-

ures, and tried not to mourn the fact that two and two stubbornly insisted on making four.

He heard the heavy door below open, then slam.

"Hiding up there again?" Cam called out.

"Yeah, having a real party."

"Some of us have real work to do."

Phillip looked at the figures dancing over his computer screen and laughed shortly. It wasn't real work to Cam, he knew, unless you had a tool in your hand.

"Best I can do," he muttered and shut the computer down. He stacked the outgoing bills on the corner of the desk, tucked the paychecks in his back pocket, then headed down.

Cam was strapping on a tool belt. He wore a ball cap backward to keep his hair out of his eyes, and it flowed beneath the down-sloped bill. Phillip watched him slide the wedding band off his finger and tuck it carefully into his front pocket.

Just as he would take it out after work, Phillip mused, and slip it back in place. Rings could catch on tools and cost a man a finger. But neither of his brothers left theirs at home. He wondered if there was some symbolism, or comfort, in having that statement of marriage on them, one way or the other, at all times.

Then he wondered why he was wondering and nudged the question, and the idea of it, aside.

Since Cam had reached the work area first, the radio wasn't tuned to the lazy blues Phillip would have chosen, but to loud, kiss-my-ass rock. Cam eyed him coolly as Phillip tugged on a tool belt of his own.

"Didn't expect to see you in so bright and early this morning. Figured you had a late night."

"Don't go there again."

"Just a comment." Anna had already chewed him out when he complained to her about Phillip's involvement with Sybill. He should be ashamed, he shouldn't interfere, he should have some compassion for his brother's feelings.

He'd rather take that brother's fist in the face any day than a hot verbal slap from his wife.

"You want to fool around with her, it's your business. She's a pleasure to look at. I'd say she's got a wide cold streak in her, though."

"You don't know her."

"And you do?" Cam lifted a hand when Phillip's eyes flashed. "Just trying to get a handle on it. It's going to matter to Seth."

"I know she's willing to do what she can so he's where he needs to be. Reading between the lines, I'd say she grew up in a repressive, restrictive atmosphere."

"A rich one."

"Yeah." Phillip strode to a pile of planks. "Yeah, private schools, chauffeurs, country clubs, servants."

"It's a little tough to feel sorry for her."

"I don't think she's looking for sympathy." He hefted a plank. "You said you wanted to get a handle on her. I'm telling you she had advantages. I don't know if she had any affection."

Cam shrugged and, deciding they'd get more accomplished working together, took the other end of the plank to fit it into place on the hull. "She doesn't strike me as deprived. She strikes me as cold."

"Restrained. Cautious." He remembered the way she reached out to him the night before. Still, it had been the first time she'd done so, the only time. He clamped down on the frustration of not being sure that Cam wasn't right. "Are you and Ethan the only ones entitled to a relationship with a woman that satisfies your hormones and your brain?"

"No." Cam lapped the ends. Deliberately he relaxed his shoulders. There was something in Phillip's voice that gave away that frustration, and something else. "No, we're not. I'll talk to Seth about her."

"I'll talk to him myself."

"All right."

"He matters to me, too."

"I know he does."

"He didn't." Phillip pulled out his hammer to nail the laps. "Not as much as he did to you. Not enough. It's different now."

"I know that, too." For the next few minutes they worked in tandem, without words. "You stood up for him anyway," Cam added when the plank was in place. "Even when he didn't matter enough."

"I did it for Dad."

"We all did it for Dad. Now we're doing it for Seth."

BY NOON, THE SKELETON OF THE hull had taken on the flesh of wood. The smooth-lap construction was labor-intensive, tedious and exacting. But it was their trademark, a choice that offered extreme structural strength and required great skill by the boatbuilder.

No one would argue that Cam was the most skilled of the three of them in woodworking. But Phillip thought he was holding his own.

Yeah, he thought, standing back to scan the exterior planking or skin of the hull. He was holding his own.

"You pick up any lunch?" Cam asked before he poured water from a jug into his mouth.

"No."

"Shit. I bet Grace packed Ethan one of those monster lunches of hers. Fried chicken, or thick slabs of honey-baked ham."

"You got a wife," Phillip pointed out.

Cam snorted, rolled his eyes. "Oh, yeah. I can just see me talking Anna into packing me a lunch every day. She'd smack me with her briefcase as she marched out the door to work. There are two of us," he considered. "We can take Ethan, especially if we catch him by surprise when he comes in."

"Let's go the easier route." Phillip dug into his pocket, pulled out a quarter. "Heads or tails?"

"Heads. Loser gets it, and buys it."

Phillip flipped the coin, caught it and slapped it onto the back of his hand. The eagle's beak seemed to sneer at him. "Damn it. What do you want?"

"Meatball sub, large chips, and six gallons of coffee."

"Fine, clog your arteries."

"Last I checked they don't stock any tofu at Crawford's. Don't know how you eat that crap. You're going to die anyway. Might as well go with a meatball sub."

"You go your way, I'll go mine." He reached in his pocket again for Cam's paycheck. "Here, don't spend it all in one place."

"Now I can retire to that little grass shack on Maui. You got Ethan's?"

"What there is of it."

"Yours?"

"I don't need it."

Cam narrowed his eyes as Phillip pulled on his jacket. "That's not the way it works."

"I'm in charge of the books, I say how it works."

"You put in your time, you take your share."

"I don't need it," Phillip said, with heat this time. "When I do, I'll take it." He stalked out, leaving Cam fuming.

"Stubborn son of a bitch," Cam muttered. "How am I supposed to rag on him when he pulls crap like that?"

He bitched plenty, Cam mused. He nagged his brothers to distraction over the pettiest detail. Then he handled the details, he thought as he capped the water jug. He'd back you into a corner, then he'd go to the wall for you.

It was enough to drive you nuts.

Now he was getting himself twisted up over a woman none of them knew they could trust if things got sticky. He, for one was going to keep a close eye on Sybill Griffin.

And not just for Seth's sake. Phillip might have the brains, but he was just as stupid as the next guy when it came to a pretty face.

"AND YOUNG KAREN LAWSON who's been working down at the hotel since she hooked up with the McKinney boy last year saw it written down, in black and white. She called her mama, and as Bitty Lawson's a good friend of mine and my longtime bridge partner—though she'll trump your ace if you don't watch her—she called me right up and let me know."

Nancy Claremont was in her element, and that element was gossip. As her husband owned a sizable chunk of St. Chris, meaning she did as well, and part of that chunk was the old barn those Quinn boys—a wild bunch if you asked her—rented for their boatyard—though God knew what else went on in there—she knew it was not only her right but her duty to pass on the succulent tidbit that had come her way the previous afternoon.

Of course, she'd used the most convenient method first. The telephone. But you didn't get the pleasure of face-to-face reaction over the phone. So she'd brought herself out, dressed in her brand-new pumpkin-colored pantsuit, fresh out of the J. C. Penney catalog.

There was no point in being the most well-off woman in St. Christopher's if you didn't flaunt it a bit. And the best place to flaunt, and to spread gossip, was Crawford's.

Second-best was the Stylerite Beauty Salon over on Market, and that, as she'd made an appointment for a cut, color, and curl, was her next stop.

Mother Crawford, a fixture in St. Chris for all of her sixty-two years, sat behind the counter in her smeared butcher apron, her tongue tucked firmly in her cheek.

She'd already heard the news—not much got by Mother, and nothing got by her for long—but she disposed herself to hear Nancy out.

"To think that child is Ray Quinn's grandson! And that writer lady with her snooty airs is the sister of that nasty girl who said all those terrible things. That boy's her nephew. Her own kin, but did she say one word about it? No, sir, she did not! Just hoity-toitying around, going off sailing with Phillip Quinn, and a lot more than sailing, if you ask me. The way young people carry on today without a snap of their fingers for morals."

She snapped her own, inches from Mother's face, and her eyes glittered with malicious delight.

Since Mother sensed that Nancy was about to veer off the subject at hand, she shrugged her wide shoulders. "Seems to me," she began, knowing the scatter of people in the store had their ears bent her way, "that there are a lot of people around this town who ought to be hanging their heads after what was being passed around about Ray. Whispering about him behind his back when he was living, and over his grave when he passed on, about him cheating on Stella, God rest her, and having truck with that DeLauter woman. Well, it wasn't true, was it?"

Her sharp eyes scanned the store, and indeed, a few heads did lower. Satisfied, she beamed her gaze hard into Nancy's glittering eyes. "Seems to me you were willing enough to believe bad about a good man like Ray Quinn."

Sincerely insulted, Nancy puffed out her chest. "Why, I never believed a word of it, Mother." Discussing such matters, she thought to herself, wasn't the same as believing them. "Truth is, a blind man couldn't have missed the way that boy's got Ray's eyes. Had to be a blood relation. Why, I said to Silas just the other day, I said, 'Silas, I wonder if that boy could be a cousin or something to Ray?'"

She'd said no such thing, of course. But she might have, if she'd thought of it.

"Never thought about him being Ray's grandson, though. Why, to think Ray had a daughter all these years."

Which, of course, proved he'd done something wrong in the first place, didn't it? She'd always suspected that Ray Quinn had been wild in his youth. Maybe even a hippie. And everyone knew what *that* meant.

Smoking marijuana, and having orgies and running around naked.

But that wasn't something she intended to bring up to Mother. That little morsel could wait until she was shampooed and tucked into the styling chair at the salon.

"And that she turned out wilder than those boys he and Stella brought home," she rattled on. "That girl over to the hotel must be just as—"

She broke off when the door jingled. Hoping for a fresh ear, she was thrilled to see Phillip Quinn walk in. Better than an addition to her audience, it was one of the actors on the very interesting stage.

Phillip only had to open the door to know what subject was under discussion. Or had been, until he stepped inside. Silence fell with a clang, and eyes darted toward him, then guiltily away.

Except for Nancy Claremont's and Mother's.

"Why, Phillip Quinn, I don't know as I've seen you since your family picnic on the Fourth of July." Nancy fluttered at him. Wild or not, he was a handsome man. Nancy considered flirting one of the best ways to loosen a man's tongue. "That was a fine day."

"Yes, it was." He walked up to the counter, knowing that stares were being bulleted at his back. "I need a couple of subs, Mother Crawford. A meatball and a turkey."

"We'll fix you up, Phil. Junior!" She shouted over at her son, who jolted at her tone despite being thirty-six and the father of three.

"Yes 'um."

"You going to ring up these people or just scratch your butt the rest of the afternoon?"

He colored, muttered under his breath, and turned his attention back to the cash register.

"You working down to the boatyard today, Phillip?"

"That's right, Mrs. Claremont."

He busied himself choosing a bag of chips for Cam, then wandered back to the dairy case to decide on yogurt for himself.

"That young boy usually comes in to pick up lunch, doesn't he?"

Phillip reached in, took out a carton at random. "He's in school today. It's Friday."

" 'Course it is." Nancy laughed, playfully patting the side of her head. "Don't know where my mind is. Fine-looking young boy. Ray musta been right proud."

"I don't doubt it."

"We've been hearing that he's got some blood relations close by."

"There's never been anything wrong with your hearing, Mrs. Claremont, that I recall. I'll need a couple of large coffees to go, Mother."

"We'll fix you up there, too. Nancy, you got more than enough news to blow around for the day. You keep trying to squeeze more out of this boy, you're going to miss your hair appointment."

"I don't know what you could be meaning." Nancy sniffed, shot

Mother a furious look, then fluffed at her hair. "But I have to be going. The husband and I are going to the Kiwanis dinner-dance tonight, and I need to look my best."

She flounced out, making a beeline for the beauty shop.

Inside, Mother narrowed her eyes. "The rest of you got business, Junior'll ring you up. But this ain't no lounge. You want to stand around and gawk, go stand outside."

Phillip disguised a chuckle as a cough when several people decided they had business elsewhere.

"That Nancy Claremont's got less sense than a peahen," Mother proclaimed. "Bad enough she dresses herself up like a pumpkin from head to foot, but she don't even know how to be subtle."

Mother turned back to Phillip and grinned. "Now, I won't say I don't have as much got-to-know as the next, but by God, if you can't try to jiggle a little information out of a body without being so blessed obvious, you're not just rude, you're stupid with it. Can't abide bad manners or a soft brain."

Phillip leaned on the counter. "You know, Mother, I've been thinking maybe I'd change my name to Jean-Claude, then move to the wine country of France, the Loire valley, and buy myself a vineyard."

She tucked her tongue in her cheek again, eyes bright. She'd heard this tale, or one of its variations, for years. "Do tell."

"I'd watch my grapes ripen in the sun. I'd eat bread that was hot and fresh, and cheese that wasn't. It would be a fine, satisfying life. But I've got just one problem."

"What's that?"

"It won't be any good unless you come with me." He grabbed her hand, kissing it lavishly while she roared with laughter.

"Boy, you are a caution. Always were." She gasped for breath, wiped her eyes. Then she sighed. "Nancy, she's a fool, but she's not mean, not deep down. Ray and Stella, they were just people to her. They were a lot more than that to me."

"I know that, Mother."

"People got something new to talk about, they're going to gum it to death."

"I know that, too." He nodded. "So did Sybill."

Mother's eyebrows lifted and fell as she realized the implication. "The girl's got guts. Good for her. Seth, he can be proud he's got blood kin that brave. And he can be proud a man like Ray was his granddaddy." She paused to put the finishing touches on the subs. "I think Ray and Stella would've liked that girl."

"Do you?" Phillip murmured.

"Yep. I like her." Mother grinned again as she quickly wrapped the subs in white paper. "She's not hoity-toity like Nancy wants to think. Girl's just shy."

Phillip had reached over for the subs, and now his mouth fell open. "Shy? Sybill?"

"Sure is. Tries hard not to be, but it costs her some. Now you get that meatball back to your brother before it gets cold."

"WHY DO I HAVE TO CARE ABOUT a bunch of queer-os who lived two hundred years ago?"

Seth had his history book open, his mouth full of grape Bubblicious, and a stubborn look in his eye. After a ten-hour day of manual labor, Phillip wasn't in the mood for one of Seth's periodic snits.

"The founding fathers of our country were not queer-os."

Seth snorted and jabbed a finger at the full-page drawing of the Continental Congress. "They're wearing dorky wigs and girly clothes. That says queer-o to me."

"It was the fashion." He knew the kid was yanking his chain, but he couldn't seem to stop his leg from jerking on cue. "And the use of the word 'queer-o' to describe anyone because of their fashion sense or their lifestyle demonstrates ignorance and intolerance."

Seth merely smiled. Sometimes he just liked making Phillip grind his teeth the way he was doing now. "A guy wears a curly wig and high heels, he deserves what he gets."

Phillip sighed. It was another reaction Seth enjoyed. He didn't really mind the history crap. He'd aced the last test, hadn't he? But it was just plain boring to have to pick out one of the queer-os and write some dopey biography.

"You know what these guys were?" Phillip demanded, then narrowed his eyes in warning when Seth opened his mouth. "Don't say it. I'll tell you what they were. Rebels, troublemakers, and tough guys."

"Tough guys? Get real."

"Meeting the way they did, drawing up papers, making speeches? They were giving England, and most especially King George, the finger." He caught a flash of amused interest in Seth's eyes. "It wasn't the tea tax, not really. That was just the platform, the excuse. They weren't going to take any shit from England anymore. That's what it came down to."

"Making speeches and writing papers isn't like fighting."

"They were making sure there was something to fight for. You have to give people an alternative. If you want them to toss out Brand X, you have to give them Brand Y, and make it better, stronger, tastier. What if I told you Bubblicious is a rip-off?" Phillip asked, inspired as he snatched up the giant pack on Seth's desk.

"I like it okay." To prove it, Seth blew an enormous purple bubble.

"Yeah, but I'm telling you that it sucks and that the people who make it are creeps. You're not going to just toss it in the trash because I say so, right?"

"Damn straight."

"But if I gave you a new choice, if I told you about this Super Bubble Blow—"

"Super Bubble Blow? Man, you slay me."

"Shut up. SBB, it's better. It lasts longer, costs less. Chewing it'll make you and your friends, your family, your neighbors happier, stronger. SBB is the gum of the future, of *your* future. SBB is right!" Phillip added, putting a ring in his voice. "Bubblicious is wrong. With SBB you'll find personal and religious freedom, and no one will ever tell you that you can only have one piece."

"Cool." Phillip was weird all right, Seth thought with a grin, but he was fun. "Where do I sign up?"

With a half laugh, Phillip tossed the gum back on the desk. "You get the picture. These guys were the brains and the blood, and it was their job to get the people excited."

The brains and the blood, Seth thought. He liked it, and figured he could work it into his report. "Okay, maybe I'll pick Patrick Henry. He doesn't look as dorky as some of the other guys."

"Good. You can access information on him on the computer. When you hit the bibliography of books on him, print it out. The library in Baltimore's bound to have more of a selection than the one at school."

"Okay."

"And your composition for English is ready to turn in tomorrow?"

"Man, you never let up."

"Let's see what you've got."

"Jeez." Grumbling all the way, Seth dug into his binder and tugged out the single sheet.

It was titled "A Dog's Life" and described a typical day through the eyes of Foolish. Phillip felt his lips twitch as the canine narrator told of his delight in chasing rabbits, his irritation with bees, the thrill of hanging out with his good and wise friend Simon.

Christ, the kid was clever, he mused.

As Foolish ended his long, demanding day curled up on his bed, which he generously shared with his boy, Phillip handed the page back. "It's great. I guess we now know how you come by your story-telling talent naturally."

Seth's lashes lowered as he carefully slipped the composition back into place. "Ray was pretty smart and all, being a college professor."

"He was pretty smart. If he'd known about you, Seth, he'd have done something about it a lot sooner."

"Yeah, well . . ." Seth gave that Quinn shoulder jerk.

"I'm going to talk to the lawyer tomorrow. We may be able to speed things up a little, with Sybill's help."

Seth picked up his pencil to doodle on his blotter. Just shapes, circles, triangles, squares. "Maybe she'll change her mind."

"No, she won't."

"People do, all the time." He'd waited for weeks, ready to run if the Quinns had changed theirs. When they hadn't, he'd started to believe. But he was always ready to run.

"Some people keep their promises, no matter what. Ray did."

"She's not Ray. She came here to spy on me."

"She came to see if you were all right."

"Well, I am. So she can go."

"It's harder to stay," Phillip said quietly. "It takes more guts to stay. People are already talking about her. You know what that's like, when people look at you out of the corners of their eyes and whisper."

"Yeah. They're just jerks."

"Maybe, but it still stings."

He knew it did, but he gripped his pencil more tightly, added pressure to his doodling. "You've just got a case on her."

"I might. She sure is a looker. But if I do have a case on her, that doesn't change the basic facts. Kid, you haven't had that many people give a good damn about you in your life."

He waited until Seth's eyes slid over to his, held. "It took me a while, maybe too long, to give a good damn myself. I did what Ray asked me to, because I loved him."

"But you didn't want to do it."

"No, I didn't want to do it. It was a pain in the ass. You were a pain in the ass. But that started to change, little by little. I still didn't want to do it, it was still a pain in the ass, but somewhere along the way I was doing it for you as much as for Ray."

"You thought maybe I was his kid, and that pissed you off."

So much, Phillip thought, for adults believing they kept their secrets and sins from children. "Yeah. That was one little angle I couldn't get rid of until yesterday. I couldn't accept the idea that he might have cheated on my mother, or that you might be his son."

"But you put my name on the sign anyway."

Phillip stared a moment, then let out a half laugh. Sometimes, he realized, you do what's right without really thinking about it, and it makes a difference. "It belonged there, just like you belong here. And Sybill already gave a good damn about you, and now we know why. When somebody cares, it's just plain stupid to push them away."

"You think I should see her and talk to her and stuff." He'd thought about it himself. "I don't know what to say."

"You saw her and talked to her before you knew. You could try it that way."

"Maybe."

"You know how Grace and Anna are all wired up about this birthday dinner of yours next week?"

"Yeah." He lowered his head a little more so the huge grin didn't show. He couldn't believe it, not really. A birthday dinner and he got to pick the food, then like a party with pals the next day. Not that he was going to call it a party, because that was really lame when you were turning eleven.

"What do you think of asking her if she'd like to come over for that? The family dinner deal."

The grin vanished. "I don't know. I guess. She probably wouldn't want to come anyway."

"Why don't I ask her? You could cop another present out of it."

"Yeah?" A smile came back, sly and slow. "She'd have to make it a good one, too."

"That's the spirit."

FIFTEEN

THE NINETY-MINUTE APPOINT-
ment with the Baltimore lawyer had left Sybill jittery and exhausted.
She thought she'd been prepared for it; after all, she'd had two and a
half days to get ready, since she'd called first thing Monday morning
and had been squeezed into his schedule on Wednesday afternoon.

At least it was over, she told herself. Or this first stage of it was
over. It had been more difficult than she'd imagined to tell a perfect
stranger, professional or not, the secrets and flaws of her family. And
herself.

Now she had to cope with a cold, chilly rain, Baltimore traffic, and
her own less-than-stellar driving skills. Because she wanted to put the
traffic and the driving off as long as possible, she left her car in the
parking garage and faced the rain as a pedestrian.

Fall had already pushed summer back a big step in the city, she
noted, shivering as she scooted across the street at the crosswalk. The
trees were starting to turn, little blushes of red and gold edging the
leaves. The temperature had plummeted with the wet weather, and
the wind lashed out, tugging at her umbrella as she approached the
harbor.

She might have preferred a dry day, so she could have wandered,
explored, appreciated the nicely rehabbed old buildings, the tidy waterfront, the historic boats moored there. But it had its appeal, even in
a hard, frigid rain.

The water was stone-gray and choppy, its edges blurring into the sky
so that it wasn't possible to tell where either ended. Most of the visi-

tors and tourists had taken shelter indoors. Any who went by, went by
in a hurry.

She felt alone and insignificant standing in the rain, looking at the
water, wondering what the hell to do next.

With a sigh, she turned and studied the shops. She was going to a
birthday party on Friday, she reminded herself. It was time she bought
her nephew a present.

It TOOK HER MORE THAN AN
hour, comparing, selecting, rejecting art supplies. Her focus was so
narrowed, she didn't note the bright glee in the clerk's eyes as she
began to pile up her choices. It had been more than six years since
she'd bought Seth a gift, she thought. She was going to make up for
that.

It had to be just the right pencils, the perfect collection of chalks.
She examined watercolor brushes as if the wrong choice would mean
the end of the world as she knew it. She tested the weight and thick-
ness of drawing paper for twenty minutes, then agonized over a case
for all the supplies.

In the end, she decided simplicity was the answer. A young boy
would likely feel more comfortable with a plain walnut case. It would
be durable, too. If he took care, it was something he would have for
years.

And maybe, after enough of those years passed, he could look at it
and think of her kindly.

"Your nephew's going to be thrilled," the clerk informed her, giddy
as she rang up the purchases. "These are quality supplies."

"He's very talented." Distracted, Sybill began to nibble on her
thumbnail, a habit she'd broken years before. "You'll pack everything
carefully and box it?"

"Of course. Janice! Would you come over and give me a hand? Are
you from the area?" she asked Sybill.

"No, no, I'm not. A friend recommended your store."

"We very much appreciate it. Janice, we need to pack and box these
supplies."

"Do you gift-wrap?"

"Oh, I'm sorry, we don't. But there's a stationery store in this center. They have a lovely selection of gift wrap and ribbon and cards."

Oh, God, was all Sybill could think. What kind of paper did one choose for an eleven-year-old boy? Ribbon? Did boys want ribbons and bows?

"That comes to five hundred eighty-three dollars and sixty-nine cents." The clerk beamed at her. "How would you like to pay for that?"

"Five—" Sybill caught herself. Obviously, she decided, she'd lost her mind. Nearly six hundred dollars for a child's birthday? Oh, yes, she'd absolutely gone insane. "Do you take Visa?" she asked weakly.

"Absolutely." Still beaming, the clerk held out her hand for the gold card.

"I wonder if you could tell me . . ." She blew out a breath as she took out her Filofax and flipped to the Q's in the address book. "How to get to this address."

"Sure, it's practically around the corner."

It would be, Sybill thought. If Phillip had lived several blocks away, she might have resisted.

I T WAS A MISTAKE. SHE WARNED herself as she struggled back into the rain, fighting with two enormous shopping bags and an uncooperative umbrella. She had no business just dropping in on him.

He might not even be home. It was seven o'clock. He was probably out to dinner. She would be better off going back to her car and driving back to the Shore. The traffic was lighter now, if the rain wasn't.

At least she should call first. But damn it, her cell phone was in her purse, and she only had two hands. It was dark and it was raining and she probably wouldn't find his building anyway. If she didn't locate it within five minutes, she would turn around and go back to the parking garage.

She found the tall, sleekly elegant building within three and despite a case of nerves, stepped gratefully into the warm, dry lobby.

It was quiet and classy, with ornamental trees in copper pots, polished wood, a few deep-cushioned chairs in neutral tones. The familiar elegance would have relieved her if she hadn't felt like a wet rat invading a luxury liner.

She had to be crazy coming here like this. Hadn't she told herself when she'd set out for Baltimore that day that she wouldn't do this? She hadn't told him about the appointment because she hadn't wanted him to know she would be in Baltimore. He'd only try to persuade her to spend time with him.

For heaven's sake, she'd just seen him on Sunday. There was no sensible reason for this desperate urge to see him now. She would go back to St. Christopher's right now, because she had made a terrible mistake.

She cursed herself as she walked to the elevator, stepped inside, and pushed the button for the sixteenth floor.

What was wrong with her? Why was she doing this?

Oh, God, what if he was home but he wasn't alone? The sheer mortification of that possibility struck her like a blow to the stomach. They'd never said anything about exclusivity. He had a perfect right to see other women. For all she knew, he had a platoon of women. Which only proved she'd lost all common sense by becoming involved with him in the first place.

She couldn't possibly drop in on him like this, unannounced, uninvited, unexpected. Everything she'd been taught about manners, protocol, acceptable social behavior ordered her to stab the down button and leave. Every ounce of pride demanded that she turn around before she was humiliated.

She had no idea what it was that overcame all of that and pushed her out of the elevator and to the door of 1605.

Don't do this, don't do this, don't do this. The order screamed in her head even as she watched her finger depress the buzzer beside his door.

Oh, God, oh, God, oh, God, what have I done? What will I say? How can I explain?

Please don't be home, was her last desperate thought seconds before the door opened.

"Sybill?" His eyes widened in surprise, his lips curved.

Lord help her, she began to babble. "I'm so sorry. I should have called. I don't mean to—I shouldn't have . . . I had to come into the city, and I was just . . ."

"Here, let me have those. You buy out the store?" He was pulling the wet bags out of her icy hands. "You're freezing. Come inside."

"I should have called. I was—"

"Don't be silly." He dumped the bags and began to peel her out of her dripping raincoat. "You should have let me know you were coming into Baltimore today. When did you get in?"

"I—about two-thirty. I had an appointment. I was just—it's raining," she blurted out, hating herself. "I'm not used to driving in traffic.

Not really used to driving at all, actually, and I was a little nervous about it."

She rambled on, while he studied her, his brows lifted. Her cheeks were flushed, but he didn't think it was from the cold. Her voice was skittish, and that was new. And interesting. She couldn't seem to figure out what to do with her hands.

Though the raincoat had protected her neat slate-gray suit, her shoes were soaked and her hair was dewed with rain.

"You're wired up, aren't you?" he murmured. He put his hands on her arms, rubbed up and down to warm them. "Relax."

"I should have called," she said for the third time. "It was rude, presumptuous—"

"No, it wasn't. A little risky, maybe. If you'd gotten here twenty minutes earlier, I wouldn't have been home yet." He drew her a little closer. "Sybill, relax."

"Okay." She closed her eyes.

Amusement flickered into his own as he watched her take slow deep breaths.

"Does that breathing stuff really work?" he asked with a chuckle.

The irritation in her voice was barely noticeable, but it was there. "Studies have proven that the flow of oxygen and mental focus relieves stress."

"I bet. I've done studies of my own. Let's try it my way." He brought his mouth to hers, rubbed gently, persuasively until hers softened, yielded, warmed. His tongue danced lightly over hers, teasing out a sigh. "Yeah, that works for me," he murmured, brushing his cheek over her damp hair. "Works just fine for me. How about you?"

"Oral stimulation is also a proven remedy for stress."

He chuckled. "I'm in danger of becoming crazy about you. How about some wine?"

She didn't care to analyze his definition of crazy just then. "I wouldn't mind one glass. I shouldn't, really. I'm driving."

Not tonight you're not, he thought, but only smiled. "Sit down. I'll be right back."

She went back to the concentrated breathing as he slipped into another room. After her nerves settled a bit, she studied the apartment.

A conversation pit in deep forest-green dominated the living area. In its center was a square coffee table. Riding over it was a large sailboat in what she recognized as Murano glass. A pair of green iron candlesticks held fat white candles.

At the far side of the room there was a small bar with a pair of black leather stools. Behind it was a vintage poster for Nuits-St.-Georges Burgundy, depicting an eighteenth-century French cavalry officer sitting on a cask with a glass, a pipe, and a very satisfied smile.

The walls were white and splashed here and there with art. A framed print of a stylish poster for Tattinger champagne, with an elegant woman, surely that was Grace Kelly, in a sleek black evening gown behind a slim flute of bubbling wine, hung over a round glass table with curved steel legs. There was a Joan Miró print, an elegant reproduction of Alphonse Mucha's *Automne*.

Lamps were both sparely modern and elegantly Deco. The carpet was thick and pale gray, the uncurtained window wide and wet with rain.

She thought the room displayed masculine, eclectic, and witty taste. She was admiring a brown leather footstool in the shape of a barnyard pig when he returned with two glasses.

"I like your pig."

"He caught my eye. Why don't you tell me about what must have been a very interesting day?"

"I didn't even ask if you had plans." She noted he was dressed in a soft black sweatshirt and jeans and wasn't wearing any shoes. But that didn't mean—

"I do now." Taking her hand he led her across to the deep cushioned U-shaped sofa. "You saw the lawyer this afternoon."

"You knew about that."

"He's a friend. He keeps me up to date." And, Phillip admitted to himself, he'd been acutely disappointed when she hadn't called him to let him know she was coming to the city. "How'd it go?"

"Well, I think. He seems confident that the guardianship will go through. I couldn't persuade my mother to make a statement, though."

"She's angry with you."

Sybill took a quick swallow of wine. "Yes, she's angry, and no doubt deeply regrets the momentary lapse that allowed her to tell me what happened between her and your father."

He took her hand. "It's difficult for you. I'm sorry."

She looked down at their linked fingers. How easily he touched, she thought absently. As if it was the most natural thing in the world. "I'm a big girl. Since it's doubtful that this little incident, however newsworthy it is in St. Christopher's, will ripple across the Atlantic to Paris, she'll get over it."

"Will you?"

"Life moves on. Once the legalities are dealt with, there won't be any motive for Gloria to make trouble for you and your family. For Seth. She will, I imagine, continue to make trouble for herself, but there's nothing I can do about that. Nothing I want to do about it."

A cold streak, Phillip wondered, or a defense? "Even after the legalities are dealt with, Seth will still be your nephew. None of us would stop you from seeing him, or being part of his life."

"I'm not a part of his life," she said flatly. "And as he makes his life, it would only be distracting and unconstructive for him to have reminders of his old life. It's a miracle that what Gloria did to him hasn't scarred him more deeply. Whatever sense of security he has, it's due to your father, to you and your family. He doesn't trust me, Phillip, and he has no reason to."

"Trust has to be earned. You have to want to earn it."

She rose, walked to the dark window and looked out on the city lights that wavered behind the rain. "When you came to live with Ray and Stella Quinn, when they were helping you change your life, remake yourself, did you maintain contact with your mother, with your friends in Baltimore?"

"My mother was a part-time whore who resented every breath I took, and my friends were dealers, junkies, and thieves. I didn't want contact with them any more than they wanted it with me."

"Regardless." She turned back to face him. "You understand my point."

"I understand it, but I don't agree with it."

"I imagine Seth does."

He set his glass aside as he rose. "He wants you there on his birthday Friday."

"You want me there," she corrected. "And I very much appreciate you for persuading Seth to allow it."

"Sybill—"

"Speaking of which," she said quickly. "I found your art store." She gestured toward the bags he'd set by the door.

"That?" He stared at the bags. "*All* of that?"

Immediately she began to nibble on her thumbnail. "It's too much, isn't it? I knew it. I got caught up. I can take some of it back or just keep it for myself. I don't take enough time to draw anymore."

He'd walked over to examine the bags, the boxes inside. "*All* of this?" With a laugh, he straightened, shook his head. "He'll love it. He'll go nuts."

"I don't want him to think of it as a bribe, like I'm trying to buy his affection. I don't know what got into me. Once I started, I couldn't seem to stop."

"If I were you, I'd stop questioning my motives for doing something nice, something impulsive, and just a bit over the top." Gently he tugged at her hand. "And stop biting your nails."

"I'm not biting my nails. I never . . ." Insulted, she looked down at her hand, saw the ragged thumbnail. "Oh, God, I'm biting my nails. I haven't done that since I was fifteen. Where's my nail file?"

Phillip edged closer to her as she grabbed her handbag and took out a small manicure set. "Were you a nervous kid?"

"Hmm?"

"A nail-biter."

"It was a bad habit, that's all." Smoothly, efficiently, she began to repair the damage.

"A nervous habit, wouldn't you say, Dr. Griffin?"

"Perhaps. But I broke it."

"Not entirely. Nail biting," he murmured, moving toward her. "Migraines."

"Only occasionally."

"Skipping meals," he continued. "Don't bother to tell me you've eaten tonight. I know better. It seems to me that your breathing and concentrating isn't quite doing the job on stress. Let's try my way again."

"I really have to go." She was already being drawn into his arms. "Before it gets too late."

"It's already too late." He brushed his lips over hers once, twice. "You really have to stay. It's dark, it's cold, it's raining," he murmured, nibbling on, toying with her lips. "And you're a terrible driver."

"I'm just . . ." The nail file slipped out of her fingers. "Out of practice."

"I want to take you to bed. I want to take you to my bed." The next kiss was deeper, longer, wetter. "I want to slip you out of that lovely little suit, piece by piece, and see what's going on under it."

"I don't know how you do this." Her breath was already coming too fast, her body going too soft. "I can't keep my thoughts aligned when you're touching me."

"I like them scattered." He slid his hands under her trim jacket until his thumbs skimmed the sides of her breasts. "I like you scattered. And trembling. It makes me want to do all sorts of things to you when you tremble."

Quick flares of heat, sharp stabs of ice were already racing over her. "What sorts of . . . things?"

He made a low, delighted sound against the side of her throat. "I'll show you," he offered, and picked her up.

"I don't do this." She pushed back her hair, staring at him as he carried her into the bedroom.

"Do what?"

"Go to a man's apartment, let him carry me to bed. I don't do this."

"We'll just consider it a change in behavioral patterns then." He kissed her thoroughly before laying her down on the bed. "Caused by . . ." He paused to light a trio of candles on an iron stand in the corner. "Direct stimulation."

"That could work." The candlelight did wonders for an already impossibly handsome face. "It's just that you're so attractive."

He chuckled and slid onto the big bed to nip at her chin. "And you're so weak."

"Not usually. Actually, my sexual appetites are slightly below average, ordinarily."

"Is that so?" He lifted her just enough to slip the jacket away.

"Yes. I've found, for myself . . . oh . . . that while a sexual interlude can be pleasant . . ." Her breath caught as his fingers slowly released the buttons of her blouse.

"Pleasant?" he prompted.

"It rarely, if ever, has more than a momentary impact. Of course, that's due to my hormonal makeup."

"Of course." He lowered his mouth to the soft swell of her breasts that rose temptingly above the cups of her bra. And licked.

"But—but—" She clenched her fists at her sides as his tongue swept under the fabric and shot off shock waves.

"You're trying to think."

"I'm trying to see if I can."

"How's it going?"

"Not very well."

"You were telling me about your hormonal makeup," he reminded her, watching her face as he tugged her skirt down over her hips.

"I was? Oh, well . . . I had a point." Somewhere, she thought vaguely, a shiver going through her as he traced a fingertip over her midriff.

He saw with delight that she wore those sexy thigh-hugging stockings again, this time in sheer smoky-black. He imagined she'd considered that the black bra and panties were proper coordinates.

He thanked God for her practical mind.

"Sybill, I love what goes on under your clothes."

He moved his mouth to her belly, tasted heat and woman, felt her muscles quiver. She made a helpless little sound in her throat as her body shifted under him.

He could take her anywhere. The power of knowing that flooded him like wine. As he took her, slowly now, wanting them both to linger at each stage, he let himself sink.

He peeled those stockings down those lovely, long thighs, following the path with his mouth all the way to her toes. Her skin was creamy, smooth, fragrant. Perfect. And only more alluring when it quivered lightly under his.

He slipped fingertips and tongue beneath that silky fantasy snug over her hips in teasing strokes so that she arched, shuddered, and moaned. Heat was there. Centered just there. Wet, arousing heat.

And when the teasing drove them both mad, he stripped that barrier aside and plunged into the hot taste of her. She cried out, her body rising, her hands fisting in his hair as he spun her to peak. When she was limp and gasping he took more.

And showed her more.

He could have anything. Everything. She was powerless to deny him, to stem the tidal wave of sensations that swamped her. The world had become him, only him. The flavor of his skin in her mouth, the texture of his hair against her flesh or in her hands, the movement of his muscle beneath her fingers.

Murmurs, his murmurs, echoed in her spinning head. The sound of her own name, a whisper of pleasure. Her breath sobbed out as she found his mouth with hers, poured everything she was into that hot flood of emotion.

Again, again, again. The urgent demand circled in her head, as she clung and gave, gave, gave.

Now it was his hands that fisted, on either side of her head as the shock of feeling slammed into him, flashing against desire, melting into a need so urgent it was pain.

She opened for him, a breathless invitation. And filling her, sinking inside her, he lifted his head and watched her face in the golden shaft of candlelight.

Her eyes were on his, her lips parted as the breath trembled through them. Something clicked, a lock opening, a connection made. He found his hands groping for hers, fingers twining together.

Slow, smooth, with each movement a fresh shock of pleasure. Soft, silky, a promise in the dark. He saw her eyes glaze, felt the tension, the ripple, and closed his mouth over hers to capture the gasp as she climaxed.

"Stay with me." He murmured it as his lips roamed her face, as his body moved in hers. "Stay with me."

What choice did she have? She was defenseless against what he brought to her, helpless to refuse what he demanded in return.

The pressure built again, an internal demand that refused to be denied. When she tumbled free, he gathered her close and fell with her.

"I WAS GOING TO COOK," HE said sometime later when she lay over him, limp and speechless. "But I think we'll order in. And eat in bed."

"All right." She kept her eyes closed, commanding herself to listen to the beat of his heart and pay no attention to the voice of her own.

"You can sleep in tomorrow." Idly he toyed with her hair. He wanted her there in the morning, badly wanted her there in the morning. It was something to think about later. "Maybe do some sightseeing or shopping. If you hang around for most of the day, you can follow me home."

"All right." She simply didn't have the strength to assert herself. Besides, she told herself, it made sense. The Baltimore Beltway was confusing, unfamiliar ground. She would enjoy spending a few hours exploring the city. It was certainly foolish to drive all the way back tonight, in the rain, in the dark.

"You're awfully agreeable."

"You caught me in a weak moment. I'm hungry, and I don't want to face driving tonight. And I miss the city, any city."

"Ah, so it's not my irresistible charm and awesome sexual prowess."

She couldn't stop the smile. "No, but they don't hurt."

"I'll make you an egg-white omelette in the morning, and you'll be my slave."

She managed to laugh. "We'll see about that."

She was afraid she was entirely too close to a slavish condition now. The heart she was desperately trying to ignore continued to insist that she'd fallen in love with him.

That, she warned herself, would be a much bigger, more permanent mistake, than knocking on his door on a rainy evening.

SIXTEEN

WHEN A TWENTY-NINE-YEAR-OLD woman changed her clothes three times before attending an eleven-year-old boy's birthday party, she was in trouble.

Sybill lectured herself on this simple fact even as she stripped off a white silk blouse—white silk, for Lord's sake, what had she been thinking of—and exchanged it for a teal turtleneck.

She was going to a simple, informal family dinner party, she reminded herself, not a diplomatic reception. Which, she admitted with a sigh, wouldn't have posed nearly as much of a social or fashion dilemma. She knew exactly what to wear, how to behave, and what was expected of her at a formal reception, a state dinner, a gala, a charity ball.

It was a pathetic statement on her narrow social experience, she concluded, that she knew neither how to dress nor how to behave at her own nephew's birthday dinner.

She slipped a long chain of silver beads over her head, took it off, cursed herself and put it on again. Underdressed, overdressed, what did it matter? She wouldn't fit in anyway. She would pretend she did, the Quinns would pretend she did, and everyone would be desperately relieved when she said her good-byes and went away.

Two hours, she told herself. She would only stay two hours. Surely she could survive that. Everyone would be polite, would avoid awkward or nasty scenes for Seth's sake.

She picked up her brush to smooth her hair back, then secured it with a clip at the nape of her neck before critically studying herself in the mirror. She looked confident, she decided. Pleasant, nonthreatening.

Except . . . maybe the color of the sweater was too vivid, too bold. Gray might be better, or brown.

Good God.

The ringing of the phone was such a welcome diversion, she all but leapt on it. "Yes, hello, Dr. Griffin."

"Syb, you're still there. I was afraid you'd taken off."

"Gloria." Her stomach plummeted to her unsteady knees. Very carefully she lowered herself to the side of the bed. "Where are you?"

"Oh, I'm around. Hey, I'm sorry I ditched you the other night. I was messed up."

Messed up, Sybill thought. It was a good term for certain conditions. From the rapid pace of Gloria's speech, she assumed her sister was messed up even now. "You stole money out of my wallet."

"I said I was messed up, didn't I? I panicked, you know, needed some cash. I'll pay you back. You talk to those Quinn bastards?"

"I had a meeting with the Quinn family, as I promised I would." Sybill uncurled the hand she'd bunched into a fist and spoke evenly. "I'd given them my word, Gloria, that both of us would meet them to discuss Seth."

"Well, I didn't give mine, did I? What'd they say? What're they going to do?"

"They say you were working as a prostitute, that you abused Seth physically, that you allowed your clients to make sexual advances toward him."

"Liars. Fucking liars. They just want to kick me around, that's all. They—"

"They said," Sybill went on, coolly now, "that you accused Professor Quinn of molesting you nearly a dozen years ago, intimated that Seth was his. That you blackmailed him, that you sold Seth to him. That he gave you more than a hundred and fifty thousand dollars."

"All bullshit."

"Not all, but part. Your part could be accurately described as bullshit. Professor Quinn didn't touch you, Gloria, not twelve years ago, not twelve months ago."

"How do you know? How the hell do you know what—"

"Mother told me that Raymond Quinn was your father."

There was silence for a moment, then only Gloria's quick breathing. "Then he owed me, didn't he? He *owed* me. Big-deal college professor with his boring little life. He owed me plenty. It was his fault. It was all his fault. All those years, he didn't give me dick. He took in scum from the street, but he didn't give me dick."

"He didn't know you existed."

"I told him, didn't I? I told him what he'd done, and who I was and what he was going to do about it. And what does he do? He just stares at me. He wants to talk to my mother. He's not going to give me a fucking dollar until he talks to my mother."

"So you went to the dean and claimed he'd molested you."

"Put the fear of God into him. Tight-assed son of a bitch."

She'd been right, Sybill thought. Her instincts when she'd walked into that room at the police station had been right after all. It was a mistake. This woman was a stranger. "And when that didn't work, you used Seth."

"Kid's got his eyes. Anybody can see that." There was a sucking noise, a hiss, as Gloria dragged on a cigarette. "Changed his tune once he got a look at the kid."

"He gave you money for Seth."

"It wasn't enough. He owed me. Listen, Sybill . . ." Her voice shifted, whined and trembled. "You don't know what it's like. I've been raising that kid on my own since he was a baby and that prick Jerry DeLauter took off. Nobody was going to help me. Our dear mother wouldn't even accept a phone call from me, and that prissy freak she married and tried to pass off as my father wouldn't either. I could've dumped the kid, you know. I could've dumped him anytime. The money Social Services doles out for a kid is pitiful."

Sybill stared out through her terrace doors. "Does it always come back to money?"

"It's easy to look down when you've got plenty of it," Gloria snapped. "You never had to hustle, you never had to worry. Perfect daughter always had plenty of everything. Now it's my turn."

"I would have helped you, Gloria. I tried to years ago when you brought Seth to New York."

"Yeah, yeah, same old tune. Get a job, straighten up, get clean, get dry. Shit, I don't want to dance to that, get it? This is my life I'm living here, baby sister, not yours. You couldn't pay me to live yours. And that's my kid, not yours."

"What's today, Gloria?"

"What? What the hell are you talking about?"

"Today is September twenty-eighth. Does that mean anything to you?"

"What the hell's it supposed to mean? It's fucking Friday."

And your son's eleventh birthday, Sybill thought and straightened her shoulders, took her stand. "You won't get Seth back, Gloria, though we're both aware that that's not your goal."

"You can't—"

"Shut up. Let's stop playing games. I know you. I haven't wanted to, I've preferred to pretend otherwise, but I know you. If you want help, I'm still willing to get you into a clinic, to pay the bill for rehab."

"I don't need your goddamn help."

"Fine, that's your choice. You won't get another penny out of the Quinns, you won't come near Seth again. I've given my deposition to their lawyer and a notarized statement to Seth's caseworker. I've told them everything, and if necessary, I'll testify in court that Seth's wishes and his best interest are served by his remaining, permanently, with the Quinns. I'll do everything I can to see that you don't use him anymore."

"You bitch." The hiss was filled with anger, but under it was shock. "You think you can screw me this way? You think you can toss me off and side with those bastards against me? I'll ruin you."

"You can certainly try, but you won't succeed. You made your deal, now it's done."

"You're just like her, aren't you?" Gloria spit the words out like bullets. "You're just like our ice cunt of a mother. Perfect society princess, and underneath you're nothing but bitch."

Maybe I am, Sybill thought wearily, maybe I'm going to have to be. "You blackmailed Raymond Quinn, who'd done nothing to harm you. It worked. At least it worked well enough for you to be paid. It won't work with his sons, Gloria. And it won't work with me. Not anymore."

"Won't it? Well, try this. I want a hundred thousand. A hundred thousand, or I'm going to the press. *National Enquirer, Hard Copy.* Let's see how fast your lousy books sell once I tell my story."

"Sales will likely increase twenty percent," Sybill said mildly. "I won't be blackmailed, Gloria. You do what you like. And think about this. You're facing criminal charges in Maryland, and there's a restraining order against you to keep you away from Seth. The Quinns have evidence. I've seen it," she continued, thinking of the letters Gloria had written. "Further criminal charges for extortion and child abuse may be brought. I'd cut my losses if I were you."

She hung up on the spew of obscenities and, closing her eyes, lowered her head between her knees. The nausea was a greasy sea in her stomach, the sneaky edge of a migraine was creeping closer. She couldn't stop the trembling. She'd held it off during the phone call, but she couldn't stop it now.

She stayed just as she was until she could control her breathing again, until the worst threat of sickness receded. Then she rose, took one of her pills to ward off the migraine and added blusher to her pale cheeks. She gathered her purse, Seth's gifts, a jacket against the chill, and left.

T HE DAY HAD BEEN ENDLESS. How was a guy supposed to sit through hours and hours of school on his birthday? I mean, he was double ones now, and everything. He was going to get pizza and french fries and chocolate cake and ice cream and probably even presents.

He'd never actually had a birthday present before, Seth mused. Not that he could remember, anyway. He'd probably end up with clothes and shit, but it would still be a present.

If anybody ever showed up.

"What's taking them so long?" Seth demanded, again.

Determined to be patient, Anna continued to slice potatoes for the homemade fries that Seth had requested as part of his birthday menu. "They'll be along."

"It's almost six. How come I had to come home after school instead of going to the boatyard?"

"Because," Anna said, and left it at that. "Stop poking into everything, will you?" she added as Seth opened the refrigerator, again. Shut it, again. "You're going to be stuffing your face soon enough."

"I'm starving."

"I'm making the fries right now, aren't I?"

"I thought Grace was going to make them."

Steely-eyed, Anna stared at him over her shoulder. "Are you suggesting that I can't make french fries?"

He was bored and restless enough to be pleased that he'd jabbed her ego. "Well, she makes really good ones."

"Oh." She turned completely around. "And I don't."

"You do okay. Anyway, we'll have the pizza." He nearly pulled it off, but snorted out a chuckle.

"Brat." Anna made a laughing dive at him. He danced away howling.

"That's the door, that's the door. I'll get it!" He raced off, leaving Anna grinning after him.

But the wicked laughter faded from his eyes when he yanked open the door and saw Sybill on the porch. "Oh. Hi."

Her heart sank, but she fixed on a polite smile. "Happy birthday."

"Yeah, thanks." Watching her cautiously, he opened the door.

"I appreciate you inviting me." At a loss, she held out both shopping bags. "Are you allowed to have your gifts?"

"Sure, I guess." Then his eyes widened. "All that?"

She nearly sighed. He sounded so much like Phillip had. "It all sort of goes together."

"Cool. Hey, it's Grace." Hampered by the bags, which he held now, he bumped past her onto the porch.

The joy in his voice, the quick, delighted smile on his face was such a marked contrast from the way he'd looked at her, Sybill's sinking heart cracked.

"Hey, Grace! Hey, Aubrey! I'll tell Anna you guys are here."

He darted inside again, leaving Sybill standing by the open door without a clue how to proceed. Grace got out of the car and smiled. "Sounds like he's excited."

"Yes, well . . ." She watched Grace set a bag on the hood of the car, followed by a large clear-plastic cake holder. Then she reached in to unstrap a babbling Aubrey from her car seat. "Do you need a hand?"

"Actually, I could use two. Just a minute, baby. If you keep wriggling . . ." She tossed another smile over her shoulder as Sybill walked over. "She's been wired all day. Seth is Aubrey's favorite person."

"Seth! He's got a birthday. We baked a cake."

"We sure did." Grace hauled Aubrey out, then passed her to an astonished Sybill. "Would you mind? She wanted to wear that dress, but the run from here to the house is bound to be a disaster."

"Oh, well . . ." Sybill found herself staring down into a beaming, angelic face and holding a bouncing little body dressed in party-pink ruffles.

"We're having a party," Aubrey told her and put both her hands on Sybill's cheeks to ensure her full attention. "I'll have a party next time when I'm three. You can come."

"Thank you."

"You smell pretty. I do, too."

"You certainly do." Sybill's initial stiffness couldn't stand up under that cheerfully charming smile. Phillip's Jeep pulled in behind Grace's, and most of the stiffness returned as Cam slid out of the passenger seat and shot her a cool, unmistakably warning look.

Aubrey let out a shriek of greeting. "Hi! Hi!"

"Hi, there, beautiful." Cam walked over, kissed Aubrey lightly on her comically pursed lips, then aimed those flinty eyes at Sybill. "Hello, Dr. Griffin."

"Sybill." Well able to interpret the chilly exchange, Phillip strode over, laid a supporting hand on her shoulder, and leaned in for the kiss Aubrey was offering. "Hi, there, sweetie."

"I have a new dress."

"And you look stunning in it."

In the way of females, Aubrey deserted Sybill without a glance and held out her arms to Phillip. He managed the transfer easily, settling her on his hip. "Been here long?" he asked Sybill.

"No, I just got here." She watched Cam carry three large cardboard boxes of pizza into the house. "Phillip, I don't want to cause any—"

"Let's go inside." He took her hand, pulling her along. "We've got to get this party going, don't we, Aub?"

"Seth gets presents. They're secrets." She whispered it and leaned in close. "What are they?"

"Uh-uh, I'm not telling." He set her down when they stepped into the house, gave her frilled bottom a friendly pat, and sent her off. She shouted for Seth and scrambled toward the kitchen. "She'll blab."

Determined to make it work, Sybill put her smile back in place. "I won't."

"Nope. You can just wait for it. I'm going to grab a fast shower before Cam beats me to it and uses all the hot water." He gave her a quick, absent kiss. "Anna'll get you a drink," he added as he headed upstairs.

"Great." On a huff of breath, Sybill steeled herself to deal with the Quinns alone.

The kitchen was pandemonium. Aubrey was squealing, Seth was talking a mile a minute. Potatoes were frying, with Grace manning the stove since Cam had Anna trapped against the refrigerator with a gleam of pure lust in his eyes.

"You know how I get when I see you in an apron."

"I know how you get when you see me breathe." And she hoped it would never change. Nonetheless, she narrowed her eyes at him. "Hands off, Quinn. I'm busy."

"You've been slaving over a hot stove. You really ought to take a shower. With me."

"I'm not going to—" She spotted the movement out of the corner of her eye. "There you are, Sybill." In a move that looked very practiced, and very effective to Sybill, Anna shifted and jammed her elbow into her husband's stomach. "What can I get you to drink?"

"Ah . . . the coffee smells wonderful, thank you."

"I'll take a beer." Cam snagged one out of the fridge. "And go clean up." He aimed that look at Sybill again, then strode out.

"Seth, stay out of those bags," Anna ordered as she pulled down a mug. "No gifts yet." She'd made the decision to keep him from opening Sybill's gifts until after dinner. She calculated that his aunt would make her excuses and run as quickly as she could manage it after the little ritual was complete.

"Man! Is it my birthday or what?"

"Yes, if you live through it. Why don't you take Aubrey into the other room? Entertain her for a while. We'll eat as soon as Ethan gets here."

"Well, where is he, anyway?" Grumbling, Seth stalked out with Aubrey on his heels and didn't catch the quick grin Grace and Anna exchanged.

"That goes for you dogs, too." Anna gave Foolish a nudge with her foot and pointed her finger. With canine sighs, both dogs clipped out of the kitchen.

"Peace." Anna closed her eyes to absorb it. "Momentary peace."

"Is there anything I can do to help?"

With a shake of her head, Anna passed over the mug of coffee. "I think we've got it under control. Ethan should be here any minute. In the big surprise." She walked to the window to look out through the gathering dark. "I hope you've brought an adolescent appetite," she added. "Tonight's menu consists of pepperoni-and-sausage pizza, peanut-oil fries, homemade hot fudge sundaes, and Grace's killer chocolate cake."

"We'll all be in the hospital," Sybill commented before she thought it through. Even as she winced, Anna was laughing.

"We who are about to die salute you. Uh-oh, there's Ethan." She'd lowered her voice to a stage whisper. At the stove, Grace dropped her slotted spoon with a clatter. "Did you burn yourself?"

"No, no." Chuckling weakly, Grace stepped back. "No, I'm, ah . . . I'm just going to run out and . . . help Ethan."

"All right but—hmmm," Anna finished when Grace hurried past

her and out the door. "Jumpy," she muttered, then hit the outside lights. "It's not quite dark yet, but it will be by the time we finish this." She salvaged the last of the fries and switched off the stove. "Cam and Phillip better put a fire under it. Oh, God, it's cute! Can you see?"

Too curious to resist, Sybill joined her at the kitchen window. She saw Grace standing on the dock, caught in the last light of the day, and Ethan just stepping onto it. "It's a boat," she murmured. "A little sailboat."

"A ten-footer. They call it a pram." Anna's smile nearly split her face. "The three of them have been building it over at Ethan's old house—the one he rents out? The tenants let them use the shed over there so Seth wouldn't know about it."

"They built it for him?"

"Whenever they could steal an hour. Oh, he's going to love it. Well, what's this?"

"What?"

"That," Anna said and stared hard through the glass. She could see Grace talking, her hands locked together, Ethan staring at her. Then he lowered his head to hers. "I hope there's not any . . ." She trailed off as Ethan drew Grace close, buried his face in her hair and rocked. And her arms came up around him. "Oh, oh." Tears flooded Anna's eyes. "She must be—she's pregnant! She's just told him. I know it. Oh, look!" She gripped Sybill's shoulder when Ethan scooped a laughing Grace up into his arms. "Isn't that beautiful?"

The two of them were wrapped around each other, making one silhouette in the last light of day. "Yes, yes, it is."

"Look at me." Laughing at herself, Anna yanked off a paper towel and blew her nose. "I'm a mess. This is going to get to me, I know it is. I'm going to want one." She blew again, sighed. "I was so sure I could wait a year or two. I'm never going to be able to wait that long now. Not for that. I can just see Cam when I—" She stopped herself. "Sorry," she said with a watery laugh.

"It's all right. It's lovely that you're so happy for them. That you're so happy for yourself. This is really a family occasion, especially now. Anna, I really should go."

"Don't be a coward," Anna said, pointing her finger. "You're here, and you're going to have to face this nightmare of indigestion and noise just like the rest of us."

"I simply think—" All she could do was close her mouth when the door burst open. Ethan was still carrying Grace and the pair of them wore huge smiles.

"Anna, we're having a baby." Ethan made the announcement with a catch in his voice.

"What, am I blind?" She brushed Ethan aside to kiss Grace first. "I've had my nose to the window. Oh, congratulations!" Then threw her arms around both of them. "I'm so happy."

"You have to be godmother." Ethan turned his face to kiss her. "We wouldn't have gotten this far without you."

"Oh, that does it." Anna burst into tears just as Phillip walked in.

"What's going on? Why's Anna crying? Jesus, Ethan, what happened to Grace?"

"I'm fine. I'm wonderful. I'm pregnant."

"No kidding?" He plucked her out of Ethan's arms to kiss her lavishly.

"What the hell is going on in here?" Cam demanded.

Still holding Grace, Phillip grinned at him. "We're having a baby."

"Oh, yeah?" He arched his eyebrow. "How does Ethan feel about the two of you?"

"Ha-ha," was Phillip's comment as he set Grace carefully on her feet.

"You feel all right?" Cam asked her.

"I feel terrific."

"You look terrific." Cam drew her into his arms, rubbed his chin over her head. And the tenderness with which he did both had Sybill blinking in surprise. "Nice going, bro," Cam murmured to Ethan.

"Thanks. Can I have my wife back now?"

"I'm nearly done." Cam held Grace at arm's length. "If he doesn't take good care of you and the little Quinn in there, I'll beat the hell out of him for you."

"Are we ever going to eat?" Seth demanded, then stopped at the kitchen doorway and stared. "Why're Anna and Grace crying?" He swept an accusing look around the room, including Sybill in the heat. "What happened?"

"We're happy." Grace sniffled and accepted the tissue that Sybill dug out of her purse. "I'm going to have a baby."

"Really? Wow. Wow. That's cool. That's way cool. Does Aub know?"

"No, Ethan and I will tell her, in a little while. But now I'm going to go get her because there's something you need to see. Outside."

"Outside." He started for the door, but Phillip stepped neatly in his path.

"Not yet."

"What is it? Come on, move. Jeez. Let me see what's out there."

"We should blindfold him," Phillip considered.

"We should gag him," was Cam's suggestion.

Ethan took care of matters by hauling Seth over his shoulder. When Grace brought Aubrey in, Ethan winked, shifted the wriggling Seth, and headed out the door.

"You're not throwing me in again!" Seth's voice rang with terrified delight and giggles. "Come on, guys, the water's really cold."

"Wimp," Cam sneered when Seth lifted his face from Ethan's back.

"If you try," Seth warned, eyes dancing with joy and challenge, "I'm taking at least one of you with me."

"Yeah, yeah, big talk." Phillip pushed Seth's face back down. "Ready?" he asked when everyone was assembled at the edge of the water. "Good. Do it, Ethan."

"Man, the water's *cold*!" Seth began, ready to scream when Ethan dropped him. But he was set on his feet and he was turned to face the pretty little wooden boat with sky-blue sails that rippled lightly in the evening wind. "What—where did that come from?"

"The sweat of our brows," Phillip said dryly while Seth gaped at the boat.

"Is it—who's buying it?"

"It's not for sale," Cam said simply.

"It . . . is it . . ." It couldn't be, he thought, while his heart thumped with nerves and hope and shock. But hope was paramount. In the past year he'd learned to hope. "Is it mine?"

"You're the only one with a birthday around here," Cam reminded him. "Don't you want a closer look?"

"It's mine?" He whispered it first, with such staggered delight and shock that Sybill felt her eyes sting. *"Mine?"* He exploded with it as he whirled around. This time the sheer joy on his face closed her throat. "To keep?"

"You're a good sailor," Ethan told him quietly. "She's a tight little boat. She's steady, but she moves."

"You built her for me." His gaze shot from Ethan's face to Phillip's to Cam's. "For me?"

"Nah, we built her for some other brat." Cam gave him a light swat on the side of the head. "What do you think? Go take a look."

"Yeah." His voice quavered as he turned. "Yeah, can I get in her? Can I sit in her?"

"For Christ's sake, she's yours, isn't she?" His voice rough with emotion, Cam grabbed Seth's hand and hauled him onto the dock.

"I think this is a guy thing," Anna murmured. "Let's give them a few minutes to pull themselves together."

"They love him so much." Sybill watched another moment as the four males made noises over a little wooden boat. "I don't think I realized it, really, until just now."

"He loves them, too." Grace pressed her cheek to Aubrey's.

AND IT WAS MORE. SYBILL thought later as she picked at the meal in the noisy kitchen. It had been that shock on Seth's face. The utter disbelief that someone loved him, could love him enough to understand his heart's desire. And understanding, make the effort to give it.

The pattern of his life, she thought wearily, had been broken, shifted, then reformed. And all before she'd really come into it. Now it was set, the way it was meant to be set.

She didn't belong here. She couldn't stay here. She couldn't bear it.

"I really should go," she said with a well-mannered smile. "I want to thank you for—"

"Seth hasn't opened your gift yet," Anna interrupted. "Why don't we let him rip, then we'll have some cake."

"Cake!" Aubrey whacked her palms on her high chair. "Blow the candles out and make a wish."

"Soon," Grace told her. "Seth, take Sybill into the living room so you can open your gift."

"Sure." He waited for Sybill to stand, then with a jerk of his shoulder started out.

"I got it in Baltimore," she began, miserably awkward, "so if it doesn't suit, if you don't like it, Phillip could exchange things for you."

"Okay." He pulled a box out of the first bag, sat Indian-style on the floor, and within seconds was tearing the paper it had taken her untold agonies to choose to shreds.

"You could have used newspaper," Phillip told her and, chuckling, nudged her into a chair.

"It's a box," Seth said, puzzled, and Sybill's heart sank at his disinterested tone.

"Yes, well . . . I kept the receipt. So you can take it back and get whatever you'd like."

"Yeah, okay." But he caught the hard beam in Phillip's eye and made an effort. "It's a nice box." But he wanted to roll his eyes. Then he idly flicked the brass hook, flipped the top. "Holy shit!"

"Christ, Seth." Cam muttered it, glancing over his shoulder as Anna walked in from the kitchen.

"Man, look at all this stuff! It's got, like, everything. Charcoals and pastels and pencils." Now he looked at Sybill with that staggered shock. "I get to have it all?"

"It goes together." Nervous, she twisted her silver beads around her finger. "You draw so well, I thought . . . You may want to experiment with other mediums. The other box has more supplies."

"More?"

"Watercolors and brushes, some paper. Ah . . ." She eased onto the floor as Seth gleefully ripped into the second box. "You may decide you like acrylics, or pen and ink, but I lean toward watercolors myself, so I thought you might like to try your hand at it."

"I don't know how to do it."

"Oh, well, it's a simple process, really." She leaned over to take one of the brushes and began to explain the basic technique. As she spoke, she forgot her nerves, smiled at him.

The light from the lamp slanted over her face, caught something, something in her eyes that jiggled at the corners of his memory.

"Did you have a picture on the wall? Flowers, white flowers in a blue vase?"

Her fingers tightened on the brush. "Yes, in my bedroom in New York. One of my watercolors. Not a very good one."

"And you had colored bottles on a table. Lots of them, different sizes and stuff."

"Perfume bottles." Her throat was closing again, so she was forced to clear it. "I used to collect them."

"You let me sleep in your bed with you." His eyes narrowed as he concentrated on the vague blips of memory. Soft smells, soft voice, colors and shapes. "You told me some story, about a frog."

The Frog Prince. Into her mind flashed the image of how a little boy had curled against her, the bedside lamp holding back the dark for both of them, his bright-blue eyes intense on her face as she'd calmed his fears with a tale of magic and happily ever after.

"You had—when you came to visit, you had bad dreams. You were just a little boy."

"I had a puppy. You bought me a puppy."

"Not a real one, just a stuffed toy." Her vision was blurring, her throat closing, her heart breaking. "You . . . you didn't have any toys with you. When I brought it home you asked me whose it was, and I told you it was yours. That's what you called it. Yours. She didn't take it when she—I have to go."

She shot to her feet. "I'm sorry. I have to go." And bolted out the door.

SEVENTEEN

SHE GOT TO HER CAR AND yanked at the door handle before she realized she'd locked it. Which was, she told herself frantically, a stupid, knee-jerk urban habit that had no more place in this pretty rural neighborhood than she did.

The next thing she realized was that she'd run out of the house without her purse, her jacket, her keys. And that she would walk back to the hotel before she would go back inside and face the Quinns again after her rude and emotional behavior.

She whirled when she heard footsteps behind her and wasn't sure if she was relieved or embarrassed to see Phillip coming toward her. She didn't know what she was, what *it* was that was bubbling up inside her, burning and swelling her heart and her throat. She only knew she had to escape it.

"I'm sorry. I know that was rude. I really have to go." In the rush to get out, the words bumped and tumbled over each other. "Would you mind getting my purse? I need my purse. My keys. I'm sorry. I hope I didn't spoil—"

Whatever was bubbling in her throat was rising higher, choking her. "I have to go."

"You're shaking." He said it gently and reached for her, but she jerked back.

"It's cold. I forgot my jacket."

"It's not that cold, Sybill. Come here."

"No, I'm leaving. I have a headache. I—no, don't touch me."

Ignoring her words, he drew her firmly against him, wrapped his arms tight around her and held on. "It's all right, baby."

"No, it's not." She wanted to scream it. Was he blind? Was he stupid? "I shouldn't have come. Your brother hates me. Seth's afraid of me. You—your—I—"

Oh, it hurt. The pressure in her chest was agony, and it was spreading. "Let me go. I don't belong here."

"Yes, you do."

He'd seen it, that connection, when she and Seth had stared at each other. Her eyes such a clear blue, his so brilliant. He'd all but heard the click.

"No one hates you. No one's afraid of you. Let go, will you?" He pressed his mouth to her temple, would have sworn he felt the pain hissing there. "Why won't you let go?"

"I'm not going to cause a scene. If you'd just get my purse, I'll go."

She was holding herself rigid as marble, but the marble was cracking, he thought, and trembling with the pressure. If she didn't let go she would explode. So he would have to push. "He remembered you. He remembered that you cared."

Through the hideous pressure there was a stab, and the stab pierced her heart. "I can't stand it. I can't bear it." Her hands gripped his shoulders, fingers clenching and unclenching. "She took him away. She took him away. It broke my heart."

She was sobbing now, her arms tight around his neck. "I know. I know it did. That's the way," he murmured, and simply picked her up, sat on the grass, and cradled her against him. "It's about damn time."

He rocked her while tears that were hot and desperate flooded out of her and soaked his shirt. Cold? he thought as the firestorm of grief whipped through her. There was nothing cold in her but the fear of emotional pain.

He didn't tell her to stop, even when the sobs shook her so violently it seemed her bones might snap. He didn't offer promises of comfort or solutions. He knew the value of purging. So he simply stroked and rocked, cradling her while she wept out the pain.

When Anna stepped out on the porch, Phillip shook his head at her, stroking still. He continued to rock her as the door shut again and left them alone.

When she'd cried herself dry, her head felt swollen and hot, her throat and stomach raw. Weak and disoriented, she lay exhausted in his arms. "I'm sorry."

"Don't be. You needed that. I don't think I've ever known anyone who needed a crying jag more."

"It doesn't solve anything."

"You know better than that." He rose and, helping her up, pulled her toward his Jeep. "Get in."

"No, I need to—"

"Get in," he repeated with just a hint of impatience. "I'll go get your purse and your jacket." He lifted her into the passenger seat. "But you're not driving." His eyes met her tired, puffy ones. "And you're not going to be alone tonight."

She didn't have the energy to argue. She felt hollowed out and insubstantial. If he took her back to the hotel, she could sleep. She'd take a pill if she had to and escape. She didn't want to think. If she started to think she might feel again. If she felt again, if any part of that flood of feeling came back, she would drown in it.

Because his face looked grim and entirely too determined when he strode out of the house with her things, Sybill accepted her own cowardice and closed her eyes.

He didn't speak, simply climbed in beside her, leaned over to secure her seat belt, then started the car. He let the blessed silence hang throughout the drive. She didn't protest when he came into the lobby with her or when he opened her purse for her key card at her door.

He took her hand again and led her directly to the bedroom. "Get undressed," he ordered. As she stared at him with those swollen, red-rimmed eyes, he added, "I'm not going to jump you, for Christ's sake. What do you take me for?"

He didn't know where the flare of temper had come from. Maybe it was looking at her like this, seeing her so utterly wrecked and defenseless. Turning on his heel, he marched into the bathroom.

Seconds later, she heard the drum of water in the tub. He came out with a glass and aspirin. "Swallow. If you don't take care of yourself, someone else has to."

The water felt like glory on her abused throat, but before she could thank him, he'd pulled the glass out of her hand and set it aside. She swayed a little, and blinked when he tugged her sweater over her head.

"You're going to take a hot bath and relax."

She was too stupefied to argue as he continued to undress her like a doll. When he laid her clothes aside, she shivered a little but didn't speak. She only stared at him when he picked her up, carried her into the bathroom and deposited her in the tub.

The water was high, and a great deal hotter than she considered healthy. Before she could get her mind around the words to mention it, he flicked off the stream.

"Sit back, shut your eyes. Do it!" he said with such unexpected force that she obeyed. She kept them closed even when she heard the door click shut behind him.

She stayed there for twenty minutes, nearly nodding off twice. Only the vague fear of drowning kept her from sinking into sleep. And the niggling idea that he would come back in, pull her out, and dry her off himself was what made her climb shakily out of the tub.

Then again, maybe he'd gone. Maybe he'd finally gotten disgusted with her outburst and left her alone. Who could blame him?

But he was standing by the terrace doors in her bedroom when she stepped out, looking out at her view of the Bay. "Thank you." She knew it was awkward, for both of them, and struggled to make the effort when he turned and stared at her. "I'm sorry—"

"You apologize again, Sybill, you're going to piss me off." He walked toward her as he spoke, laid his hands on her shoulders. He cocked his eyebrows when she jumped. "Better," he decided, running his fingers over her shoulders and neck, "but not perfect. Lie down."

He sighed, pulled her toward the bed. "I'm not after sex. I do have some small level of restraint, and I can call on it when I'm faced with an emotionally and physically exhausted woman. On your stomach. Come on."

She slid onto the bed and couldn't quite muffle the moan when his fingers began to knead along her shoulder blades.

"You're a psychologist," he reminded her. "What happens to someone who represses their feelings on a regular basis?"

"Physically or emotionally?"

He laughed a little, straddled her, then got seriously down to work. "I'll tell you what happens, doc. They get headaches, heartburn, stomach pains. If and when the dam breaks, it all floods out so hard and so fast that they make themselves sick."

He tugged the robe off her shoulders and used the heels of his hands to press the muscles.

"You're angry with me."

"No, I'm not, Sybill. Not with you. Tell me about when Seth stayed with you."

"It was a long time ago."

"He was four," Phillip prompted and concentrated on the muscles that had just tensed. "You were in New York. Same place you have now?"

"Yes. Central Park West. It's a quiet neighborhood. Safe."

Exclusive, Phillip thought. No trendy East Village for Dr. Griffin. "Couple of bedrooms?"

"Yes. I use the second as my office."

He could almost see it. Tidy, organized, attractive. "I guess that's where Seth slept."

"No, Gloria took that room. We put Seth on the living room sofa. He was just a little boy."

"They just showed up on your doorstep one day."

"More or less. I hadn't seen her in years. I knew about Seth. She'd called me when the man she'd married left her. I sent her money off and on. I didn't want her to come. I never said she couldn't, but I didn't want her to come. She's so . . . disruptive, so difficult."

"But she did come."

"Yes. I came back from a lecture one afternoon and she was waiting outside the building. She was furious because the doorman wouldn't let her in, wouldn't let her go up to my apartment. Seth was crying, and she was screaming. It was just . . ." She sighed. "Typical, I suppose."

"But you let her in."

"I couldn't just send her away. All she had was this little boy and a backpack. She begged me to let them stay for a while. She said she'd been hitchhiking. That she was broke. She started crying, and Seth just crawled onto the couch and fell asleep. He must have been exhausted."

"How long did they stay?"

"A few weeks." Her mind began to drift between then and now, sliding back and forth in time. "I was going to help her get a job, but she said she needed to rest first. She said she'd been sick. Then she said a truck driver in Oklahoma had raped her. I knew she was lying, but . . ."

"She was your sister."

"No, no." She said it wearily. "If I'd been honest, I would have admitted that that had stopped mattering years before. But Seth was . . . He hardly spoke. I didn't know anything about children, but I got a book and it indicated he should have been much more verbal."

He nearly smiled. It was so easy to picture her selecting the proper book, studying it, trying to put everything in order.

"He was like this little ghost," she murmured. "This little shadow in the apartment. When Gloria would go out for any length of time and leave him with me, he'd creep out a little. And the first night she didn't come home until morning, he had a nightmare."

"And you let him sleep with you and told him a story."

"*The Frog Prince.* My nanny told it to me. She liked fairy tales. He was afraid of the dark. I used to be afraid of the dark." Her voice was thick and slow with fatigue. "I used to want to sleep in my parents' bed when I was afraid, but I wasn't allowed to. But . . . I didn't think it would hurt him, just for a little while."

"No." Now he could see her, a young girl with dark hair and light eyes, trembling in the dark. "It wouldn't have hurt."

"He used to like to look at my perfume bottles. He liked the colors and the shapes. I bought him crayons. He always liked to draw pictures."

"You got him a stuffed dog."

"He liked to watch the dogs being walked in the park. He was so sweet when I gave it to him. He carried it around everywhere. He slept with it."

"You fell in love with him."

"I loved him so much. I don't know how it happened. It was only a few weeks."

"Time doesn't always factor in." He skimmed her hair back so he could see her profile. The curve of her cheek, the angle of her brow. "It doesn't always play a part."

"It's supposed to, but it didn't. I didn't care that she took my things. I didn't care that she stole from me when she left. But she took him. She didn't even let me say good-bye to him. She took him, and she left his little dog because she knew it would hurt me. She knew I would think about him crying for it at night, and worry. So I had to stop. I had to stop thinking about it. I had to stop thinking about him."

"It's all right. That part's all over now." He stroked gently, nudging her closer to sleep. "She won't hurt Seth anymore. Or you."

"I was stupid."

"No, you weren't." He stroked her neck, her shoulders, felt her body rise and fall on a long, long sigh. "Go to sleep."

"Don't go."

"No, I'm not." He frowned at how fragile the nape of her neck looked under his fingers. "I'm not going anywhere."

And that was a problem, he realized as he smoothed his hands down her arms, over her back. He wanted to stay with her, to be with her. He wanted to watch her sleep just the way she was sleeping now, deep and still. He wanted to be the one who held her when she cried, for he doubted that she cried often, or that she had anyone to hold her when she did.

He wanted to watch those quiet lake eyes of hers go bright with laughter, that lovely, soft mouth curve with it. He could spend hours listening to the way her voice changed tones, from warm amusement to prim formality to earnestness.

He liked the way she looked in the morning, vaguely surprised to see him beside her. And at night, with pleasure and passion flickering over her face.

She hadn't a clue how revealing that face was, he thought, as he tugged down the covers, shifting her until he could spread them over her. Oh, it was subtle, like her scent. A man had to get close, very close, before he understood. But he'd gotten close, very close, without either of them realizing it. And he'd seen the way she'd watched his family, with wistfulness, with yearning.

Always staying a step back, always the observer.

And he'd seen the way she'd watched Seth. With love, and with longing, and again from a distance.

So as not to intrude? To protect herself? He thought it was a combination of both. He wasn't quite sure exactly what went on in her heart, in her mind. But he was determined to find out.

"I think I might be in love with you, Sybill." He said it quietly as he stretched out beside her. "Damn if that doesn't complicate things for both of us."

She woke in the dark. And for a moment, just a flash, she was a child again and afraid of all those things that lurked in the shadows. She had to press her lips together, very hard, until it hurt. Because if she cried out one of the servants would hear and might tell her mother. Her mother would be annoyed. Her mother wouldn't like it that she'd cried about the dark again.

Then she remembered. She wasn't a child. There was nothing lurking in the shadows but more shadows. She was a grown woman who knew it was foolish to be afraid of the dark when there was so much else to fear.

Oh, she'd made a fool of herself, she thought, as more memories slipped through. A terrible fool of herself. Letting herself become upset that way. Worse, letting it show until she'd had no control, none whatsoever. Instead of maintaining her composure, she'd rushed out of the house like an idiot.

Inexcusable.

Then she'd cried all over Phillip. Wept like a baby right in the front yard as if she'd . . .

Phillip.

Mortification had her moaning aloud, covering her face with her hands. She sucked in a gasp when an arm came around her.

"Ssh."

She recognized his touch, his scent even before he drew her against him. Before his mouth brushed her temple, before his body fit comfortingly to hers.

"It's all right," he murmured.

"I—I thought you'd gone."

"I said I'd stay." He slitted his eyes open, scanned the dull red glow of the bedside alarm. "Three A.M. hotel time. Should have figured it."

"I didn't mean to wake you." As her eyes grew accustomed to the dark, she could make out the sweep of his cheekbone, the ridge of his nose, the shape of his mouth. Her fingers itched to touch.

"When I wake up in the middle of the night in bed with a beautiful woman, it's hard to mind."

She smiled, relieved that he wasn't going to press her about her earlier behavior. It could just be the two of them now. No yesterday to mourn over, no tomorrow to worry about.

"I imagine you've had a lot of practice."

"Some things you want to get just right."

His voice was so warm, his arm so strong, his body so firm. "When you wake up in the middle of the night in bed with a woman, and she wants to seduce you, do you mind?"

"Hardly ever."

"Well, if you wouldn't mind . . ." She shifted, slid her body over his, found his lips with her lips, his tongue with her tongue.

"I'll let you know as soon as I start to mind."

Her laugh was low and warm. Gratitude moved through her, for what he'd done for her, what he'd come to be to her. She wanted so badly to show him.

It was dark. She could be anything she wanted to be in the dark.

"Maybe I won't stop if you do."

"Threats?" He was every bit as surprised, and aroused, by the teasing purr of her voice as he was by the deliberate, circling trail of her fingertips down his body. "You don't scare me."

"I can." She began to follow the trail with her mouth. "I will."

"Give it your best shot. Jesus." His eyes all but crossed. "Bull's-eye."

She laughed again and lapped at him like a cat. When his body quivered, and his breathing grew thick and ragged, she scraped her nails slowly up his sides and down again.

What a wonder the male form was, she thought, dreamily exploring it. Hard, smooth, the planes and angles so perfectly fashioned to mate with woman. With her.

Silky here, then rough. Firm, then yielding. She could make him want and ache just as he made her want and ache. She could give, she could take just as he did and all the wonderful and wicked things people did in the dark, she could do.

He'd go mad if she continued. He'd die if she stopped. Her mouth was hot and restless, and everywhere. Those elegant fingers had the blood raging through his veins. As their flesh grew damp, her body slipped and slid over his, a pale silhouette in the dark.

She was any woman. The only woman. He craved her like life.

Dreamlike, she rose up over him, shrugging out of her robe, arching her back, shaking her hair back. What soared through her now was freedom. Power. Lust. Her eyes gleamed, catlike against the dark, bewitching him.

She lowered herself, taking him inside her slowly, dimly aware of what effort it cost him to allow her to set the pace. Her breath caught, released on a moaning sigh of pleasure. Caught again, released again when his hands captured her breasts, squeezed, possessed.

She rocked, small movements, torturously slow, arousing herself with the power. And kept her eyes on his. He shuddered beneath her, his muscles bunched, his body tight between her thighs. Strong, she thought, he was so strong. Strong enough to let her take him as she chose.

She skimmed her hands over his chest, then lowered. Her hair curtained their faces as her mouth closed hard over his. A tangle of tongues and teeth and breath.

The orgasm rolled through her like a wave, growing, building, then sweeping her up and over. She reared back with it, body bowing, and rode it out.

Then she rode him.

He gripped her hips, his fingers digging in as she surged over him. All reckless speed and clashing light now, all heat and greed. His mind emptied, his lungs screamed, and his body climbed desperately toward release.

When he found it, it was brutal and brilliant.

She seemed to melt over him, her body as soft and hot and fluid as a pool of liquid wax. Her heart thudded hard against the frantic beat of his own. He couldn't speak, couldn't find the air to push the words free. But the ones that shimmered on his tongue were three that he'd been careful never to say to a woman.

Triumph still glowed inside her. She stretched, lazy and satisfied as a cat, then curled herself against him. "That," she said sleepily, "was exactly right."

"What?"

She chuckled softly and ended on a yawn. "I may not have scared you, but I fried your brain."

"No question." A sex-scrambled brain. Men who started thinking about love, much less bringing the word up when they were hot and naked and wrapped around a woman, just got themselves in trouble.

"First time I ever liked waking up at three A.M." Already half asleep, she pillowed her head on his shoulder. She shifted. "Cold," she muttered.

He reached down and tugged up the tangled sheets and blankets. She nipped an edge with her fingers, pulled them up to her chin.

For the second time in one night, Phillip lay awake, staring at the ceiling while she slept deep and still beside him.

EIGHTEEN

IT WAS BARELY LIGHT WHEN
Phillip crawled out of bed. He didn't bother to moan. What good
would it do? Just because he'd barely slept, his mind was fogged with
fatigue and worry, and he had an entire day of backbreaking manual
labor ahead of him was no reason to complain.

The fact that there was no coffee was a damn good reason to complain.

Sybill stirred as he started to dress. "You have to go to the boatyard?"

"Yeah." He rolled his tongue over his teeth as he jerked up his
slacks. Christ, he didn't even have a toothbrush with him.

"Do you want me to order up some breakfast? Coffee?"

Coffee. The word alone was like a siren's song in his blood.

But he grabbed his shirt. If she ordered coffee, he would have to
talk to her. He didn't think it was a smart move to have a conversation
when he was in such a foul mood. And why was he in a foul mood? he
asked himself. Because he hadn't slept and she'd managed to sneak
through his legendary defenses while he wasn't looking and make him
fall in love with her.

"I'll get some at home." His voice was clipped and edgy. "I have to
go back and change anyway." Which was why he was up so damn
early.

The sheets rustled as she sat up. He watched her out of the corner
of his eye and reached for his socks. She looked tousled and tumbled
and temptingly soft.

Yeah, she was sneaky all right. Hitting him over the head like that with her vulnerability, sobbing in his arms that way and looking so damned hurt and defenseless. Then waking up in the middle of the night and turning into some sort of a sex-fantasy goddess.

Now she was offering him coffee. She had a hell of a nerve.

"I appreciate you staying last night. It helped."

"I'm here to serve," he said shortly.

"I . . ." She gnawed on her bottom lip, alerted and confused by his tone. "It was a difficult day for both of us. I suppose I'd have been wiser to stay away. I was already a little off balance after Gloria's call, and then—"

His head shot up. "What? Gloria called you?"

"Yes." And now, Sybill thought, she'd only proven why that was information best kept to herself. He was upset. Everyone was going to be upset.

"She called you? Yesterday?" With his temper simmering, he picked up his shoe, examined it. "And you didn't think that it was worth mentioning before this?"

"I didn't see any point in it." Because her hands couldn't seem to keep still, she pushed at her hair, tugged at the sheet. "I wasn't going to mention it at all, actually."

"Weren't you? Maybe you forgot, momentarily, that Seth is my family's responsibility. That we have a right to know if your sister's going to cause more trouble. A need to know," he said, rising as his anger rapidly approached flash point. "So that we can protect him."

"She won't do anything to—"

"How the hell do you know?" He exploded with it, rounding on her so that she clutched the sheets in white-knuckled fingers. "How can you know? By *observing* from ten paces back. Goddamn it, Sybill, this isn't a fucking exercise. This is life. What the hell did she want?"

She wanted to shrink, as she always did from anger. She coated her heart and her voice with ice, as she always did to face it. "She wanted money, of course. She wanted me to demand it from you, to give her more myself. She shouted at me, too, and swore at me, just as you are. It appears that staying ten paces back has put me directly in the middle."

"I want to know if and when she contacts you again. What did you tell her?"

Sybill reached for her robe, and her hand was steady. "I told her that your family would not give her anything. And neither would I. That I had spoken with your lawyer. That I had added, and would continue to add, my weight and influence to see that Seth remains a permanent part of your family."

"That's something, then," he muttered, frowning at her as she pulled on her robe.

"It's the least I can do, isn't it?" Her tone was frigid, distant and final. "Excuse me." She strode into the bathroom, shut the door.

From where he stood, Phillip heard the deliberate click of the lock. "Well, fine, that's just fine." He snarled at the door, grabbed his jacket, then got the hell out before he made matters any worse than they already were.

THEY DIDN'T GET ANY BETTER when he arrived home to find less than half a cup of coffee left in the pot. When he discovered midway through his shower that Cam had obviously used most of the hot water, he decided that just made it all perfect.

Then he stepped into his room, a towel slung around his hips, and found Seth sitting on the side of his bed.

Definitely perfect.

"Hey." Seth eyed him steadily.

"You're up early."

"I thought I'd maybe go in with you for a couple of hours."

Phillip turned to pull underwear and jeans out of his dresser. "You aren't working today. You've got your friends coming over later for the party."

"That's not till this afternoon." Seth lifted a shoulder. "There's time."

"Suit yourself."

He'd expected Phillip to be steamed. He had a thing for Sybill, didn't he? Seth reminded himself. It had been tough to come in here, to wait, to know he'd have to say something.

So he said the single thing that was most on his mind. "I didn't mean to make her cry."

Shit, was all Phillip could think. He yanked on his Jockeys. He wasn't going to get out of this. "You didn't. She was just due for a cry, that's all."

"I guess she's pretty pissed off."

"No, she's not." Resigned to it now, Phillip pulled on his jeans.

"Look, women are hard to understand under the best of circumstances. These circumstances pretty much suck."

"I guess." Maybe he wasn't so steamed after all. "I just sort of remembered some stuff." Seth stared at the scars on Phillip's chest because it was easier than looking into his eyes. And because, well, the scars were so cool. "Then she got so whacked out about it and everything."

"Some people don't know what to do with feelings." He sighed, sat on the bed beside Seth, and was bitterly ashamed of himself. He'd blasted Sybill right between the eyes because *he* hadn't known what to do with his feelings. "So they cry, or they yell, or they go off and sulk in a corner. She cares about you, but she doesn't know exactly what to do about it. Or what you want her to do about it."

"I don't know. She's . . . she's not like Gloria." His voice rose a pitch. "She's decent. Ray was decent, too, and I've got—they're like relatives, right? So I've got . . ."

Understanding came quickly and squeezed his heart. "You've got Ray's eyes." Phillip kept his voice matter-of-fact, knowing Seth would believe him if he said it right. "The color and the shape, but that something that was behind them, too. The something that was decent. You've got a sharp brain, just like Sybill. It thinks, it analyzes, it wonders. And under all that, it tries to do what's right. What's decent. You've got both of them in you." He nudged Seth's shoulder with his own. "Pretty cool, huh?"

"Yeah." The smile bloomed. "It's cool."

"Okay, scram, or we're never going to get out of here."

H E ARRIVED AT THE BOATYARD nearly forty-five minutes behind Cam and expected to get grief for it. Cam was already at the shaper, rabbeting the next run of planks. Bruce Springsteen shouted from the radio about his glory days. In defense, Phillip turned the volume down. Instantly Cam's head came up.

"I can't hear it over the tool unless it's loud."

"None of us will be able to hear if you keep blasting our ears for hours every day."

"What? Did you say something?"

"Ha-ha."

"Well, we're cheerful, aren't we?" Cam reached over and switched off the power. "So, how's Sybill?"

"Don't start on me."

Cam angled his head while Seth shifted his gaze from man to man and anticipated the entertainment value of a Quinn battle. "I asked a simple question."

"She'll survive." Phillip snatched up a tool belt. "I realize you'd prefer to see her run out of town on a rail, but you'll have to make do with the fact that I gave her a verbal bashing this morning rather than a physical one."

"Why the hell did you do that?"

"Because she pissed me off!" Phillip shouted. "Because it all pisses me off. Especially you."

"Fine, you want to try for a physical bashing, I'm available. But I asked a goddamn simple question." Cam pulled the board off the shaper and heaved it toward the stack, where it landed with a clatter. "She already took a punch in the gut yesterday. Why the hell would you add to it this morning?"

"You're defending her?" Phillip stepped forward until they were nose to nose. "You're defending her, after all the shit you've handed me over her?"

"I've got eyes, don't I? I saw her face last night. What the hell do you take me for?" He jabbed a finger into Phillip's chest. "Anybody who'd kick a woman when she's that torn up ought to have his neck snapped."

"You son of a—" Phillip's fist was clenched and halfway through the swing before he stopped himself. He would have enjoyed a few bloody rounds, especially since Ethan wasn't there to break it up. But not when he was the one who deserved to be bloodied.

He unclenched his fist, spreading his fingers as he turned away to try to find some control. He saw Seth watching him with dark, interested eyes and snarled. "Don't you start."

"I didn't say a word."

"Look, I took care of her, okay?" He dragged a hand through his hair and aimed his rationalization at both of them. "I let her cry it out, patted her hand. I dumped her into a hot tub, tucked her into bed. I stayed with her. Maybe I got an hour's sleep out of the deal, so I'm feeling just a little testy right now."

"Why'd you yell at her?" Seth wanted to know.

"Okay." He took a steadying breath, pressed his fingers to his tired eyes. "This morning she told me that Gloria had called her. Yesterday. Maybe I overreacted, but damn it, she should have told us."

"What did she want?" Seth's lips had gone white. Instinctively, Cam stepped over and laid a hand on his shoulder.

"Don't let her spook you, kid. You're beyond that now. What's the deal?" he demanded of Phillip.

"I didn't get details. I was too busy blasting Sybill for not telling me sooner. The gist of it was money." Phillip shifted his gaze to Seth, spoke directly to him. "She told Gloria to kiss ass. No money, no nothing, no how. She told her she'd been to the lawyer and was making sure you stayed just where you are."

"Your aunt's no pushover," Cam said easily, giving Seth's shoulder a quick squeeze. "She's got spine."

"Yeah." Seth straightened his own. "She's okay."

"Your brother over there," Cam continued, nodding toward Phillip. "He's an asshole, but the rest of us have sense enough to know that Sybill didn't bring up the phone call yesterday because it was a party. She didn't want anybody to get upset. A guy doesn't turn eleven every day."

"So I screwed up." Muttering to himself, Phillip grabbed a plank and prepared to beat out his frustrations with nail and wood. "I'll fix it."

Sᴙʙɪʟʟ NEEDED TO DO SOME FIXing of her own. It had taken her most of the day to work up both the courage and the plan. She pulled into the Quinn driveway just after four, and was relieved not to see Phillip's Jeep.

He'd be at the boatyard for another hour at least, she calculated. Seth would be with him. As it was Saturday night, they would most likely stop on the way home, pick up some takeout.

It was their pattern, and she knew her behavioral patterns, even if she didn't seem to be able to fully connect with the people who were doing the behaving.

Ten paces back, she thought, and was hurt all over again.

Annoyed, she ordered herself out of the car. She would do what she had come to do. It should take no more than fifteen minutes to apologize to Anna, for the apology to be accepted, at least outwardly. She would explain about the call from Gloria, in detail, so that it could be documented. Then she would leave.

She would be back at her hotel, buried in her work, long before Phillip arrived on the scene.

She knocked briskly on the door.

"It's open," came the response. "I'd rather kill myself than get up."

Warily, Sybill reached for the knob, hesitated, then opened the door. All she could do was stare.

The Quinn living room was usually cluttered, always appeared lived-in, but just now it appeared to have been lived in by a rampaging platoon of insane elves.

Paper plates, plastic cups, several of them dumped or spilled, littered the floor and the tables. Small plastic men were strewn everywhere as if a war had been waged, and the casualties were horrendous. Obviously fatal accidents had taken place with model cars and trucks. Shreds of wrapping paper were sprinkled over all like confetti on a particularly wild New Year's Eve.

Sprawled in a chair, surveying the damage, was Anna. Her hair was in her face, and her face was pale.

"Oh, great," she muttered, turning narrowed eyes to Sybill. "Now she shows up."

"I—I'm sorry?"

"Easy for you to say. I've just spent two and a half hours battling ten eleven-year-old boys. No—not boys," she corrected between her teeth. "Animals, beasts. Spawns of Satan. I just sent Grace home with orders to lie down. I'm afraid this experience might affect the baby. He could be born a mutant."

The children's party, Sybill remembered, her dazzled eyes scanning the room. She'd forgotten. "It's over?"

"It will never be over. I will wake up at night for the rest of my life, screaming, until they cart me off to a padded room. I have ice cream in my hair. There's some sort of . . . mass on the kitchen table. I'm afraid to go in there. I think it moved. Three boys managed to fall in the water and had to be dragged out and dried off. They'll probably catch pneumonia and we'll be sued. One of those creatures who disguised himself as a young boy ate approximately sixty-five pieces of cake, then got into my car—I don't know how he got by me, they're like lightning—and proceeded to throw up."

"Oh, dear." Sybill knew it wasn't a laughing matter. It shocked her to realize that her stomach muscles were quivering. "I'm so sorry. Can I help you, ah, clean up?"

"I'm not touching any of it. Those men—the one who claims to be my husband and his idiot brothers—they're going to do it. They're going to scrub and clean and wipe and shovel. They're going to do it all. They knew," she said in a vicious whisper. "They knew what a boy's birthday party would mean. How was I to know? But they did, and they hid themselves away down at that boatyard, using that lame excuse about contract deadlines. They left me and Grace alone with this, this unspeakable duty." She shut her eyes. "Oh, the horror."

Anna was silent for a moment, her eyes still closed. "Go ahead. You can laugh. I'm too weak to get up and belt you."

"You worked so hard to do this for Seth."

"He had the time of his life." Anna's lips curved as she opened her eyes. "And since I'm going to make Cam and his brothers clean it up, I'm feeling pretty good about it, all in all. How are you?"

"I'm fine. I came to apologize for last night."

"Apologize for what?"

The question threw her off rhythm. She was already running behind schedule, she thought, distracted by the chaos and Anna's rambling monologue. Sybill cleared her throat and began again. "For last night. It was rude of me to leave without thanking you for—"

"Sybill, I'm too tired to listen to nonsense. You weren't rude, you have nothing to apologize for, and you'll annoy me if you keep this up. You were upset, and you had a perfect right to be."

And that blew Sybill's carefully prepared speech all to hell. "I honestly don't understand why people in this family won't listen to, much less accept, a sincere apology for regrettable behavior."

"Boy, if that's the tone you use when you lecture," Anna observed with admiration, "your audience must sit at attention. But to answer your question, I suppose we don't because we so often indulge in what could be termed regrettable behavior ourselves. I'd ask you to sit down, but those are really lovely slacks and I have no idea what nasty surprises there are on any of the cushions."

"I don't intend to stay."

"You couldn't see your face," Anna said more gently. "When he looked up at you, when he told you what he remembered. But I could see it, Sybill. I could see it was a great deal more than duty or responsibility or a valiant attempt to do what was right that brought you here. It must have crushed you when she took him away all those years ago."

"I can't do this again." The burn of tears scalded the back of her eyes. "I just can't do this again."

"You don't have to," Anna murmured. "I just want you to know I understand. In my work I see so many damaged people. Battered women, abused children, men who are at the end of their ropes, the elderly we so blithely displace. I care, Sybill. I care about every one of them who come to me for help."

She sighed a little and spread her fingers. "But in order to help them, I have to hold part of myself back, be objective, realistic, practical. If I threw all my emotions into every one of my cases, I couldn't do my job. I'd burn out, burn up. I understand the need for a little distance."

"Yes." The painful tension drained out of Sybill's shoulders. "Of course you do."

"It was different with Seth," Anna went on. "Right from the first minute, everything about him pulled at me. I couldn't stop it. I tried, but I couldn't. I've thought about that, and I believe, sincerely, that my feelings for him were there, just there, even before I met him. We were meant to be a part of each other's lives. He was meant to be part of this family, and this family was meant to be mine."

Risking the consequences, Sybill eased down on the arm of the sofa. "I wanted to tell you . . . you're so good with him. You and Grace. You're so good for him. The relationship he has with his brothers is wonderful, and it's vital. That strong male influence is important for a boy. But the female, what you and Grace give him, is just as vital."

"You have something to give him, too. He's outside," Anna told her. "Drooling over his boat."

"I don't want to upset him. I really have to go."

"Running away last night was understandable and acceptable." Anna's gaze was direct, level and challenging. "Running now isn't."

"You must be very good at your job," Sybill said after a moment.

"I'm damn good at it. Go talk to him. If I manage to get out of this chair in this lifetime, I'll put some fresh coffee on."

It wasn't easy. But then Sybill supposed it wasn't meant to be. Crossing that lawn toward the boy who sat in the pretty little boat, so obviously dreaming of fast sails.

Foolish saw her first and, alerted, raced toward her, barking. She braced herself and put a hand out, hoping to ward him off. Foolish skimmed his head under it, turning the defensive gesture into a stroke.

His fur was so soft and warm, his eyes so adoring, his face so fittingly silly that she relaxed into a smile. "You really are foolish, aren't you?"

He sat, batting at her with his paw until she took it and shook. Satisfied, he raced back toward the boat, where Seth watched and waited.

"Hi." He stayed where he was, pulling on the line and making the small triangle of sail sway.

"Hello. Have you taken it out yet?"

"Nah. Anna wouldn't let me and any of the guys go out in her today." He jerked a shoulder. "Like we'd drown or something."

"But you had a good time at your party."

"It was cool. Anna's a little pissed—" He stopped and looked toward the house. She really hated it when he swore. "She's pretty steamed about Jake barfing in her car, so I figured I'd hang out here until she levels."

"That's probably very sensible."

Then silence fell, heavy, as they both looked out over the water and wondered what to say.

Sybill braced herself. "Seth, I didn't say good-bye to you last night. I shouldn't have left the way I did."

"It's okay." He shrugged again.

"I didn't think you remembered me. Or any of the time you stayed with me in New York."

"I thought I'd made it up." It was too hard to sit in the boat and look so far up. He climbed out, then sat on the dock to dangle his legs. "Sometimes I'd dream about some of it. Like the stuffed dog and stuff."

"Yours," she murmured.

"Yeah, that's pretty lame. She didn't talk about you or anything, so I thought I'd just made it up."

"Sometimes . . ." She took the risk and sat beside him. "Sometimes it was almost like that for me, too. I still have the dog."

"You kept it?"

"It was all I had left of you. You mattered to me. I know it may not seem like that now, but you did. I didn't want you to."

"Because I was hers?"

"Partly." She had to be honest, had to give him that, at least. "She was never kind, Seth. Something was twisted in her. It seemed that she could never be happy unless the people closest to her weren't. I didn't want her back in my life. I'd planned to give her a day or two, then arrange to have the two of you moved to a shelter. That way I would fulfill my family obligation and protect my own lifestyle."

"But you didn't."

"I made excuses at first. Just one more night. Then I admitted that I was letting her stay because I wanted to keep you there. If I found her a job, helped her get an apartment, worked with her to put her life back together, I could keep you close. I'd never had—you were the . . ."

She ordered herself to take one cleansing breath and just say it. "You loved me. You were the first person who ever did. I didn't want to lose that. And when I did, I pulled myself back, right back to where I'd been before you came. I was thinking much more of myself than of you. I'd like to make up for that, a little, by thinking of you now."

He looked away from her, down at the feet he was kicking back and forth over the water. "Phil said how she called and you told her to kiss ass."

"Not precisely in those words."

"But that's what you meant, right?"

"I guess it was." She nearly smiled. "Yes."

"You guys got the same mother, right, but, like, different fathers?"

"Yes, that's right."

"Do you know who my father was?"

"I never met him, no."

"No, I mean do you know who he was? She was always making up different guys and names and shit. And stuff," he corrected. "I just wondered, that's all."

"I only know his name was Jeremy DeLauter. They weren't married long, and—"

"Married?" His gaze flew back to hers. "She never got married. She was just BS-ing you."

"No, I saw the marriage license. She had it with her when she came to New York. She thought I could help her track him down and sue him for child support."

He considered a moment, absorbing the possibility. "Maybe. It doesn't matter. I figured she just took the name from some guy she lived with sometime. If he got hooked up with her, he must've been a loser."

"I could arrange for a search. I'm sure we could locate him. It would take some time."

"I don't want that." There wasn't any panic in his voice, just disinterest. "I was just wondering if you knew him, that's all. I got a family now." He lifted his arm as Foolish nosed into his armpit, and wrapped it around the dog's neck.

"Yes, you do." Aching a little, she started to rise. She hesitated, her eye drawn toward a flash of white. She saw the heron soar, gliding over the water just at the edge of the trees. Then it was gone, around the bend, leaving barely a ripple on the air.

A lovely thing, she thought. A lovely spot. A harbor for troubled souls, for young boys who only needed a chance to become men. Perhaps she couldn't thank Ray and Stella Quinn for what they'd done here, but she could show her gratitude by stepping aside now and letting their sons finish the job with Seth.

"Well, I should go."

"The art stuff you gave me, it's really great."

"I'm glad you like it. You have talent."

"I fooled around some with the charcoal last night." She hesitated again. "Oh?"

"I'm not getting it right." He twisted his head to look up at her. "It's a lot different than a pencil. Maybe you could show me how to do it."

She stared hard over the water because she knew he wasn't asking. He was offering. Now, it seemed, she was being given a chance, and a choice. "Yes, I could show you."

"Now?"

"Yes." She concentrated on keeping her voice even. "I could show you now."

"Cool."

NINETEEN

So, he'd been a little hard on her, Phillip told himself. Maybe he felt that she should have told him immediately that Gloria had contacted her. Party or no party, she could have taken him aside and filled him in. But he shouldn't have jumped all over her and then walked out.

Still, in his own defense, he'd felt raw and annoyed and unsettled. He'd spent the first part of the night worried about her, and the second part worried about himself. Was he supposed to be happy that she'd wormed her way through his defenses? Was he supposed to jump for joy that in a matter of weeks she'd managed to drill a hole in the highly polished shield he'd maintained so expertly for over thirty years?

He didn't think so.

But he was willing to admit that he hadn't behaved well. He was even willing to offer a peace token in the form of vintage champagne and long-stemmed roses.

He'd packed the basket himself. Two bottles of Dom, well chilled, two crystal flutes—he wasn't about to insult that brilliant French monk with hotel glasses—the beluga he'd craftily hidden, for just such an occasion, inside an empty carton of plain low-fat yogurt, knowing that no one in his family would touch it.

He'd made the toast points himself and had selected both the blush-pink roses and the vase with care.

He thought she might be a tad resistant to the visit. It never hurt to pave the way with champagne and flowers. And since he intended to do a little worming himself, they couldn't hurt. He was going to loosen her up, he decided, talk to her, and more, get her talking. He wasn't leaving until he had a much clearer view on just who Sybill Griffin was.

He rapped cheerfully on her door. That was going to be his approach—casual cheer. He shot a quick, charming smile at the peephole when he heard footsteps, saw the vague, telltale shadow.

And he stood as those footsteps receded.

Okay. Maybe more than a tad resistant, he concluded, and knocked again. "Come on, Sybill. I know you're there. I want to talk to you."

Silence, he discovered, didn't have to be empty. It could be crowded with ice.

Okay, fine, he thought, scowling at the door. She wanted to do it the hard way.

He set the basket beside the door, then marched back down the hall to the fire stairs and started down. For what he had in mind it was wiser not to be seen leaving the lobby.

"Ticked her off good, didn't you?" Ray commented as he jogged down the steps beside his son.

"Christ almighty." Phillip glared into his father's face. "Next time why don't you just shoot me in the head? It'd be less embarrassing than to die of a heart attack at my age."

"Your heart's strong enough. So, she's not speaking to you."

"She'll talk to me," Phillip said grimly.

"Bribing with bubbly?" Ray jerked a thumb behind him.

"It works."

"The flowers are a good touch. I could usually get around your mother with flowers. Quicker if I groveled."

"I'm not groveling." On that he was firm. "It was just as much her fault."

"It's never just as much their fault," Ray said with a wink. "The sooner you accept that, the sooner you'll get makeup sex."

"Jesus, Dad." He could only rub a hand over his face. "I'm not going to talk to you about sex."

"Why not? Wouldn't be the first time." He sighed as they came to the ground level. "Seems to me your mother and I talked to you plenty, and talked to you straight, about sex. Gave you your first condoms, too."

"That was then," Phillip muttered. "I've got the hang of it now."

Ray let out a rippling, delighted laugh. "I bet you do. But then again, sex isn't the prime motive here. It's always a motive," he added.

"We're men, we can't help it. Lady up there, she's got you worried, though, because it's not just about sex. It's about love."

"I'm not in love with her. Exactly. I'm just . . . involved."

"Love always was a tough one for you." Ray stepped out into the windy night, zipped up the frayed sideline jacket he wore over his jeans. "When it came to females, that is. Anytime things started to head toward serious, you'd start moving fast and loose in the opposite direction." He grinned at Phillip. "Looks to me like you're moving straight ahead this time."

"She's Seth's aunt." Annoyance pricked at the back of his neck as he walked around the building. "If she's going to be part of his life, our lives, I need to understand her."

"Seth's part of it. But you slapped her back this morning because you were scared."

Phillip planted his feet, legs spread, rolled his shoulders as he studied Ray's face. "Number one, I can't believe I'm standing here arguing with you. Number two, it occurs to me that you were a hell of a lot better at letting me run my own life when you were alive than you are as a dead man."

Ray only smiled. "Well, I've got what you might call a broader point of view now. I want you happy, Phil. I'm not going to move on until I'm sure the people who matter to me are happy. I'm ready to move on," he said quietly. "To be with your mother."

"Have you—did you . . . How is she?"

"She's waiting for me." The glow slipped over Ray's face and into his eyes. "And she's never been what you could call the waiting type."

"I miss her, so much."

"I know. So do I. She'd be flattered, and annoyed, too, that under it all you've never been willing to settle for less than the kind of woman she was."

Staggered, because it was true, and a secret that he'd kept carefully locked up, Phillip stared. "It's not that, not altogether that."

"Part of that, then." Ray nodded. "You have to find your own, Phil. And make your own. You're getting there. You did a fine job with Seth today. So did she," he said, glancing up at the light shining through Sybill's bedroom window. "You make a fine team, even when you're pulling in different directions. That's because you both care, more than you might understand."

"Did you know he was your grandson?"

"No. Not at first." He sighed now. "When Gloria found me she hit me with all of it at once. I never knew about her, and there she was, shouting, swearing, accusing, demanding. Couldn't calm her down or make sense of it. Next thing I knew she'd gone to the dean with that story about how I'd molested her. She's a troubled young woman."

"She's a bitch."

Ray only moved his shoulders. "If I'd known about her sooner . . . well, that's done. I couldn't save Gloria, but I could save Seth. One look at him and I knew. So I paid her. Maybe that was wrong, but the boy needed me. It took me weeks to track down Barbara. All I wanted from her was confirmation. I wrote to her, three times. Even called Paris, but she wouldn't speak to me. I was still working on that when I had the accident. Stupid," he admitted. "I let Gloria upset me. I was angry with her, myself, everything, worried about Seth, about how the three of you would take it when I explained it all. Driving too fast, not paying attention. Well."

"We would have stood with you."

"I know that. I let myself forget it, and that was stupid, too. Stella was gone, the three of you had your own lives, and I let myself brood, and forget. You're standing with Seth now, and that's more important."

"We're nearly there. With Sybill adding her voice, the permanent guardianship's a given."

"She's adding more than her voice, and she'll add more yet. She's stronger than she gives herself credit for. Than anyone gives her credit for."

In a swift change of mood, Ray clucked his tongue, shook his head. "I guess you're going up there."

"That's the plan."

"Never quite lost that unfortunate skill. Maybe this time that's a good thing. That girl could use some surprises in her life." Ray winked again. "Watch your step."

"You're not going to come up, are you?"

"No." Ray slapped Phillip's shoulder and let out a hearty laugh. "Some things a father just doesn't need to see."

"Good. But since you're here, make it easier for me. Give me a boost up to that first balcony."

"Sure. They can't arrest me, can they?"

Ray cupped his hands, giving Phillip's foot a helpful push, then stood back to watch him make the climb. He watched, and he smiled. "I'm going to miss you," he said quietly and faded into shadows.

• • •

IN THE PARLOR. SYBILL CON-
centrated fiercely on her work. She didn't give a damn if it had been
petty, unreasonable behavior to ignore Phillip's knock. She'd had
enough emotional upheaval for one weekend. And besides, he'd given
up quickly enough, hadn't he?

She listened to the wind rattle against her windows, set her teeth,
and pounded the keyboard.

> The import of internal news appears to outweigh that of the exter-
> nal. While television, newspapers, and other information sources
> are as readily available in the small community as they are in large
> urban areas, the actions and involvements of one's neighbors take
> precedent when the population is limited.
>
> Information is passed on, with varying degrees of accuracy,
> through word of mouth. Gossip is an accepted form of communica-
> tion. The network is admirably quick and efficient.
>
> Disattending—the pretense of not hearing a private conversation
> in a public place—is not as prevalent in the small community as in
> the large city. However, in transient areas such as hotels, disattend-
> ing is still a consistent and acceptable behavioral pattern. I would
> conclude that the reason for this is the regular comings and goings
> of outsiders in this type of area. Overt attention is paid, however, in
> other areas such as

Her fingers froze, her mouth dropped open, as she watched Phillip
slide her terrace door open and step inside.

"What—"

"The locks on these things are pathetic," he said. He walked to the
front door, opened it, and picked up the basket and vase of flowers
he'd left there. "I figured I could risk these. We don't get a lot of
thievery around here. You might want to add that to your notes." He
set the vase of roses on her desk.

"You climbed up the building?" She could only stare at him,
amazed.

"The wind's a bitch, too." He opened the basket, took out the first
bottle. "I could use a drink. How about you?"

"You climbed up the building?"

"We've already established that." He opened the wine with an expert and muffled pop.

"You can't . . ." She gestured wildly. "Just break in here, open champagne."

"I just did." He poured two glasses and discovered it didn't do his ego any harm to have her gaping at him. "I'm sorry about this morning, Sybill." Smiling, he offered her a glass of champagne. "I was feeling pretty rough, and I took it out on you."

"So you apologize by breaking into my room."

"I didn't break anything. Besides, you weren't going to open the door, and the flowers wanted to be in here. So did I. Truce?" he said and waited.

He'd climbed up the building. She still couldn't get over it. No one had ever committed such a bold and foolish act for her. She stared at him, into those golden angel eyes, and felt herself softening. "I have work."

He grinned because he saw the yielding. "I have beluga."

She tapped her fingers on the wrist rest of her keyboard. "Flowers, champagne, caviar. Do you usually come so well equipped when you break and enter?"

"Only when I want to apologize and throw myself on the mercy of a beautiful woman. Got any mercy to spare, Sybill?"

"I suppose I might. I wasn't keeping Gloria's phone call from you, Phillip."

"I know you weren't. Believe me, if I hadn't figured that out myself, Cam would have beaten it into my head this morning."

"Cam." She blinked in shock. "He doesn't like me."

"You're wrong. He was worried about you. Can I persuade you to take a break from work?"

"All right." She saved her file, shut down the machine. "I'm glad we're not angry with each other. It only complicates things. I saw Seth this afternoon."

"So I hear."

She accepted the wine, sipped. "Did you and your brothers clean up the house?"

He gave her a pained and pitiful look. "I don't want to talk about it. I'm going to have nightmares as it is." He took her hand, drew her over to the sofa. "Let's talk about something less frightening. Seth showed me the charcoal sketch of his boat that you helped him with."

"He's really good. He catches on so quickly. Really listens, pays attention. He's got a fine eye for detail and perspective."

"I saw the one you did of the house, too." Casually, Phillip leaned forward for the bottle and topped off her wine. "You're really good, too. I'm surprised you didn't pursue art as a profession."

"I had lessons as a girl. Art, music, dance. I took a few courses in college." Desperately relieved that they were no longer at odds, she settled back and enjoyed her wine. "It wasn't anything serious. I'd always known I'd go into psychology."

"Always?"

"More or less. The arts aren't for people like me."

"Why?"

The question confused her, put her on guard. "It wasn't practical. Did you say you had beluga in there?"

There, he thought, the first step back. He'd simply have to go around her. "Mmm-hmm." He took out the container and the toast points, refilled her glass. "What instrument do you play?"

"Piano."

"Yeah? Me, too." He shot her an easy smile. "We'll have to work up a duet. My parents loved music. All of us play something."

"It's important that a child learn to appreciate music."

"Sure, it's fun." He spread a toast point, offered it. "Sometimes the five of us would kill a Saturday night playing together."

"You all played together? That was nice. I always hated playing in front of anyone. It's so easy to make a mistake."

"So what if you did? Nobody's going to cut off your fingers for hitting a sour note."

"My mother would be mortified, and that would be worse than—" She caught herself, frowned into her wine, started to set it aside. He moved smoothly, adding more to her glass.

"My mother really loved to play the piano. That's why I picked it up at first. I wanted to share something with her specifically. I was so in love with her. We all were, but for me she was everything strong and right and kind about women. I wanted her to be proud of me. Whenever I saw that she was, whenever she told me she was, it was the most amazing feeling."

"Some people strive all their lives for their parents' approval and never come close to gaining their pride." There was something bitter and cold in her voice. She caught it herself and managed a weak laugh. "I'm drinking too much. It's going to my head."

Deliberately he filled her glass again. "You're among friends."

"Overindulging in alcohol—even lovely alcohol—is an abuse."

"Overindulging on a regular basis is an abuse," he corrected. "Ever been drunk, Sybill?"

"Of course not."

"You're due." He tapped his glass to hers. "Tell me about the first time you tasted champagne."

"I don't remember. We were often served watered wine at dinner when we were children. It was important that we learn to appreciate the proper wines, how they were served, what to serve them with, the correct glass for red, the correct glass for white. I could easily have coordinated a formal dinner party for twenty when I was twelve."

"Really?"

She laughed a little, let the wine froth in her head. "It's an important skill. Can you imagine the horror if one bungles the seating? Or serves an inferior wine with the main course? An evening in ruins, reputations in tatters. People expect a certain level of tedium at such affairs, but not a substandard Merlot."

"You attended a lot of formal dinner parties?"

"Yes, indeed. First, several smaller, what you might term 'practice' ones with intimates of my parents, so that I could be judged ready. When I was sixteen, my mother gave a large, important dinner for the French ambassador and his wife. That was my first official appearance. I was terrified.'

"Not enough practice?"

"Oh, I had plenty of practice, hours of instruction on protocol. I was just so painfully shy."

"Were you?" he murmured, tucking her hair behind her ear. Score one for Mother Crawford, he thought.

"So silly. But any time I had to face people that way, my stomach would seize up and my heart would pound so hard. I lived in terror that I would spill something, say something I shouldn't, or have nothing to say at all."

"Did you tell your parents?"

"Tell them what?"

"That you were afraid?"

"Oh." She waved her hand at that, as if it were the most absurd of questions, then picked up the bottle to pour more champagne. "What would be the point? I had to do what was expected of me."

"Why? What would happen if you didn't? Would they beat you, lock you in a closet?"

"Of course not. They weren't monsters. They'd be disappointed, they'd disapprove. It was horrible when they looked at you that way—

tight-lipped, cold-eyed—as if you were defective. It was easier just to get through it, and after a while, you learned how to deal with it."

"Observe rather than participate," he said quietly.

"I've made a good career out of it. Maybe I didn't fulfill my obligations by making an important marriage and giving a lifetime of those beastly dinner parties and raising a pair of well-behaved, properly bred children," she said with rising heat. "But I made good use of my education and a good career, which I'm certainly more suited for than the other. I'm out of wine."

"Let's slow down a little—"

"Why?" She laughed and plucked out the second bottle herself. "We're among friends. I'm getting drunk, and I think I like it."

What the hell, Phillip thought and took the bottle from her to open it. He'd wanted to dig under that proper and polished surface of hers. Now that he was there, there was no point in backing off.

"But you were married once," he reminded her.

"I told you it didn't count. It was *not* an important marriage. It was an impulse, a small and failed attempt at rebellion. I make a poor rebel. Mmm." She swallowed champagne, gestured with her glass. "I was supposed to marry one of the sons of my father's associate from Britain."

"Which one?"

"Oh, either. They were both quite acceptable. Distant relations of the queen. My mother was quite determined to have her daughter associated by marriage with royalty. It would have been a triumph. Of course I was only fourteen, so she had plenty of time to work out the plan, the timing. I believe she'd decided I could become engaged, formally, to one or the other when I was eighteen. Marriage at twenty, first child at twenty-two. She had it all worked out."

"But you didn't cooperate."

"I didn't get the chance. I might very well have cooperated. I found it very difficult to oppose her." She brooded over that for a moment, then washed it away with more champagne. "But Gloria seduced them both, at the same time, in the front parlor while my parents were attending the opera. I believe it was Vivaldi. Anyway . . ." She waved her hand again, drank again. "They came home, found this situation. There was quite a scene. I snuck downstairs and watched part of it. They were naked—not my parents."

"Naturally."

"High on something, too. There was a lot of shouting, threatening, pleading—this from the Oxford twins. Did I mention they were twins?"

"No, you didn't."

"Identical. Blond, pale, lantern-jawed. Gloria didn't give two damns about them, of course. She did it, knowing they'd be caught, because my mother had chosen them for me. She hated me. Gloria, not my mother." Her brow knit. "My mother didn't hate me."

"What happened?"

"The twins were sent home in disgrace and Gloria was punished. Which led, inevitably, to her striking back by accusing my father's friend of seducing her, which led to another miserable scene and her finally running off. It was certainly less disruptive with her gone, but it gave my parents more time to concentrate on forging me. I used to wonder why they saw me more as creation than child. Why they couldn't love me. But then . . ." She settled back again. "I'm not very lovable. No one's ever loved me."

Aching for her, the woman and the child, he set his glass aside and framed her face gently with his hands. "You're wrong."

"No, I'm not." Her smile was soaked in wine. "I'm a professional. I know these things. My parents never loved me, certainly Gloria didn't. The husband, who didn't count, didn't love me. There wasn't even one of those kindly, good-hearted servants you read about in books, who held me against her soft, generous bosom and loved me. No one even bothered to pretend enough to use the words. You, on the other hand, are very lovable." She ran her free hand up his chest. "I've never had sex when I've been drunk. What do you suppose it's like?"

"Sybill." He caught her hand before she could distract him. "They underestimated and undervalued you. You shouldn't do the same to yourself."

"Phillip." She leaned forward, managed to nip his bottom lip between her teeth. "My life's been a predictable bore. Until you. The first time you kissed me, my mind just clicked off. No one ever did that to me before. And when you touch me . . ." Slowly she brought their joined hands to her breast. "My skin gets hot and my heart pounds, and my insides get loose and liquid. You climbed up the building." Her mouth roamed over his jaw. "You brought me roses. You wanted me, didn't you?"

"Yes, I wanted you, but not just—"

"Take me." She let her head fall back so she could look into those wonderful eyes. "I've never said that to a man before. Imagine that.

Take me, Phillip." And the words were part plea, part promise. "Just take me."

The empty glass slipped out of her fingers as she wrapped her arms around him. Helpless to resist, he lowered her to the sofa. And took.

THE DULL ACHE BEHIND HER eyes, the more lively one dancing inside her temples, was no more than she deserved, Sybill decided as she tried to drown both of them under the hot spray of the shower.

She would never, as God was her witness, overindulge in any form of alcohol again.

She only wished the aftermath of drink had resulted in memory loss as well, as a hangover. But she remembered, much too clearly, the way she'd prattled on about herself. The things she'd told Phillip. Humiliating, private things, things she rarely even told herself.

Now she had to face him. She had to face him and the fact that in one short weekend she had wept in his arms, then had given him both her body and her most carefully guarded secrets.

And she had to face the fact that she was hopelessly, and dangerously, in love with him.

Which was totally irrational, of course. The very fact that she believed she could have developed such strong feelings for him in such a short amount of time and association was precisely why those emotions were hopeless. And dangerous.

Obviously she wasn't thinking clearly. This barrage of feelings that had tumbled into her so quickly made it all but impossible to maintain an objective distance and analyze.

Once Seth was settled, once all the details were arranged, she would have to find that distance again. The simplest and most logical method was to begin with geographical distance and go back to New York.

Undoubtedly she would come to her senses once she'd picked up the threads of her own life again and slipped back into a comfortable, familiar routine.

However miserably dull that seemed just now.

She took the time to brush her wet hair back from her face, to carefully cream her skin, adjust the lapels of her robe. If she couldn't quite take full advantage of her breathing techniques to compose herself, it was hardly any wonder, what with the drag of the hangover.

But she stepped out of the bathroom with her features calmly arranged, then walked into the parlor, where Phillip was just pouring coffee from the room service tray.

"I thought you could use this."

"Yes, thank you." She carefully censored her gaze to avoid the empty champagne bottle and the scatter of clothing that she'd been too drunk to pick up the night before.

"Did you take any aspirin?"

"Yes. I'll be fine." She said it stiffly, accepted the cup of coffee and sat with the desperate care of an invalid. She knew she was pale, hollow-eyed. She'd gotten a good look at herself in the steamy mirror.

And she got a good look at Phillip now. He wasn't pale at all, she noted, nor was he hollow-eyed.

A lesser woman would despise him for it.

As she sipped her coffee and studied him, her muddled mind began to clear. How many times, she wondered, had he refilled her glass the night before? How many times had he refilled his own? It seemed to her there was a wide discrepancy between the two.

Resentment began to stir as she watched him generously heap jam on a piece of toast. Even the thought of food had her shaky stomach lurching.

"Hungry?" she said sweetly.

"Starving." He took the lid off a plate of scrambled eggs. "You should try to eat a little."

She'd rather die. "Sleep well?"

"Yeah."

"And aren't we bright-eyed and chipper this morning?"

He caught the tone, slanted her a cautious look. He'd wanted to take it slow, give her some time to recover before they discussed anything. But it appeared that she was recovering rapidly.

"You had a little more to drink than I did," he began.

"You got me drunk. It was deliberate. You charmed your way in here and started pouring champagne into me."

"I hardly held your nose and poured it down your throat."

"You used an apology as an excuse." Her hands began to shake, so she slammed the coffee onto the table. "You must have known I'd be angry with you, and you thought you'd just ease your way into my bed with Dom Perignon."

"The sex was your idea," he reminded her, insulted. "I wanted to talk to you. And the fact is, I got more out of you after you were buzzed than I ever would have otherwise. So I loosened you up." And damn if he was going to feel guilty over it. "And you let me in."

"Loosened me up," she whispered, getting slowly to her feet.

"I wanted to know who you are. I have a right to know."

"You—you did plan it. You planned to come in here, to charm me into drinking just a little too much so you could pry into my personal life."

"I care about you." He moved toward her, but she slapped his hand away.

"Don't. I'm not stupid enough to fall for that again."

"I do care about you. And now I know more, and understand more about you. What's wrong with that, Sybill?"

"You tricked me."

"Maybe I did." He took her arms, keeping a firm grip when she tried to pull back. "Just hold on. You had a privileged, structured childhood. I didn't. You had advantages, servants, culture. I didn't. Do you think less of me because until I was twelve I ran the streets?"

"No. But this has nothing to do with that."

"No one loved me either," he continued. "Not until I was twelve. So I know what it's like on both sides. Do you expect me to think less of you because you survived the cold?"

"I'm not going to discuss it."

"That's not going to work anymore. Here's emotion for you, Sybill." He brought his mouth down on hers, dragging her into the kiss, into the swirl. "Maybe I don't know what to do about it yet either. But it's there. You've seen my scars. They're right out there. Now I've seen yours."

He was doing it again, making her weaken and want. She could rest her head on his shoulder, have his arms come around to hold her. She only had to ask. And couldn't.

"There's no need to feel sorry for me."

"Oh, baby." Gently this time, he touched his lips to hers. "Yes, there is. And I admire what you managed to become despite it all."

"I was drinking too much," she said quickly. "I made my parents sound cold and unfeeling."

"Did either of them ever tell you they loved you?"

She opened her mouth, then sighed. "We simply weren't a demonstrative family. Not every family is like yours. Not every family shows their feelings and touches and . . ." She trailed off, hearing the trace of panicked defense in her own voice. For what, she wondered wearily. For whom?

"No, neither of them ever said that to me. Or to Gloria, as far as I know. And any decent therapist would conclude that their children reacted to this restrictive, overly formal, and demanding atmosphere by choosing different extremes. Gloria chose wild behavior as a bid for attention. I conformed in a bid for approval. She equated sex with affection and power and fantasized about being desired and forced by men in authority, including her legal and her biological fathers. I avoided intimacy in sex out of fear of failure and selected a field of study where I could safely observe behavior without risk of emotional involvement. Is that clear enough?"

"The operative word, I'd say, is 'chose.' She chose to hurt, you chose not to be hurt."

"That's accurate."

"But you haven't been able to keep it up. You risked being hurt with Seth. And you're risking being hurt with me." He touched her cheek. "I don't want to hurt you, Sybill."

It was very likely too late to prevent that, she thought, but she gave in enough to rest her head on his shoulder. She didn't have to ask for his arms to come around her. "Let's just see what happens next," she decided.

TWENTY

Fear, Sybill wrote, *is a common human emotion. And being human, it is as complex and difficult to analyze as love and hate, greed, passion. Emotions, and their causes and effects, are not my particular field of study. Behavior is both learned and instinctive and very often contains no true emotional root. Behavior is much more simple, if no more basic, than emotion.*

I'm afraid.

I'm alone in this hotel, a grown woman, educated, intelligent, sensible, and capable. Yet I'm afraid to pick up the phone on the desk and call my own mother.

A few days ago, I wouldn't have termed it fear, but reluctance, perhaps avoidance. A few days ago I would have argued, and argued well, that contact with her over the issue of Seth would only cause disruption in the order of things and produce no constructive results. Therefore, contact would be useless.

A few days ago, I could have rationalized that my feelings for Seth stemmed from a sense of moral and familial obligation.

A few days ago, I could, and did, refuse to acknowledge my envy of the Quinns with their noisy and unstructured and undisciplined interactive behavior. I would have admitted that their behavior and their unorthodox relationship were interesting, but never would I have admitted that I had a yearning to somehow slip into that pattern and become part of it.

Of course, I can't. I accept that.

A few days ago, I attempted to refute the depth and the meaning of my feelings for Phillip. Love, I told myself, does not come so quickly or so intensely. This is attraction, desire, even lust, but not love. It's easier to refute than to face. I'm afraid of love, of what it demands, what it asks, what it takes. And I'm more afraid, much more, of not being loved in return.

Still, I can accept this. I understand perfectly the limitations of my relationship with Phillip. We are both adults who have made our own patterns and our own choices. He has his needs and his life, as I do mine. I can be grateful that our paths crossed. I've learned a great deal in the short time I've known him. A great deal I've learned has been about myself.

I don't believe I'll be quite the same as I was.

I don't want to be. But in order to change, truly, to grow, there are actions that must be taken.

It helps to write this out, even though the order and sense are faulty.

Phillip called just now from Baltimore. I thought he sounded tired, yet excited. He had a meeting with his attorney about his father's life insurance claim. For months now, the insurance company has refused to settle. They instigated an investigation into Professor Quinn's death and held off paying the claim over the suspicion of suicide. Financially, of course, it put a strain on the Quinns with Seth to provide for and a new business to run, but they have doggedly pursued legal action over this issue.

I don't think I realized until today how vital it is to them to win this battle. Not for the money, as I originally assumed, but to clear any shadow on their father's name. I don't believe suicide is always an act of cowardice. I once considered it myself. Had the proper note written, the necessary pills in my hand. But I was only sixteen and understandably foolish. Naturally I tore the letter up, disposed of the pills, and put the matter aside.

Suicide would have been rude. Inconvenient for my family.

Doesn't that sound bitter? I had no idea I'd harbored all this anger.

But the Quinns, I've learned, considered the taking of one's own life selfish, cowardly. They have refused all along to accept or to allow others to believe that this man they love so much was capable of such a singular selfish act. Now, it appears, they will win this battle.

The insurance company has offered to settle. Phillip believes my deposition may have swayed them toward this response. He may be right. Of course, the Quinns are, perhaps genetically, ill-suited to *settlements. All or nothing, is precisely how Phillip put it to me. He believes, as does his attorney, that they will have all very shortly.*

I'm happy for them. Though I never had the privilege of meeting Raymond and Stella Quinn, I feel I know them through my association with their family. Professor Quinn deserves to rest in peace. Just as Seth deserves to take the Quinn name and to have the security of a family who will love and care for him.

I can do something to ensure that all of that happens. I will have to make this call. I will have to take a stand. Oh, my hands shake just at the possibility. I'm such a coward. No, Seth would call me a wimp. That's somehow worse.

She terrifies me. There it is in black and white. My own mother terrifies me. She never raised a hand to me, rarely raised her voice, yet she shoved me into a mold of her own making. I barely struggled.

My father? He was too busy being important to notice.

Oh, yes, I see a great deal of anger here.

I can call her, I can use the very status that she insisted I achieve to gain what I want from her. I'm a respected scientist, in some small way a public figure. If I tell her I'll use that, if I make her believe I will, unless she provides a written statement to the Quinns' attorney, detailing the circumstances of Gloria's birth, admitting that Professor Quinn attempted several times to contact her for verification of Gloria's paternity, she will despise me. But she will do it.

I only have to pick up the phone to do for Seth what I failed to do years ago. I can give him a home, a family, and the knowledge that he has nothing to fear.

"SON OF A BITCH." PHILLIP wiped sweat off his forehead with the back of his hand. Blood from a nasty but shallow scrape smeared over his skin. He grinned like an idiot at the hull he and his brothers had just turned. "That's a big bastard."

"It's a beautiful bastard." Cam rolled his aching shoulders. The turning of the hull meant more than progress. It meant success. Boats by Quinn was doing it again, and they were doing it right.

"She's got a fine line." Ethan ran a calloused hand over the planking. "A pretty shape to her."

"When I start thinking a hull looks sexy," Cam decided, "I'm going home to my wife. Well, we can score her waterline and get back to work, or we can just admire her for a while."

"You score her waterline," Phillip suggested. "I'm going up and running the paperwork for the draw. It's time to hit your old racing pal up for some cash. We can use it."

"You cut the paychecks?" Ethan asked him.

"Yeah."

"Yours?"

"I don't—"

"Need it," Cam finished. "Cut one anyway, goddamn it. Buy your sexy lady some bauble with it. Blow it on some overpriced wine or lay it on the throw of the dice. But cut your check this week." He studied the hull again. "It means something this week."

"Maybe it does," Phillip agreed.

"The insurance company's going to fold their hand," Cam added. "We're going to win there."

"People are already changing their tune." Ethan rubbed a layer of sawdust off the planking. "The ones who wanted to whistle lies under their breath. We've already won there. You worked the hardest to make sure we did," he said to Phillip.

"I'm just the detail man. Either one of you tried to have more than a five-minute conversation with a lawyer . . . well, you'd nod off from boredom, Ethan, and Cam would end up punching him. I won by default."

"Maybe." Cam grinned at him. "But you skated out of a lot of the real work by talking on the phone, writing letters, zinging off faxes. It just comes down to you being secretary. Without the great legs and ass."

"Not only is that sexist, but I do have great legs and a terrific ass."

"Oh, yeah? Let's see 'em." He moved fast, diving and taking Phillip down onto that reputedly terrific ass.

Foolish scrambled up from his nap by the lumber and raced over to join in.

"Christ! Are you crazy!" Laughter prevented Phillip from rolling free. "Get off me, you moron."

"Give me a hand here, Ethan." Cam grinned, swearing as Foolish lapped eagerly at his face. Phillip struggled half-heartedly when Cam sat on him. "Come on," he urged when Ethan merely shook his head. "When's the last time you pantsed somebody?"

"Been a while." Ethan considered as Phillip began to struggle in earnest. "Maybe the last time was Junior Crawford at his bachelor party."

"Well, that's ten years ago, anyway." Cam grunted as Phillip nearly succeeded in bucking him off. "Come on, he's put on some muscle the last few months. And he's feisty."

"Maybe for old time's sake." Getting into the spirit, Ethan evaded a couple of well-aimed kicks and got a firm hold on the waistband of Phillip's jeans.

"Excuse me," was the best Sybill could manage when she walked in on air blue with curses and the sight of Phillip being held down on the beaten-wood floor while his brothers . . . well, she couldn't quite tell what they were trying to do.

"Hey." Cam avoided a fist to the jaw, barely, and grinned hugely at her. "Want to give us a hand? We're just trying to get his pants off. He was bragging about his legs."

"I . . . hmmm."

"Let him up now, Cam. You're embarrassing her."

"Hell, Ethan, she's seen his legs before." But without Ethan lending his weight, it was either let go or get bloody. It seemed simpler, if less fun, to let go. "We'll finish up later."

"My brothers forgot they're out of high school." Phillip got to his feet, brushing off his jeans and his dignity. "They were feeling a little rambunctious because we turned the hull."

"Oh." She shifted her attention to the boat, and her eyes widened. "You've made so much progress."

"It's got a ways to go yet." Ethan studied it himself, visualizing it complete. "Deck, cabin, bridge, belowdecks. Man wants a damn hotel suite in there."

"As long as he's paying for it." Phillip crossed to Sybill, ran a hand down her hair. "Sorry I got in too late to see you last night."

"That's all right. I know you've been busy with work and the lawyer." She shifted her purse from hand to hand. "Actually I have something that may help. With the lawyer, with both situations. Well . . ."

She reached into her purse and took out a manila envelope. "It's a statement from my mother. Two copies, both notarized. I had her overnight them. I didn't want to say anything until they'd arrived, and I'd read them to see . . . I think they'll be useful."

"What's the deal?" Cam demanded as Phillip quickly skimmed the neatly typed two-page statement.

"It confirms that Gloria was Dad's biological daughter. That he was unaware of it and that he attempted to contact Barbara Griffin several times during a period from last December to this March. There's a letter from Dad written to her in January, telling her about Seth, his agreement with Gloria to take custody."

"I read your father's letter," Sybill told him. "Perhaps I shouldn't have, but I did. If he was angry with my mother, it didn't show in the words. He just wanted her to tell him if it was true. He was going to help Seth anyway, but he wanted to be able to give him his birthright. A man who worried that much about a child would hardly have taken his own life. He had too much to give, and was too ready to give it. I'm so sorry."

" 'He just needs a chance, and a choice,' " Ethan read when Phillip passed the letters to him, then cleared his throat. " 'I couldn't give one to Gloria, if she's mine, and she won't take it now. But I'll see that Seth has both. Whether he's mine by blood or not, he's mine nonetheless now.' It sounds like him. Seth should read this."

"Why did she agree to this now, Sybill?" Phillip asked her.

"I convinced her that it was best for all concerned."

"No." He caught her chin in his hand, lifted her face to his. "There's more. I know there is."

"I promised her that her name, and the details, would be kept as private as possible." She made a restless little movement, then let out a breath. "And I threatened to write a book telling the entire story if she didn't do this."

"You blackmailed her," Phillip said with stunned admiration.

"I gave her a choice. She chose this one."

"It was hard for you."

"It was necessary."

Now he put both of his hands on her face, gently. "It was hard, and brave, and brilliant."

"Logical," she began, then shut her eyes. "And yes, hard. She and my father are very angry. They may not forgive me. They're capable of not forgiving."

"They don't deserve you."

"The point is Seth deserves you, so . . ." She trailed off as he closed his mouth over hers.

"Okay, move aside." Cam elbowed Phillip away and took Sybill by the shoulders. "You did good," he said, then kissed her with a firmness that made her blink.

"Oh," was all she managed.

"Your turn," Cam stated, then gave her a gentle nudge toward Ethan.

"My parents would have been proud of you." He kissed her in turn, then patted her shoulders when her eyes filled.

"Oh, no, don't let her do that." Instantly, Cam took her arm and pulled her back to Phillip. "No crying in here, no crying allowed in the boatyard."

"Cam gets jittery when women cry."

"I'm not crying."

"They always say that," Cam muttered, "but they never mean it. Outside. Anybody who cries has to do it outside. It's a new rule."

Chuckling, Phillip pulled Sybill toward the door. "Come on. I want a minute alone with you anyway."

"I'm not crying. I just never expected your brothers to . . . it's not usual for me to be—" She stopped herself. "It's very nice to be shown you're appreciated and liked."

"I appreciate you." He drew her close. "I like you."

"And it's very nice." She indulged in the luxury of both. "I've already spoken with your attorney and with Anna. I didn't want to fax the papers from the hotel as I did give my word the contents would be kept private. But both of them agree that this last document should move everything along. Anna believes that your petition for permanent guardianship will go through as early as next week."

"That soon?"

"There's nothing in the way of it. You and your brothers are Professor Quinn's legal sons. Seth is his grandchild. His mother agreed, in writing, to transfer custody. Reneging on that might stall the decree, but no one believes at this point that it would change it. Seth is eleven, and at his age his desires would be taken into account. Anna's going to push for a hearing early next week."

"It seems strange, it all coming together like this. All at once."

"Yes." She looked up as a flock of geese swept overhead. Seasons change, she thought. "I thought I would walk down to the school. I'd like to talk to him, tell him some of this myself."

"I think that's a good idea. You timed it well."

"I'm good at schedules."

"How about scheduling a family meal tonight at the Quinns, to celebrate?"

"Yes, all right. I'll walk him back here."

"Great. Hold on a minute." He went back inside, returning moments later with a very energetic Foolish on a red leash. "He could use a walk, too."

"Oh, well, I . . ."

"He knows the way. All you have to do is hold on to this end." Amused, Phillip stuck the leash in her hand, then watched her eyes go wide as Foolish made his dash. "Tell him to heel," Phillip shouted as Sybill trotted after the dog. "He won't, but it'll sound like you know what you're doing."

"This is not funny." She muttered it as she jogged awkwardly after Foolish. "Slow down. Heel! God."

He not only slowed, but stopped, burying his nose in a hedge with such determination she was terrified he would race through it and take her with him. But he only lifted his leg and looked immensely pleased with himself.

By her count, he lifted his leg eight times before they turned the corner down from the school and she caught sight of the buses. "What kind of a bladder do you have?" she demanded, looking hopefully for Seth while she struggled to cling to the leash and prevent Foolish from rocketing toward the crowd of children pouring out of the building. "No. Sit. Stay. You might bite someone."

Foolish slanted her a look that seemed to say, Please, get serious. But he sat, smacking her heels rhythmically with his tail. "He'll be along in a minute," she began, then let out a yelp as Foolish leaped up and raced forward. He'd spotted Seth first and was running on love.

"No, no, no, no," Sybill panted uselessly just as Seth caught sight of them. He let out a yelp himself, of pure joy, and dashed toward the dog as if they'd been cruelly separated for years.

"Hey! Hi!" Seth laughed as Foolish made one adoring leap and bathed his face. "How's it going, boy? Good dog. You're a good dog." Belatedly, he looked over at Sybill. "Hey."

"Hey, yourself. Here." She shoved the leash into his hand. "Not that he pays any attention to it."

"We've kind of had trouble with leash training."

"No kidding." But she managed a smile now to include Seth and Danny and Will when they hurried up behind him. "I thought I'd walk back to the boatyard with you. I wanted to talk to you."

"Sure, that's cool."

She stepped determinedly out of Foolish's path, then quickly back again as a bright-red sports car screamed up to the curb and stopped with a wild squeal of brakes. Before she could snarl at the driver that he was in a school zone, she saw Gloria in the passenger seat.

Sybill's movement was fast and instinctive. She put Seth protectively behind her.

"Well, well, well," Gloria drawled and eyed them both out of the window.

"Go get your brothers," Sybill ordered Seth. "Go right now."

But he couldn't move. He could only stand and stare while the fear settled in his stomach like balls of ice. "I won't go with her. I won't go. I won't."

"No, you won't." She took his hand firmly in hers. "Danny, Will, run to the boatyard right now. Tell the Quinns we need them. Hurry. Go straight there."

She heard the smack of running sneakers on the sidewalk but didn't look. She kept her eyes trained on her sister as Gloria slipped out of the car.

"Hey, kid. Miss me?"

"What do you want, Gloria?"

"Everything I can get." She fisted a hand on the hip of her lipstick-red jeans and winked at Seth. "Wanna go for a ride, kiddo? We can do some catching up."

"I'm not going anywhere with you." He wished he had run. He had a place in the woods, a place he'd picked out and fixed up. A hiding place. But it was too far away. Then he felt Sybill's hand, warm and strong on his. "I'm not ever going with you again."

"You'll do what the hell I tell you." Fury flashed in her eyes as she started forward. For the first time in his life, Foolish bared his teeth and growled a vicious threat. "Call off that fucking dog."

"No," Sybill said it simply, quietly, and felt a surge of love for Foolish. "I'd keep my distance, Gloria. He'll bite." She scanned the car, the leather-jacketed man behind its wheel, beating a rhythm on the dash to the blasting radio. "It looks like you landed on your feet."

"Yeah, Pete's okay. We're heading out to California. He's got connections. I need cash."

"You're not going to get it here."

Gloria pulled out a cigarette, smiling at Sybill as she lit it. "Look, I don't want the kid, but I'm going to take him unless I get a stake. The Quinns'll pay to get him back. Everybody's happy, no harm done. If you mess with me on this, Syb, I'm going to tell Pete to get out of the car."

Foolish shifted from growling to snarling. Sharp canine teeth bared. Sybill raised a brow. "Go ahead. Tell him."

"I want what's due me, goddamn it."

"You've had more than your due all your life."

"Bullshit! It was you who got everything. The perfect daughter. I hate your fucking guts. I've hated you all my life." She grabbed Sybill by the front of her jacket and all but spit in her face. "I wish you were dead."

"I know that. Now take your hands off me."

"You think you can make me?" With a laugh, Gloria shoved Sybill back a step. "You never had the guts before, did you? You'll take it, and you'll take it, and you'll give me what I want, just like always. Shut that dog up!" she shouted at Seth as Foolish strained at the leash and snapped wildly. "Shut him up and get in the goddamn car before I—"

Sybill didn't see her own hand come up, didn't realize the order had gone from her brain to her arm. But she felt her muscles tighten, her rage erupt, and then Gloria was sprawled on the ground gaping at her.

"You get in the goddamn car," she said evenly, not even looking at the Jeep that screeched up to the curb. Not blinking when Foolish dragged himself and Seth closer and growled low in his throat at the woman on the ground. "You go to California, or you go to hell, but you stay away from this boy, and you stay away from me. Keep out of this," she snapped at Phillip as he and his brothers burst out of the Jeep.

"Get in the car and go, Gloria, or I'll pay you back right now for everything you ever did to Seth. Everything you ever did to me. Get up and go, or when the cops get here to take you in for jumping bail, when we add charges of child abuse and extortion, there won't be much left of you to put in a cell."

When Gloria didn't move, Sybill reached down and, with a strength born of fury, hauled her to her feet. "Get in the car and go, and don't ever try to get near this boy again. You won't get through me, Gloria. I swear to you."

"I don't want the damn kid. I just want some money."

"Cut your losses. I'm not going to bother holding that dog or the Quinns back after another thirty seconds. Want to take all of us on?"

"Gloria, are you coming or not?" The driver flicked his cigarette out the car window. "I don't have all day to hang around this bumfuck town."

"Yeah, I'm coming." She tossed her head. "You're welcome to him. All he ever did was slow me down and get in my way. I'm going to score big in L.A. I don't need anything from you."

"Good," Sybill murmured as Gloria climbed back in the car. "Because you'll never get anything from me again."

"You knocked her down." Seth wasn't shaking, nor was he pale now. As the sports car shrieked away, the look he sent Sybill was filled with gratitude, and with awe. "You knocked her down."

"I guess I did. Are you all right?"

"She never even looked at me, really. Foolish was going to bite her."

"He's a wonderful dog." When he leaped on her now, she pressed her face into the warmth of his neck. "He's a fabulous dog."

"But you knocked her down. Sybill knocked her right on her butt," he shouted as Phillip and his brothers walked over.

"So I saw." Phillip put a hand to her cheek. "Nice going, champ. How do you feel?"

"I feel . . . fine," she realized. No cramping, no chills, no sick headache. "I feel just fine." Then she blinked as Seth threw his arms around her.

"You were great. She's never coming back. You scared the shit out of her."

The bubbly little laugh that rose into her throat caught her by surprise. Leaning down, she buried her face in Seth's hair. "Everything's just the way it's supposed to be now."

"Let's go home." Phillip slid his arm around her shoulders. "Let's all go home."

"HE's GOING TO BE TELLING that story for days," Phillip decided. "Weeks."

"He's already embellishing on it." Amazingly serene, Sybill walked with Phillip by the water's edge while the heroic Foolish romped in the yard behind them with Simon. "The way he tells it now, I beat Gloria to a pulp and Foolish lapped up the blood."

"You don't sound all that displeased by it."

"I never knocked anyone down before in my life. Never stood my ground that way. I wish I could say I did it all for Seth, but I think part of it was for me, too. She won't come back, Phillip. She lost. She is lost."

"I don't think Seth will ever be afraid of her again."

"He's home. This is a good place." She turned in a circle to take in the trim house, the woods going deep with twilight, the last sparkle of the sun on the water. "I'll miss it when I'm back in New York."

"New York? You're not going for a while yet."

"Actually, I'm planning on going back right after the hearing next week." It was something she'd made up her mind on. She needed to resume her own life. Staying longer would accomplish nothing but adding to the emotional mess.

"Wait. Why?"

"I have work."

"You're working here." Where did the panic come from? he wondered. Who pushed the button?

"I have meetings with my publisher that I've put off. I need to get back. I can't live in a hotel forever, and Seth's settled now."

"He needs you around. He—"

"I'll visit. And I'm hoping he'll be allowed to come see me occasionally." She'd worked it all out in her head, and now she turned to smile at him. "I promised to take him to a Yankees game next spring."

It was as if it were already done, he realized, struggling against that panic. As if she were already gone. "You've talked to him about it."

"Yes, I thought I should let him know."

"And this is how you let me know?" he shot back. "It's been nice, pal, see you around?"

"I'm not sure I'm following."

"Nothing. Nothing to follow." He walked away. He wanted his own life back, too, didn't he? Here was his chance. End of complications. All he had to do was wish her well and wave good-bye. "That's what I want. It's always been what I wanted."

"Excuse me?"

"I'm not looking for anything else. Neither one of us was." He whirled back to her, temper glinting in his eyes. "Right?"

"I'm not sure what you mean."

"You've got your life, I've got mine. We just followed the current, and here we are. Time to get out of the water."

No, she decided, she wasn't following him. "All right."

"Well, then." Assuring himself that he was fine with it, he was calm. He was even pleased. He started back toward her.

The last of the sun shimmered over her hair, into those impossibly clear eyes, shadowed the hollow of her throat above the collar of her blouse. "No." He heard himself say it, and his mouth went dry.

"No?"

"A minute, just one minute." He walked away again, this time to the edge of the water. He stood there, staring down like a man contemplating diving in well over his head. "What's wrong with Baltimore?"

"Baltimore? Nothing."

"It's got museums, good restaurants, character, theater."

"It's a very nice city," Sybill said cautiously.

"Why can't you work there? If you have to go into New York for a meeting, you can hop the shuttle or the train. Hell, you can drive it in under four hours."

"I'm sure that's true. If you're suggesting I relocate to Baltimore—"

"It's perfect. You'd still be living in the city, but you'd be able to see Seth whenever you wanted."

And you, she thought, yearning toward the picture. But she shook her head. It would kill her to go on this way. And she knew it would spoil the happiness she'd had, the new self she'd discovered. "It's just not practical, Phillip."

"Of course it's practical." He turned around, strode back to her. "It's perfectly practical. What's impractical is going back to New York, putting up that distance again. It's not going to work, Sybill. It's just not going to work."

"There's no point in discussing it now."

"Do you think this is easy for me?" he exploded. "I *have* to stay here. I have commitments, responsibilities, to say nothing of roots. I've got no choice. Why can't you bend?"

"I don't understand."

"I have to spell it out? Damn it." He took her by the shoulders, gave her a quick, impatient shake. "Don't you get it? I love you. You can't expect me to let you walk away. You have to stay. The hell with your life and my life. Your family, my family. I want *our* life. I want *our* family."

She stared at him, the blood ringing in her ears. "What? What?"

"You heard what I said."

"You said . . . you said you loved me. Do you mean it?"

"No, I'm lying."

"I . . . I've already knocked one person down today. I can do it again." Just then, she thought she could do anything. Anything at all. It didn't matter if there was fury in his eyes, if his fingers were digging into her arms. If he looked fit to kill. She could handle this. She could handle him. She could handle anything.

"If you meant it," she said, her voice admirably cool, "I'd like you to say it again. I've never heard it before."

"I love you." Calming, he touched his lips to her brow. "I want you." To each temple. "I need you to stay with me." Then her mouth. "Give me more time to show you what we'll be like together."

"I know what we'll be like together. I want what we'll be like together." She let out a shuddering breath, resisted the urge to close her eyes. She needed to see his face, to remember it exactly as it was at this moment, with the sun sinking, the sky going peach and rose, and a flock of birds winging overhead. "I love you. I was afraid to tell you. I don't know why. I don't think I'm afraid of anything now. Are you going to ask me to marry you?"

"I was about to muddle my way through that part." On impulse, he pulled out the simple white band holding back her hair and tossed it over her shoulders where the dogs gave loud and delighted chase. "I want your hair in my hands," he murmured, threading his fingers through the thick, rich brown. "All my life I said I would never do this because there would never be a woman who would make me need to or want to. I was wrong. I found one. I found mine. Marry me, Sybill."

"All my life I said I would never do this because there would never be a man who'd need me or want me, or matter enough to make me want. I was wrong. I found you. Marry me, Phillip, and soon."

"How does next Saturday strike you?"

"Oh." Emotion flooded her heart, poured into it, out of it, warm and smooth and real. "Yes!" She leaped, throwing her arms around him.

He spun her in a circle, and for a moment, just for a flash, he thought he saw two figures standing on the dock. The man with silver hair and brilliantly blue eyes, the woman with freckles dancing over her face and wild red hair blowing in the evening breeze. Their hands were linked. They were there, then they were gone.

"This one counts," he murmured, holding her hard and close. "This one counts for both of us."